Be My Baby

Laura Greaves is an award-winning author and journalist who announced her intention to be a writer at the age of seven, largely because of her dual obsessions with *Anne of Green Gables* and *Murder, She Wrote*.

She is also the author of the romantic comedy novel *The Ex-Factor* and bestselling non-fiction book *Incredible Dog Journeys*.

Laura lives on Sydney's Northern Beaches with her family, as well as two incorrigible (but seriously cute) dogs. Her continuing *Anne of Green Gables* fixation is matched only by her dog obsession, which is why you will always find at least one four-legged friend in Laura's books.

Connect with Laura:

lauragreaves.com
facebook.com/lauragreaveswritesbooks
instagram.com/lauragreavesauthor
twitter.com/Laura_Greaves

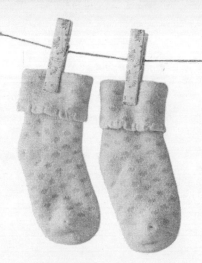

Be My Baby

LAURA GREAVES

MICHAEL JOSEPH
an imprint of
PENGUIN BOOKS

MICHAEL JOSEPH

UK | USA | Canada | Ireland | Australia
India | New Zealand | South Africa | China

Penguin Books is part of the Penguin Random House group of companies whose addresses can be found at global.penguinrandomhouse.com.

Penguin
Random House
Australia

First published by Penguin Random House Australia Pty Ltd, 2014
This edition published by Penguin Random House Australia Pty Ltd, 2017

Cover design by Louisa Maggio © Penguin Random House Australia Pty Ltd
Text design by Louisa Maggio © Penguin Random House Australia Pty Ltd
Cover photographs: Roses on desk: mykeyruna/Shutterstock; Stains of lipstick: BERNATSKAYA OXANA/Shutterstock; Paper cup: Africa Studio/Shutterstock; Crack: Shcherbakov Roman/Shutterstock; Pink socks hanging on line with clothespins and Vintage scene: Ramon Antinolo/Shutterstock.
Typeset in Sabon by Louisa Maggio, Penguin Random House Australia Pty Ltd
Colour separation by Splitting Image Colour Studio, Clayton, Victoria
Printed and bound in Australia by Griffin Press, an accredited ISO AS/NZS 14001 Environmental Management Systems printer.

National Library of Australia
Cataloguing-in-Publication data:

Greaves, Laura, author.
Be my baby / Laura Greaves.
9780143785606 (paperback)

Australians–England–London–Fiction.
Sponsors–Fiction.
Child rearing–Fiction.
Work-life balance–Fiction

penguin.com.au

MIX
Paper from
responsible sources
FSC
www.fsc.org   FSC® C009448

To all mothers, everywhere –
whether biological, adoptive, foster, step, single,
coupled, heterosexual or otherwise –
you're doing a great job.

Anna

I want to throttle her. I want to reach across the oceans and continents between us, grab her by her pudgy neck and squeeze it until her eyeballs bulge like a goldfish's. I want to shake her by the shoulders until she's dizzy. I want to slap her, scream at her, clench my fists and stamp my feet until she realises what a colossal idiot she is. Instead, I employ my extensive journalistic vocabulary and say, 'Huh?'

'I said I'm pregnant,' Helena repeats patiently. 'Sixteen weeks along.'

'Sixteen weeks! And you're only telling me now?'

Pregnant. Just the word sends chills up my spine.

She sighs. 'Well, I only found out myself at twelve weeks. And I've been trying to speak to you for a month. Haven't you got my phone messages or my emails? You're not the easiest person to get hold of, Anna.'

Helena, quite rightly, sounds peeved. I cringe inwardly, remembering the countless unreturned messages on my voicemail and 'call me!' emails in my inbox. I'd meant to phone her, really

I had. Life had just got in the way.

'Anyway,' she goes on, 'you're going to be an aunty!'

Now is not the time to point out that, as we're not actually related, I'll only ever be an aunty in the 'moustache-like-a-chimney-brush spinster family friend' sense of the word.

'But Hel, are you sure you're pregnant? You don't even have a boyfriend.' Because obviously this makes all the difference.

'Yes, I'm sure,' she says, giggling. 'Just because you inhabit a haven of, ahem, domestic bliss, Anna, doesn't mean the rest of us aren't getting a bit occasionally. It's Adam's.'

Adam . . . Adam. The nightclub bouncer with the lazy eye? No, that was Darren. The brickie's labourer who lived above the chip shop? But he was well over sixteen weeks past his use-by date. Adam. The mechanic with the —

'Oh God, you don't mean the mechanic with the souped-up Escort? The one who claimed to be half French but thought Versailles was a type of conjunctivitis? The one —' I lower my voice to a whisper, 'Helena, he's not the one with the teenage girlfriend?' Even through 24 000 kilometres of ocean and fibre-optic cable, I can feel my best friend cringe.

'She was nineteen, Anna, not thirteen. And they'd broken up, so she was his *ex*-girlfriend,' Helena says. 'I knew he wasn't The One. I never intended it to be anything more than a fling, a bit of fun. I guess I just didn't realise I'm so damn fertile.'

I'd also put money on the fact that she didn't want to ruin the moment by asking him to put a condom on his adolescent-shagging appendage, but this isn't the time to point that out either.

'So . . . what are you going to do?' I ask, gritting my teeth and praying she's not going to tell me she wants to —

'Keep it,' Helena says.

Again, my thoughts swing to violence. Perhaps a swift kick to the shin will bring her to her senses. How is it that she can't see what a truly ludicrous idea this is? Of course she wants to keep it. Helena has wanted children as long as I've known her and her desire to spawn has only grown stronger as she's grown older. This is despite the fact that she's never had a long-term relationship, still lives with her parents and once near-drowned a guinea pig trying to give it an aromatherapy bath. She can't make toast but she can make whole people. How about that.

'Are you sure it's the best thing, Hel?' I say, trying to be diplomatic when I really want to scream 'Abort! Abort!' space shuttle-style. 'You're only twenty-five and you have so many plans. What about going back to university? What about travelling?'

What about not ending up on a housing commission estate with only toothless women called Chardonnay-Krystle for company? I want to add.

'I can still do all those things. I'll just have a child in tow. We'll be citizens of the world,' she says dreamily.

I can only sigh. Helena has never been one to let reality get in the way of her lofty ambitions. At last count she'd embarked on – and dropped out of – four separate university degrees. Apparently her desire to be a photographer/lawyer/economist/photographer wasn't quite so powerful as her desire to avoid doing any actual work.

'Okay, so what about Adam? Have you told him?'

'Er . . . yeah. He's not quite so optimistic about impending parenthood.'

'What does that mean, Helena?'

Silence.

'Hel?'

'Look, he's told me to get rid of it, okay? But that's not important. What *is* important is I'm going to have this baby no matter what anyone says, including Adam and including my mother.'

Oh God. Her mother. Frosty isn't the word for Brigitta Stanley. When Helena was thirteen and carrying a bit of puppy fat, Brigitta kindly suggested she familiarise herself with the ancient art of thrusting her fingers down her throat after every meal. The woman makes the Islamic State seem forgiving.

'How did you tell her?' I whisper, as though merely discussing Brigitta will conjure her up at my desk.

'I didn't. I told Dad and let him tell her,' she says.

'How did she take it?'

'How do you think? Called me a failure. Demanded I terminate the pregnancy. Said if I go through with it she'll disown me. You know how she is.'

I'm sure my heart actually shatters at the resigned tone in Helena's voice. She would have expected nothing better from her mother.

'Oh Hel, I'm so sorry,' I offer.

'It's fine, Anna. I can do this by myself. I know I can.'

'You won't have to. I may be 24 000 kilometres away but I'll do anything and everything I can for you.' I'm not quite sure where this strength of resolve has suddenly bubbled up from, but I'm running with it.

'Actually,' Helena says. 'There is something I wanted to ask you. When she's born, would you —'

'Wait – *she*?' The pitch of my voice causes several colleagues to turn and stare. 'You're having a girl?'

'Oh my God, didn't I tell you that? I just found out,' she says, and I can hear the excitement in her voice. 'They usually can't tell you 'til twenty weeks, but the woman doing the scan said she could see the gender and asked if I wanted to know. I was so sure I didn't, but as I looked at this tiny blob moving around on the screen I just had to know whether it was my first glimpse of my son or my daughter.'

In spite of myself, I'm visualising pink Babygro suits and a pair of adorable miniature Reebok trainers I'm sure I saw in the fashion editor's cupboard.

'But listen, Anna,' Helena continues, 'I wanted to ask you if you would be her godmother.'

In my shocked state, I seem to have slipped into some alternate universe, a surreal place where my best friend has just asked me to assume partial responsibility for a child's spiritual wellbeing. A creeping panic rises like bile in my throat.

'I'm sorry – what?'

'Come on, Anna. You're my best friend in the whole wide world and the only person I knew I could count on to support my decision to have this baby,' Helena pleads. 'I can't think of a better woman to warn my daughter off dodgy guys and teach her the difference between Marc Jacobs and Tom Ford.'

This is interesting. It reminds me of a terminally dull airline pilot I dated briefly. I quickly learned to tune out his sleep-inducing droning about aircraft technicalities, but one tidbit did stick in my mind: the Collision Avoidance System. Basically, if you're thundering through the sky in a pressurised tin can, also known as a 747, and another 747 is about to slice through the cabin, a computerised voice in the cockpit will politely ask the captain to 'climb, climb'.

I had always liked to think of my ability to steer clear of children as my own Collision Avoidance System. Kids always seem to be in my airspace – friends' bubs, screeching brats on the Tube – but whenever one gets close enough to interrupt the in-flight movie of my life I 'climb, climb' as fast as humanly possible. I am not a 'kid person'. Never have been. And now here's Helena, trying to force one such missile directly into my flight path.

'Uh, Hel, are you sure about this? I mean, I hardly have a child-friendly lifestyle. I never get to bed before two a.m., I'm constantly surrounded by coke-snorting degenerates —'

'Also known as celebrities,' Helena interrupts with a giggle.

'Whatever. And I spend all my money on cocktails and clothes. I can barely look after myself. Are you sure you want to let me within corrupting distance of a child? *Your* child?' She has to realise what a mistake this would be.

There's a pause. 'Well . . . yes. While you're in London, all those things are true, but one day you'll come back to Adelaide and that will change,' Helena says softly.

I roll my eyes. This is how my mother's 'When are you going to come home and settle down' speech always starts.

'And in the meantime you'll be the fabulous London godmother who sends her tiny Ralph Lauren twin-sets and sparkly Dolce & Gabbana party shoes. But you won't have to be here to watch her throw up on them.'

Her tone is upbeat but suddenly Helena sounds so far away, so frightened, that I want to cry for her – and kick myself for being such a judgy, cold-hearted cow. Whatever my own feelings about children may be, they're no justification for abandoning my best friend.

'Of course I'll be her godmother, Hel. I'd be honoured,' I say, valiantly ignoring the little voice in my head whispering, *What are you thinking?*

Right, there's work to be done. Must stop trawling eBay for some sort of manual on how not to scar a godchild for life and focus on more pressing issues.

Issue *du jour* is Cat Hubbard, singer, songwriter and current darling of the Primrose Hill social set, who dragged herself up from apparently nowhere to land at the top of the charts with her first album. She seems too good to be true and, as *The Mirror*'s crack showbiz correspondent, it's my job to prove that she is — before those hacks at celebscandalz.com beat me to it.

I try to ignore the uncomfortable sensation in my stomach as I rouse my computer from sleep mode and pull up my notes on Cat. I know what that feeling is: guilt. Despite having spent the past three years gleefully laying bare celebrities' misdeeds for the benefit of a ravenous British public, I've never quite managed to shake the feeling that my job is, well, a bit icky. I'm hardly making the world a better place, am I? Revealing to Vera Housewife that Katie Price has got hitched yet again or that Jeremy Clarkson has said some new boneheaded thing isn't going to end world hunger or bring peace to the Middle East. Unlike some of my colleagues, who genuinely seem to believe they're performing some sort of benevolent public service, I know that what I do is a bit scummy. And it seems even grubbier and less necessary these days, with an ever-increasing number of celebrity gossip websites breaking and updating the 'news' a thousand times faster than the print media can anyway. Why wait for a newspaper when you can simply refresh your internet browser for real-time updates on who Kylie Jenner is dating?

It wasn't where I saw my career going as a fresh-faced eighteen-year-old the day I started my cadetship on the local rag in my Aussie hometown, Adelaide. I thought I'd become a hard-nosed news reporter, uncovering corruption in big business and blowing the lid off political conspiracies left, right and centre. But after five years of working almost constant graveyard crime shifts, I'd brought down no governments and caused the collapse of precisely zero multinational conglomerates. What I did have, however, were far too many memories of mangled car wrecks, family homes reduced to ash and decomposing bodies uncovered by dog walkers in lonely fields.

Arriving in London and observing its zealous worship of celebrities – talented or otherwise – was a breath of fresh air. I developed an appetite for glitz and glamour that couldn't be sated, no matter how many copies of *Closer* magazine I bought or how long I spent debating whether the latest D-list celebrity hook-up was the real deal. I took the first vaguely celeb-oriented job I was offered, running the entertainment pages on a newspaper in London's leafy commuter belt. Unfortunately, it wasn't the sort of place that attracted the uber-famous. Instead of writing about Harry Styles or Katy Perry, my bread and butter was ageing stand-up comedians and whichever for-mer *EastEnders* actor was starring in the local panto at Christmas. After two years of it, and having spent every Sunday working free-lance shifts at *The Mirror*, I practically French-kissed the news editor when he offered me my job running the showbiz desk.

I'm good at what I do, there's no doubt about that. But the longer I do it, the less enticing the boozy lunches and free tickets and trips away become. No matter how much I try to deny it, I'm becoming uncomfortably aware of the inconvenient fact that the celebrities I write about are people, too.

I shake my head, trying to chase away my maudlin thoughts. It's Helena's news that's made me all introspective. How will I explain to my goddaughter that I revel in others' misfortune – for a living?

'Anna?' The hairs on the back of my neck bristle at the singsong voice. Nicki Ford-Smith perches one firm buttock on the corner of my desk, sweeps her white-blonde hair over one shoulder as if she's in a Herbal Essences commercial and fixes me with her vacuous gaze.

Ugh.

'Yeah?' I tap furiously away at my keyboard, trying to give the impression of productivity.

'Um, I was just wondering how you're, like, getting on with the Cat Hubbard piece?'

'Oh fine,' I lie breezily, not looking at her. The mere sight of Nicki's five foot ten bronzed frame makes me want to dive for a packet of chocolate biscuits. 'I've got a couple of good leads on for-mer classmates and the woman who works in her local drycleaner reckons she once brought in a dress with a dubious stain.'

Nicki bares her perfect teeth – I couldn't really call it a smile. 'Great,' she says flatly. 'Look, I hope you don't mind but I made a few calls of my own and I've, like, come across a couple of bits and pieces.'

Here it comes: the stiletto in the back.

'I'm sure you'll dig up something much better but, just in case, I could always put together a few paragraphs on her, uh, husband.'

Bullseye. 'She's married?'

'Not any more,' Nicki says with a toss of her mane. I'm reminded how long it's been since I've had a haircut. 'But she was, back when she was, like, nineteen. I mentioned it to Girish and he's keen to run with it if, you know, you haven't got anything better.'

'How do you know this?'

'Oh, I have a couple of friends in Primrose Hill.' There are those teeth again.

I glance at the clock – forty minutes to deadline. I could make a fuss about this glorified secretary – sorry, *entertainment desk assistant* – hijacking my story. Or I could go to WH Smith and buy *What to Expect When You're Expecting* for Helena, followed by an intravenous gin and tonic for myself.

'Sounds good,' I say, flashing my fakest smile back. 'If you could knock a page lead together, I'll save my angle for tomorrow.'

I feel a heavy hand clasp my shoulder. 'See that you have an angle, Anna,' says Girish Thakkar, fearsome news editor. 'It seems to have been awfully quiet in the world of celebrity this week.'

'Will do, Girish. Not a problem,' I say with far more confidence than is justified.

Girish frowns. Nicki's pearly whites glint under the fluorescent lighting.

Ugh.

I grab my bag and make a run for it, scurrying out of the building before Nicki has the chance to launch phase two of her showbiz coup. Still reeling from Helena's announcement, I fumble for my mobile phone and punch in Finn's number.

'Yeah?'

'Hey gorgeous, it's just me. You will never, ever guess what's happened.'

Finn sighs. 'Look, Anna, I'm really busy here. Whatever celebrity drama is unfolding, can't it wait 'til I get home?'

'Well, no, Finn, it can't,' I say, my stomach lurching at the obvious irritation in his voice.

'What then?'

'Helena's pregnant!'

'Uh-huh.' I can hear the click-clack of his computer keyboard in the background.

'Uh-huh? Finn, this . . . Are you typing?'

'No.' The click-clack stops.

'Hey, will you listen to me, please? This is big news. It won't kill you to give me your undivided attention for thirty seconds.'

'Fine,' Finn says wearily. 'Helena's pregnant. I didn't think she had a boyfriend?'

'She doesn't. It was, uh, unplanned. But she's going to have the baby and she's really, really excited and I'm thrilled for her.' Even to my own ears I sound mildly hysterical.

'Well, that's great. Is there anything else because I —'

'Yes, there is something else actually,' I snap. 'She's asked me to be the baby's godmother.'

Silence.

'Finn? Are you still there?'

'Yes, I'm here,' he says, and I detect a definite note of mirth in his voice. 'And how did you respond to this offer?'

'I said yes, of course,' I say, indignant. 'I'm honoured that she asked me.'

'But Anna, you don't even like kids.'

His tone is hesitant. He's asking me to read between the lines. He doesn't want to have to say I'll be a terrible godmother. As if I hadn't already worked that one out for myself.

'I don't dislike them,' I venture. 'I'm an only child; I just haven't had much experience with kids. I can't quite figure out how to work them.'

Finn snorts with laughter. 'And you'll make a good godmother because . . . ?'

His smugness is really starting to grate. *Is this how I sounded to Helena?* I feel sick at the thought. 'Because,' I say hotly, 'Helena is my best friend and she thinks I can do this. And her baby will be different. I'll be involved in her life from the start so we'll get on just fine.'

'How can you be involved, Anna? Helena and her baby will be in Adelaide. You'll be in London. It's not like you can pop round for walks in the park.'

I don't respond.

'Anyway, I've gotta go. I've got a piece leading the six o'clock bulletin,' he says.

'So does that mean you'll be home at a decent hour?'

Finn pauses. 'Er, actually, I was going to have a couple of drinks with the lads after work. You don't mind, do you?'

Suddenly I'm very, very tired. 'No, Finn,' I say. 'I don't mind.'

'Great.' And he hangs up without saying goodbye.

Good mood suitably dampened, I mooch into the Tube station. As recent conversations with my boyfriend of five years go, that one was pretty good. I'm almost resigned to the fact that I'm obviously far from the most interesting thing in Finn's life these days. The trouble is, despite my apparently glamorous existence, he's still the most interesting thing in mine.

My stomach does a little flip-flop as I recall the barely disguised boredom in his voice. I'll go baby shopping tomorrow, I decide; right now all I want is my couch, my dog and some cheesy chick flick.

The red message light on the phone is blinking as I step in the front door. Before I have a chance to dial voicemail, I'm kneecapped by a tiny black missile. Nui, my Boston terrier, flings himself at me as though he hasn't seen a human being in decades, as opposed to the four hours since his lunchtime dog walker left. I scoop him up and let his rough little tongue cover my face in kisses, enjoying the fact that Finn's not there to tell me – again – how unhygienic it is.

Nui doesn't like Finn, and Finn can't bear it so he pretends he doesn't like Nui. Even though we bought him together, choosing the fuzziest black fur ball from a writhing mass of fuzzy black fur balls in a child's playpen in the breeder's kitchen (how's that for unhygienic?), he never took to Finn the way he did to me. Oh, he'll take as many tummy scratches and chewy rawhide treats as Finn cares to dispense, but the moment he's done Nui will be back next to me on his favourite sofa cushion. It drives Finn mad, particularly as he named our pet. Nui means 'big' in Tahitian. The actual Nui is tiny – he only weighs seven kilos – and Finn thought he was being terribly clever. But, I have to admit, the name suits him. Nui has a *lot* of personality; he's a big dog in a little dog's body.

'At least someone's pleased to see me,' I murmur as I set Nui down. He skitters off into the kitchen, claws clicking on the floor-boards. The landline rings. And I'd been so close to that G&T.

The phone screen says 'Unknown Number', which would usu-ally earn the call a one-way ticket to voicemail. But it could be Helena again, and I want to apologise for my lukewarm response to her news earlier, so I pick up the phone.

'I suppose you've known about this for weeks?' a clipped voice hisses before I've even said hello.

Christ. Forget the tonic and double the gin. 'Brigitta, what a nice surprise. It's been quite a while.' *Please don't yell at me*, I silently add.

'I've left seven messages. I've been up all night. Why haven't you returned my calls?'

'Well, I've just walked in the door. I've been at work, Brigitta,' I venture.

'Ah yes, work. Gainful employment. Something Helena will

never see the likes of again once she's a dole-bludging single mother.'
Her voice is even more ear-splittingly shrill than usual.

'Look, Brigitta, you should really be talking to Helena. I've only
just found out myself. I can't get involved in this.'

'But I have to talk to you, Anna,' she rails. 'You're the only one I
can talk to because you, my dear, are the only one that idiot daughter
of mine will listen to. You know she's always looked up to you, since
high school. When you moved to London I thought perhaps she
might finally be motivated to do something with her own life. And
instead she's done this. You simply *must* change her mind.'

I cringe at the steel in Brigitta's voice. How had Helena stood her
ground in the face of this?

I take a deep breath. 'It's not up to me to change her mind, and
I really don't think I could if I tried. Helena is going to do this; she's
going to be a mother. And you know what? I think she'll be a really
good one.'

Brigitta scoffs. 'A good one! That poor child is ruined before it —'

'She,' I offer.

'Before *she* has even arrived. Helena will fail, Anna. She will fail
at parenting like she's failed at everything else.'

There's a hammering at the front door. *Thank you, God.*

'Uh, I have to go now, Brigitta. I have company,' I babble as I lean
into the hall to crack open the front door, herding an ecstatic Nui
away with my foot and gesturing at whoever's there to come inside.

'I always told her she'd been swapped at birth! If only it were
true!'

'Okay then, bye.' I slam the receiver back into its cradle and flop
on to the sofa. I release my chestnut hair from its practical work bun
and it spills down my back in messy waves. Squeezing my eyes shut,
I attempt to teleport myself to a dimension free from pregnant best
friends and their psychotic families.

'Um, hello?'

My eyes spring open at the forceful greeting. It's Luke Parker from next door or, as Finn and I have not-so-affectionately named him, Parcel Nazi. He fills the sitting room doorway, dark eyebrows arched in a way that suggests he's entirely unimpressed. It seems to be his default setting; Luke has been wearing a scowl virtually every time I've seen him since he moved in a year ago. It's a shame, really; he'd almost be handsome if he smiled every now and then.

Quickly, I scan Luke's rangy frame to try and locate the source of today's annoyance. It doesn't take long to spot it. He's clutching a bulky, brown paper-wrapped parcel that looks suspiciously like —

'Jimmy Choos!' I squeal, leaping up. 'Oh, I forgot I'd ordered these. They were on sale on this great designer sample website and I just had —'

'Yeah, that's great. Look Annie, I —'

'Ann*a*.'

'Right. Well, look, obviously you're some sort of cyberspace benefactress, single-handedly keeping the footwear industry in business, but the thing is, I work from home and I'm really sick of being interrupted five times a day by couriers who can't deliver this crap to your house because you're not here,' he says.

Clearly I've angered the gods. How many more people are going to be inexplicably rude to me today? Of course, where Parcel Nazi is concerned, it's not entirely unexpected. Based on my previous experience, it seems he just can't help being a prat.

'Do you think,' Luke goes on, wearily running a hand through his mop of dark hair (it's bordering on mullet – I'd say something if I wasn't convinced he'd throw the Choos at me), 'that you could have these things delivered to your office instead?'

He doesn't wait for a response but drops the parcel on the floor, turns on his heel and stomps out. I go to the window and watch him huff along the footpath to the next house in the terrace, muttering to himself. The slam of his front door reverberates in my sitting room windowpane.

I rescue the parcel and unwrap the shoes. Beautiful. As if I'd have such stunning specimens delivered to the office; they'd mysteriously vanish in the mailroom, I'm sure. How could anyone harbour hostility towards such divine accessories? I pause. It really is unreasonable. And I'm not having it. Not today.

Shoes in hand, I yank open the front door, hop the low dividing wall that separates our front gardens and, with a barking Nui in pursuit, rap sharply on Luke's door. He opens it warily.

'If I were you, Luke,' I spit, 'I would look on these visits from couriers as an opportunity to work on your social skills. Because, from where I'm standing, you're not much of a people person.'

He stares at me, dumbfounded, his stupid bushy hair flopping over one blue eye.

'Thank you for bringing me my shoes. It's much appreciated, *neighbour*.' I saunter back to my own house and throw my meagre remaining energy into flinging the door closed. A panel of leadlight glass cracks. Nui yelps and dives under the couch.

Waiter? Make it a triple.

Helena

'Now you listen to me, young lady. Mummy has a million and one things to do tomorrow, and she's not going to manage any of them unless she gets some rest. So, please, will you stop wriggling about and just GO TO SLEEP!'

My daughter doesn't reply but continues to pump her little legs like she's on an exercise bike. She can't reply, to be fair. She hasn't actually been born yet. But I definitely think I'm getting my 'don't mess with mummy' tone down pat.

I heave myself out of bed and pause, swaying slightly while I relocate my centre of gravity. I'm aware of a dull ache in my lower back. I never imagined how difficult doing normal stuff like standing would be with this enormous belly attached.

I am knackered. There's no other way to say it. I've been existing on three hours of sleep a night, if I'm lucky, for the last month. I have bigger bags under my eyes than the Louis Vuitton trunks Rachel Zoe takes to fashion week. My hair is both greasy and a fetching two-tone shade; I'm too shattered to wash it and the highlights have been growing out since I fell pregnant. My child is keeping me up all night and she's still in the bloody womb.

When I tell people what a sleep thief Ivy is – that'll be her name, Ivy – most of them give me that conspiratorial 'you ain't seen nothin' yet' smile. Even worse are the know-it-alls who insist that having a four-kilo circus freak practising somersaults in my guts is in some way a good thing. 'She'll be such an active baby,' they coo. 'You'll shed your baby weight in no time tearing around after her!'

Baby weight. That's another thing. As far as I can tell, 'baby weight' is the actual mass of this tiny person I'm growing. I can cope with baby weight. What I find more difficult to embrace is 'knocked up, alone and eating to compensate' weight. As a vegetarian, I should probably be positively glowing from the mounds of fresh fruit and vegetables I should probably be eating. I should have a stylish little baby bump while the rest of me remains lithe and cellulite-free, like any stick-thin actress playing a pregnant woman in any Hollywood film, with what looks like a basketball under her jumper. Because that's *so* realistic.

Instead, I have thighs like bollards, a whole collection of chins, and bingo wings so big I could take flight. One more cheese sandwich (the vegetarian's failsafe) and I'll have to be forklifted out of my bedroom window when I go into labour.

If I ever go into labour, that is. Obviously I realise it has to happen at some point, but right now it feels like a remote possibility. Ivy is nine days late. Four more days and my obstetrician will insist on inducing me. You might think, from the way Ivy's wriggling around inside me, that she's itching to hit the ground running, yet she seems to have no inclination to swap my warm, cosy belly for the bright lights beyond.

I can't blame her, really. What's waiting for her in the real world? A grandmother who regards Ivy's very existence as a personal affront and a grandfather who may well be thrilled at the prospect of a chubby baby to bounce on his knee, but daren't show it for fear of icy recrimination from said grandmother. Then there's Ivy's father, but the less said about him the better. I stopped kidding myself months ago that he'd be at my hospital bedside with a cool flannel and a bunch of lilies.

At least there's me. It might not be much, but my daughter will always, always have me.

I waddle into the lounge room, which takes all of three seconds. Space is just a fantasy when your meagre study allowance and occasional furtive handouts from your dad are paying for your bachelorette pad. Still, every square centimetre of my flat widens the buffer zone between me and my mother.

Anna's latest care package sits unopened on the worn arm of the sofa. I'd meant to rip into it when I staggered in from uni – because resuming my visual arts degree while heavily pregnant was *such* a bright idea – but Ivy had been mercifully still so I'd taken the opportunity to sneak a ten-minute snooze in front of *Home and Away* instead. Now, the thought of a funny note from my best friend is like finding water in the desert.

I tear into the padded bag and a shower of small, beautifully wrapped packages cascades out, as well as a thick envelope in that heavy, expensive paper Anna always uses. I should start with the letter – Anna has no doubt written one of her heartfelt notes – but the pressies are too enticing. After all, it's four a.m. and I feel like I'm on spin cycle; I deserve a treat.

I carefully unwrap the largest gift, mindful of the time Anna will have spent preparing it. My breath catches as I unfold a tiny pair of cheongsam-style pyjamas in vibrant fuchsia silk. *Found these in New York*, says a note pinned to the front. *Couldn't resist!*

New York indeed. I didn't even know Anna had been away, but then she's always gallivanting off somewhere. Once upon a time I'd have been hitting the road with her; we'd always planned to travel together. We were even supposed to go to London together – Anna and Hel take on the world! – but it didn't pan out. I'd just started uni and was serious about whichever guy I was seeing at the time. Anna and Finn were practically married and suddenly the idea of boozing our way around Blighty was less appealing to the two of them than becoming proper corporate Londoners, working like dogs to save enough cash for a deposit on a house back home.

Turns out it was a sensible strategy. She'll come back here in a year or two – or five, knowing Anna – with a shedload of dosh and a CV to die for. And it's not like she's completely forsaken seeing the world in favour of the daily grind. She and Finn are masters of the dirty weekend – they have to be, what with him being obsessed with his job – and she's forever flitting off to Cannes or Milan on the trail of some celebrity scandal.

Meanwhile, my days are filled with dull university lectures, interminable tirades from my mother and resigned measurement of my ever-expanding waistline (114 centimetres at last count). But I'm happy with my choices, I really am. If I hadn't stayed in Adelaide I'd never have met Adam, and now I wouldn't be expecting Ivy. And even though I haven't seen Adam since the day I told him I was pregnant, I wouldn't change a thing. I may be the only one who knows it right now, but Ivy is the best thing that has ever happened to me.

As if to show she agrees, my daughter aims a kick at my belly button. My satin nightie – another gift from Anna which arrived promptly after I'd moaned to her about what a heifer I'd become – ripples as Ivy's tiny foot pushes against my skin. The throbbing pain in my back has crept to my front, like I've been wrapped in an overly enthusiastic bear hug. Looks like sleep isn't on the agenda for either of us tonight.

No worries – there's still more loot to tear into. I lift the next parcel from the pile, a rectangular box wrapped in brown paper and tied with string. The wrapping is embossed with inked baby booties and rattles. I can just picture Anna hunched over her coffee table, meticulously stamping away. ('In-store gift wrapping is for lazy people,' she always says.) Her attention to detail is so Type A it's terrifying.

I gingerly peel back the paper and lift the lid from the box. Inside, housed snugly in a nest of tissue paper, are a pair of itsy-bitsy Reeboks, white with pink swirls. I smile wryly, registering Anna's point. She's a runner – no, not just a runner. Anna is a running evangelist. She extols the benefits of pounding the pavement like some nutty preacher on a street corner.

I've seen many a guy at a party, having initially feigned interest in jogging in the hope it would earn him a fumble inside Anna's C cups, looking increasingly desperate as she rattles off statistics and training schedules and the advantages of this sports drink versus that one. They just can't seem to make the connection between the raven-haired, kitten heel-wearing girly girl they're ogling and the obsessive endorphin junkie talking at them. It's a paradox I've always suspected Anna secretly loves.

Now, clearly, she wants my daughter to grow up to have the same mind-numbing effect on men in social situations. I giggle; Anna has never been backward in coming forward.

There's a little Aladdin's cave of goodies still to pore over: a minuscule beaded gypsy skirt (*From Istanbul!* says Anna's note), a silver charm bracelet so dainty it barely fits over my sausage-like thumb, face paints (*Don't worry, they're water-based!*) and a tiny music box that plays Anna's favourite piece of classical music: the theme from that awful 70s tearjerker, *Love Story*.

A lump forms in my throat. They're perfect, all of them. And they're even more perfect in my dingy flat at four a.m., when my mental checklist of people ever likely to give my baby such thoughtful presents seems pitifully short. What I wouldn't give to be opening these with Anna at my side, chastising me for tearing her carefully created wrapping paper or hooting with laughter as she recounts the stories of her trips to New York or Istanbul.

But there's still Anna's letter, on its substantial, creamy paper. She'll have written something profound, something life-affirming, something that will make me believe I'm a fabulous, independent single mum-to-be like Kate Hudson, rather than an exhausted miscreant who can't keep a man, like some reject from a reality TV show.

Sliding the paper, with its knife-edge creases, from the envelope, I see another Post-it stuck to the first page. *Sorry Hel*, it says in Anna's neat hand. *This one's for Ivy, too!*

Oh.

To my fave goddaughter, the letter begins.

On 14 April, you changed my life! When your mum rang that day to tell me the news – that YOU would soon be joining us – I'll admit I was a tiny bit surprised. Okay, I was completely and utterly blown away. Your mum didn't even have a boyfriend but I knew that made no difference. She's a star, your mum. She has more love for you in the freckle next to her right ear than so many mothers have in their whole body.

But what's really bowled me over, young Ivy, is the way you've given me a whole new outlook on life. I've never really been a big fan of little people —

I can't help it, I let out a hoot. Anna saying she's 'not a big fan' of kids is like Kim Kardashian saying she doesn't really go for the natural look.

— but with you it's different. I already feel we have a real connection and you've not even arrived! I think about you often; when I wander into Gap Kids or Monsoon I automatically seek out the twirliest dresses and I'm keeping all my favourite outfits for when you

grow up (they'll be vintage by then!)

*Ivy, I'm going to try my very, very best to be the kind
of godmother you deserve. I want to be there for you – even if,
technically, I'm half a world away – and teach you things. And
I hope you'll teach me things, too. I may be a positively ancient
twenty-five but I look forward to growing up again with you.*

*Lots of love, Aunty Anna (ooh, that makes me sound
so old!)*

I fold Anna's letter and slip it back into its envelope, then place
it carefully on the coffee table. Pursing my lips, I stare at the velvety
stock, which is blank except for a flowery 'Ivy!' with a heart where
the dot of the exclamation mark should be. My belly hurts. I'm
tired. And now I feel completely deflated to boot.

There's a strange feeling nibbling at the edges of my thoughts,
and I know precisely what it is. It's the same feeling I would get
when, as an insecure teenager, I'd make myself feel momentarily
superior by uttering a snide comment to Anna about some fat, unat-
tractive or, heaven forbid, poorly dressed girl we'd spotted in the
street. We'd snigger as she walked by, cloaked as we were in our own
perfection, but then, inevitably, my heart would sink. Perhaps this
girl would wave and smile at a friend across the road, or she'd pull
out her mobile phone and start chatting animatedly to her boyfriend.
That's when the feeling would hit: the realisation that she was a nice,
normal girl and I was a bitter, cynical and – worse – smug bitch.

I'm feeling that way now because of Anna's letter. Because it's a
lovely, sincere message to my unborn child and all I can think is: Is
she *serious*?

Ivy has changed *Anna's* life? My baby has given *Anna* a whole
new outlook? As for this mythical connection they share, Anna
should try carting Ivy around inside her for nine months – she
wouldn't be so eager to be connected then. And if she thinks wasting

money on designer baby clothes Ivy will grow out of in a month proves what a dedicated godmother she'll be, well, it's not exactly what I had in mind.

How can Anna be so self-involved? My pregnancy is not about her. If Ivy is changing anyone's life, it's *mine*. It's a wonder Anna managed to get her head out of her backside long enough to write my daughter a letter in the first place.

These thoughts are swiftly followed by a wave of disgust. I've spent the last half-hour opening gifts Anna has quite literally gone to the ends of the earth for and yet I'm sitting here, enormous and uncomfortable, feeling my best friend is exactly like my mother: she just doesn't get it.

My mother is so concerned with the havoc she's convinced Ivy will wreak on my life that she's entirely blind to what good my daughter will do. Ivy will be someone I'll love and who'll – hopefully – love me no matter what. Mum thinks it's all about my not having a husband or a career or much money. But that's just surface stuff; those things won't matter when I've got a little person with no one in the world to rely on except me.

It's preposterous, of course, to think that Anna doesn't understand any of this. Anna gets it – gets me – more than anyone. She's been my best friend for a decade and has seen the best and the very, very worst of me. Ever since the first day of Year Nine when Anna, who had transferred from another school, flounced into the seat next to me in English and breathed, 'Where did you get those earrings?' we've been through everything together. I've lost count of the number of times she's snuck me in through her bedroom window at midnight after yet another hellish row with my mother, silencing her own parents with a glance when they've found me curled up on their couch the next morning. She's been there through my umpteen dodgy relationships and even more almost-relationships and flings that left me heartbroken. And every time I've dropped out of uni or got myself all fired up about a new course that's definitely, absolutely going to lead to my dream career, she's allowed herself only the briefest roll of the eyes before yelping and enthusing right along with me.

So why am I feeling like this? Why do I have this heavy feeling in my abdomen, like I've eaten a house brick?

Come to think of it, why *do* I still have this pain in my belly? It feels like someone is tightening a belt around my middle. I thought it'd gone but now it's come back.

It's come back.

It went away and then came back.

Oh my God. I'm in labour.

As I heave myself up from the arm of the couch I realise my nightie is suspiciously damp. Sure enough, when I stand up there's a trickle of fluid down my inner thigh that tells me my waters have broken. As if to emphasise the point that labour has officially begun, a twisting pain suddenly pierces my belly. It builds to an agonising crescendo, like the worst menstrual cramps I've ever experienced multiplied by a nasty bout of gastro, with the after-effects of a bad curry thrown in for good measure. I grip the back of the sofa and try not to faint as beads of sweat prickle on my forehead.

Then, almost as rudely as it barged in, the pain vanishes. I use the respite to lumber towards the telephone and punch in my parents' number. It rings and rings, each extended trill sounding more and more mocking. It's almost five a.m. and they're fifty-something retirees; they can't possibly be out.

'Pick up the bloody phone, you idiots,' I shout into the receiver. 'How often do you get calls in the middle of the night, people? It's obviously important!'

But still it rings. And rings.

And then it dawns on me: I am the only person who would be calling at this hour; they must assume it's me. But they're not answering.

Their pregnant – overdue, in fact – daughter is telephoning them at five a.m. and they're choosing not to pick up the phone. It's my mother's last chance to make her feelings known: *you've disgraced yourself and your family*, I can almost hear her hissing, *now you can deal with the consequences*.

I can picture my dad, having reached for the receiver and had his hand slapped away, sitting up in bed praying for the ringing to stop while my mother rolls over and pretends to go back to sleep. I know he'll give it ten minutes or so, then get up under the pretence of going to the toilet and sneak into the kitchen to call me back. Trouble is, I don't think I can wait that long.

Another wave of pain crashes over me. This can't be good; it's been only two minutes since the last contraction. I have no idea what to do next. My heart is racing and I feel sick. What was I thinking? I can't do this. I don't even know who to call when I'm in labour – what am I going to do when I've got an actual child to cope with? Who was I kidding to think I could handle this alone? It's a joke. I'm a joke.

The contraction subsides just as the phone rings. Mum must have started snoring more quickly than usual.

'Dad!'

'Hey babes, it's Anna,' comes the tinny reply. 'Oh bollocks, what time is it there? I always get the bloody time difference messed up.'

'Anna! Oh An, I'm in labour. Well, I think I am. I'm in terrible pain and I think my waters broke and I tried to call my parents but they're not answering because they're punishing me, I know they are, and I don't know what —'

'Helena, stop. Calm down, hon. Take some deep breaths.' Anna's voice is level and soothing. I inhale deeply.

'Okay, now I want you to hang up the phone and sit down wherever you are. I'm going to call an ambulance, and then I'll call you right back.' Without waiting for my response, Anna hangs up.

I flop on to the floor as yet another contraction pummels my insides. Through the pain and fatigue I'm still acutely aware of a lingering sense of shame. Moments ago I'd been berating Anna in my mind yet somehow she'd known to call me – she *never* gets the time difference wrong – and was now taking charge from the other side of the planet.

The phone rings again. 'Hello?' I answer weakly.

'The ambulance will be there in just a few minutes. They asked me to ask you to have your hospital bag with you if you can. Saves them having to look for it,' Anna says.

'My hospital bag?'

'Yeah, you know, the bag with a fresh nightie, clean knickers, your toothbrush. The new mum's essentials.'

God, I've forgotten to pack my hospital bag. I've had an extra nine days' grace and I haven't even been organised enough to chuck some undies in a backpack.

'I, uh, I don't have a hospital bag.' I can't help it, fat tears begin to roll down my cheeks. 'I'm crap at this, Anna,' I wail. 'I can't even look after myself. Why did I ever think I could look after a baby?'

'Helena, I realise this might seem like an odd thing to say in this particular situation, but you can't worry right now about what kind of mother you're going to be,' Anna says carefully.

'What? I'm in labour. I think now is the time!'

'No, Hel, it's not. You've got the rest of today and all day tomorrow and the rest of this baby's life to worry about that. At this exact moment, just think about yourself. Just think about relaxing as much as you can and getting to the hospital and getting through this, one little bit at a time,' she says.

I hear the howl of an ambulance siren in the street below.

'But this is the easy part. Any minute now Ivy's going to be here and I've got nothing to offer her except me. Her fat, useless, unwed mother,' I sob.

There's a hammering at the door. 'Miss Stanley?' comes a deep male voice. 'It's the ambulance service.'

I'm gripped by another contraction and momentarily can't reply.

'Anna, they're here and I'm having a contraction and I can't get up to unlock the door,' I manage to rasp at last.

'Don't worry, Hel. I've told them where the spare key is. They'll let themselves in.'

'How do you know where I keep the spare key?'

'Helena, you've been keeping your spare key under that weird pot you made in Year Ten art since we were sixteen,' she says, laughing.

I giggle but before I can answer the front door swings open and two men dressed in reflective green coveralls hurry in.

'Miss Stanley?' says one with a warm smile.

'Helena,' I say weakly.

'Okay, Helena. I'm Stuart. How are you feeling?'

'Have you seen that bit in *Alien* when the slimy monster bursts out of John Hurt's stomach? Kind of like that.'

Stuart chuckles as he presses two fingers to my neck to take my pulse.

'I'm going to go now,' Anna says in my ear. 'These guys will look after you and I'll call you in the hospital.'

'Okay,' I whisper.

'I love you, Hel. You're an incredible person and you are going to be an incredible mother. Don't waste another second thinking any different.' She hangs up.

'Can you tell me how many weeks you are, Helena?' Stuart asks.

'Forty-one.' He's cute; shame I'm practically monosyllabic.

'And how far apart are your contractions?'

'About two minutes.'

'Right, let's get you up.'

Stuart and his mate brace themselves on either side of me and hoist me up. They guide me to the sofa and ease me back into it.

'Okay, Helena,' Stuart says matter-of-factly. 'I think this baby of yours is in a bit of a hurry and I'd say it's fairly unlikely we'll make it to the hospital before she decides to join us.'

My throat tightens in panic, just as my abdomen tightens with yet another contraction. I groan in a particularly unladylike fashion.

'What we're going to do is get you down into the ambulance, where we'll be able to deliver the baby en route if we need to. How does that sound?'

I want to tell Stuart that sounds like a swell idea. I want to say, 'You know what, Stuart? The idea of being surrounded by trained professionals, fancy machines and pain-relieving drugs sounds pretty darn good right now. Let's do it!'

But I can't say any of that because I'm paralysed by terror and agonising, maddening pain in equal measure. A new sensation is juddering through my body: the urge to push. I don't think I'm doing the pushing – but there's definitely pushing going on.

Stuart sees the look on my face and, his eyes flickering an apology, hitches up my now ruined satin sheath. Oh, the shame.

'She's crowning,' he says gravely to the other paramedic. 'Change of plan, Helena,' he says with a grin. 'We're not going to need to go anywhere just yet. Your baby's coming right now.'

Finn

Jez is positively beaming. He's sporting a grin so wide and unwavering it's like his face has been hijacked by it. It's a little disconcerting, if I'm honest. I expected Jez to slouch into the pub with the defeated gait of a broken man, his broad shoulders hunched and feet shuffling. Instead, he bounds – there's no other word for it – to the bar and slaps me on the back so hard I almost drop my pint.

'Finn, me auld mate! How the bloody hell are ye?' the lumbering Glaswegian yelps, flinging one arm across my shoulders. 'It's been too bloody long, pal!'

Aha, here comes the real story. The maniacal grin must be Jez's reaction to being allowed out of the house for the first time in three months; any moment now it will be replaced by a grey pallor as he admits to what I secretly suspect: fatherhood is killing him.

'It has indeed, Jez, it has indeed. It's bad enough that I hardly see you at work these days, without beers being off the menu as well,' I say. 'Ellie got you up to your nuts in shitty nappies?' I can't suppress my smirk. Wait until I tell him about my interview, then he'll really regret tying himself down.

'Naw, man. It's no' like that. Ellie's great wi' the wean. It's just me, like. I hate bein' away fae the bairn,' Jez says.

'Sorry Jez, I just about understood "wean". You're going to have to repeat the rest of that in English.'

'Bloody Aussies,' he says, the Cheshire-cat grin broader than ever. 'I'm just saying, like, my Danny's a top little lad. So funny'n that, the things he does. I don't want tae miss anything.'

Jez slaps me on the back again and turns to flag down the barman, leaving me to stare slack-jawed at this stranger impersonating my best friend. I feel like I've been dragged into some awful 1950s sci-fi flick, *Invasion of the Body Snatchers* or something. Except that instead of screaming townsfolk being replaced by slimy pod-people, my mate Jez has metamorphosed from the ultimate beer-swilling workaholic into some sort of house husband. And worse, he seems quite pleased with himself.

'I cannae tell ye, man, just how great it's been wi' me'n Ellie since Danny came along,' Jez says, turning back to me and slurping the head off his pint. 'We're so much closer'n that. Gettin' on great these days.'

I shake my head in disbelief. 'Wait, let me see if I understand this. Jez, the bloke who's been trying to ditch his missus almost the entire two years I've known him, hasn't been out on the beers in three months by *choice*?'

Jez has the good grace to look mildly sheepish. 'I know, Finn, I know. It's come as a pretty big surprise to me'n all. I can't explain it. Becoming a father's just, like, not at all what I expected. It's bloody great,' he says.

'But what about you and Ellie? I thought you said there was no future in it, baby or no baby?'

'Aye, I did, I did. But it's different now, ye know? I think I was just bored before. Me'n Ellie've been together since school'n I reckon I just thought the grass were greener,' Jez says, pensively running a hand over his shaved head.

'But how have sleepless nights and no sex fixed that?'

'Who said anything about no sex?' he says with a wink.

I can't believe what I'm hearing. Ever since my first day at the network, when Jez lobbed a football at my head from across the office and shouted 'G'day Bruce! How's it goin', cobber?' in his almost incomprehensible Scottish burr, he's been the yardstick by which I've judged how domestic is too domestic.

In two years, I've met his fiancée, Ellie, maybe four times, and then only when I've been picking Jez up or dropping him off at their house in Chiswick. He's never brought her to a work do or let her join us in the pub. Jez is – or was – firmly of the belief that the boozer is a place for men and their mates; if a girlfriend warrants an invite it's only because all the other blokes will have their birds there as well.

Jez is the mate I can always rely on to meet me for beers at a moment's notice when I need a bit of space from Anna. He's the one who thinks nothing of telling me my girlfriend's 'a great-lookin' lassie' one moment, and then turning around and announcing that five years with the same woman is too long and I should 'cut her loose'.

Anna thinks Jez is a sexist pig. He's not really – he just likes to keep his social life and his home life separate. 'But,' Anna will always argue, 'your partner *is* your social life. The whole point of being in a relationship is so you'll always have someone to go out with.'

But now it looks like Anna might be right. Jez actually choosing Ellie and their newborn son over a night on the tiles is just unheard of. And it makes me very uncomfortable.

'But . . . but you said no amount of nagging from Ellie was going to keep you at home with a snot-nosed kid?' There's a note of desperation in my voice.

'Steady there, pal. Danny's a crackin' little boy,' Jez returns, his smile fading momentarily. 'I know it sounds weird but I just feel like I've grown up a bit, ye know? I mean, I'm thirty-three and I've got a top bird and a bairn tae think about. I owe it to both of 'um tae make the effort.'

We're both silent for a moment, trying to absorb the enormity of Jez's total personality overhaul. I hope this doesn't mean we're going to have to talk about babies and relationships instead of cars and football from now on. I get enough of that from Anna. In the six months since Helena had Ivy, it feels like Anna has talked about nothing else. If I didn't know her better, I'd swear she was getting clucky. I shudder involuntarily at the thought.

'So, how's Anna?' Jez pipes up. And so it begins.

'She's, uh, okay. Fine. She's fine,' I mutter.

'Ye don't sound too sure about that, mate.'

'It's just that we've not been seeing that much of each other. I've been working a lot, so she's been giving me a bit of grief,' I say. 'And now I've got this job interview.'

'Ye should make more time fae Anna, Finn. It must be hard fae the lass, what wi' her family and her new little goddaughter back in Australia,' Jez says solemnly.

I splutter into my beer. I've dropped the magic word: 'interview'. Jez is supposed to grab hold of it like the frustrated domestic weirdo he's surely become. Instead he's telling me to spend more time at home? And since when does he give a toss about Anna's goddaughter? My head is spinning; this is without doubt the most surreal conversation I've ever had with my best mate.

'Er, right. But anyway, I've got this interview,' I say meekly.

'Oh yeah?' Jez looks at his watch.

'Yeah, it's for a senior reporting job on a new current affairs show.'

'Sounds grand, mate.'

'Yeah. Only trouble is it's in Belfast.'

Jez fixes me with his blue eyes. 'Belfast? What does Anna think about that?'

'I haven't told her yet. I don't think there's much point, you know, until after the interview. Why get her all worked up unless I'm offered the job?'

I study Jez carefully for a reaction. Three months ago I'd have known exactly how he'd respond. He'd say: 'Aye pal, go for it. Ye don't need grief from the missus if you're not actually goin'.' Now I'm not sure what he'll say, although based on the last few minutes, I think I can guess.

'Ye should tell her, Finn. You're in this together. She has a right to know,' he says matter-of-factly.

I scowl at Jez, who sips his beer contentedly. I know I'll have to tell Anna about the job eventually. The Belfast producer seemed pretty serious when she rang this morning to 'ascertain my interest' in the position. But I won't know just how serious until I fly out to Northern Ireland next week to meet with her. Why rock the boat before that?

What I do know is precisely how Anna will react to the news when I eventually tell her. She won't be happy for me, that's for sure. She'll just bluster on about the practicalities: how it would be crazy for her to throw in her well-paid and highly coveted job to come with me; how my moving to Belfast without her will mean she can't afford the rent on our Victorian terrace; how we'll see even less of each other than we do now (*if that's even possible*, I can almost hear her saying).

She'll probably cry, call me selfish, inconsiderate and all the rest of it. Then she'll tell me how coming to London was never supposed to be about furthering our careers but about having adventures together, seeing the world together, planning our lives *together*. She'll remind me how hard it was to persuade me to come to the UK with her in the first place, pointing out I'd have happily spent the rest of my working life on the suburban Adelaide newspaper where we met if she hadn't dragged me out of my comfort zone.

'You were a big fish in a small pond,' she'll proclaim. 'You'd never have moved out of your mum's house if it wasn't for me. And now look at you – a senior TV journalist with a posh house in Richmond!'

It's the truth, of course – but that's just the problem. I had been reluctant to leave Adelaide, where I was comfortable and I knew people and they knew me. But I was more reluctant to let Anna leave me. So I followed her to London where, again, she was proved right: the opportunities for me here seem endless. I walked into my job within a month of arriving and have been dazzling the powers-that-be, if I say so myself, ever since. It's nice to have Anna to come home to at the end of every day, but in London I've found a renewed hunger for journalism that I can tell has her pretty miffed.

'Ask yourself this, mate: if you're offered the job, will ye take it?' Jez asks.

I pause, pretending to think about the question, though I don't need to. I know the answer: yes. If I'm offered the job in Belfast I will take it. Even though I know Anna probably won't follow. I tell Jez as much.

'I don't get it,' he says. 'It's just a job. Do you want to split from Anna?'

Do I? I love her but we've been together so long. When we met, Anna was just twenty and a couple of years into her cadetship at the paper. She was fun, that had been my first impression. She thought nothing of working the late shift, then heading to the pub at midnight and knocking back G&Ts into the small hours. And she was so full of ideas. She'd decide on a whim that something interested her – pottery, swing dancing, learning Italian – and buy every book she could find on the subject, devouring knowledge like a locust devours crops.

Five years later and somehow Anna's flights of fancy seem not so much spontaneous as immature, like she's trying to prove – to me? to herself? – that she's still as fun-loving as she ever was. But I've watched her ironing the bed sheets and seen the file of clippings from interior design magazines she keeps in the bottom of her wardrobe. I know the real Anna. She's Martha Stewart in Paris Hilton's clothing.

This job, putting a bit of distance between us, could be just the thing to get us back on track. Maybe all I need is the chance to miss her again.

Anna is asleep – or at least pretending to be – when I finally slink into the bedroom at two a.m., stinking of stale beer and ciggies.

Like a detective, I can tell what kind of day my girlfriend has had by the various piles of clothing strewn across the threadbare carpet. Her work clothes – sensible black trousers, strappy top thing and vertiginous heels – have been flung in all directions. On the furthest side of the bedroom (though I can smell it from the doorway) is her running gear. Sweaty leggings, muddy sneakers and the ratty Van Halen T-shirt I've consigned to the kitchen bin at least three times lie quietly festering next to Anna's bath towel.

So, I deduce, she was stuck late at work but was determined to squeeze in a run before tonight's C-list bash. I wonder what it was this time – the announcement of the latest bunch of has-beens to be chucked into the jungle or the desert or some tropical island, perhaps? The opening of an envelope, more like. Whatever the occasion, she's obviously been busy. I hate to wake her, but I have to tell her about my interview. My mind's made up.

I know Anna is baffled by my soaring enthusiasm for my work. After all, five years ago my bread and butter was dull local council stories – articles about irate dog owners or Barry and Betty Lunchbucket's battle to make the bin men take their lawn clippings on the same day as their old newspapers. Now I'm interviewing radical clerics, door-stepping MPs and reporting from outside Buckingham Palace – stuff that really matters.

I can't quite work out how it's happened myself but I like feeling my opinions count for something. I walk into the office every morning thinking, *This is it, this will be the day they unmask me and reveal to all the world that I'm just some jumped-up hack with a trendy haircut and a knack for putting a fresh spin on old ideas.* But they haven't found me out yet.

I can't tell Anna any of this though. She won't get that moving to a new network – albeit one in Northern Ireland – will mean I can move through the ranks much more quickly. Getting in at ground level on a new show means I could be a co-presenter within a year. I'm almost thirty; if I don't get my chance soon it may never come.

I look over at my sleeping girlfriend, who's snoring lightly and flexing the fingers of her right hand as though typing. Does this happen to all couples? Are the things that attract you to someone, like their passion for their job, ultimately the things that grate the most?

'Anna,' I whisper, leaning over to stroke her dark hair back from her face. She stirs, stretching her lean body like a cat, but doesn't wake.

'An, wake up,' I say, louder now. 'Come on, sweets.'

Anna opens her eyes groggily and looks at me, perplexed, as though she's seen me somewhere but can't quite place me. Then, suddenly, she sits bolt upright.

'Oh, Finn, I'm so worried —'

'Shh, I know. I'm sorry. I was out with Jez and I just lost track of —'

But Anna is shaking her head. 'No, Finn. It's Helena. I'm so worried about her. We had the strangest phone conversation tonight and it's got me really rattled,' she says.

'Uh, okay. What did she say?' I ask, trying to mask the relief in my voice. I will tell her about the interview – soon – but for now it looks like I've been given a reprieve.

'It's not really what she said. It's more what she *didn't* say,' Anna replies. 'She's usually so chatty on the phone but tonight she was really quiet. It was all one-word answers and grunts.'

'Grunts?'

'Yeah, like she couldn't be bothered putting whole sentences together. I asked her how Ivy's been sleeping. "Fine." Whether her mum and dad have been to see her. "Dad has." If she'd had any time for study. "A bit."'

'So? She answered your questions. What's the problem?'

'The problem is I usually can't get a word in edgeways when I talk to Hel. A month ago she talked for twenty minutes about how the colour of Ivy's poo varies according to whether she's had breast milk or formula,' she says.

I arrange my face into what I hope is an understanding expression when, in actual fact, the combination of six pints and talk of technicolour infant mess is causing my stomach to churn. 'Uh-huh,' is all I can manage.

'But tonight it was as if she just didn't have the energy, or the inclination, to talk to me.'

'Don't take this the wrong way, An, but maybe she didn't,' I venture. 'She has a six-month-old baby. She's probably exhausted.'

The look on Anna's face tells me the sensible answer wasn't the one she was looking for. I can't help it, baby talk just leaves me cold and I've already endured almost seven hours of it from Jez. I thought Anna's goddaughter being half a world away might temper her enthusiasm for the subject, but she's become a bona fide baby bore since Ivy was born. I'm not quite sure what's caused Anna to morph from resolutely child *un*friendly to gooey over anything baby-related, but it's tedious to say the least.

'I'm worried it's more serious than that,' she says.

'What do you mean?'

'I'm worried Helena may have postnatal depression.'

'Well, lots of women get that, don't they? It's easily treated,' I say lightly.

'Sure, it's easily treated for women who feel they can seek treatment. Women with good self-esteem and a support network of family and friends who'll help them through something like this.'

'Well, Helena's got you,' I offer.

'But I'm no use to her over here, am I? And it's not like she's got much support in Adelaide either. You know Brigitta hasn't been to see Ivy yet? In six months. Didn't even send flowers when Hel was in hospital.' Anna doesn't try to hide her disgust.

'What about the baby's father?' I ask, and instantly know I've said the wrong thing. Anna gives me a withering look that screams *don't you* ever *listen to a word I say?* She doesn't answer the question.

'I'm just worried it's starting to dawn on Helena that she's pretty much alone.' She winces as she says it, like she's condemning her best friend to a life of microwave meals-for-one and talking to her cats.

'Did she say anything else?' I'm not sure why this matters; I'm clamouring to contribute something useful.

'Yes. Just before we hung up she said she had to go. Then she said goodbye,' Anna says meaningfully.

'Well, isn't that what people generally say when they end a phone call?'

'But that's just it, Finn,' she says, exasperated. 'Hel never says stuff like that. She'll say, "Ooh, *Neighbours* is on. Catch ya" or "S'pose I'd better drag myself to the gym. Laters." Saying "goodbye" made it sound like she was going . . . away.' Tears well in Anna's eyes. 'I'm worried she'll do something stupid,' she sputters.

I have absolutely no idea what to say. Why isn't there a manual for these kinds of conversations?

'Er, but I thought she loves being a mum?' A feeble effort.

'So did I. At least, that's what she always tells me,' Anna says. 'But after tonight I'm wondering if she just says that stuff for my benefit. Like she's trying to convince me of it. Or convince herself.'

Anna burrows her face into my chest and I wrap my arms around her. The words 'job interview' are still loitering at the back of my mind. I've never been particularly good at saying the right thing at the right moment but even I know now isn't the time to announce, 'Bummer about your friend. Hey, I might be moving to Belfast!'

Then, suddenly – mercifully – I have a brainwave.

'Look, why don't I ring Helena's mum? I'll tell her about your conversation with Hel and ask her to go round and check on her,' I say gently.

Anna shakes her head sadly. 'Brigitta won't go, Finn. She doesn't give a damn about Helena any more.'

'She will go,' I say forcefully. 'I'll make sure of it.'

At last, Anna's cheeks dimple as she smiles. 'Thank you,' she whispers.

She swathes herself in my bathrobe and follows me into the sitting room as I pick up the phone. My heart thuds uncomfortably. Religious zealots, crooked politicians and international despots pale in comparison to Brigitta Stanley.

She picks up the phone after one ring. 'Yes?'

'Hello, Br . . . um, Mrs, er . . . Brigitta. This is Finn Cassidy. Anna's boyfriend?'

'Finn, yes. Have you heard anything?' Brigitta says flatly.

I cast a quick glance at Anna, who is balanced on the edge of the couch. This is definitely not the greeting I had expected.

'I'm not sure I understand,' I say. Anna leans forward intently.

'You mean Anna hasn't read my email?' Brigitta says, her voice rising an octave.

'Well, no. It's two in the morning here.'

'I realise that, young man, which is why I emailed Anna instead of telephoning,' she snaps. 'I know the pair of you keep unsociable hours, I thought perhaps she might check her inbox last thing.'

'No, sorry. We just —'

'What is it then?'

'Excuse me?' I'm getting flustered. Brigitta is truly bamboozling.

'If you haven't read the email, why are you calling me?' she says, speaking patronisingly slowly, presumably so that my tiny brain can comprehend.

'Oh, right. I'm calling on Anna's behalf, really. She spoke to Helena earlier today and was worried by a couple of things she said,' I tell her.

'What things?' Brigitta demands.

'Anna seems to think Helena may be feeling a bit down. She —' I pause. Brigitta may be the devil incarnate but I can't bring myself to blurt out 'We think your daughter might be considering jumping off a cliff.' I try again. 'Anna thinks it's really important that Helena has people around her at the moment,' I say.

'Oh God,' is Brigitta's response.

'It might be a good idea for you to go and see her today. Could you do that?'

There's a pause. Anna is pacing the sitting room floor, twisting her dark hair around the fingers of one hand and gesticulating wildly with the other. She's mouthing things I can't understand.

'No,' Brigitta says at last.

Now I'm lost for words. 'No? You won't go and see Helena?'

Anna stops dead, her face contorted into a mask of pure fury. She lunges for the phone.

I snatch it out of her reach. 'Are you joking?'

'I wish I was. I would love to see my daughter, Finn. And my granddaughter,' Brigitta sighs. 'But I can't. That's what my email was about. Helena and Ivy are missing.'

Anna

When Helena crawled up through the fog of childbirth two days after Ivy's arrival, the first thing she'd asked me was how I was able to call an ambulance for her from the other side of the planet.

The answer, of course, is because I'm organised. And because I know Helena inside out. I knew that however well prepared she thought she was for Ivy's arrival, she would somehow be caught unawares.

Hel seems to go through life being blindsided by unexpected happenings. Like that afternoon, aged fourteen, when she spent hours perfecting her makeup and straightening her hair so that she could ride her bike seductively past her crush's house, only to hit a pothole and tumble arse over elbow into the gutter in front of him and six of his friends. Or the time she tried to save money by bleaching her waist-length hair at home and ended up with a ginger crop that made her look like Ronald McDonald.

Or the time she leapt into bed with a thoroughly unsuitable bloke and wound up pregnant. But that's beside the point.

The point is things just seem to happen to Helena, despite her best intentions. And that's why, as soon as she told me she was expecting a baby, I made sure my own mother was on standby in Adelaide to dial 000 on Helena's behalf if I gave the word.

When Helena first asked me to be Ivy's godmother, I agreed more out of a sense of obligation than any real desire to be involved in her daughter's life. Though I'd never admit it to Finn, I suspected he was right when he pointed out all those months ago that the basic facts of geography would make it virtually impossible for me to offer any real guidance as Ivy grows up. But the more I thought about it, the more I realised it doesn't have to be that way. We have Skype and FaceTime these days, not to mention email and social media and dirt-cheap international phone calls. I can be a weekly or even daily presence in Ivy's life. I can read her stories before she goes to sleep at night and play peekaboo for hours on end. Maybe I can foster ambition and drive in her too; encourage her not to throw in the towel when things get tough. Maybe I can step up and be there for Helena, and make an actual difference to her daughter at the same time.

But I can't do any of that until I know where Helena and Ivy are. And right now I don't know what to do, don't know who to call. Before he even spoke, the strangled look on Finn's face as he placed the phone carefully back in its cradle following his call to Brigitta told me action was required, and so I've morphed into a human whirlwind. And still no amount of pacing, opening and closing of cupboards or rifling through stacks of papers can organise my absent best friend into being happy and safe.

'Come on, babe, just relax. You're not going to help anyone by trashing the house. Let me make you a cuppa and we'll talk about it,' Finn says, reaching out for me.

I wriggle free of his embrace. 'I don't want a bloody cuppa. I can't just sit here, Finn. I have to *do* something,' I snap.

'What do you want to do, Anna? Fly home to Australia this second?'

He's trying to calm me down, to reason with me. As if that's even a remote possibility at a time like this. Helena and Ivy could be anywhere, and he wants to mull over the possibilities over tea and biscuits?

I sink on to the sofa, struggling to draw breath past the ocean of terror in my chest. I'd spoken to Helena not six hours ago and I knew something wasn't right. Why didn't I do something then? Why didn't I pick up the phone and scream at Brigitta until she agreed to shelve her petty pride and go to her daughter? I bury my face in my hands; my fingers are deathly cold.

'Where *are* you, Helena?' I wail. My reply is a knock at the front door.

'If that's Parcel Nazi telling us to keep the noise down I swear to God I will —'

'I'll get it,' Finn offers. 'You keep . . . doing whatever it is you're doing.'

I hear him pad into the hall, the drag of the deadbolt, the front door swinging open. Nui's growl. Then silence.

'Anna?' Finn calls eventually. 'I think you'd better come out here.'

Sighing, I stomp into the hall. Then I freeze, my mouth agape. There, looking bleary-eyed yet murderous, is Luke. Standing next to him, tiny and huddled and clutching a tightly swaddled Ivy to her chest, is Helena.

It might have been two years since I last saw her, and I know she's had a rough ride since, but I think it's fair to say Helena has never looked worse. Like me, Hel has always been able to turn even the most innocuous snack swiftly into cellulite (that's why I run so much), but now she is frighteningly thin. The voluptuous 50s pin-up figure I've always envied has disappeared. Now her shapeless T-shirt and faded tracksuit bottoms hang off her wasted frame and her once resplendent bust careens southward in a futile search for underwire.

It feels like hours pass before she lifts her gaze from my front step and looks at me from beneath her dirty blonde fringe. Her blue eyes are ringed with bruise-black circles and her skin is sallow. If not for the squirming bundle in her arms I'd think my best friend was a drug addict.

'Is this yours?' Luke snaps, elbowing her forward.

Helena looks up at me, silently imploring, as though the power of speech has deserted her.

I shoot Parcel Nazi the most venomous look I can muster and he has the sense to look away.

'Now is not the time,' I hiss, wrapping my arm around Helena's shoulder and drawing her into the hall. Ivy, until now eerily quiet, lets out a cry and Luke's face softens momentarily.

'Sorry,' he mumbles. 'It's just late and . . . I was sleeping and your friend started hammering on my door and —'

'Save it,' I say as I shake my head, stunned that he thinks I give a toss about his half-arsed apology. I close the door in his face.

Finn has vanished and I hear the kettle hissing in the kitchen. Ivy's cries grow louder and more urgent; she's wrestled her arms free of their snug prison and is waving them purposefully, like a student on a protest march. Helena makes no effort to comfort her daughter. She still hasn't uttered a word.

'I'm so glad you're here,' I say at last, because I am, even if I can't quite grasp how she can possibly be standing in my hallway when she should be half a world away.

A trace of a smile flickers across her face. 'Really?' she whispers.

Suddenly, I come back to life. The surrealness of the situation lingers, but the paralysing fear I'd felt just moments ago has passed. Helena is safe. My goddaughter is safe.

I wrap them both in a hug so fierce I fear I might break Hel, but

Ivy quiets and her mother uses her free arm to hug me back.

'Come on,' I murmur and lead them into the sitting room.

Helena immediately sinks on to the couch, Ivy lolling haphaz-ardly beside her. Without asking, I scoop the squirming infant up into a firm embrace. Is this how you're supposed to hold babies? I have no idea but Hel doesn't move to correct me.

'Hello there,' I whisper to Ivy. 'I'm pleased to meet you at last.'

She peers curiously up at me, her blue eyes as round as saucers.

Finn creeps in bearing two steaming cups of tea. He sets them down on a side table then hovers, unsure whether to slip away qui-etly or ask the question that is clearly burning on his lips.

'Hello Finn,' Helena says dully, offering him a half smile. 'How's things?'

Finn casts me a sidelong glance. He wants my permission; against my better judgement, I give it with a slight nod.

'We've been really worried, Helena,' he begins carefully, and I'm grateful he's chosen the delicate approach. 'We're really happy you're safe . . . but . . . why are you here? How did you even get here?'

Ivy, by now solemnly absorbing her new surroundings, grabs a fistful of my hair and yanks. I bite my lip to stifle a yelp. Those six-month-old arms are like little pistons.

Helena sighs. 'I couldn't take it any more. I had to get away,' she says simply. 'So I took my dad's credit card and booked a one-way flight.'

Wait 'til Brigitta hears about that one.

'But Hel, I spoke to you just a few hours ago. Where were you then? Why didn't you tell me you were coming?'

'I was at Heathrow,' she says with a shrug. 'We'd just arrived. I was going to tell you on the phone but, I don't know, it seemed ridiculous. So we got on the Tube and rode around for a few hours. I had to think about whether coming to you was the right thing.'

Perhaps a decision that might have been best made *before* she'd boarded a twenty-four-hour flight.

'What do you mean?'

'Well, I didn't know if you'd want me – us – here.'

She isn't making sense. I've been virtually mad with worry since she hung up the phone nearly seven hours ago. I would have given my life savings and sold my entire shoe collection to have her little rumpled body on my sofa. How can she not know that?

'Why would you doubt that?' Finn pipes up.

Helena purses her lips. She looks at Finn, then at me, her best friend cradling her sweet-smelling baby daughter.

'Well,' she says finally, 'because I need to ask you both something. Something big.'

From the corner of my eye I see Finn shoot me a startled look. *Wait, Anna,* I can tell he's thinking. *Don't agree to anything we can't deliver.*

'Of course, Hel,' I say. 'Just name it.' Finn's shoulders drop a little further.

Hel takes a deep breath, drawing herself up slightly and glancing at her daughter, whose eyelids are now drooping despite her unfamiliar environment and the suffocating tension in the air. How wonderfully simple life must seem to Ivy.

'The last few months have been hard,' Helena says carefully. 'Really hard. I thought that when Ivy was born, even though we wouldn't have much, we'd be okay. But we're not okay. *I'm* not okay.'

My best friend looks up at me, her eyes willing me to understand, to spare her having to explain exactly why she's not coping, why the now peacefully sleeping bundle in my arms doesn't make her happy. But I don't understand. Helena is going to have to do better than this. 'What do you mean you're not okay?'

She shakes her head slowly and I know she's close to tears.

Carefully, so as not to wake Ivy, I sit down next to Helena on the couch. 'Tell me, hon.'

'I love my daughter. I love her *so much* but I just don't think it's enough. There's only me to care for her and I don't think I'm enough,' she says sadly. 'Ivy needs – she deserves – a father and grandparents and a whole world of people who love her. The last six months it's just been me and her in my horrid little flat and that's the best I can do for her. What kind of life is that?'

'It won't be like that forever, Hel,' I say gently. 'Ivy could go into daycare a few days a week so you can go back to uni or find a job. You'll meet loads of new people. Hey, you might even meet some hunky professor and fall madly in love.'

Helena looks at me as if I've just suggested Richard Branson will walk through the door and offer her a million pounds to be his new CEO. Glib reassurance is clearly not the way forward in this particular situation.

'Okay, so it's tough right now. But things will get better,' I say. 'You've got to talk to your parents, ask for more support. Maybe your mum could look after Ivy a couple of days a week. You know, to give you a break?'

I'd been hoping to see Helena smile again but the crazed grin that spreads across her face at my suggestion is more alarming than reassuring. 'Ha!' she snorts. 'You're honestly suggesting I allow *that woman* to come anywhere near my daughter? Anna, I know you've been away a while but surely your memories of my mother haven't faded so quickly?'

I can't help it, I'm beginning to lose patience. Helena has turned up on my doorstep – 24 000 kilometres from her own – in the middle of the night with her infant daughter in tow. She's had me out of my mind with worry, offered no real reason for her bizarre behaviour and now evidently doesn't want my advice. And my right arm has gone completely numb; for such a small person, Ivy is *really* heavy.

'I'm sorry, Hel. I don't know what to say to make you feel better.' I'm fighting to contain my ire. Helena just shrugs.

'What was it you wanted to ask us?' Finn asks, as I shift Ivy gingerly to my other arm. Her downy pink beanie slips into Helena's lap, but she doesn't move to replace it.

'Oh, right. Um.' Helena's gaze swings from Finn to me and back to Finn, as though she's weighing up who'll be more receptive to her request. Eventually she settles on me. 'Anna,' she says, twisting towards me. 'I know I can be a good mum to Ivy in time . . .'

In time? Where is she going with this?

'But it's – *she's* – too much for me right now. I need to get away for a bit, to sort my head out. I've got family in Scotland, a great aunt, and she says I can stay with her for a few weeks.'

'Okay, so you and Ivy will go to Scotland. You'll get some fresh air and peace and quiet. You'll clear your head. That sounds great,' I say, a little too brightly, because there's a kernel of dread in the pit of my stomach.

'Well, actually, I think it would be better, for me and for Ivy, if I went by myself.'

Silence.

Helena looks steadily at me, waiting for the penny to drop. But I don't want that penny to go anywhere. I suspect it has a baby attached to it.

'Hang on a minute,' Finn blusters. 'Are you saying you want to leave Ivy *here*? With us?'

'Yes.'

'No way! We can't have a baby, Helena. We both work full time,' Finn practically shouts, his voice oddly shrill. His eyes are wide with horror and his mouth hangs agape; my boyfriend is truly terrified by the thought of sharing his home with a small child. Good to know.

'But it would only be for a couple of weeks. Two or three. A month at the most,' Helena pleads.

'You have *got* to be —'

'Finn! Shh!' I gesture towards the miraculously still sleeping Ivy. 'Will you let Helena speak?'

He looks at me, aghast. 'You're not seriously considering this, are you, Anna?'

I can't be, can I? In practical terms, it's a truly ridiculous idea. I work all hours; what would I do with Ivy during the day (and, frequently, most of the night)? I can't see Finn leaping to offer to use up precious annual-leave days changing nappies and mopping up sick. He's way too into his career these days. Even outside of work, my lifestyle is far from child-friendly: I drink too much and swear too much and blast terrible 80s rock music late at night. I have no money to speak of and I'm pretty sure taking care of a baby isn't an inexpensive exercise. Then there's the small problem of my knowing absolutely nothing about children. What do they eat? When do they sleep? Maybe they're like puppies and can't be taken out of the house before a certain age. Plus, Finn clearly hates the idea and it's his house too.

But then I look at Ivy, snuffling quietly in her sleep. And I look at Helena, who's trying so hard and loves her daughter so much but still thinks she's failing. She hasn't touched Ivy for the last half-hour because she's so scared she'll ruin her. And I think that if there's anything I can do to erase that fear from my best friend's heart, I have to do it. I'm Ivy's godmother, after all.

'Okay. Four weeks. Ivy can stay with us.'

'What?!' Finn throws me a murderous look and storms from the sitting room.

Helena's shoulders start to shake and fat tears roll down her cheeks. 'Thank you,' she whispers.

The first rays of dawn are beginning to illuminate the London skyline by the time a sort of calm finally descends on the house. I'm shattered, but perversely glad my first night of pseudo-mother-hood has been sleepless; I've got to get used to it sooner or later. Ivy woke briefly but settled after a bottle and, after promising to give me a crash course in child-rearing before she boards her train to Inverness, Helena has retreated with her daughter to the spare bedroom. Which just leaves Finn.

I know he's awake because I've spent the last few hours listening to the bedroom floorboards creak as he paces overhead. I understand why he's angry at my agreeing to babysit indefinitely but I just don't have the energy to thrash it out right now. Wearily, I climb the stairs, hoping when he sees the dark circles under my eyes he'll be kind enough to wait until at least midday to yell at me.

'Do you have any idea what you've let yourself in for?' he spits as I step into the bedroom. That'll be a no on the yelling postponement then.

'Finn, can we do this in the morning? Please?'

'No, Anna, we can't! How could you make Helena a promise like this without discussing it with me first?' His green eyes flash with anger.

Suddenly, a rush of adrenaline makes me feel wide awake. 'What do you mean "discuss", Finn? You mean you'd have said no and I'd just be expected to go along with it, right?'

Finn's lip curls arrogantly. 'Oh, don't start, Anna. You know agreeing to take care of Ivy was bloody ridiculous. Don't try to put this on me.'

I fling back the doona and throw myself into bed. I don't know what irritates me more: Finn's total lack of support, or his implication that I'm incapable of looking after a baby. I turn and face the wall but I can still feel him glaring at me.

'You don't know Helena like I do. She's been through some hard times in her life but she's always managed. The fact that she's come all this way to ask for help means she really, really needs it. I'm not about to send her packing.'

There's silence behind me. At last, I've got through to him. Then Finn clears his throat.

'The thing is,' he says haltingly, 'I'm not going to be much use to you through this.'

I sigh and roll to face him. 'Look, I'm no child expert either. But we'll manage somehow.'

'Ah, no, that's not what I meant.' He suddenly looks deeply guilty.

'Well, what *do* you mean?' I ask, both suspicious and scared. What is he really saying – that he won't help me? Surely he can't be willing to split up over this.

He comes to sit on the bed and takes a deep breath. 'What I mean is I have an interview on Tuesday for a new job. In Belfast. And if I get the offer, I'm going to take it.'

Anna

What feels like three minutes after I've finally drifted off to sleep, Ivy's plaintive cries seep into my consciousness. She wails tentatively at first, no doubt confused at finding herself in the crook of her mother's arm on a lumpy futon instead of nestled in her own cosy crib. I listen for sounds of movement, for a sign that Helena is cuddling her daughter closer to calm her, or shuffling about as she retrieves a clean nappy. But I hear only the wood pigeons chortling in the back garden; the spare room is apparently still. Maybe Hel's trying that controlled crying thing, I think as I roll over and jam my pillow over my ears. But it's no use: I'm officially awake.

As the haze of sleep clears from my head, Ivy's howls grow louder. Or does her little voice only seem to have risen to an ear-splitting crescendo because I'm exhausted and overwrought? The memory of last night's – this morning's? – spectacular blow-up with Finn comes flooding back. I groan and slide a foot across the mattress towards him; as always after sleeping on an argument, I'm ready to forgive and forget. I wriggle my toes in the hope a show of affection might persuade Finn to go and knock on Helena's door. But Finn's side of the bed is empty and cold. He's asleep on the couch downstairs, where I banished him at six a.m. after he told me he finds me boring.

'You're going to do what?' I'd said when Finn dropped his bombshell.

'I'm going to take the job if it's offered.'

'In Belfast?'

'Yes.'

'The Belfast in Northern Ireland?'

'That's the one.' He'd spoken calmly, steadily holding my gaze as if daring me to let him have it.

'And were you planning on discussing this with me at any point?' I asked, on the verge of tears for the first time despite the evening's events.

Finn shook his head, exasperated. 'What would be the point, Anna? This is such an amazing opportunity for me but I knew you wouldn't see that. You'd just fixate on my having to move away.'

'Of *course* I would, Finn!' I exploded, my throat tight. 'I can't believe you want to leave me in London by myself just for some job!'

'It's not just some job!' Finn shouted back. 'It's a senior reporting job on a brand-new show. I could be co-host within a year. And you'd hardly be by yourself, would you? You've got loads of mates here.'

'It's hardly the same as having my boyfriend here, is it? I just can't believe you'd make a decision like that without even telling me. You are so selfish! Coming to London was never about our careers, Finn, it was about —'

I stopped speaking when he rolled his eyes.

'Oh, don't start that again. "It was about having adventures together." I've heard it all before,' he said, raking his hands through his sandy blonde hair. 'But life's not exactly one big adventure now, is it?'

'What's that supposed to mean?'

He looked away then, pacing the floor and wringing his hands. 'Well, it's all about work, isn't it? For both of us. When was the last time we had a night on the tiles or went away for a weekend?'

I just stared at him, dumbfounded. How had I become the bad guy in this scenario?

'And when you are home all you want to do is go running or fawn over the bloody dog!' As if Nui knew he was being talked about, he jerked to attention and let out an affronted *whuff*.

Finn was shouting by then, making me wince as I thought of the sleeping baby in the next room. The last thing I wanted was a screaming child thrown into this situation.

'Oh please, Finn, that is so unfair!' I hissed back in a stage whisper. 'I go running to de-stress and because, as you once so kindly put it, I have thighs like tree trunks. And I'm not the only one who works long hours. I "fawn" over Nui because he's the only company I have most of the time!'

'Whatever,' Finn mumbled. 'I knew you wouldn't understand. Is it any wonder I want a change from this? God, Anna, you've just become so boring.'

The second the words had left his mouth, a startled expression crossed Finn's face. He'd stepped way over the line. He was in trouble. And he knew it. Without another word, he'd picked up his pillow, yanked the worn throw rug from the end of the bed and slunk out of the bedroom to sleep downstairs. Which, come morning, would ordinarily please me under the circumstances – i.e. his being a total arse – but, as Ivy's keening reaches 'strangled cat' proportions in the next room, I think I'd happily forgive him if only he'd make it stop.

Defeated, I roll over and peer blearily at my bedside clock. It says ten a.m., which can't be correct because if it was really ten o'clock I'd be at my desk, eating toast with Marmite and planning the day's celebrity ambush.

Oh crap.

Hauling myself into a sitting position, I fumble for my mobile and dial the office.

'Anna Harding's line, Nicki Ford-Smith speaking!' my nemesis trills.

'Nicki, it's Anna. I'm —'

'Oh Anna, where are you? I was *so* worried,' she coos.

I roll my eyes. Sure she was worried – worried I was merely stuck on the Tube as opposed to a preferably gruesome fate that would necessitate her stealing my job.

'What's all that noise? Is that a *baby*?'

Ivy sounds absolutely hysterical now. Why the hell isn't Helena doing something? I know she's depressed, but lying there while her daughter hollers like this is cruel. As for Finn, letting a child scream herself hoarse to make a point is beyond petty. Then I remember – Finn has no doubt left for work. Nice of him to wake me.

'Er, look Nicki, something's come up and I'm running late,' I tell her, squishing my finger against my free ear to try to dull the racket. 'I'll be in by lunchtime. Can you please tell Girish I have a doctor's appointment or something?'

'Of course I will. But Anna, what about your interview?'

'What interview?'

'It says here in your diary: *BC, 10.30*. Who's BC?'

Oh. My. God. I completely forgot. If not for Ivy in the next room I'd let fly at this moment with a string of expletives that would have Parcel Nazi banging on the front door demanding quiet within seconds.

BC. Benedict Cumberbatch. *The* Benedict Cumberbatch. One of the biggest TV and movie stars in the world. A bona fide megastar and notoriously unfond of tabloid journalists who, after I'd spent months diligently sucking up to his publicist, had agreed to meet me to talk exclusively about the long-awaited new series of *Sherlock*. A certified geek sex symbol who is probably on his way to Canary Wharf right now while I languish in Richmond, in my pyjamas, with a pocket-sized atomic bomb screaming bloody murder in the next room.

If it were any other actor I'd phone his publicist, spin some story about being off sick with the flu or being sent on assignment to Greenland and reschedule the interview. But *the* Benedict Cumberbatch won't take kindly to having his schedule disrupted, that much I'm sure of. He'll pull out of the interview and the WORLD EXCLUSIVE the paper has been plugging on its front page all week will go spectacularly down the gurgler. I'll be sacked, obviously. Nicki Ford-Smith will get my job and I'll have no choice but to go write obits for the *Puddletown Express*. Or follow Finn to Belfast with my tail between my legs. Neither of which is an appealing prospect at this point. Which means there's only one option.

'You'll have to do it, Nicki,' I sigh. 'BC is Benedict Cumberbatch. He's coming in to talk about the new *Sherlock*. You'll find my questions and research material in my top drawer.'

There's silence at the end of the line. Then, 'Benedict Cumberbatch?'

'Yes.'

'Coming here in twenty minutes?'

'Yes. Look Nicki, if you don't think you're up to this I can phone a freelancer —'

'No! Nonononononono. I can do it. I'm ready,' she squeals.

'Fine. Call me when you're done.' I slam the phone down.

Handing Benedict Cumberbatch to Nicki on a platter hurts. It hurts a lot. But I have to put that out of my mind and sort out the chaos that's enveloped my house. Poor Ivy is still bellowing and now Nui is scratching fiercely at the bedroom door, not so subtly reminding me he's not yet had a chance to relieve his bladder this morning.

'Helena!' I screech as I heave myself out of bed. As I fling the bedroom door open, I catch a glimpse of myself in the mirror hanging on the back of it. My hair resembles a bird's nest and there are deep purple rings around my hazel eyes. My usually olive skin is pale and wan. Even my freckles look washed out. I look exactly like a woman who's had three hours' sleep after her missing best friend turns up in the middle of the night on her doorstep with a baby. It's probably a good thing I'm not meeting Benedict Cumberbatch today looking like this. I wouldn't want to scare the poor guy.

Nui charges down the stairs like he's spotted a juicy lamb bone at the bottom. Still not a peep out of Helena. I race after my dog, who's now pawing frantically at the doggy door. I unlatch it and let him out – his sense of relief as he cocks his leg against his favourite tree is palpable – then bound back upstairs.

'Hel!' I pound on the door to the spare bedroom. 'Helena! Ivy has been screaming for a good twenty minutes. Don't you think you should do something?'

Still she doesn't respond.

'Oh, for goodness sake.' I push the door open and step into the room. There's baby clothes and blankets strewn everywhere, and a crimson-faced Ivy weeping desolately on the futon. But no Helena.

'Shit.'

There are no adult-sized shoes or clothing in the room and Helena's tattered backpack is nowhere to be seen. There's just Ivy, tangled in the blankets Helena has used to construct a makeshift cradle on the bed. Wailing because she's hungry and frightened. Wailing because she's alone.

I scoop her up, holding her as close as I can without squishing her. Her little body judders and shakes with the force of her sobs but their ferocity seems to ease slightly as I rock her gently and rub her back. I'm so desperate to soothe this fragile speck of a person that I'm barely aware of the cold fury gripping my insides. Unless I find Helena downstairs in the kitchen or she comes bustling in the front door in the next thirty seconds bearing plastic bags full of *Wiggles* DVDs and baby shampoo, I will never, *ever* forgive her for this.

How could she do this to her daughter? How could she do it to *me*? She's not herself, I know that, but there is no excuse for abandoning her child.

And what the hell am I supposed to do with Ivy? I might have agreed to mind her, but not without some sort of guidance, a crash tutorial in basic child rearing. At the very least, Helena could have left me a contact phone number. I'm an only child; I'd never even held a baby until I started my first job, when colleagues on maternity leave would bring their wrinkly little creations into the office to be ooohed and ahhhed over. I need hints, tips, suggestions. I need a library of books and a list of telephone helplines and websites. I'm a journalist, for crying out loud – I can't go into a situation like this without extensive research. I need to know what I'm dealing with.

'Shh, possum. Aunty Anna's here,' I whisper in Ivy's perfectly shell-shaped ear. Aunty Anna. It sounds strange and foreign. I wonder if Ivy can feel my fear. Babies are very receptive to that sort of thing, aren't they? Or is that dogs?

Ivy's cries have dwindled to the occasional high-pitched mewl. 'There, you're okay now. You just wanted a cuddle, didn't you? You just missed your mum.'

A lump rises in my throat as I say the words. I miss Ivy's mum, too. Not the hollowed-out version of Helena who's run away from her child but the feisty, fearless Hel I used to know, the one who would take any situation and roll with it. The one who would pick herself up after being dumped or laugh off Brigitta's latest character assassination, slip on her little black dress and go dancing. I miss the Helena who, a year ago, looked upon motherhood as her next big adventure. I miss Ivy's mother and I miss my friend. And I don't know when I'll see either of them again.

I can feel Ivy's tummy grumbling beneath her pink terry-cloth sleep suit. I also detect a suspiciously ripe odour emanating from her business end. Helena has at least had the good sense to leave behind her baby bag and I rifle through it with one arm while still jiggling Ivy in my other. The bag contains Ivy's dummy, a collection of balled-up clothes and precisely one nappy. There's no formula or wet wipes, no toys, no rattle or teddy bear. Helena either left Adelaide in a hell of a hurry, or her mind hasn't been on her daughter for quite a while.

I grab the nappy then step across the hallway into the bathroom and snatch up a facewasher – Finn's, I note meanly. Though she must be ravenous, Ivy is at last mercifully quiet and watches me with interest as I lay her back on the bed and wriggle her out of her suit. Taking a deep breath, I unpeel the tabs on her fully laden nappy.

I don't want to look but, even if I had the ability to change a nappy with my eyes closed, it'd be pointless – the stench alerts me to the contents well before I actually see it.

'Good God!' It's not the amount of poo that astonishes me, or even the colour (though it's far from pretty). It's the sheer reach of the stuff. Ivy's minuscule; I think I expected to find a similarly petite little parcel in her nappy. But it's just *everywhere*. From her legs to halfway up her back, it's like a noxious weed has taken root. I'm surprised she doesn't have poo in her hair.

'Please don't let it be like this every time,' I gasp, gagging and trying not to breathe in as I clean Ivy as quickly as possible with the facewasher (which will go straight in the bin, tempting as it may be to simply rinse it and put it back in the shower for Finn).

Suddenly, Ivy starts to laugh. She chuckles a cry of impish joy, like she's planned the whole thing.

'I'm glad you find this funny!'

She burbles and chatters and, in spite of myself, I dissolve into giggles as I strap her into the clean nappy. 'You cheeky little minx,' I chastise. 'I hope you don't think Aunty Anna's going to be a pushover.' The title sounds slightly less bizarre this time. Maybe I could get used to it.

I'm about to dress Ivy in a fresh jumpsuit when I catch sight of the deep blue, late April sky beyond the spare room window. It's a warm morning and Ivy is rolling around on the bed, apparently happy as a clam in just her nappy. I decide to let her go semi-starkers. I pick her up, surprised by how velvety her skin feels against my own bare arms, and we walk downstairs.

At the sound of my footsteps, Nui propels himself through the doggy door and into the kitchen. He stops in his tracks, looking thoroughly nonplussed when he sees me cradling a small creature that isn't him. After a beat, he turns on his heels – all four of them – and flounces back out to the garden. Drama queen.

There's a tin of formula on the worktop and, next to it, a note. This should be good, I think. But the note isn't from Helena, it's from Finn.

> *Anna,*
> *I'm sorry. I didn't mean the things I said last night.*
> *You're not boring. You're beautiful – and you're right.*
> *I should have discussed the job thing with you. I still think*
> *if it's offered, that taking the job is the right thing to do.*
> *Belfast isn't that far away – I could come back every*
> *weekend, or you could come visit me.*
> *But if you really don't want me to consider it, I won't.*
> *I love you.*
> *Finn xx*

I feel a sudden rush of affection for my boyfriend and press his note to my chest. Ivy, eyes wide and interested now that she's moved beyond the four bare magnolia walls of the spare bedroom, snatches the note and tries to jam it into her mouth.

I shouldn't have been so hard on Finn last night, I think as I prise the paper from its dribbly captor. I was so tired and freaked out by having a baby land in my lap that I didn't even give him a chance to explain. I'm sure he didn't intend to keep the news of his job interview from me; there was hardly a right time to bring it up with everything else that was going on. As for saying he'll take the job if it's offered . . . well, I'm sure he doesn't mean it. He was probably just trying to get my attention. That's so like Finn – making a bold pronouncement so that all eyes are on him, then ironing out the details later. He'll come home this evening and we'll sit down and discuss it like adults. The most important thing is that Finn loves me and I love him. Our relationship is too important to let a stupid job interview throw a spanner in the works.

A spark of irritation lingers as I glance at the wall clock and see it's nearly eleven a.m. It would have been nice if Finn had hung around this morning to help out with Ivy. I won't make it into the office before the editors' afternoon conference at this rate. Then again, he probably assumed Helena would be here to ease my transition into full-blown godmothering. So did I.

'We'll work it out tonight,' I resolve aloud. Ivy regards me closely. She must think I'm an absolute nutcase. I smile brightly at her and silently vow to try harder to appear at least vaguely normal.

'Bee-*atch*!' comes a voice from the hall. Nui streaks in through the doggy door, barking furiously, and tears off to identify the voice's owner. I don't need to follow; I'd know that throaty greeting anywhere. It's Jen, my across-the-road neighbour and running partner.

'Where the hell were you this morning?' she shrieks as she bounds into the kitchen, still in her leggings and trainers. 'We had a running date, you lazy cow!' Then, clocking Ivy, she stops dead. 'What *the fark* is that?'

I frown at Jen but resist the temptation to cover Ivy's ears. She'll hear a lot worse if she stays with me for long.

'This is Ivy, my goddaughter.' I give Jen the edited version of last night's events.

'Christ almighty,' she says, switching into mother mode and stepping forward to take Ivy from me. I shake my arms with relief – I'd been losing the feeling in my hands – and unscrew the lid from the formula tin.

Jen is one of my few Australian friends in London, and my only mate with children. Originally from Brisbane, she was working as a waitress in a cocktail bar, like that 80s song says, when she met Andrew, the investment banker and consummate City boy who's now her husband. Within a year, he'd swapped his Clerkenwell flat for their renovated terrace and Jen was pregnant with Milo, now three. Elodie followed eighteen months later. On the surface, Jen is the ultimate Richmond-upon-Thames mother. She's whippet-thin, drives an unnecessarily large four-wheel drive and looks a million dollars all the time. She has a nanny three days a week, which is how she manages to join me on my hour-long circuits of Richmond Park. But all Jen has to do is open her mouth and it's clear that while you can take the girl out of Brisbane, you'll never get Brisbane out of this girl.

She loves Milo and Elodie fiercely but she's not precious about them. Jen may wrinkle her nose as she passes a Matalan outlet, preferring to buy all of her children's clothes from organic fair trade artisans on Etsy, but more often than not Milo will be covered with playground dirt and Elodie will have mashed banana in her hair. She's no-nonsense, and that's why I adore her.

'Jesus, Anna, when you didn't show up for our run this morning I just assumed you'd been out late at one of your celebrity dos, so I figured I'd let you snooze. I had no idea you'd had motherhood foisted upon you overnight,' she says, her head on an awkward slant as Ivy tugs on a fistful of her curly auburn hair.

'Yeah, well, it was a bit of a surprise to me, too,' I say, managing a wry grin. 'I'm so glad you're here though, Jen. I've got absolutely no idea what I'm doing. You've got to help me.'

I hold up the plastic scoopy thing I've found in the tin of formula.

'For example, what am I supposed to do with this?'

Jen laughs and gently hands Ivy back to me. Ivy has been angel-ically quiet despite what must be an intense hunger. In fact, I think, narrowing my eyes suspiciously, she seems rather amused by my ineptitude. Jen sends me upstairs for Ivy's bottle and when I return she's whipped up a batch of formula and written down her method in moron-proof steps. I pop the bottle into Ivy's mouth and she begins to gulp hungrily.

'Right, what else do you need? Did mum-of-the-year leave you anything at all?' she asks.

I open my mouth to defend Helena but stop myself. Jen is right – Helena has left me and Ivy up the proverbial creek. Aside from Ivy's bottle, the formula and some clothes, I'm completely *sans* baby goods. Before Jen arrived I'd been wondering whether the washing basket could double as a crib.

I shake my head. 'No,' I tell Jen. 'We're pretty much screwed.'

'Give me fifteen minutes,' she says with a grin and skips out.

The front door clicks open and there comes the low murmur of a male voice. 'Oh hello,' Jen says coolly, then, 'Anna, you've got another visitor. I'll be back in a sec!'

I sigh irritably. Now what? Making it to the office is becoming a seriously remote possibility.

Luke pops his head around the kitchen door, prompting Nui to growl as menacingly as a Boston terrier can. I'm pleased to note Luke looks as bleary-eyed as I feel. At least this will be quick; whatever he's got to complain about, I'm definitely not in the mood to hear it.

'Hi,' he mumbles at the floor.

I don't answer. *You're on my turf now*, I feel like saying. *Take me on and see what happens.*

'I just, uh, wanted to apologise for last night. I got the impres-sion I didn't help whatever was going down. So I'm sorry,' he says, raising his cobalt eyes to meet mine.

I'm shocked. I'd expected a tirade about his late-night caller or, at the very least, a rant about the raised voices and screaming baby that surely interrupted his sleep. I didn't expect humility or contrition. I sure as hell did not expect 'I'm sorry'.

'Well, okay. Thanks for that. I'm sorry you got dragged into it,' I tell him haltingly.

He visibly relaxes and offers a small grin. 'So . . .' Luke's gaze lingers on Ivy, still guzzling from her bottle in my arms. 'Is everything all right?'

I pause. I consider offering him a coffee – and an olive branch – and pouring out the whole story. But I'm not quite ready to let him off the hook. One apparently sincere apology does not make up for twelve months of being decidedly un-neighbourly. Even if Luke does look kind of cute with his sweet smile and fresh-out-of-bed hair sticking up at mad angles.

I mentally slap myself. Cute? *Luke?* It's lack of sleep and my fight with Finn that's got me thinking such crazy thoughts. I've got to get a grip – and get to work.

'Er, yeah, we're all fine. I'm going to be minding my goddaughter for a while,' I say, flashing him a quick smile. 'She's a bit shaken up so I apologise in advance if she cries a lot over the next few days.'

'Oh, that's fine, Anna,' Luke says, smiling back.

What! He's not bothered about a wailing infant *and* he's remembered my name. Who is this guy and what has he done with Parcel Nazi?

'Just, you know, give me a shout if you need anything.'

I assure him I will – even though I'd sooner eat mud than ask Luke for help – and usher him towards the front door. As I wave him down the garden path, Jen totters up it carrying a bassinet and hauling a pram that's bursting with baby paraphernalia.

'Okay, so,' she says, lumping it all into the hallway and pushing a stray curl from her flushed face. 'We've got the pram, the bassinet, a baby bath, a change mat, some toys, spare bottles, a carrying sling and some cloth nappies for emergencies. But take my advice, hon, use disposables. The last thing you want to do with your weekends is spend them scraping shit off towelling.'

I wrinkle my nose at Jen's charming turn of phrase. I can't believe the amount of loot she's brought me. It looks like a branch of Mothercare has exploded in my hall. I'd love to spend the rest of the day figuring out what to do with it all but time is charging ahead.

'I don't know what I'm going to do with Ivy this afternoon,' I say. 'I've got to go into work. I already had to miss an interview with Benedict Cumberbatch this morning and —'

Jen gasps in genuine horror. 'You did *not!*'

I nod sadly. 'That's not the worst bit. I had to ask Nicki Ford-Smith to do it instead.'

'Ugh,' says Jen loyally.

'Girish will already be on the warpath over that, so I've got to get there this afternoon.' An idea strikes me. 'Jen, I don't suppose . . . I mean, I hate to ask but . . .'

'Consider it done,' she says, holding up both hands to spare me having to grovel. 'What's one more, eh? Compared to my two terrors, this little pixie will be a cinch.' She runs the backs of her fingers along Ivy's cheek.

'Thanks, mate. For that and for all this,' I gesture towards the baby gear. 'Once this is all sorted out, I swear I'll be your on-call babysitter for the rest of my life.'

Jen giggles. 'You'll regret saying that, you know!'

Given my ham-fisted attempts at parenting this morning, she's probably right. But I can't worry about that now – I've got a career to salvage.

Helena

'Ladies and gentlemen, we will shortly be arriving at Inverness, where this service terminates. Please make sure you take all your personal belongings with you when leaving the train.'

The crowded train slows as the rolling green countryside is swallowed up by the grey outskirts of Inverness. I'm surprised by the rows of squat grey houses whizzing past the train's smeared picture windows. Their drab facades match the steel-grey, overcast sky. Beams of watery sunlight leak through the cloud but do little to cheer up the sullen city – or me. In my mind's eye, I'd seen Inverness as a romantic Highland village filled with storybook cottages and wandering bagpipers. Yet another example of reality spectacularly failing to live up to my imagination.

As the train shudders to a stop at Inverness station and impatient passengers leap into the aisle, I shoulder my backpack and reach instinctively for Ivy's baby bag. But, of course, it's not there and neither is Ivy. Instead of my daughter, wide-eyed and observant, the seat next to me is occupied by a greasy-haired teenager who has tinny death metal blaring from his iPod headphones. He slings his battered satchel over his shoulder, hitting me in the stomach. Casting a surly glance back at me, he scans my own lank locks, my faded navy-blue hoodie and saggy khaki combat trousers, and leaves the train with a smirk.

Leaving Ivy wasn't such a hideous thing to do, I think as I pick my way down the litter-strewn aisle. Not really. It's not like I actually abandoned her. Anna was in the next room, Finn was sleeping downstairs. That rat-faced dog was sniffing about. I made sure she was warm and secure; nothing was going to happen to her. It was the best thing, my just leaving. Definitely the best thing. If I'd hung around until everyone woke up, there'd have been a big, emotional scene and that wouldn't have been good for any of us. Anna, though she'd said last night that she understood why I had to get away, would still have tried to change my mind this morning. She would have thought the simple fact of my being in London, under the wing of my best friend, would make it all okay. She's like that, Anna – always thinks a good night's sleep and a nice cup of tea can cure the world's ills. She's either an eternal optimist or utterly deluded.

But it's not like I'm proud of leaving my daughter without saying goodbye. I would have liked Ivy to wake up to a cuddle and a kiss from her mum. It would have been nice to sit in Anna's sunny kitchen and tell her that Ivy loves peach puree but hates mashed-up peas, or that stroking the bridge of her nose will almost always send her to sleep. But when I woke up this morning in Anna's spare bedroom, with its relentlessly cheerful yellow walls, I pulled back the curtains and knew I had to just go. It was a criminally gorgeous day: the sky was a blinding, almost navy blue and a light breeze tickled the daisies in Anna's little garden. I could hear birds chirping and children playing. It was like I'd woken up in a Werthers Originals commercial; I half expected to see a kindly old man helping a little boy to build a sailboat from Paddle Pop sticks.

What I saw instead when I turned away from the window was a room scarred by the detritus of a woman who doesn't have a clue. A tatty backpack stuffed with whatever was on my bedroom floor when I made the decision to flee Adelaide. A hastily packed baby bag containing almost nothing of use to a six-month-old child. And me, of course: a basket case with a stolen credit card and not the faintest idea what she's doing.

So I went. I went because Ivy deserved to start a new day with a fighting chance.

I step down from the train onto a platform teeming with people. Men in sharp suits exchange firm handshakes with business associates. Young girls wearing far too little clothing for the brisk Highland spring are wrapped up in bear hugs by their boyfriends. A woman who looks about my age, holding the hand of a squirming toddler, thrusts a clutch of shopping bags to her own waiting mother and plants a kiss on her cheek. I feel like a voyeur watching these happy homecomings. In the odd half-light of the late afternoon, I feel I might have stepped back in time to a sepia-toned reunion of war heroes and their sweethearts. I don't expect the woman who has come to collect me from the train will be nearly as happy about my arrival.

Quickly, the crowds start to disperse and I start to panic. Few people remain on the platform and none of them looks like my great aunt, Edme. At least, none of them looks like the woman in the fifteen-year-old photograph of her that I swiped from my parents' mantelpiece as I sprinted out their front door two days ago with my father's credit card in my pocket and my mother's shrill admonitions in my ears. The woman in the picture had been curvaceous and bawdy-looking, her grey-flecked red hair pinned in a loose bun at the nape of her neck as she danced with a cigarette in her left hand and a bottle of beer in her right. She looked like the sort of woman who, given half a chance, would have snuck away from that family gathering to go and snog the gardener behind the potting shed. Edme is my father's aunt – his father's younger sister – and the only one of the Scottish Stanleys still living. My father's parents migrated from the Highlands hamlet of Gairloch to Australia in the early 1950s and Dad and his four older sisters grew up bona fide Aussies. My grandparents never lost their thick Scottish accents but my dad somehow acquired an accent that sounds like a combination of Alf Stewart and Steve Irwin. My mother, with her aristocratic ancestors and plummy speech, visibly cringes every time he opens his mouth. Which is probably why, these days, he doesn't say much at all.

No, there's definitely no one on the platform who looks like the Aunt Edme in the photograph, or the fifteen-years-older version of her I've constructed in my mind. She's now aged in her late seventies and still living on the rambling family farm, Strahan, so I'm looking for a tall, robust woman with wild hair and ruddy cheeks. Wearing an Aran jumper and riding boots. And possibly a kilt. I've really got to stop watching reruns of *Monarch of the Glen*.

But the only people still milling around are station staff, a couple of schoolgirls loudly and passionately debating the merits of Beyoncé versus Rihanna, and a pale, skinny bloke with a shaved head wearing a truly awful brown suit. My gaze lingers on the suit for a split second – where would you even buy something so horrid? – and the thin man looks up and meets my eye. Astonishingly, a bright smile spreads across his face and he strides purposefully towards me.

I freeze. Obviously he's mistaken me for someone else. Now there's going to be an awkward conversation involving him being mortified by his error and me trying to escape before Edme spots me talking to someone dressed like a dog's breakfast.

'Helena?' he says in a deep and distinctly un-Scottish voice. He extends a hand but I'm too surprised to shake it.

'Er . . . yeah?'

He smiles even more broadly and crows' feet deepen at the

edges of his hazel eyes. He's not bad looking up close, though his pallid complexion and that suit do a good job of tempering any real attractiveness.

'I'm Oliver. I work with Miss Stanley at the school.' He looks at me expectantly, still grinning, his hand dangling limply between us until he sees me glance at it and shoves it into his pocket.

The school? I'm lost. As far as I know, Edme is an artist. Over the years my dad occasionally spoke of watching from his window during family holidays at Strahan and seeing her charging out into the garden on a fine morning with her sketchbook and charcoals. She would return at dusk with a black-smudged face and a sheaf of drawings, which she would sometimes sell through a local gallery. What with her art and the income from her farming tenants, Dad said Edme had always done quite well for herself. So what is a seventy-something artist doing working in a school?

'Your great aunt is our art teacher,' Oliver says, sensing my baf-flement. 'She's teaching her last class of the day right now, in fact, which is why she asked me to come and collect you. I was in town today for a meeting anyway.'

'Uh, right then. Good,' I say, snapping out of my stupor at last. 'Pleased to meet you, Oliver. Thanks for coming to get me.'

I push my confusion aside and force myself to sound pleasant. It's not Oliver's fault my father hasn't spoken to his aunt in almost a decade and really has no idea what Edme's life is like now. Communication has never been my family's strong suit.

Oliver grins again, lifts my backpack from my shoulder and hooks it over his own. 'It's my pleasure,' he says warmly. 'My car's parked just round the corner.'

He turns and walks towards the exit and as I trail a few steps behind his lanky form it suddenly occurs to me that I'm about to get into a car with a total stranger. Sure, he *says* he knows Edme – but the things he's said about her don't gel at all with what I know about my great-aunt. What if he's just making it up? What if he doesn't know her at all? What if he's a wandering psychopath – and in a suit like that, it's plausible – who overheard Edme talking about me in the local pub, offed her and has decided I'll be next? What if he dumps my body in a loch and no one ever finds it, and Ivy grows up thinking her mother never loved her and Anna hates me forever?

My heart is thudding in my chest and my breaths are coming in short, shallow gasps. A wave of dizziness sweeps over me and I stumble slightly. Oliver – if that's even his real name – turns and regards me curiously.

'Helena? Are you all right? You look very pale.' He's one to talk.

I try to laugh, to show him I'm calm and in control and that he'll have a fight on his hands if he thinks he can have his murderous way with me. But my casual chuckle comes out like a choked bray and now a strange blackness is seeping into the edges of my field of vision. Oliver frowns and takes a step back towards me. I try to raise a hand to ward him off but my limbs are as heavy as anvils. Sweat beads on my forehead and I feel a scream welling up in the pit of my stomach. Before I can open my mouth to let it out, I'm falling. Down, down, down, tumbling and twisting and somersaulting into darkness.

I come around minutes later with my face pressed against the frigid concrete of the station platform and my arm twisted uncomfortably beneath me. I can hear a chorus of whispering voices, with Oliver's baritone rising above the muted cacophony.

'If you can hear me, Helena, try to open your eyes now,' he's saying gently.

I do as he asks and his face looms into view, worry lines etched on his brow. I lift my head slightly and he visibly relaxes as he helps me sit up. The murmuring bystanders wander away, looking slightly miffed that I haven't lapsed into a coma or swallowed my tongue.

'You fainted,' Oliver says unnecessarily. 'How do you feel?'

I raise a hand to the throbbing lump that marks the spot where my forehead met the pavement. What the hell just happened? One moment I'd been fine; the next, I'm resorting to unconsciousness as a means of escaping a potential serial killer. Looking at Oliver now, at what seems to be the genuine concern in his eyes, my momentary fear of him seems not only irrational, but utterly ridiculous.

'I don't know how I feel,' I tell him honestly as I stagger to my feet.

Oliver's eyes roam over my body and I automatically hunch my shoulders and wrap my arms around myself, hiding from his gaze.

'Have you eaten today?' he asks. Why, does he think my fat bum caused me to faint?

'Of course I have. I had . . .' But have I? I was in such a hurry to leave Anna's this morning I wasn't about to creep into her kitchen and whip up a stack of pancakes. And I was so tired after the flight last night that I sank into sleep without even thinking of food. Come to think of it, I hadn't eaten much on the plane either; Ivy was fractious and I spent most of the flight trying to settle her and avoid the angry looks of my fellow passengers. My stomach unleashes a timely growl as I realise it's been at least two days since my last proper meal.

'You know what? I'm bloody starving. Could we grab a sandwich or something?'

Oliver glances at his watch and runs a hand over his close-cropped brown hair. He's been in my presence less than ten minutes but obviously he's already had a gutful of me and my drama. He probably just wants to bundle me into his car, floor it the one hundred kilometres to Gairloch and fling me at Edme's door. Then get as far away as possible.

'I've got a better idea. There's a lovely little pub on the way home, about forty miles from here. If you can wait another hour, I'll treat you to an early dinner,' he says.

I no longer think he's going to kill me, but a pity dinner seems an equally awful proposition. But I need food, and the thought of a heaped plate, an open fire and perhaps a wee dram of something alcoholic is too good to refuse.

'That would be lovely,' I tell him, and I mean it.

An hour and a half of winding Highland roads and chocolate-box scenery later, Oliver's battered VW Golf pulls into the car park of The Red Cap and Boobrie pub. I laugh aloud as I read the ludicrous name.

'What kind of crazy place have you brought me to, mister?' I tease. Oliver's ready grin reappears as he leads me into the pub. I haven't said much since climbing into his car in Inverness and Oliver thankfully hasn't asked too many questions. He occasionally piped up with a snippet about this loch or that hill but otherwise we drove in companionable silence. Any lingering suspicion about his intentions has vanished; I feel strangely but pleasantly at ease in Oliver's presence.

'A boobrie is a mythical Highland waterbird which is said to haunt lakes and wells,' he says. 'And the Red Cap, well, he's a really nasty fellow. He wears iron boots but moves at great speed. He has claws for hands and lives in ruined castles.' Oliver's voice becomes an exaggerated horror-movie voiceover. 'They say his cap is stained red with the blood of his victims. *Mwah ha ha ha ha!*'

'So this is a pretty cheerful establishment then?' I say with a giggle.

'You'll like it, I promise. It's one of the best places I've found since I've lived up here,' he says.

He orders a glass of red wine for me and a pint of Guinness for himself, then ushers me to a table by the exposed stone back wall of the bar. He slides a menu across the table to me and opens his own.

'So you're not from the Highlands originally?' I ask casually as I scan the main courses. It's a stupid question – his accent is unmistakably English – but I don't want to launch into a full-scale interrogation before the guy's even had a sip of his beer.

'Aye, I am actually,' he says. 'Grew up in Ullapool, right up the top of the country. My father was a fisherman. But I moved down to London to live with my mum when I was sixteen, after my dad died. I only came back to Scotland last year.'

'Oh, I'm sorry,' I say, wishing I hadn't asked. 'I didn't mean . . . I wasn't . . . it's just, you don't sound Scottish.'

'I tried hard to lose the accent. I went to college in North London and university at Cambridge and I didn't think looking and sounding like a football hooligan would do my cause much good,' he says good-naturedly.

'And what cause was that?'

The jolly-looking barmaid appears at our table, a pencil poised over the notepad in her hand. Oliver orders a steak. I haven't made up my mind what I want to eat but I don't want the interruption to put Oliver off telling me his story; I'm hooked. I ask for the first vegetarian dish my gaze falls upon, macaroni and cheese.

'I didn't want to end up like my dad. He was a hard man, an alcoholic. He basically drank himself to death. I wanted more for myself. I'm not like him, but the way I looked' – he waves a hand to indicate his imposing height and rangy frame – 'and sounded, people formed their own opinions about me. So I changed.'

'You went to Cambridge and became a . . . teacher?' I venture. I know Oliver works in a school but he hasn't told me what he actually does.

He nods and takes a gulp of his Guinness. 'Yeah. And the funny thing is, my first few jobs were in some really tough inner-London schools, where looking and speaking like a hard nut probably would have made my job much easier.' He laughs and shakes his head in mock ruefulness.

'So why did you come back to Scotland?'

Oliver's smile fades and he shrugs his shoulders. 'The jury's still out on that one. Officially I came back to take up the deputy head teacher position at Gairloch High. But it was more than that, if I'm honest. I had a rough time in this neck of the woods growing up; I guess I felt I owed it to myself to try to create some good memories of the place.'

He looks surprised, like the thoughts he's just put into words weren't yet fully formed in his mind. I feel a little sheepish. I'd never have guessed Oliver was so driven and highly educated and I'd definitely never have picked him for a high school deputy principal. He looks too young for a start, though on closer inspection I'd say he's probably in his early thirties. It's his thinness that fools, I decide. I can easily picture him in skinny black jeans and a Radiohead T-shirt, queuing outside the beer tent at a music festival. But standing before an assembly hall full of scowling teenagers? In that suit? That image is much harder to conjure up.

'But enough about me, as they say. What brings you to cosmopolitan Gairloch?'

The waitress reappears at that moment with our drinks and a bread basket. I take a sip of my wine and swallow slowly, savouring the tart taste and stalling for time as I decide what I'm going to tell Oliver. Who knows what Edme has told him already? All I said to her when I telephoned from Heathrow yesterday was that I'm travelling and thought I'd come up to see her. I've no doubt she knows I have a child – one of my dad's blabbermouth sisters would surely have gleefully told her about Alan's daughter's illegitimate spawn – but I didn't mention Ivy and Edme didn't ask. Still, that doesn't mean she hasn't told Oliver everything she knows. I don't imagine there's much discretion in a hamlet the size of Gairloch.

'It's a long story,' I begin carefully. 'I had some . . . problems back in Adelaide and I needed a bit of a break.' I hope I sound lighthearted. I hope Oliver can't tell I'm only sharing a fraction of the story.

'Was it . . . were they relationship problems?' he asks, staring intently into his pint glass.

'Um, sort of.' Is he testing me? Waiting to see how much I'll reveal? 'There was a guy but it didn't work out. We had, ah, different ideas about where our relationship was going.' *He wanted me to abort my daughter*, I know I should add, but I don't.

Oliver nods, satisfied, and bites into a crusty brown roll. There, I've done it. I've lied about Ivy. Well, not lied, exactly – more like omitted.

Oh, who am I kidding? I've denied my daughter's very existence and I fear there's no coming back from that.

Anna

My belongings aren't in bin liners, which I choose to take as a good sign. Notebook still on desk, meeting shoes (stupidly high stilettos that would be lethal if worn on actual streets) still under chair where I flung them after my last agonising red carpet event, dog-eared picture of a shirtless David Beckham still tacked to pinboard (phew). For the moment at least, it seems I still have a job. There's no sign of Girish and, even better, no sound of him – when he's on the warpath he can usually be heard swearing from the lobby, twenty-two floors below.

'It's fine, you're fine,' I mutter to myself as I scurry to my desk and hit the power button on my Mac. 'You're only five hours late for work. It happens.'

I take a deep breath and flip to today's date in my diary. There it is, like a punch in the face: *BC, 10.30*. Oh Benedict, my lovely, lovely Benedict. Geek-gorgeous Benedict who, in my head at least, would have taken one look at me this morning and vowed never to love another. Talented Benedict, who would choke back tears during his inevitable Academy Award acceptance speech as he thanked me for always being there. Sexy Benedict, who would gather me up in his arms and —

'Practically stuck his tongue down my throat!'

Bloody Benedict, who had no doubt helpfully given Nicki Ford-Smith the story of her career and finished mine off in the process.

'I know! I couldn't belieeeeve it! I was all, "Nice to meet you too, Mr Cumberbatch." It was HYSTERICAL,' Nicki shrieks into her mobile phone as she sashays across the office. '*And* he's invited me to the premiere tonight. I know! That's how huge this TV show is – it's getting a proper premiere in a cinema!'

She catches sight of me as she flounces into her seat and covers the mouthpiece.

'Girish wants to see you,' she hisses in a stage whisper. 'He said for you to fetch him out of conference as soon as you got in.'

I nod meekly. What was I thinking, imagining I'd got away with it? With my luck so far today it was a wonder Girish hadn't turned up at my house himself and dragged me into the office by my hair. I click open my email and try to look unfazed as I stall for time, my mind racing. Should I tell the truth? 'I'm sorry I didn't get to work until three p.m., Girish, but I was babysitting.' I don't think so.

My computer pings as an email drops into my inbox. I breathe a sigh of relief – reading it will put another thirty seconds between me and certain professional death.

An, it begins. *B/fast show interview brought forward. Flying Monday. Talk soon. F x.*

F indeed. Eff right off, mate.

'I don't know – maybe the Gucci? Or the Chloe? Or maybe I should buy something new after work – it is a premiere after all!' Nicki howls with laughter. Finally she ends her call and turns to me with a look on her face saccharine-smug enough to make Mother Teresa want to retch in Heaven. Seeing me glowering back at her, she quickly rearranges her features so as to approximate vague concern.

'Is everything okay, Anna?' she asks, furrowing her brow (which I wouldn't have thought possible given her fortnightly trips to the beautician for 'waxing').

'Oh yeah, no worries,' I say in what I hope is a breezy fashion. 'Had a bit of family drama last night' – well, Helena is family insofar as she's wretched and self-absorbed and evidently doesn't care a jot about my feelings – 'but it's all cool now.'

Nicki nods with the practised sympathy of someone who's recently read a *Cosmo* article entitled 'Be a Better Friend!'

'Does this have something to do with the baby I could hear when you called this morning?'

I hesitate. I know Nicki's questions are motivated purely by her own agenda. She's on a fact-finding mission, a recce she hopes will offer up new and interesting ways to undermine me. It's search and destroy; she wants the coordinates of my career so she can napalm it into oblivion. I'm loath to help direct her crosshairs but it's probably inevitable she or someone else at work will find out about Ivy sooner or later. I have a feeling life will be easier for me in the long run if I fess up about my unexpected visit from the stork at the outset.

'Yes,' I concede eventually. 'I'm godmother to my best friend's baby, Ivy, and she's going to be staying with me for a little while.'

Nicki can barely disguise the gleeful glint in her eyes. 'Well, that's great. I'm sure it'll be a blast having them both there.' She has a far more convincing handle on the 'breezy' thing than I do.

'Actually, it's just Ivy. Helena, that's my best friend, she had some, er, things to deal with so I'm just, you know, doing the god-motherly thing.' *Do not say another word, Anna.*

'Wow, it's really nice of you to help Helena like that,' Nicki says. She looks perplexed, as though the idea of helping a friend isn't a concept she's devoted much thought to lately. Or ever. She leans forward conspiratorially. 'And don't worry about things here. Feel free to delegate to me whenever you like. Like this morning – Ben was a darling.'

Ben. My mate Benedict is now Nicki's mate Ben. She studies her perfectly manicured talons as she lets her barb sink in.

'Yeah, thanks for covering me on that,' I mutter. 'Went well, did it?'

'Oh, it was great,' she says, her eyes flashing. 'He's *such* a gentleman and just, like, so *dedicated* to his craft.'

His craft indeed. I'll bet her interview with Benedict was the first time Nicki has ever heard the word used in relation to filmmaking. Quality cinematic performances aren't generally high on the list of priorities of people who claim *Sharknado* as their favourite movie.

'And he's really funny and self-depreciating —'

'Self-deprecating.'

'Right. And so we just, like, got along famously.'

'Glad to hear it.' I get up from my chair; my upchuck reflex is just about at breaking point. 'Leave your copy on my desk when you're done and I'll have a read through. I'd best get on and see Girish.'

'I've already sent the story through. Girish wanted it ASAP since it's, like, going on the front page and everything,' she babbles, trotting beside me as I weave through the desks towards the glass-walled conference room. 'My first splash! Can you belieeeve it?'

'No, Nicki, I really can't.'

Girish sees me lurking and gestures for me to enter the room. I gulp and push the door open. He sits at one end of a long mahogany table, its surface so highly buffed the other section editors' double chins are reflected in all their glory.

I've always hated being called into conference. Held twice a day, it's ostensibly a meeting in which the content of the next day's newspaper is discussed. In reality, it's just an excuse for a bunch of fat middle-aged bores to ogle topless photos of soap stars on holiday and slap each other on the back for stitching up politicians and dodgy TV repairmen. Until I worked on a national newspaper, I thought elections were decided by voters, and criminals were caught by the police. Now I know the truth – newspaper editors are only slightly less powerful than God. Or so they'd have you believe.

'Anna, what the fuck are you playing at?' Girish blusters.

I wince. Though he's never one to mince his words, he's not usually rude or aggressive. He's showing off for his mates. Nigel, the paper's editor-in-chief, regards me with a mixture of boredom and contempt. I don't think he's actually spoken to me in the entire time I've worked for him.

'Sorry, Girish? I don't follow.' I'm stalling for time. There's no way I'll survive this attack of the egos unscathed but buying a moment for my brain to engage could mean the difference between life and death.

'You don't follow? Well, let me be a little clearer. Would you mind explaining to us why, a) you're five hours late for work, and b) you let the dozy cow who answers your phone handle our biggest exclusive of the year?'

Even though my professional life is on the line, I can't resist a tiny smile at Girish's description of Nicki.

'I'm really sorry, Girish. I had a bit of an emergency and couldn't get here. I felt' – my throat threatens to close up as I say the word – '*confident* Nicki could handle it.'

A vein throbs on Girish's forehead. I haven't noticed until now how genuinely livid he looks. Surely Nicki can't have done that badly?

'It seems your confidence was misplaced on this occasion, Anna,' he says ominously. The other editors grunt and wobble their jowls in assent.

'Why? What did she write?' I can feel panic setting in.

Girish looks at Nigel who, with one pudgy finger, grimly slides a sheaf of typewritten papers across the table towards me.

'She wrote a feature about Benedict Cumberbatch's new show,' Nigel says.

She didn't. She *cannot* be that stupid! I snatch up the story and scan it in desperation. She's called him a 'prodigious talent', a 'consummate professional'. She's described at length how he came to be cast in the role. She's practically had a literary orgasm over his 'glowing skin and cheeky smile'. What she hasn't done is dig up any dirt on his marriage, got him to talk about his young children, or implied any on-set tensions between him and his co-stars. Our readers eat that stuff up, but it's nowhere to be seen. This is worse than I thought.

Nicki had one of the world's biggest screen stars in the palm of her hand and has written a perfectly nice article about his new TV show. There's not a whiff of scandal. Not a hint of sex. Not even an inkling of an irate response to a question that cut too close to the bone. After months of effort on my part persuading Benedict Cumberbatch to sit down with one of the muck-rakingest rags on the planet, Nicki has faithfully recounted every charming word he said. I'm screwed.

'Your little emergency has cost this newspaper one of our biggest ever scoops,' Girish rails. 'We can't print this! No one gives a shit that Benedict Cumberbatch is doing another series of some show that's been around for years. They want to know whether his marriage is on the rocks or if he's secretly gay!' He snatches Nicki's story from my hand and hurls it on to the table in disgust. 'Any one of the gossip sites could trump this rubbish with literally *anything* they can find out about him.'

'Yeah. Yes, you're right.,' I say, looking wildly around the room on the off-chance one of the other editors is feeling benevolent enough to step in and save me. But they all just stare back at me, blatantly amused by my public torture.

'So? What do you intend to do about this?' Girish goes on.

Words start tumbling from my mouth before they've been vetted by my brain. 'Tonight's the premiere in Leicester Square,' I hear myself saying. 'Nicki was invited but I'll go in her place. I'll get the story. I'll make this right, boss.'

Girish looks at Nigel and, mercifully, the editor looks mildly assuaged. 'Fine,' Nigel says. 'Right, Chris. What's news in sport?'

And that's that. Girish shoots me another murderous look and I skulk back to my desk.

Ordinarily, this would be no big deal. I've been to dozens of premieres, bowled up to countless stars much bigger than Benedict Cumberbatch. I'm not intimidated by famous people. At least, 'Showbiz Anna' is not intimidated by famous people. While 'Real Anna' won't enter a busy pub unless a convoluted exchange of text messages has confirmed someone she knows is already there, Showbiz Anna knows most celebs are just averagely talented but more driven versions of normal people. When I step into Showbiz Anna's shoes, I'm bold as brass. If it's dirt Girish wants, dirt is what Showbiz Anna will deliver.

But tonight's premiere poses two key problems. The first is Nicki Ford-Smith. She's not going to give up her chance to be seen on the red carpet alongside Benedict Cumberbatch without a fight. The second problem is Ivy. I pick up my desk phone and punch in Jen's number.

'Oh darl, this one is such a little sweetheart,' she says when she hears my voice. 'Ivy's been good as gold all day. Milo and El are absolutely in love with her. Milo's already asked if we can keep her!'

I breathe a sigh of relief. Perhaps this won't be quite the logistical nightmare I feared. 'I don't suppose you could, Jen? Keep her, I mean. Just for a few hours this evening.' I give Jen the abridged version of the Benedict Cumberbatch debacle.

'Bloody hell, Anna, that's bollocks. When is that stupid little stick insect going to get the boot?'

'Unfortunately I think this looks a lot worse for me than it does for Nicki,' I say glumly. 'Which is why I'll clean your house for the rest of the year if you'll help me out tonight.' I cross my fingers.

Jen chuckles. 'Tempting as that is, I can't, hon. I'm really, really sorry but we're visiting Andrew's parents in Dorset this weekend. We're leaving as soon as he gets home tonight,' she says. 'Won't Finn be home?'

I haven't even thought of asking Finn to watch Ivy. The thought of him interacting with a child seems vaguely absurd. And he'll probably be working late anyway. But still, what choice have I got?

I thank Jen and hang up, then dial Finn's mobile.

'Finn's phone. Fiona speaking,' says a broad Irish voice.

Who? 'Oh, uh, hello. Is Finn there, please?'

'I'm sorry, Anna. He's just stepped away from the table. Can I get him to call you back?' the voice says pleasantly.

'Yes, please. It's quite urgent, so . . . Sorry, how do you know who I am?'

Fiona laughs softly. 'Your name came up on the screen and Finn's just been telling me all about you over lunch,' she says. 'I look forward to meeting you when you come out to visit.'

'Right . . . So . . . visit where?'

'Well, Belfast, of course. We're thrilled Finn has decided to join the *Belfast Breakfast* team.'

Who *is* this woman? I feel like I've joined a conversation half-way through and no one can be bothered filling me in.

'What do you mean he's joining your team? His interview isn't until next week.' Hadn't Finn's email said Monday?

Fiona laughs her tinkly giggle again. 'It was supposed to be next week, but we decided we just couldn't wait the weekend to get Finn on board. I flew into London first thing, whisked him off to lunch and made him an offer he couldn't refuse,' she says.

I suddenly feel like I can't breathe. She can't be serious.

'Now, I hope you won't mind my borrowing Finn this evening, Anna. We have lots of brainstorming to do for our new show.'

Suddenly, I hear Finn's voice in the background. Fiona covers the mouthpiece with her hand but I hear her muffled voice say, 'It's Anna. I'm afraid I may have ruined the surprise. Shall I pass her over?'

Then she takes her hand away to hand Finn the phone and I hear his reply. 'Christ no! She'll kill me.'

I slam the phone into its cradle, hot tears stinging my eyes. Finn has taken the job in Belfast. A mere six hours after promising we'd discuss it, and that he'd stay if I want him to, he's sold his loyalty to me, to our relationship, for lunch in a fancy restaurant.

My mobile starts buzzing and Finn's name flashes on the screen; I reject the call. I feel shaken and hollow, too stunned to do anything but stare dumbly at my Mac monitor. This time yesterday I had a relationship and a career. Now both seem to be hanging by a thread.

But I do have a baby to take care of and a premiere to attend. Finn is probably feeling ashamed enough to be guilted into ditching this Fiona person and staying with Ivy tonight but I can't bring myself to speak to him. Jen has her own family to care for. I wouldn't trust any of my other friends with a house plant, let alone an infant, and Helena is God knows where doing God knows what.

For a split second I consider calling Parcel Nazi, throwing myself at his feet and vowing never again to let Nui wee in his flower beds if he'll just watch Ivy for a couple of hours. But I hardly know Luke, and my infrequent dealings with him have been largely unpleasant. He may have seemed half human this morning but the guy can't even cope with my post landing on his doorstep – I doubt he'd be overly enthusiastic to find my goddaughter there. I'm left with only one option: Ivy will have to make her red carpet debut with me.

The numbness starts to dissipate, and in its place is fierce, cold rage. Damn Helena! Why couldn't she be stronger? Why couldn't she put her airy-fairy melancholy aside and just do the right thing by her daughter? This should not be my problem.

I hear the rustle of plastic bags behind me and whip round to see Nicki tottering along with what looks like half of House of Fraser in her arms.

'Sooo,' she says excitedly as she retrieves two minuscule scraps of fabric from a bag. 'Do you think the D&G or the Gucci?' She holds a tiny dress in each hand. I blink dumbly and she shakes the frocks at me. 'For the premiere? I know high fashion's not, like, your thing Anna, but if —'

'You can put them both away,' I snarl through clenched teeth. 'Put your teeny frocks and your stripper shoes and your pointlessly small clutch back in those bags and get the hell out of my sight.'

Nicki looks as shocked as if I'd slapped her. 'What? Why?'

I stand and square up to her, aware that the rest of the newsroom has its collective jaw on the floor as it watches our exchange. '*You* are not going to the premiere. I am. I gave you a huge opportunity with that Benedict Cumberbatch interview, you moron, and you cocked it up beyond belief. So now I have to clean up your mess and it's the absolute last thing I need.'

Nicki stares at me a heartbeat longer, then narrows her eyes. 'Fine,' she says. 'Fine. You go to the premiere. But don't you dare pretend giving me that interview was some kind of ultrasonic act.'

'Altruistic.'

'Whatever. You were desperate because your personal life was in chaos as usual, and I did you a favour. You may have forgotten that, Anna, but don't you worry – I'll remember *this*.'

Finn

'I'll be earning twice what I am now so I can keep up my share of the rent and you won't have to move. It's strictly Monday to Friday so I'll be back every weekend. They're putting me up in an apartment in the centre of Belfast so you'll have the perfect crash pad for shopping weekends.'

I tick the benefits off on my fingers as I rattle them off. I infuse my voice with enthusiasm and practise my most upbeat facial expressions. But it's no good. The face that stares back from the bathroom mirror still looks shifty and guilt-ridden. Try as I might, I can't hide the gleam in my eye that shouts 'I can't wait to start this job!' I might as well spare myself the effort and just take out an ad in *The Mirror* that reads: 'Dear Anna, bollocks to our relationship. Love Finn.' Because no matter how I try to spin this, that's all she'll hear.

I turn away from the mirror. 'What would you do?' I ask the bathroom attendant. He hands me a crisp linen napkin, a hopeful expression on his face, clearly praying dry hands will make the bloke who's been talking to his reflection for the last ten minutes go back to his table. But he's out of luck, because I can't face that yet either.

Waiting at the table is Fiona O'Donnell, executive producer of *Belfast Breakfast* and the woman who's just agreed to pretty much every professional demand I could think of. Great salary, car, flash apartment, dressing room, clothing allowance – done. And, best of all, I'm going to be the show's co-host. I hadn't really even been serious when I asked for that, expecting her to laugh me out of the restaurant and tell me it's senior reporter or it's nothing. But she's handed it to me on a silver platter with a side order of whatever the hell I want, and now she's out there waiting patiently for me to dazzle her with my witty repartee and groundbreaking ideas for hard-hitting journalism. She's also no doubt expecting me to explain why a phone call from my girlfriend has me cowering in a toilet.

I offer the attendant a weak smile and, as I lock myself in a cubicle, I'm sure I hear a sigh escape his lips. I lower the toilet lid and sit on it. Damn these posh restaurants and their pleasant bathrooms. They make it even harder for spineless arseholes who accept jobs they've promised their girlfriends they won't to go out and face the music.

I didn't mean to take the job. Honest. When I left the house this morning, tired and grumpy as I was, I really was ready to give up the opportunity. Our relationship may have hit a rocky patch but I know it's going to take more than the occasional weekend together to fix it. Anna deserves more from me than that, especially now she has Ivy to deal with. I meant what I wrote in my note – at the very least, I planned to discuss the job offer with her before I thought about it any further. But then Fiona turned up.

In my defence, I'd like to see any man get swept off to lunch by such an attractive and persuasive woman and not agree to everything she says. Fiona is charming and glamorous, with ash-blonde hair blowdried to a perfect sheen and disarmingly pale blue eyes. She's dressed head to toe in expensive-looking black clothes that Anna could no doubt identify as Marc Jacobs or Prada with just a glance. She's clearly the sort of woman who expects to get what she wants – the doorman at The Ivy greeted Fiona by name as she strutted in, and ushered her straight to an intimate corner table. She didn't even have a reservation (even Anna would be impressed by that). The woman has power and, well, balls. She ordered a 200-quid bottle of wine without looking at the menu. I got a little tipsy on the wine but mostly it's Fiona O'Donnell who is intoxicating.

But that's not the whole truth. The truth is that, even though I really did intend to talk over the job offer with Anna, I guess I also wanted to give her a taste of her own medicine. As I heard the words 'I'll take it' come tumbling out of my mouth in response to Fiona's job offer, a big part of my brain was shouting, 'What in God's name are you doing?!' But another, equally big part was smirking. 'So Anna thinks she can foist a kid on me without my say-so? Let's see how *she* feels being on the receiving end of a stupidly rash decision.'

Helena didn't help matters. I saw her this morning. She woke me up as she tried to creep past my makeshift bed on the sofa – without her baby.

'Helena,' I hissed. 'Where do you think you're going? Where's Ivy?'

At least she had the decency to look ashamed. In fact, with her tearstained face and black-shadowed eyes, she looked positively distraught.

'Please don't wake Anna, Finn,' Helena pleaded. 'It's best this way. I'm a walking disaster. The sooner I get out of here and let Anna and Ivy get on with it, the better off we'll all be.'

Even though I was groggy with sleep, Helena's words sent ripples of anger coursing through me. 'Oh, *we'll* all be better off, will we? In case you hadn't noticed, Helena, "all of us" includes *me*.' I was fighting to keep my voice level. 'I'm part of this fun little scenario and I fail to see how I'll be better off if I let you do a runner and saddle Anna with your kid without even a word.'

Helena's pitiable gaze turned steely and she laughed a derisive snort. 'Will you listen to yourself?' she spat. 'It's all about *you*, isn't it, Finn? In one breath you're telling me how we're all in this together and in the next it's Anna alone who'll be "saddled" with Ivy.'

I started to defend myself but Helena held up her hands. 'Save it,' she said. 'I didn't expect your support. In fact, if I thought for one second you'd actually be involved in caring for Ivy, I'd have thought twice about bringing her here. It's only knowing your head is too far up your arse to have anything to do with her that convinced me.'

'What's that supposed to mean?'

Helena shook her head sadly. 'Anna is Ivy's godmother because she'll teach my daughter about kindness and generosity and being a good person. That's who she is. I think Ivy can do without lessons in narcissism and how to be a prize tool.' And she stepped through the front door into the pre-dawn gloom.

Which is how I came to be hiding in a toilet, a prize tool who's probably just flushed away his relationship out of petty pride.

'Christ no, she'll kill me,' I'd said to Fiona when Anna called.

And if she does, I'll deserve it. I may have killed the last of the love between us.

Anna

Jen appears to have interpreted my request for 'something pretty' for Ivy to wear to the premiere to mean 'something Biblical'. My goddaughter is decked out in Elodie's christening dress, a sweeping cream gown of silk and French lace. Probably antique, undoubtedly worth more than I'll be paid this month. No pressure, then.

It's not exactly practical children's attire and will look ridiculously out of place on the red carpet but, as I have about three minutes to get to the premiere and probably would have taped a Sainsbury's bag on Ivy if it were left up to me, I'm ridiculously grateful. I snatch Ivy from Jen's arms, flinging air kisses and thank yous in her direction as I struggle to bundle my wriggling goddaughter into the child seat in the waiting taxi. We just might make it.

'Anna,' calls a voice. I turn and see Luke striding down the footpath towards me, a grave expression on his face. Nothing new there.

'Hi Luke,' I say, hoping he'll pick up the implied can't-you-see-I'm-running-horrendously-late in my greeting and retreat. No such luck. Instead, he stops dead in front of me and says, 'Wow.'

Wow? What does he mean, wow? Is that sarcasm? I can never

tell with Luke. His gaze roams over my dishevelled form and I look down in panic. I've hurled myself into one of my party failsafes, a navy-blue silk gown that may or may not be Chloe. (The label assures me it is but, since I bought it on eBay for a hundred quid, I'll never be entirely convinced.) Nevertheless, I think the frock suits me, even if it is the basis of an outfit that was thrown together in the twelve minutes I had at my disposal between arriving home to collect Ivy and rushing out the door. I thought I looked vaguely presentable; now Luke's 'wow' has spun me into a frenzied search for missed splotches of baby food or clumps of dog hair.

'What? Wow what?' I plead, when my hunt turns up nothing.

Luke blinks in surprise. 'Nothing. Just, er, you look nice.'

Now it's my turn to gape. A strange warm feeling unfurls in my chest. I think it's delight. Sensing my shock, Luke shakes his shaggy head slightly and continues. 'Er, anyway, your dog barked all afternoon so —'

'Are you kidding me?'

'Um, no. I just —'

'Have a look at what's going on here, Luke. Do I seem like a woman who has time to stand here and be told off because her dog barks occasionally?'

Oh, poor Nui. He's a confirmed 'indoor dog' but I must have shut him outside in my rush to get to the office this afternoon. I can only imagine the racket he made as he demanded to be let back in. But I'm not about to offer Luke an apology. Is there *nothing* this guy won't complain about? That inkling of pleasure I felt a moment ago vanishes in an instant.

'I wasn't —'

'Dogs bark, Luke. You know, if you really can't function without absolute silence, you might want to rethink living in London. We live under the Heathrow flight path, for goodness sake. Are you going to start standing in your garden, shaking your fist at the planes?' I know I'm goading him, but I can't resist. I can't remember the last person who wound me up as much as he does. I expect Luke to take the bait and rant back at me. Instead, he smiles. A big, warm grin that lights up his whole face.

'As I was saying, your dog barked all afternoon so I hopped your back fence and brought him over to my place,' he says. 'He seemed kind of lonely. I hope you don't mind.'

'Oh.'

'Yeah. He's still there now. I was just coming to tell you in case you were worried he'd got out,' Luke goes on, his smile growing even broader. 'I can see you're on your way somewhere, so I'm happy to hang on to him for the evening if you like. Unless your bloke will be home soon?' He stops speaking and waits, still grinning, for me to regain my composure. He's obviously enjoying this.

My instinct is not to give him the satisfaction of helping me out. This is the second time today he's left me gobsmacked with his apparent personality transplant, and I'm still not sure what to make of it. But I really could use his help. I'm already going to have to travel at warp speed to reach the premiere in time and Ivy is growing fractious in the taxi. Nui does need feeding (I've forgotten that, too – it seems my dogmothering skills are right up there with my godmothering abilities). And God knows what time Finn will wander home after his earlier performance.

'Actually, that would be great.' I offer Luke a smile in return.

He looks at me expectantly. 'I think the word you're looking for is thank you,' he says sternly.

'Of course! Thank you. I really appreciate it, um, Luke.' Saying his name aloud feels odd. I've really only hurled it at him in anger before; now it feels like we've broken through some invisible barrier, and using his name kindly feels strangely intimate.

'It's my pleasure,' he says, and I think he actually means it.

Ivy lets out an irritated squawk, reminding me that my window for saving my job is closing fast. 'I've got to go,' I tell Luke. I peel the front door key from my key ring. 'Nui's food is in the cabinet under the sink. If he gets really annoying, feel free to put him back in the house. Finn should be home eventually.'

Luke takes the key and glances into the taxi, where Ivy is doggedly trying to squirm free of the child seat. 'You know, I'm happy to look after your goddaughter as well if you like,' he says. 'I'm great with kids.'

Much as I want to hug him with gratitude, fling Ivy at him and race off in the taxi, I shake my head. Ivy is in my care; leaving her with Luke would be irresponsible. What would Helena think if she knew I'd foisted her daughter on to a virtual stranger? Then again, given recent events, she'd likely see nothing wrong with it.

'I probably should take you up on that, since I'm on my way to possibly the most child-unfriendly event in the world,' I say. 'But it's been a chaotic couple of days for Ivy. I think it's best I keep her with me.'

'No worries,' Luke says with a nod. 'The offer's always open. Now, I'd best get back to that dog of yours.'

With a wave, he turns and walks back to his house. I watch him retreat, still trying to process this 'new' Luke. If I wasn't such a cynic, I might actually entertain the idea of being friends with my neighbour.

The taxi driver leans impatiently on his horn. 'Oi! We goin' or what?'

I leap into the cab, offering a silent prayer to the god of movie stars as the driver squeals the tyres. *Please let Benedict Cumberbatch be as helpful as Luke.* If going to this premiere was low on my list of priorities before Finn's bombshell, it is absolutely the last thing I want to do now.

Christ no, she'll kill me. My boyfriend's words play over and over in my head. He has to know I heard him, but he hasn't called me back since I rejected his call. He didn't text or email or send an

'I'm an arse' bouquet to the office. I half expected him to be on the doorstep when I arrived home, ready to grovel. Finn's quite good at grovelling – he's had ample opportunity to hone his technique over the last five years. But the house was empty. Which is probably lucky for him. I don't know what I'd have done first. Hit him? Thrown things? Smashed something? Thrown something at him and hope it hit him and smashed?

Mostly I think I'd have screamed. And yelled. And screamed some more. Over and over again, until Finn realised how he's ripping my heart out by turning his back on us just as everything's turning to twenty-four-carat crap.

In any event, I don't have time to think about it or plot my revenge now. I can feel my rage curling itself into a neat little ball in the pit of my stomach, where it will slumber, purring, until Finn turns up to poke it with a sharp stick.

Leicester Square is a cacophony of screaming millennials and hollering paparazzi. 'Benedict! Benedict! Over here, Benedict!' Their chant rises up like a mantra.

With Ivy on my hip (the pram didn't really go with my dress) I push through the masses to the red carpet. It's flanked by burly security guards, all muttering furtively into their earpieces. Behind them, a sea of flashbulbs explodes as Benedict Cumberbatch strides towards the cinema entrance. Nicki was right – there's definitely a sort of glow around him. He radiates health, wealth and charisma the way I radiate garlic the day after a quality Indian takeaway.

Ivy grizzled for most of the car trip, until I fed her a bottle of formula helpfully prepared by Jen, but now she's watching the circus with interest. Her rosy-pink lips form a surprised 'o' and she nestles closer into me. Strange as it feels to have a baby in my arms, I'm already growing to like the sensation of her warm little body against my chest. And she is a beautiful-looking little girl. Most babies seem to look like prunes until they're at least six months old, when the lucky ones start to resemble something almost human and the unlucky little blighters start showing signs of inheriting Dad's monobrow or Mum's weak chin.

It always surprises me to see women I'd thought were in their right minds cooing over offspring who resemble a cross between Gandhi and a semi-dried tomato. I suspect they're made to sign a contract in the hospital that requires them to babble on about their baby's beauty even when the baby in question was clearly last in line on the day the attractive features were being handed out. Fortunately, Ivy's beauty is obvious to everyone who sees her. She even has Helena's dimples. I never had the pleasure of meeting Ivy's father, but from what Hel's said it seems what he lacked in common decency he made up for with good genes.

With my free hand I flash my invitation and the security monolith steps aside to allow me onto the red carpet. Mr Movie Star is pressing the flesh with hysterical young girls a few paces ahead of me, which gives me a chance to formulate a plan.

Though my mission is to find a story to replace Nicki's useless interview with Benedict, I don't actually plan to speak to him. I can hardly bowl up to him and say, 'Oh hi, Ben! Listen, that insightful interview you gave my ditzy colleague this morning is no good to us, so be a sport and give me something juicy, won't you?'

The only way I'll get my career-saving story is to hang back and observe. Watch who he talks to, who tosses furtive glances his way from across the room, who gossips about him in the toilets. Then I'll piece together a story from what I know, and make up the bits I don't. Welcome to the world of tabloid journalism.

Benedict moves to enter the cinema and I stick a few paces behind him. If I can remain quiet and unobtrusive, it might just work. And that all depends on Ivy.

'Buh!' she suddenly announces, then dissolves into a fit of giggles. A dozen expensively coiffed heads swivel in our direction – I guess the sound of a chatty baby isn't what you'd expect to hear at a premiere. Fortunately Benedict's isn't among them.

'What a gorgeous baby!' A statuesque brunette breaks away from her gaggle of beautiful people and makes a beeline for Ivy. It's Cat Hubbard, the next target on my hit list after all the available dirt on Benedict has been dug up. Aside from Nicki's nugget nearly a year ago about Cat's short-lived marriage, and the comprehensively raked-over stuff about the drug problem she's now conquered, my search for a scoop on Cat Hubbard has so far proved fruitless. But my showbiz hack's instincts tell me a star as big as Cat can't possibly be as squeaky-clean as she now appears. None of them are.

'How old is she?' Cat asks, waggling a finger in front of Ivy's nose.

'Five months. No, six months.'

Cat smiles. 'It's hard to keep track at this age, isn't it? They change so much every day.'

'They sure do,' I say emphatically, because it seems like the thing to say. Well, Ivy does look a *little* bit different today from how she did yesterday.

'Oh, you're just too cute, aren't you?' she coos. Ivy arches towards Cat and waves her arms. 'Do you mind?' Cat asks me, poised to catch her.

'Of course not.' Gingerly, I hand Ivy over. She promptly attaches her mouth to Cat's nose and gums furiously. Could this child be more embarrassing?

'Have you got some teeth coming though, missy?' Cat asks in a singsong voice, detaching Ivy from her face and offering the tip of her little finger to be chewed instead. 'What's her name?'

'Ivy.'

'That was my great-grandmother's name! Gorgeous. I'm Cat,

by the way,' she says with a grin.

'I know, I'm . . . a big fan,' I reply. Some instinct tells me not to reveal my hack reporter credentials while Cat has my goddaughter in her arms. 'I'm Anna.'

'Well, Anna, it's nice to meet you. Did you work on the film?'

'Ah, no . . . I'm, er, a writer.' Again, not strictly a lie.

'Really? That's brilliant. Well done,' Cat says warmly. Then, looking at Ivy, 'And well done on having such a beautiful little girl. You're very lucky.'

Ivy blows a raspberry and wrinkles her nose in delight. I can't help but laugh. 'I sure am.'

Cat hands Ivy back to me and adjusts her couture dress. 'God, I hate this thing,' she says. 'I'm leaving as soon as the lights go down. I've got my jeans in the car.'

I'm suddenly struck by the surrealness of the situation. I'm standing at an A-list movie premiere – well, a TV premiere in a movie theatre – clutching someone else's baby and listening to a chart-topping singer moan about her frock.

As if she's read my mind, Cat stops fussing with her dress and takes a long look around her. 'Does your head in, doesn't it?'

'God, yes.' Cat is rapidly becoming my favourite celebrity. Maybe she genuinely *is* as cool as she appears to be.

'Right,' she says, drawing herself up to her impressive full height and squaring her shoulders. 'The sooner I get in there the sooner I can blow this joint.' She moves off, then stops. 'Great to meet you, Anna. I'm having an album launch party on the twenty-third at the 100 Club. Why don't you come along? Your little one's welcome too.'

This is the first invite to a celebrity bash I've ever received from an actual celebrity. Usually I have to suck up to PRs or, worse, gate-crash. Girish will be thrilled. 'I'd love to. Thanks, Cat.'

She smiles again and disappears into the crowd.

I follow Benedict discreetly into the cinema and find a seat a couple of rows behind him. The rest of the media are seated upstairs on the balcony but having a proper invitation means I can sit with the major players. I watch him carefully. The moments I spent chatting to Cat meant I missed out on watching who he spoke to, so I'm behind the eight ball. If he leaves during the screening I'll have to chase him down and actually talk to him. He's not likely to volunteer anything salacious but even an innocuous comment can be spun into something titillating. Unless you're Nicki Ford-Smith, obviously.

The lights dim and the opening credits begin to roll across the screen. A spontaneous cheer erupts from the crowd as Benedict's name appears. I steal a glance to see how he reacts but he appears unmoved. Could he be nervous? The cheering merges into a smattering of applause, which seems to startle Ivy. She lets out a soft whimper and turns her face up towards mine. Her eyes are as wide as saucers, glistening in the darkened auditorium. She whimpers again, as if she's asking, 'What's this all about then?'

'It's all right, petal,' I whisper in her ear, drawing her closer to me. The woman in the next seat shoots a sharp glance in my direction. Ivy responds by yelping a little louder and several people turn to scowl at us. I feel my chest tighten with anxiety. In my dash to get Ivy and myself into town in time to catch Benedict on the red carpet, the fact that I have to keep a six-month-old amused – and quiet – through a movie-length TV premiere didn't really register. I have no idea how I'm going to do it, or if it's even possible. Who brings a tiny baby to a cinema, much less a fancy premiere? Theatres have those 'mums 'n' bubs' sessions precisely to avoid situations like this.

Ivy's mewling is growing louder and more annoyed. 'Shh, Ivy. There there, baby,' I breathe, gently rocking her and sending telepathic pleas to pipe down. Ivy fixes me with her limpid gaze and pauses for a moment. Then she takes a deep breath, screws up her face and —

'WaaaaaAAAAAaaahhhh!'

The death stares are now accompanied by tutting and head-shaking. None of it has any effect on Ivy, who sucks in another lungful of air and releases it as an ear-splitting scream. I check her nappy – dry and stink-free. She finished her bottle not half an hour ago so she can't be hungry. I rock her more quickly; still she screams. I rub her belly; she yelps like a cat with its tail stuck in a door. I roll my eyes and offer my best 'Kids!' smiles to the people who huff and mutter and look pointedly at my goddaughter, as if that alone has the power to silence her.

'Wah-wah-wah-waaaaAAAAhhh!'

Even Benedict has turned to frown at us now. Perhaps Ivy is offering her critique of the episode – surely if it was any good people would be looking at it rather than us.

'Oh Ivy, shush, darling. Please, please, *please* be quiet.'

I lift her from her position cradled in my arms and turn her so she's facing over my shoulder. Instantly, she's quiet. *Thank you, God*. She snuffles and snorts in my ear and her little head wobbles as she takes in the frowning faces in the row behind us. 'There you go! You just wanted to have a look around, didn't you!'

'Oh for God's sake!' The sour-faced crone next to me leans over. 'Your bloody screaming kid is bad enough,' she hisses, her gin-tinged breath stinging my nostrils. 'Do you think you could refrain from giving the rest of us a running bloody commentary on what it's doing?'

'Excuse me? *It?*'

The woman rolls her eyes. 'Don't get all high and bloody mighty with me. You're the idiot who brought a screaming brat to a premiere.'

I feel my insides clench in anger as I open my mouth to give the hag a serve. Fortunately, Ivy seems to have had the same reaction and saves me the trouble. She bobbles her little head around to face the witch and lets loose a torrent of thick, milky sick all over the woman's gown.

'Christ!' Cruella de Vil leaps out of her seat, frantically pawing at the rivulets of yellowy goo dripping down her dress. 'You stupid bitch! This is Matthew Williamson!'

'Congratulations!' a voice pipes up at the back of the auditorium. 'Now shut up and sit down!'

But Cruella's having none of it. 'You disgusting woman! It's ruined! I'll be sending you the bill!' she shouts.

'Why? I didn't spew on your dress, *it* did.'

At the mention of spew, Ivy turns to me and flashes a megawatt smile. If I wasn't already besotted, I'd have fallen in love with her in that moment. She's defiled the silly cow's frock and, what's more, she's immensely proud of herself. Bless her little cotton socks.

'You shouldn't have been let in! Who brings a baby to a premiere?'

'Shut up!'

'Get over it, you freak!'

'Down in front!'

The surrounding chorus of disapproval is doing nothing to dampen the woman's enthusiasm for telling me off. 'Outside!' she says. 'Outside now!'

'Why, are you going to open up a can of whoopass?' I'm encouraged to hear a few muffled chuckles from nearby seats. Is she for real? Even Ivy appears bored by her histrionics.

'What seems to be the problem here, ladies?' One of the security behemoths is crouching beside my seat, speaking in that soft yet menacing voice rent-a-cops are so fond of.

Ms Crazy clambers over me and grips his arm. 'This fucking moron brought her kid and it's just puked all over me,' she whines, still yelling.

'I will ask you to lower your voice and refrain from using that type of language,' he tells her, then turns to me. 'Is this true?' he asks, a hint of a smile playing across his lips.

'Look at her dress, mate. Do you think it's true?' It's not like me to be insolent to people in authority (even people who don't really have any authority at all) but I just can't take the situation seriously. And judging by the uproarious giggles now coming from Ivy, she can't either.

'Ma'am, I think you'd better come with me,' he says, standing up and gesturing for me to do the same.

'Me? Why? She's the one behaving like a madwoman. There's no law against bringing a baby to a cinema.'

I can see my chance of speaking to Benedict, which was always slim at best, dwindling to impossibility. Although given he (and everyone else in the cinema) is now regarding me with an expression approaching outright hostility, that's probably a good thing.

'No, there's no law against it. But I'm weighing up the probabilities here and I reckon it's more likely you'll go quietly than she will,' the man says. He has a point.

So, with Ivy still hooting with laughter in my arms, I follow him meekly out of the cinema. Cruella stands with her arms folded and smugly watches me go. I'm not normally a violent person but I'd love to wipe that smile right off her face. Instead, I settle for the bitchiest remark I can muster. 'I don't know what you're looking so pleased about. You're the one who has to sit here for the next ninety minutes reeking of vomit.'

Ejected into Leicester Square, the cinema doors slamming dramatically behind me, I feel strangely euphoric. I've failed in my mission to crucify Benedict Cumberbatch, and my head may very well be on the chopping block as a result. Girish will have to run Nicki's dull interview and she'll see it as another weapon in the arsenal she's planning to use to oust me from my job. But, actually, I couldn't care less.

I don't know what I was thinking, imagining I could carry on as normal with a tiny baby in tow. It's not fair to me or to Ivy. It's not fair to Helena either – her midnight flit wasn't helpful, but it doesn't change the fact that I promised to care for her daughter as best I can. And then there's this mess with Finn to sort out – that's not going to happen overnight. I'm owed a holiday; bugger it, I'm going to take it.

I pull out my mobile phone and dial Girish's number. My call diverts to his voicemail.

'Hi Girish, it's Anna. I've just been thrown out of the Benedict Cumberbatch premiere because my goddaughter spewed on some chick from *EastEnders* or something. I don't have a story to replace Nicki's so you'll have to run with that. I'm sure this will make you apoplectic but actually it's a well-written feature and it wouldn't kill *The Mirror* to get its mind out of the gutter every once in a while. Meanwhile, I will be taking two weeks off, as of right now. The emergency I mentioned this morning, the one you didn't want to hear about? Well, her name is Ivy, she's six months old and she needs me. Call it a holiday, call it personal leave, call it maternity leave if you want. The point is, I'll see you in a fortnight.'

Helena

Since Ivy was born, there have been good days and bad ones. Maybe I'm crazy but I expected the day after I left Ivy in London with Anna to be a good one. I thought I would feel somehow lighter, content in the knowledge that my daughter is being well cared for and that I have days stretching ahead of me in which I have nothing to do but think, walk and get my head together. Call me callous but I think I expected to feel relieved, to feel free. Instead, I wake on my first morning in Aunt Edme's house feeling like I've been run over by a great big truck, emotionally speaking. Crammed into a rock-hard single bed in a draughty guest room that looks like it hasn't seen a duster in several decades, the weight of my failures as a mother – and a human being – press down on my chest. Leaving Ivy wasn't brave or right or even slightly justifiable. It was wrong. It was weak. It was cowardly.

Aunt Edme wasted no time in telling me she agrees. My worries about when – or if – to tell my great-aunt about Ivy were pointless; as soon as my dad realised his missing MasterCard had been used to book an international flight and saw the photo of Edme was missing from the mantlepiece, he put two and two together. By the time Oliver delivered me to Edme's door, she'd had several phone calls from my mother, and greeted me with a face like thunder. (I'm not sure whether this was because of what she'd learned or because simply speaking to my mother seems to have that effect on most people.)

'Hello, Helena,' she'd said with a tight-lipped smile that disappeared the instant Oliver's tail lights were swallowed by the darkness. 'It's been a long time. My, haven't you been a busy girl?'

'Aunt Edme!' I said with false warmth, swooping in to peck her papery cheek. 'It's wonderful to see you. Thanks so much for having me to stay.'

'Little one not with you?' She peered over my shoulder, as if I might have Ivy secreted in my back pocket.

'No, she's in London with her godmother. Anna couldn't bear to let her go!' I was quite amazed at how easily the lies tripped off my tongue. If only I could use my powers for good instead of evil. Edme saw straight through my fibs, at any rate.

'Is that so?' she said with a snort. 'Listen, young lady, I've said you can stay here and I never go back on my word. But I think your behaviour is reprehensible and you'll get no sympathy from me.'

She turned abruptly and marched into the house, leaving me dumbstruck on the doorstep. When she realised I wasn't following she beckoned sharply and issued an irritated tut. I scurried after her, up a creaky staircase and down a dark, narrow passageway to a closed door. She opened it, shooed me inside and closed it again without another word. I heard her purposeful footsteps striding away down the hall. Her contempt was palpable. I wondered how Oliver had managed to spend several hours with me and not say anything; it seemed inevitable she'd have told him all about me. Old people love to spread scandal.

I don't know what Edme found more disagreeable – that I'd

had a bastard child in the first place, that I didn't mention said child when I phoned from Heathrow or that she wasn't with me now. My parents don't know Anna has Ivy, and Edme clearly expected to see her. But given the icy reception I'd received, I'm doubly glad Ivy's not here. Anna might not have been thrilled about the prospect of taking care of Ivy but I'm pretty sure she won't shut her in a tiny room with décor lifted straight from the pages of *Monastery Monthly*.

At least the room has a view. Daylight reveals that Edme's cottage, which is actually more like a ramshackle mansion, sits in the middle of a green field, with acres of waving grass front and back and not a neighbour in sight. Her property slopes down towards a winding road and, beyond that, a sheer cliff drops away into the most unearthly body of water I've ever seen. Gairloch – the actual loch the village takes its name from – is vast and silent, and so still its surface displays a perfect reflection of the surrounding hills. It's a stunning vista, and if I didn't feel like I'm at the bottom of a deep, dark well, I might find it uplifting.

Oh yes, today is most certainly not a good day. On a good day I might feel compelled to get out among all that natural beauty, to wander and explore and feel the frigid Highland breeze sting my face. On a good day I'd relish the peace and quiet, the vacant hours that might help me make sense of the mess in my head.

I *do* want to leave the cottage, but only to escape Edme's reproachful glares. And besides, there's a chance I'll get lost in the endless countryside and, as night falls, freeze to death on some forgotten hillside. I don't actually want to harm myself, I'm certain of that. But sometimes I can't help thinking everyone would be a lot better off if I wasn't around to keep screwing things up.

There's a sharp rap at the bedroom door. 'Helena? Are you awake?' I shiver; there's not an ounce of friendliness in that voice. It's scarcely past dawn, so there's every chance I'd still be asleep. Which is no doubt precisely what's brought my great-aunt to the door.

'Yeah.' I'm not up to even faux-civility.

'Good. I need you to go into the village and pick up some things,' she says. 'I'd go myself but I've marking to be going on with.'

I peer at the ancient bedside clock. Barely half past six. Is the woman mad?

'Er, will anything be open at this hour?'

I can practically feel her bristle through the heavy oak door. 'We're all farmers and fishermen around here, Helena. You won't find any of us lolling in bed all day. We're all up with the sun,' she says curtly. 'Besides, it's a two-mile walk into the village. The shops will be open by the time you get there.' She clomps away.

I heave myself out of bed with a sigh. Something tells me playing my 'basket case' card won't wash with Edme. Or with any of the 'farmers and fishermen' in Gairloch, for that matter. This is not a place where 'I'm depressed' is likely to elicit any response other than 'Get on with it.'

I pull on my jeans, boots, two long-sleeved T-shirts, a chunky wool jumper and my parka. The problem with being so skinny these days is I'm always bloody freezing. The sky beyond my window is a brilliant blue but the early-morning sunlight is watery; like Edme's heart, the Highlands sun offers no warmth whatsoever. I scrape my blonde hair into a low ponytail and jam a beanie over it. It's not exactly a glamorous look, but it should keep the bone-chilling Scottish cold at bay.

Edme has left a ten-pound note and a handwritten shopping list on the floor outside my bedroom door. At this bottom of the list she has scrawled: *Village – turn right at gate.* Sounds easy enough.

I meander down the driveway and dutifully turn right at the end. The road is narrow and windy, hugging the cliff face; the eerily still loch sweeps out to my left. I'm glad it was dark when Oliver dropped me off last night – I think I'd have been revisiting my pub dinner had I known what a precarious position I was in.

The morning light is brittle and the air smells of cold. It all feels a bit otherworldly and suddenly I know why: it's silent. I don't mean 'city silent', when the traffic calms briefly and all that's left is the occasional bark of a dog or a snippet of conversation drifting into the night through an open dining-room window. I mean *properly* silent. There's no chirping birds, no gentle lapping of water on the shores of the loch far below me, no rustling breeze. Even the grass waves soundlessly. The quiet drapes over everything like a heavy shroud. It feels like I'm watching a breathtaking nature documentary with the volume switched off.

To say it feels slightly odd to literally be able to hear a pin drop is a crashing understatement. Babies make a lot of noise. I know that's not exactly a newsflash but I don't think people realise just how constant the noise is. Ivy actually doesn't cry much (though when she does, I'm pretty sure she can be heard from deep space) but she's always making a racket. She gurgles and chats to herself for hours. She shakes her toys and slaps her fat little hands on tabletops. She blows raspberries and claps her feet together. And she laughs a lot. Pretty much everything amuses Ivy; she seems to have a real appreciation for the absurd. I guess I should be heartened that having a total misery guts for a mother hasn't quashed her joy for life just yet.

I'm about three feet from Edme's front gate when the tears start. I don't notice them at first; they slide over my cheeks as quietly as everything else in this desolate place. But then I feel my throat constrict and my chest starts to heave, and before I know it I'm sobbing for Australia. Or Scotland. The thing is, I don't even know why I'm crying. Obviously I have plenty of reasons to wail, but it's not any one of them in particular, as far as I can tell. I'm not crying because I'm a useless mother or because I miss my daughter. I'm not crying because I'm alone in a strange country, an unwelcome guest in the home of a woman who looks at me like I'm something unpleasant she's scraped off the sole of her shoe. I'm not even crying because

I'm skint and friendless and my parents have disowned me. It's none of these things. And all of these things. And a million other things, failings and injustices I haven't even thought of yet. So I just cry and walk, walk and cry. After a while I start to feel a little better. It's reassuring somehow, the way this strange, silent landscape just ignores my distress, swallowing up my tears and offering nothing to comfort me.

A sudden crunching on the gravel road behind me makes me spin around, startled. It's a tiny sound, but in this vast, noiseless void it's as loud as a gunshot. A man cycles towards me on an old-fashioned fixed gear bicycle. As he draws nearer, I realise it's Oliver.

'Morning, Helena,' he says with a smile. 'I just called at the cottage and Edme said you were coming into the village. I'm glad I've caught you.'

'You are? You did – go to the cottage, I mean? At this hour?' I cringe inwardly. *Way to make scintillating conversation there, Hel.* I can't help it – Oliver's appearance has me flustered. Gone is yesterday's charity-shop suit. Today Oliver's rangy frame is clad in skinny jeans, battered Converse trainers and a faded Rolling Stones T-shirt over a long-sleeved top (apparently not everyone finds the Scottish Highlands as excruciatingly freezing as I do). His shaven head is covered by a woolly beanie and he has a guitar slung over one shoulder. I'm stunned by the transformation. The geeky teacher has been replaced by some sort of wandering indie minstrel, and he's completely gorgeous.

'I'm sorry if I seemed a bit abrupt when I dropped you off last night,' he goes on, mercifully ignoring the fact that I'm standing there like a stunned mullet. 'I just realised how long we'd been and I knew Edme would be impatient to see you.' He ducks his head and offers a cheeky smile. 'She can be quite a formidable woman.'

I release the breath I didn't realise I've been holding. 'That's one way to put it,' I reply, trying to wipe my tearstained face as subtly as possible. If Oliver notices my red eyes and blotchy complexion, he doesn't let on.

He climbs off his bike. 'Can I walk you the rest of the way to town?'

'That would be lovely.'

What is this, the 1850s? Since when do blokes on bicycles offer to walk me anywhere? And since when do I call things 'lovely'?

'Going busking?' I point to Oliver's guitar.

'I wouldn't make much! There are only about three people in Gairloch,' he says with a chuckle. 'No, I'm off to set up the community hall. I teach guitar to a few of the local kids there on Saturday mornings. We're a small school and don't have the budget for a music teacher, and this keeps them out of trouble. You might have noticed there's not a whole lot to do around here.'

'Bit of Mick and Keith on the agenda today then?' I nod towards the instantly recognisable set of pouting lips on Oliver's T-shirt.

'You're a Stones fan?' he asks as we continue walking towards town. He looks surprised and maybe a little impressed.

'They're probably my favourite band in the universe,' I say. I'm telling the truth – I've loved the Rolling Stones my whole life. And it has nothing to do with the fact that I'm currently picturing Oliver's T-shirt crumpled on the bedroom floor of Edme's spartan guest room. That'd definitely brighten the place up a bit.

'Mine too! Sadly, these kids are more interested in being the next Arctic Monkeys.' He shakes his head in mock dismay and wheels his bike to a stop in front of a squat grey building. 'This is my stop,' he says.

I'm surprised. I could picture this building as the foreman's office on a building site – but as a nursery for future rock stars? It doesn't look particularly inspiring.

'I know,' says Oliver, clocking my dubious expression. 'The kids refuse to meet on school premises on a Saturday, so this is our only option.'

'At least you don't have neighbours to annoy,' I say. The hall is on the far outskirts of the village; the next building I can see is at least a hundred metres away. 'The kids can make as much racket as they like.'

'And they do!' Oliver pauses. 'Listen, you don't fancy coming in, do you? I'll only be an hour. Then we could grab a coffee or something?' He sounds nonchalant but – am I dreaming? – looks ever so slightly hopeful.

I open my mouth to tell him I can't imagine a better way to spend a Saturday morning than watching a bunch of surly fifteen-year-olds massacring 'I Bet You Look Good on the Dance Floor'. But something stops me, and it's not the mental picture of Edme, tapping her foot and scanning the driveway as she waits for me to return with her haggis or shortbread or whatever it is she has on her list.

It's the unknown. I still don't know whether Oliver knows about Ivy. After Edme's chilly reception last night, I was sure he must. But he hasn't said anything, so maybe she hasn't either. Of course, if he doesn't know that I have a baby, that makes me all the more awful for spending time with him and not admitting she exists. Then again, if he *does* know I have a child, he's either trying to catch me lying or he has a thing for unwed mothers. I don't know which is creepier. It's all too much for my addled brain to process. Delicious though he is, Oliver represents yet more opportunity for confusion and angst, and I have more than enough of both already.

'I'd love to but I can't.' I smile as warmly as I can, hoping he won't take it as a complete brush-off. 'Edme and I didn't exactly start off on the right foot last night, so I'd best do the shopping and get back to her.'

His brow furrows momentarily. 'Fair enough,' he says cheerfully. 'I can think of better ways to spend my Saturday than listening to a bunch of kids shredding "I Bet You Look Good on the Dance Floor", too.'

Dear God, give me strength. The man may very well be perfect.

'Another time then?' he continues, and I find myself nodding my agreement, my must-not-fancy-Oliver vow of two seconds ago promptly forgotten.

Oliver unlocks the hall doors and disappears inside with a wave. I continue into the village, surprised to see Edme was right: though it's just shy of seven-thirty, Gairloch's smattering of stores is well and truly open for business. A teenager stacks bundles of newspapers outside the newsagency-cum-post office. In front of the bakery, two middle-aged women gossip amiably while their small white dogs sniff each other's backsides.

I retrieve Edme's crumpled shopping list from my pocket and head for the butcher. There's no haggis on the list, sadly – just boring steaks and sausages. Then I collect her mail from her post office box, pick up a carton of milk and buy a bottle of cooking sherry. I can't help chuckling as, bottles clinking, I begin the long walk home. Only in Scotland can I buy booze before the sun is properly up.

As I pass the community hall, a wall of crunchy guitar and feed-back rushes out to greet me. Through the window, I spy Oliver's head bobbing in time to the music and I'm tempted to stand there and watch him. Thankfully, the thought of him catching me staring and writing me off as completely nuts is enough to spur me onward.

Edme's cottage is a hive of activity when I finally dawdle back an hour later. The TV is blaring in the compact sitting room and there are paintbrushes and lumps of charcoal scattered over every surface. I hear clattering in the kitchen so I creep down the hall. Loud talk-back radio drones from the ancient wireless on the bench top. The floor is littered with pots, pans and crockery – some of it broken. Edme's corpulent grey cat, Hector, cowers under a dining chair.

And there, in the midst of the chaos, is Edme – stark naked and, evidently, stark raving mad. The acrid smell of alcohol is unmistakable and, on closer inspection, I notice empty spirits bottles among the morass on the floor. Cooking sherry indeed.

'Edme?' I venture. She whirls around, a crazed expression on her face.

'Oh, it's *you*,' she spits, her eyes narrowing. 'I suppose you used it all?' She plants her hands on her hips, giving me a close-up view of things I really don't want to see.

'Used all of what, Edme?'

'The hot water! Foolish girl. I went up to have a bath and there's no hot water. I've had to come down and look for a kettle to boil some.' She seems to have been distracted in her hunt for the kettle by an equally urgent search for the bottom of a bottle. I've been gone just two hours; I can't believe how plastered she is. Something tells me her state is the product of more than a single morning's work. Was she drunk when I arrived last night?

'No, Edme, I haven't had a bath yet this morning. I've been in the village, remember? Perhaps there's a problem with the boiler?' I don't know why I'm wasting my breath trying to reason with her. The look on her face tells me this is an argument I have no chance of winning.

'Liar! Such an evil little fibber.' She points an accusing finger. I'm annoyed to feel tears prickle behind my eyes. Edme probably won't even remember this exchange later this afternoon; I'll be damned if I'm going to let her make me cry.

'Look, why don't you go and have a lie-down and I'll sort out the hot water,' I say, picking my way through the carnage on the floor. I grasp her elbow with one hand and place the other on her leathery back. If nothing else, I just want the woman to cover up. I give her a gentle push and she stumbles forward.

'I expect you've seen Oliver. He came here looking for you,' she slurs, ricocheting off a hall table.

'Yes, we walked into the village together.' I really, *really* hope she was clothed when Oliver came calling. Oliver didn't say anything, but he's probably too much of a gentleman to tell me if he'd seen his employee in her birthday suit.

'Well, don't you go getting any ideas. He's taken.' Though my head knows there's every chance she's talking utter nonsense, my heart sinks. 'Lives with Niamh Browne, the geography teacher. Pretty little thing. No illegitimate children. Quite the fashionable couple, they are.' Edme smirks at me as she heaves herself up the stairs.

'Well, that's lovely,' I lie, my voice hollow. 'And don't you worry, Aunty. I'm not exactly in the market for a boyfriend right now.'

Edme flops into her unmade bed and I cover her with the duvet, thrilled that her old-lady wrinkly bits are at last under wraps. 'Good thing,' she murmurs as sleep begins to take hold. 'Because I've told him all about you and your bastard bairn. He wouldn't look twice at a slut like you.'

Two hours later, the tears still won't stop. I hate to give Edme the satisfaction but the bitter old hag is still comatose upstairs so I'm free to blub in peace. I nurse a large tumbler of her 'cooking' sherry in my lap. Not even ten a.m. and I'm hitting the bottle.

I can't stop replaying her words over in my mind. Is Edme right? Am I a slut? It's true that Ivy's father, Adam, wasn't my first. He wasn't even my second. Or my third. There was a handful of guys before him and none of them lasted long. Come to think of it, none of them stuck around much beyond a couple of rolls in the hay. But I thought I was in love with each of them – it's not like I fell into bed with just anyone for the hell of it. Edme is wrong. I thought they loved me; some of them even said they did. Adam vanished the instant I told him I was pregnant, so it's not like I ever had the chance to make it work with him, to give Ivy a proper father. I may have made some less than inspired choices when it comes to men, but I never realised it at the time. I've got 20/20 hindsight – lucky me.

The doorbell rings. I take a long gulp of sherry before getting up to answer it. I'm hot, and my head feels fuzzy, whether from the booze or the crying I'm not sure. Edme's house is oppressively warm.

'Another time,' says Oliver cheerily the moment the door swings open.

'Huh?'

'You said you'd have coffee with me another time and that was' – he checks his watch – 'three hours ago. So it's officially now another time.' He smiles proudly.

I stare at him for a moment, open-mouthed. Then I crumple into a neat little heap on the front step and dissolve into sobs once more. I'm making an unfortunate habit of collapsing in front of this guy.

'Hey, hey,' Oliver says, crouching next to me and drawing me into his arms. It feels unbelievably good. 'I'm sorry. It was just my rubbish attempt at being charming. You don't have to have coffee with me.' I can hear the urgency and concern in his voice and it's almost unbearable.

'You know about me,' I splutter when I've finally regained the power of speech. 'You know I have a baby. Edme told me she told you.'

'Aye, I do know that,' he says quietly.

'So . . . so why are you being so nice to me? Don't you think I'm a horrible person? I lied about my own daughter,' I wail.

Oliver loosens his grip and turns me to face him. 'You didn't lie to me, Helena,' he says. 'We only met yesterday. Why would you tell me everything about yourself straight away? I didn't give you my life story.'

'You sort of did, actually.'

Oliver smiles. 'What can I say? I'm an open book,' he says. 'But choosing not to explain a very personal situation to a total stranger doesn't make you a liar.'

'But why would you want to have coffee with a screwed-up single mother?'

'Who says you're screwed up?'

'Oh, come on. This isn't the first time you've caught me crying hysterically. Or had me collapse at your feet. That's not exactly normal behaviour. And anyway —' *Don't say it, don't say it, don't say it!* 'Anyway, you have a girlfriend.'

There, it's out there.

Oliver blinks in surprise. 'I don't have a girlfriend,' he says.

Now it's my turn to look confused. 'But Edme said . . . the geography teacher . . . you live together?' Any minute now I'll rediscover my ability to construct whole sentences.

'Niamh?' Oliver shakes his head. 'She's just my flatmate. A colleague. Edme's having you on, Helena.'

My fists clench. If my aunt doesn't already have a headache when she wakes, she will when I've finished with her.

'So you don't think I'm a harlot?'

Smiling, Oliver shakes his head.

'And you don't have a girlfriend?'

'No. No girlfriend.'

'Then . . . what *is* this?'

He shrugs. 'This is just what it is. You seem like a nice person and, well, I may be wrong but you also seem like you could do with some cheering up,' he says.

He's definitely not wrong there. But still. Something tells me coffee, tea, even a glass of water with Oliver could open a can of worms that would be best kept firmly closed.

'Think of it as a public service,' he goes on. 'You're one of about four people in Gairloch aged under eighty. Half an hour in your company may be the only thing that gets me through another year here. Do it for the sake of my sanity!'

I smile in spite of my inner turmoil. 'Oh, all right then,' I say with a sigh. To hell with it. Bad decisions are my specialty; what's one more going to matter at this point? I'm in a strange place, and as Oliver says, it's 'another time'.

Anna

'Absolutely not.'

'Anna . . .'

'No!'

'Oh, come *on*. You've barely left the house in four days! Enough with the moping.' Jen jerks her head towards the stairs, which are lined with boxes of Finn's belongings. Muffled thuds and curses emanate from the bedroom as he packs his suitcase. It's Wednesday, not even a week since Finn accepted his new job, and it seems like he can't get out of London fast enough. 'He'll be back next weekend,' Jen says gently.

'I don't care. I'm not going.'

'It'll be fun!'

I shoot Jen my most incredulous look and she at least has the sense to look sheepish.

'Okay, so maybe it won't be *fun*, as such,' she admits. 'Not the sort of fun you're used to anyway. I can pretty much guarantee there'll be no tequila slammers or clandestine rendezvous in the cloakroom.'

'You're doing a great job of selling it to me, Jen.' I try to hide my smile. 'Though I am pleased to hear Starbucks has a cloakroom now. How chic.'

Jen rolls her eyes and points to Ivy, who is gurgling happily to herself in a bouncy chair on the floor. 'Where did this chair come from?' she asks.

'You.'

'Who have you been practically living with since this child landed in your lap?'

'You.'

'And who gave you the playsuit she's wearing? And those keys she's gumming?'

'You and you. I get it – I owe you.' I give an exaggerated sigh. 'Though you might want to get those keys back if you're planning on driving anywhere today.'

'I *am* planning on driving, actually,' Jen says testily. 'And I'm planning on having you and your brat in the car with me and my brats.'

'But that's just it, Jen. She's not my brat, is she? Don't you think it will look a bit weird if I turn up at your mothers' group with a child that's not my own?' I can just see the Richmond mothers (or their nannies), in their twin-sets and pearls, diving for their mobile phones to report the nutter playing mummy to someone else's baby.

'Oh, who cares about those bitches,' says Jen. 'I only go there to silently mock them anyway. We'll just tell them you're my cousin visiting from Brisbane or something. The point is they all have little kids and they've made all the same mistakes you're making.'

'What mistakes? I happen to think I'm doing very well given the lack of training.'

'Anna, you tried to feed a six-month-old baby a chicken tikka masala.'

'So?'

'She has no teeth!' Jen throws up her hands in despair.

She has a point. I've been muddling through for the best part of a week but there have been more than a few near misses. Maybe an intensive parenting workshop isn't such a bad idea. And a caffeine hit is definitely a good idea, given Ivy has apparently decided sleep is optional these days.

'Okay,' I sigh again. 'I'll go to your stupid mothers' group. But only because it's such a nice day and I'm getting a bit cabin feverish hanging around the house all the time. I'm telling you now, though, if anyone tries to make me sign up for baby yoga or baby orchestra or baby economics, I'm out of there.'

The Richmond branch of Starbucks looks more like a freaky farmyard than a coffee shop when we arrive half an hour later. Spray-tanned, blow-dried mothers are stationed at tables that form a sort of perimeter fence around a herd of small people absorbed in Lego blocks, colouring books and Bratz dolls. The younger babies snooze in prams with enormous off-road tyres – presumably for traversing the wilds of Richmond high street – or perch on their mothers' knees. The racket is deafening.

'Hi ladies,' says Jen as she breezes in. Milo and Elodie immediately toddle off to join the other animals. The women smile hello at Jen and regard me coolly. 'This is my cousin, Anna, and her, uh, Ivy. They're visiting from Australia.'

In the playpen, Milo looks up from perusing a selection of colouring books, a quizzical expression on his face. I smile and silently plead with him to keep my little secret, vowing to explain the concept of 'white lies' to him when we get home.

A few mums murmur hello. Jen plops down beside a woman whose honey-coloured highlights are almost an exact match for the bejewelled gold knuckledusters adorning her fingers.

'Have a seat, cuz.' Jen grins broadly, patting the empty chair next to her.

Knuckledusters offers a bored smile. What was I thinking, letting Jen harangue me into this?

'I'll just grab a coffee first,' I say, thrusting Ivy into Jen's arms. 'Latte?' Jen nods and I escape to the counter.

Ten minutes later I'm clutching two coffees and loitering by the condiments stand trying to set a world record for slowest addition of sugar and application of chocolate sprinkles.

'Caught you,' says a deep voice behind me. I turn; it's Luke, and damn if he doesn't look moderately attractive once again. I shake my head, inwardly berating myself. Finn's imminent departure has knocked me off my axis. Now is not the time to go developing an inappropriate crush on my formerly awful neighbour. I must keep reminding myself that Luke's poisonous personality precludes him from achieving bona fide 'dreamy' status. But dressed in charcoal suit trousers and an open-neck white shirt, he's not half bad.

'Trying to avoid them?' he says, nodding towards the herd.

'What are you doing here?' I ask, ignoring his question.

'I had a meeting with a client. I was going to stop off for a coffee but when I saw the playgroup going on over there,' he holds up his cardboard cup, 'I decided to make it a takeaway.'

I follow his gaze back to the mothers group, where at least three women have guzzling children attached to their breasts. One of them, I note with consternation, is Jen. Surely that can't be right. Milo is three – he's practically an adult! Is this what Ivy is supposed to be doing? I search her out among the morass of other infants, looking for signs she's feeling deprived or emotionally stunted. But she's sitting propped up against Jen's feet, doggedly trying to grab the nose of the kid next to her, and seems happy enough.

'Tempted?' says Luke.

I turn to him, horrified. 'To breastfeed?'

'No!' he says, though I definitely see his eyes flick to my chest. He holds up his cup again. 'To make yours a takeaway and get out of here.'

'Oh.' I shake my head, trying to dislodge from my mind a vivid image involving Luke and me, braless, that has suddenly lodged there. 'God, yes, this is my idea of hell.'

'Come on then,' he says. 'Grab your coffee and let's go for a stroll by the river.'

My fingers twitch on the handle of my mug. I'm tempted, and not just because Luke really does cut a fine figure in his 'business casual' attire. Suddenly, I feel an overwhelming desire to spend a few uncomplicated minutes making idle conversation about something other than babies, bad boyfriends or my shaky career. 'I can't,' I tell him with a sigh. 'I'm here with Jen. From across the road. I can't just leave Ivy with her and take off.'

'She won't mind. We'll be back in twenty minutes,' Luke persists.

Am I seriously considering taking a riverside promenade with Parcel Nazi? This time last week, the only place I'd have willingly gone with Luke was the local real estate agency, to help him find a new house as far away from mine as possible. Spending my morning in a cramped coffee shop with a dozen rowdy kids and their frosty mothers may not be my idea of a good time but surely *Luke* isn't a more appealing prospect?

Since when does he want to hang out with me anyway? The man was mean about my shoes – clearly I'm not his sort of person any more than he's mine. I really can't work out what's going on here, what's changed between us, but something has definitely shifted. What with Finn moving to Belfast amid repeated promises that our relationship will endure, and Luke apparently vying for the Neighbour of the Year title, I've had enough mixed messages to last quite a while.

'What's going on here?' I ask.

'Sorry?'

'Here.' I wave my hand between the two of us. 'What's going on?'

'Well, it's a coffee shop. Generally, people come here to drink coffee,' Luke says slowly.

I make a face. 'Funny guy. You know what I mean.'

Luke shakes his shaggy head. 'I don't think I do, actually, Anna,' he says with a shrug.

'I *mean* why are you being nice to me all of a sudden? We've been living next door to each other for over a year, during which time our communication has pretty much consisted of you calling me Annie and delivering my shopping in a haughty fashion. Now you're suddenly dogsitting and getting my name right and suggesting strolls by the river. What. Is. Going. On?' *And why do I like it so much in spite of myself*, I want to add. I fold my arms across my chest, partly to project what I hope is a don't-mess-with-me demeanour and partly to obstruct Luke's view should his gaze go wandering again.

He looks away and thrusts his hands into his pockets. He opens his mouth, then closes it again. Finally he says, 'Can't we just say I've seen the error of my ways?'

'Er, no. We can't. Spill it.'

He sighs and looks at his feet. If we were outside I'm sure he'd scuff his toe in the dirt and say, 'Aw, shucks.'

'Okay, look,' he says instead. 'I know I haven't been the friendliest of neighbours.'

I can't resist saying, 'Ha!'

'But I'd read your column in *The Mirror* and I was forever having to sign for your shoes and handbags and whatever and I guess I just had you pegged as a certain type of girl.'

'And what kind of girl is that?' I say darkly.

'A vapid, giggly, gossip-loving, expensive shoe-buying girl.'

'I see. And what's changed?'

He shrugs again. 'Well, you came round and yelled at me that day and I started to think I might have been a bit harsh,' he says.

'You reckon?' I feel my cheeks starting to flush. I wasn't expecting this kind of honesty.

'And then your friend turned up on my doorstep the other night and now you have her baby —'

'Yeah?' If he's going to try and analyse Helena or pass judgement on the Ivy situation, I fear the contents of my mug will soon be spattered all over his crisp white shirt.

'Well, I'm not sure how that's come about but I can imagine it's pretty overwhelming. I have some, ah, experience with kids, so I thought if I could help you out in some way it might make up for my being a bit of a prat in the past.'

As if on cue, Jen appears at my side, prising her latte from my grip and depositing Ivy in my free arm. 'These idiots are getting on my tits,' she mutters. 'Leave in ten?' I nod. 'Hello Luke,' she says primly before plastering a big fake smile on her face and swanning back to the group.

'No walk then?' Luke says quietly.

'Not today. Sorry,' I reply, offering him a tiny smile. 'But I appreciate what you said and I may take you up on your offer of help. God knows I need it.'

Luke waggles his fingers in Ivy's face and she chuckles gleefully. 'Nah, you seem to be doing a pretty good job.' That warm feeling blooms in my chest again. How ironic that the first person to compliment my pseudo-parenting skills is the last person I'd ever imagined hearing a kind word from.

Luke picks up the laptop bag at his feet and I turn to follow Jen. But something stops me.

'Luke?'

He stops walking and looks at me expectantly.

'The thing is, I *am* giggly and gossip-obsessed and fond of pricey footwear,' I tell him. 'But that doesn't make me vapid or stupid or any less worthy of civil treatment than, say, a brain surgeon. There's nothing wrong with having a few frivolous interests.'

He gives me the strangest look, like I've just told him the sky's blue and he sees for the first time that, yes, it really is.

'You're right. I'm sorry,' he says simply.

'Anna, let's roll!' Jen calls over the growing roar of toddlers.

I hand Luke my untouched coffee and shift Ivy to my other hip. I'm suddenly terribly tired of butting heads with my neighbour. Holding grudges is exhausting. Luke's latest apology feels like his hundredth and he genuinely seems to want to make amends. I could definitely use another friend at this point; is it such a bad thing if he happens to be easy on the eyes into the bargain?

'You know what? Don't worry about it,' I say. 'Let's pretend you haven't been a jerk and I haven't been a superficial, shoe-loving gossip columnist for the past twelve months and just start from scratch.'

Luke's face brightens. 'So, like . . . we could be mates?' he says.

Ivy claps her pudgy hands together in assent. 'Looks like it,' I say, laughing at her.

'Ahhh!' Ivy says with a bobble of her little head.

And that's that.

My benevolent mood vanishes the moment Jen pulls up in front of my house and I see Finn's boxes have migrated from the staircase to the front porch. They seem to have multiplied and I catch myself hoping they're full of his video games, cricket gear and Taylor Swift CDs. I can definitely do without that stuff. He's sitting astride one of them, looking irritated.

'Do you want me to come in with you?' Jen asks softly.

'No,' I say with a sigh. 'There's nothing we can say to each other that hasn't already been said.' I slide out of the car and open the back door to unbuckle Ivy's car capsule – another loaner from Jen. 'I guess he's really going.' I don't know whether I'm telling Jen or myself.

'Come over later,' she says. 'We'll crack open a bottle of red and discuss at length why all men are arseholes.'

'Not Daddy!' Milo crows from the back seat.

'No sweetheart, not Daddy.' Jen rolls her eyes and whispers, 'Sometimes Daddy.'

I slam the door and Jen drives further up the street in search of a parking space. I walk slowly up the garden path towards Finn, grateful that Ivy is snoozing in her car seat. Finn hasn't exactly been pleased to have a baby in the house this week. Meanwhile, I've been glad to have her there to keep me from thinking about this moment, the moment he officially chooses his job over me.

'The moving van will be here any second and my taxi's due in five minutes,' he says. 'I was hoping we'd have more time to talk.' His tone is faintly accusing, as if this scenario is entirely of my creation.

'What else have we got to talk about?' I squeeze past him, setting Ivy's carrier on the hall floor and letting an ecstatic Nui into the front garden to sniff around.

Finn takes my hand in his. 'I just want to make sure you understand,' he says, his voice softening, 'that I love you.'

I take a deep breath and clench my jaw – anything to stop me blurting out, 'Why don't you flipping well act like it then!' Or something equally petulant.

'Nothing will change that, whether I live in Belfast or bloody Outer Mongolia,' Finn goes on. 'It's still you and me, An. It always will be.'

Tears prick the corners of my eyes. The words trip so silkily off his tongue and he's giving me puppy-dog eyes so earnest they put Nui to shame. I so want to believe him. It's not like there aren't thousands, maybe millions, of women out there in long-distance relationships. They all seem to just get on with it. Why can't I be like them, bright and breezy and living my life content in the knowledge there's a man who's in love with me? In Northern Ireland, but in love with me nonetheless.

I know why. It's because Finn's words sound hollow. Since he accepted this job nearly a week ago he's made daily declarations every bit as heartfelt as this. But he's still going. What if his proclamations of love are simply fuelled by guilt? What if it's all just hot air? It's easy to call promises over your shoulder as you sprint out the door, when you're not the one left staring at the empty side of the bed where your boyfriend used to be. And the worst bit is I know that even if I could find the words to explain all of this to Finn, he still wouldn't get it.

Fortunately I'm spared having to string a sentence together by the belching arrival of a battered white van. A leather-faced bald man roughly the size and build of a refrigerator emerges from it, and when his gruff 'Cassidy?' is rewarded with a nod from Finn, he begins hefting his boxes into the back. As Finn ducks back inside the house to bring out his luggage, Luke comes striding up the street. Nui, who was apparently much quicker than me in setting aside his Luke-related hostility, trots out to sniff his trouser legs.

'Hey-ho, neighbour!' Luke calls, doffing an imaginary cap and stooping to give the dog an affectionate scratch. I flash a watery smile in return. It must look as unconvincing as it feels because Luke's brow immediately furrows. 'You okay?' he asks.

I try to nod, but find myself shaking my head as the threatened tears well up and spill over. The moving guy grunts as he lugs a box past me. At least I'm not the only one embarrassed by my melodramatic show of emotion.

Luke steps through the garden gate, then back on to the footpath, as though he's unsure whether the terms of our freshly inked friendship contract permit him to try to comfort me. Finn's return makes up his mind; he takes another step back and shakes his leg to dislodge Nui, who has progressed from sniffing to gnawing.

'I'll catch you later,' he says, ignoring Finn as he walks briskly to his own house.

Finn watches him go with narrowed eyes. 'I thought you hated that bloke,' he says once Luke's front door has closed behind him.

Before I can respond, the moving guy slams the van doors and says, 'Right, that's all of 'em. Sign 'ere.' He thrusts a clipboard and a stubby pencil at Finn.

Finn initials the document and the sweaty mover lumbers back to his van and peels away in a cloud of exhaust. A moment later, Finn's black cab pulls up and something inside me disconnects. I've always been this way with goodbyes. The lump in my throat feels like a golf ball, but I want him to just kiss my cheek, get in the taxi and leave. I can't bear another lovey-dovey speech or a grand, end-of-the-movie farewell.

But this is Finn. 'I guess this is it then,' he says thickly.

I want to laugh at the cliché. What's next, *I'll never forget you*?

'I guess it is,' I reply.

He wraps me in a bear hug. 'I love you,' he whispers into my hair. 'No amount of distance will ever change that.'

'Ain't No Mountain High Enough' suddenly starts playing in my head. I'm tempted to offer Finn some crackers to go with his cheese.

'I know,' I say, hugging him back.

He pulls back, holding me at arm's length, and fixes me with a meaningful gaze. Then he loops his satchel over his shoulder, picks up his duffel bag and gets in the taxi. As it pulls away from the kerb, he presses his palm to the window. It's so hideously contrived, and it's the last straw. I start howling, which starts Nui howling, which wakes Ivy in the hall and she starts howling. I scoop Nui up and run into the house, sobbing harder with every step. I set the dog down and he scurries straight to his pillow next to the sofa. He curls into a tiny ball and peers at me, clearly perturbed by my sudden hysteria. Ivy's screaming bloody murder but I don't lift her out of her capsule. I'm learning to differentiate between her cries now and can tell this isn't 'I'm hungry' or 'My nappy is full of something you really don't want to deal with'. This is a 'You frightened the living daylights out of me just now, lady!' cry. She's irate and letting me know it. I don't mind; I'd kind of like to kick my legs and wave my arms and scream the place down too. Before I can assume the position, there's a knock at the door. Nui immediately bounds into the hallway, yapping. Ivy, startled by the flurry of activity, is momentarily quiet.

'It's not a good time, Jen,' I call in my reedy, I've-been-wailing-like-an-infant voice. 'I'll come round later.' Even the promise of chocolate and hard liquor isn't enough to make me want to face the world at this moment.

'It's Luke,' comes the reply.

The sound of his deep voice makes me cry even harder. Of course it's my moderately attractive and newly pleasant next-door neighbour on the doorstep instead of my boyfriend. Of course Finn didn't reach the end of the road, realise his mistake and order the taxi to turn around. Of course he's not going to stride into the sitting room, gather me up in his arms and promise never to leave me again. Until Luke spoke, I didn't even realise I was watching that fantasy film reel in my mind. But now Luke is here, not Finn, just in time to see me blotchy and mascara-streaked and in the midst of a boyfriend-induced nervous breakdown.

'Come in.'

He does. And walks straight past me to Ivy's capsule, where she's still crying with gusto. He unfastens the straps and gently lifts her out, cradling her close to his chest and rubbing her back. 'You need some time to yourself,' Luke says, looking at me at last. 'I'm going to take Ivy to the park for a walk.'

My newly minted friend is clearly telling, not asking, and even in the midst of my meltdown this gets right on my nerves.

'Oh, are you?' I challenge.

'Yes.' Luke looks around for Ivy's pram and spots it in the hall. With one hand, he wheels it into the sitting room and settles Ivy in the seat. 'I think you could do with the peace and quiet and she'll enjoy spending an hour with someone who's . . . a little more relaxed. I'll take the dog as well if you like.'

His audacity is mindboggling. My tears dry up instantly. 'Um, sorry, but who the hell do you think you are?'

Luke actually looks surprised. Until he reads the hurt and anger on my face. 'I didn't mean to imply you're not up to looking after Ivy,' he says quickly. 'I just thought you could use a break.'

'And what gave you that impression?'

'Well, I saw your fella leave just now and I know you're upset.'

'Do you? You know how I feel about my boyfriend taking a job in another country without telling me, packing half the house into his suitcase and pissing off?'

'Of course not,' Luke says, looking at me like he wishes the floor would open up and swallow him. 'But . . . well, we live in terraced houses, Anna. I heard you crying. And Ivy too.'

'So what? I was crying. Do I have "Rescue Me" tattooed on my face or something?' I fire back, trying not to think about what else Luke must have heard through the common wall recently.

I don't quite know why I'm being so awful. The thing is, he's right. I really could use an hour or two to wail and wallow and cut Finn's face out of photographs. And Ivy shouldn't have to watch me behave like a screaming banshee. But the fact that Luke thinks he can just breeze into my house and tell me what's good for me makes my blood boil. I've had enough of that from Finn, trying to sell his new job to me like it's some grand golden opportunity for both of us. Like I'm too stupid to see that it's all about him.

'And what on earth makes you think I'd let you just swan off with my goddaughter anyway? I don't know anything about you.'

'Remember I told you this morning I have lots of experience with kids?' Luke says hopefully.

'Gee, that's reassuring. I'm sure a child molester would never think of telling a parent he's great with kids!' Not that I'm actually a parent, but still.

Now it's Luke's turn to look hurt and I instantly wish I could take the words back. 'I'm sorry,' he says feebly. 'I have this compulsion to try and fix things. I just wanted to do something nice for you.'

My frozen heart defrosts a little at the genuine sentiment in his words. I knew the moment he walked in the door he wasn't criticising my baby know-how; that he was just trying to help, albeit in typically bumbling man fashion. But I'm sick of help in all its forms. I'm sick of having to be the one who helps her best friend sort her life out, who tries to help her colleague keep a job she doesn't deserve, who smiles and nods and helps her boyfriend feel justified in abandoning her. And I'm sick of people's ham-fisted attempts to help me cope because they think I can't do it on my own.

'I'm sorry I was so mean,' I say at last. 'Don't you find it odd that so many of our conversations seem to involve you apologising to me, Luke? How about, instead of constantly trying to make it up to me, you just think before you open your mouth in the first place?'

He lets out a whoosh of breath. 'I think that's probably the best advice I've ever been given,' he says with a quirky smile.

Ivy emits a sputtering cry from her pram. The look on her little face plainly says, 'Er, hello? Am I getting a walk or not?'

Luke looks at me with raised eyebrows. 'I'm going to try this again,' he says. 'Anna, would you like me to take Ivy for a walk and give you a breather for an hour or so?'

I ponder his question. Strangely, I don't feel like wailing or wallowing or cutting Finn's face out of photographs any more. It's amazing what a good rant can do for the spirit.

'I think Ivy would love a walk,' I tell him. 'But I could use some fresh air myself. If you don't mind, I'll come with you.'

Finn

This morning I was woken by my radio alarm clock instead of a screaming baby. Of course, the alarm sounded at three-forty-five a.m. and Ivy doesn't usually wake 'til after six, but it still felt good having a lilting Irish burr rouse me from sleep instead of Ivy's earsplitting squeal. When I got out of bed my feet found plush wall-to-wall carpeting, not kids' toys (which always seem to have more corners and sharp edges when stepped on than I would think safe for children).

The sleek stainless-steel fridge in my new kitchen was filled with champagne and pastries – a welcome gift from Fiona O'Donnell, my new executive producer – rather than Tupperware containers of pureed god-knows-what. At four-thirty a.m., a black BMW pulled up at the main entrance of my building and a courteous Irishman drove me to work without reproachful glares or frosty one-word answers to my questions. It's only my first day, but so far Belfast craps all over London.

'Finn!' Fiona greets me warmly as I enter the *Belfast Breakfast* studios. 'Welcome aboard. How are you feeling? Tired?'

'Surprisingly no. I've had my fair share of early starts lately.' Understatement of the decade.

'Well then, you've got one up on me. I've been working in breakfast television for eight years and I still can't get used to the ungodly hours.' Fiona runs her hands wearily through her blonde hair. 'Some mornings it's all I can do to stick a bit of lippy on.'

She's clearly fishing for compliments. She looks stunning, from her blow-dried mane to the alarmingly pointy tips of her brown boots. But I'm happy to oblige my new boss. 'Don't be silly, you look great,' I tell her.

Fiona smiles coyly. 'Thanks, Finn,' she says. 'Now, let's get you to make-up.' She beckons a production assistant, who trots to her side. The young girl looks vaguely familiar from yesterday's production meeting but the *Belfast Breakfast* team is so vast, I can't remember her name. Not that it matters; she doesn't say a word to me as she leads me through a maze of corridors to my dressing room.

That's right, I have a dressing room now. In London I had to stash my coat in a desk drawer; in Belfast I have a spacious dressing room replete with a spotlit make-up table, a sofa, a flat-screen television and my own coffee machine. Lolling in the make-up chair is a skinny woman with blue hair and facial piercings who introduces herself as Roisin, my make-up artist. My make-up artist!

As Roisin gets to work, I choose not to think about the dubiously orange pancake foundation she's slathering on to my nose and forehead and instead let myself have a moment of feeling absolutely, unbelievably thrilled. I can't believe I spent years grafting at the BBC, with its endless budget cuts and two make-up artists available on an only-if-the-hosts-don't-need-them basis, when the spoils of commercial television were out here all along, just waiting to be plundered.

Roisin finishes artfully arranging my hair just as the dour production assistant returns. 'Five minutes,' she says glumly.

Clearly not a morning person either.

I unzip my hoodie and slip on the pressed lilac shirt hanging on the back of the door. It's not exactly my colour – Jez would rip the piss out of me if he saw it – but Fiona says pastels work well on TV and make me more appealing to the female demographic. Or something. It's quite possible I look an absolute tit. But I don't care. I didn't pay for this shirt or the other four swinging on the hook. I didn't pay for the Italian silk ties or the Armani suits I'll wear with them either; the network has bought me a whole new wardrobe. I've arrived. And I'm doing it in purple.

I retrace my steps through the labyrinthine corridors and emerge into someone's lounge room. At least, that's what the *Belfast Breakfast* set looks like. My co-host, Mary Eames, sits on a plush beige sofa, her feet and hands neatly crossed. She turns her face up towards her own make-up artist, who is feverishly administering a last-minute dusting of powder. To be shiny on breakfast television, I'm quickly learning, is sinful in the extreme, like hesitating for even a moment when a woman asks, 'Do I look fat in this?'

Mary's note cards are scattered across an oak side table that also bears an enormous vase of pink lilies. Anna would love those.

I feel a sudden pang. What's Anna doing right now? Is she still sleeping, sprawled across the bed the way she always does when I'm not there, as though her body is glad of my absence? Or is she up with Ivy, padding around the shadowy house, softly singing terrible 80s power ballads in that utterly tuneless voice the baby seems to love?

'Is there something wrong with the sofa, Finn?' comes Mary's voice, outrageously cheerful for this hour of the morning.

'Er, no. Why?'

'Well, you're standing there staring at it like it's made of beer. Don't you fancy sitting next to me then?' Mary pats the couch next to her and flashes a playful smile.

I shake my head. *Sharpen up, Cassidy.* 'Sorry, Mary, I was in my own little world.' I sit beside her and the floor manager swoops in to affix my earpiece.

'How're you doing there, Finn?' Fiona's voice purrs in my ear. I aim a thumbs-up at the darkened windows of the upstairs production room. 'Great,' she says. 'Break a leg, babe.'

The floor staff hush as the quasi-jazz riffs of the show's theme song blare into the studio. The red light atop camera one blinks on.

'Good morning, Belfast, and welcome to your brand-spanking-new breakfast program. I'm Mary Eames.'

'And I'm Finn Cassidy, and as you may be able to tell, I'm not from around here.'

Fiona chuckles in my ear. 'Cute.'

Mary launches into her patter about what's coming up on the show, then throws to the six a.m. news bulletin.

'Whew!' she says when we hear the newsreader's disembodied voice piped over the speakers from a neighbouring studio. 'That's always the scariest bit. We're away now!'

A vision of Anna drifts through my mind. She's curled up on the sofa, her ratty bathrobe thrown over that godawful Van Halen T-shirt, cradling a mug of tea in one hand and her goddaughter in the other. I wish she could see me now; she'd realise this is worth all the angst.

'We're back in ten,' comes Fiona's voice.

Yes, we're away.

Three hours later, I've interviewed a ballet dancer, a celebrity chef, a dog trainer and Bob Geldof (less interesting than the dog guy) and my first show is in the bag. The jaunty jazz fades out, the baking hot spotlights are turned off and normal fluorescent strip lights flicker on in their place. I feel exhilarated. Knackered but exhilarated. I can't wait to phone Anna and tell her all about it.

'Great work, team,' says the floor manager, Roland, leading his staff in a round of applause. 'We had a few of the usual technical teething problems here and there but, on the whole, that was a nice first broadcast.' His team beams at the praise; I suspect 'supportive and complimentary' isn't Roland's default setting.

The same can't be said for Fiona, who bursts on to the set with her hands clasped to her chest like she's clutching a BAFTA. 'Oh, well *done*, guys! That was perfect, just perfect! Mary, you're gorgeous. Finn, the suits loved you,' she gushes, referring to the faceless executives who run the network.

'Really? I wasn't too . . .'

'Australian?' Mary suggests.

'Yeah.'

'Not at all!' Fiona says. 'You're our point of difference, Finn. People were ringing the switchboard complaining they couldn't understand you. They love it!'

I'm not quite sure I follow her logic, but before I have the chance to think about it Fiona claps her hands together and shouts, 'Right! To the pub!'

Everyone laughs, removing headsets and picking up satchels as they follow Fiona out the door.

'Is she serious?' I ask Mary.

She looks at me, puzzled. 'Of course.'

'But it's nine in the morning.'

Mary smiles knowingly. 'Ah, Finn. You're in Ireland now. We go on a bender after every show.'

'You do?'

She whacks me playfully across the head with her note cards. 'Of course not, you pillock! This is just a one-off to celebrate the first show.'

I heave a sigh of relief. 'Good. I mean, I like a drink as much as the next Aussie but a daily booze-a-thon is asking a bit much.'

'Fair dues,' Mary says with a shrug. 'Today will be a big one though, so you'd better get your drinking shoes on.'

By lunchtime, I can barely stand. In fact, I can barely even sit, so it's fortunate that I'm wedged between Fiona and a 150-kilogram sound technician called Frank.

'So what do you make of our fair city so far?' Fiona asks. She doesn't sound remotely inebriated even though I've watched her sink at least four pints of Guinness.

'S'great. Great city. Great people. Great 'partment,' I slur.

'Not missing London too much then?'

'Nah.' *Insightful comment there, Cassidy.*

'What about your lovely girlfriend? Amelia?'

'Anna.'

'Right.' Fiona smiles slightly. 'Not pining for Anna?'

'Not really,' I reply, then immediately clamp my hands over my mouth. Did I say that out loud?

Fiona chuckles. 'Hey, it's okay,' she says. 'I get it. Everything here is new and exciting. You probably just haven't had time to miss her yet.'

This would be my cue to nod and make a concerned face and say, 'You're probably right' and come off looking halfway human. But this beer is like truth serum.

'No, it's not that. I was glad to get away from her.'

Fiona purses her lips. 'Really?'

Stop now, stop now, stop now. 'Yeah, she's not very support-ive of my career. She didn't want me to take this job and she let me know it at every available opportunity.'

'Is that right?' Fiona looks at me with concern. Both of her.

'And now she's got this baby.' The vehement way I spit out the word surprises me. I drain the dregs of my pint and gesture to

Roland, who's watching from the bar, to order me another.

'What baby?' Fiona asks.

'Oh, it's her goddaughter. Her best friend got knocked up, then lost the plot and left her kid with Anna while she ran off to find herself or something.'

There's a long pause, and then Fiona says, 'So, you took this job against your girlfriend's wishes and left her literally holding the baby?'

I consider this for a moment. It sounds quite bad when she puts it like that. 'Yes.' My voice sounds small and guilty. I scan Fiona's face for a reaction, for signs she's suddenly realised how despicable I truly am and is going to sack me on the spot. But instead of berating me or turning her back in disgust, Fiona slides her hand from the table and rests it on my thigh.

'I admire your determination, Finn,' she says quietly, giving my leg a squeeze. 'You're obviously very ambitious. That was clear the moment we met.'

'It was?' I don't know whether it's the innumerable pints or Fiona's hand resting so casually on my leg, but my head suddenly starts to spin.

Fiona nods and leans in close. I can smell her spicy perfume and feel her breath on my neck. 'You can go far in this business if you want to, Finn,' she says. 'Just stick with me.'

Helena

Ewan McGregor. After three casual coffees, a long lunch and a bracing country stroll in the past ten days, it's finally occurred to me who Oliver looks like: Ewan McGregor. With a shaved head, circa *Trainspotting*, not *Star Wars*. Except, you know, less like a heroin addict.

This is very bad news. Before I realised that my only friend in Gairloch looks uncannily like a movie star (and making matters worse, a movie star who rides big, manly motorbikes), the coffees, the lunch and the hike were nothing more than nice distractions. They were just easy chitchat with a guy who happens to like the same bands as me. Breaks in my long days of sitting and thinking, thinking and sitting. (And crying – I still haven't quite managed to get a handle on that.)

Well, okay, my meetings with Oliver have probably always been more than 'distractions'. They've been much-needed respite, if I'm honest. An hour spent lingering over a cappuccino with him is an hour I haven't had to spend swimming against the tide of frosty looks and pointed silences in Edme's cottage. They've been hours free from my great-aunt's blunt questions about when I intend to return to Ivy, and from her drunken rages, which are an almost daily treat.

So hanging out with Oliver makes my soul feel a little lighter, makes my black heart feel slightly less decayed. But now that I've realised he looks like Ewan McGregor that's all ruined, isn't it? How can I roll out of bed, stick a sweatshirt and sneakers on with my pyjama bottoms and slope off to meet him for coffee now? How can I turn up at his place for lunch with nothing to show for myself but a half-empty bottle of sherry swiped from Edme's pantry? I can't, is the answer.

Now that the full extent of Oliver's hotness has become clear to me, I'll have to start wearing make-up and washing my hair and try-ing even harder not to become a blubbering wreck in front of him. Because his likeness to Ewan McGregor means Oliver has ceased to be My Friend Oliver and become Oliver, The Guy I Fancy.

There's no getting around this. I can't unfancy someone once I start fancying him. It can't be undone, no matter how many sensible conversations I have with myself in which I point out all the reasons why fancying Oliver will wreck everything.

REASONS WHY FANCYING OLIVER WILL WRECK EVERYTHING

1. I will start inventing flimsy reasons to see him, which he will notice and find disturbing.
2. I will suddenly start dressing up for our meetings which, given the stark contrast with my appearance to date, he will notice and find disturbing.
3. I will develop a high-pitched and irritating nervous laugh, which will become my default response to everything he says. He will notice and find this disturbing, too.
4. Whenever he's within six feet of me, I will become engrossed in lewd daydreams involving him and lose the power of speech.

5. In an attempt to appear alluring and mysterious, I will stop
    telling Oliver my deepest, darkest thoughts and feelings and
    instead resort to a stream of inanities about the weather and
    the football, neither of which I know anything about. This will
    suck for him and for me.

It's the last one that bothers me most of all. In the hours we've spent
together, Oliver has plumbed deeper recesses of my soul than anyone except Anna. I've found myself telling him things I've barely
even allowed myself to think, let alone say aloud.

It was only five minutes into that first cup of coffee that I poured
out the sorry tale of Ivy's conception. I was convinced Oliver would
leap out of the nearest window and flee when I told him that Ivy's
father, Adam, was a part-time mechanic and full-time pothead.

But he didn't leap. He just listened. And he kept listening when
I awkwardly admitted Ivy was the result of a two-minute fumble
in the back of Adam's Escort on our third – and final – date. He
listened as I recounted Adam's attempts to dissuade me from continuing with the pregnancy. Anger flashed in Oliver's eyes as I dredged
up the late-night phone calls with their whispered threats.

There's just something about Oliver that makes me comfortable
spilling my guts. But when I go all girlie and ridiculous, and I
inevitably will, that will all change. I'll forget he already knows
many of my dark secrets (and hope he forgets, too) and start acting all breezy and carefree as I try to make him see me as an enticing
Cool Girl rather than as damaged goods.

Because that's what I am, and I know it. Not because I'm an
unemployed, (temporarily) underweight unwed mother. If there was
some parallel universe in which Oliver was remotely likely to be
interested in me romantically, those things wouldn't be deal-break-
ers. He'd be brilliant with Ivy, I'm sure of it.

No, what makes me damaged isn't the fact that I have a child;

it's the person I've become since I had her. The crying, the moping, the feeling that if I just lay down in my bed and didn't get up again, nobody in my life would be any worse off. The 'depression', if I'm being clinical about it. These aren't things most men would include on their list of 'ideal woman' criteria. (And if they did, I'd be kind of worried.)

So now I'm going to launch Operation Allure and stop telling Oliver the things that confuse and frighten me. Because he might like me more if I'm less 'me'. I'll just have to find some other way of working through the mad clutter in my brain, someone else to unload all this on. Someone just like Oliver – kind, funny, compassionate – but who bears no resemblance to Ewan McGregor. Someone like Anna.

This is the twelfth morning I've woken up in the hard, narrow bed in Edme's musty guest room and I still haven't rung Anna. I haven't even sent her a text message or an email to let her know where I am. She knows I'm in Scotland but, unless she's spoken to my mother, she won't know I'm in Gairloch.

I'm guessing Anna hasn't rung my parents, because if Mum had given her Edme's number I've no doubt she'd have been on the phone within hours of my arrival, reading me the riot act for skipping out on her and Ivy. I know Anna too well to believe she could know where I am and just leave me to it. Her fierce sense of right and wrong just wouldn't allow it. Her profession may suggest otherwise but I know that, in Anna's book, there are some lines you just do not cross – and abandoning a friend in a difficult situation is one of them. In Anna's mind, I'm pretty sure my midnight runner is a sackable offence.

But even though I know Anna will be livid, I also know she'll be frantic. And so today I pick up the ancient bakelite telephone on Edme's hall table.

Anna answers on the fourth ring. 'Hello?'

'Anna . . .' I have a speech prepared but the words stick in my throat.

'Hel? HELENA? WHERE ARE YOU?' Anna unleashes a torrent of shouted questions, exclamations and expletives, her voice rising in volume and pitch with every word.

'I'm in a village in the Highlands called Gairloch,' I shout back in a bid to be heard over her rage. 'I'm fine!'

There's a sudden, ominous silence. 'You're *fine*?'

This is going to be worse than I thought.

'Well . . . I mean . . . I'm okay.'

'Oh *good*.' Anna's voice drips with sarcasm. 'Because when you did a bunk in the middle of the night without your child and then dropped off the face of the planet for a fortnight I was a tiny bit concerned something may have been awry.'

Only Anna could manage to get a word like 'awry' into a bollocking.

'I know. I'm . . . I'm sorry.'

'You're sorry?'

'Of course!'

'And you're fine?'

'Yes.'

More silence. 'And . . .?'

'And . . .' Christ, what does she want from me? 'How are you?'

'Oh, I'm just *great*,' she drawls. 'I've been abandoned by my best friend and my boyfriend. The dog now prefers my next-door neighbour and my career's probably in the crapper. But hey, at least your kid likes me.'

My heart sparks slightly at the mention of Ivy, but I can't bring myself to ask Anna how she's doing. Perverse as it sounds, the only way I've been able to cope with being away from my daughter for this long is by not thinking about her. I feel like I just might be making some progress up here, talking things through with Oliver and slowly getting a handle on everything that's brought me to this point. If Anna tells me Ivy's been grizzly without me or has had a fever or, even worse, has been as happy as a clam since I left, I know I'll go to pieces.

'What's happened with Finn?' I ask.

Anna snorts derisively, letting me know she's on to my avoidance tactics. 'He got a job in Belfast. He's gone.'

'Gone? You broke up?'

She sighs. 'No . . . I don't think so . . . oh, I don't know.' Her voice cracks.

I'm suddenly consumed by shame. Anna sounds weary and defeated, like she's been fighting an epic battle and can't be bothered with it any more. I know that feeling well, but it's never occurred to me that my best friend might be suffering, too. Of course I knew Anna hasn't spent much time around babies, but she's always been the capable, organised one; I figured she'd just cope with Ivy. I hadn't factored arsehole boyfriends, fair-weather dogs and precarious careers into the equation. What a selfish cow I've been.

'Oh An, I didn't realise. I'm so —'

'Yeah, yeah, you're sorry.' Heat flashes in her voice once more. Suddenly, Ivy starts howling in the background. 'Look, I've got to go,' Anna says distractedly. 'I'll see you in a fortnight.'

Click. The dial tone buzzes in my ear.

Operation Allure will have to wait another day. I dial Oliver's number.

'Helena?' He shouts his greeting over a chorus of appalling singing voices.

'More music practice?'

'Even better, choir. What's up?'

'Oh, nothing . . .'

'Hels. Come on.'

He's been abbreviating my name since our lunch 'date' last week, at which much wine (me) and beer (him) was consumed and enough skeletons freed from cupboards — first loves, heartbreaks, sexual experiences – to breed a certain level of familiarity. Now I'm Hels, he's Oli and we've each dug up enough dirt on each other to never forsake the friendship.

'Nothing, really. I just wondered if you fancied coming round for dinner? I could do with seeing a friendly face.'

'Sure, but . . .' His sentence is drowned out as the Von Crap singers reach an eardrum-perforating crescendo.

'Sorry, I didn't quite catch that.'

'Great, guys. From the top,' Oliver calls to his students. Their voices mercifully recede as he steps out of the room. 'I said I'd love to have dinner but why don't you come to my place instead? Niamh's out tonight.'

Niamh's out? *Niamh's out?* Oliver's flatmate – who is actually perfectly lovely and not at all the possessive wench Edme's description of her had conjured in my mind – is the only reason I can be in his house without doing or saying something I'll regret. Niamh is my safety net. With her there, in her ubiquitous slippers and bobbly cardigan, chatting animatedly about her day, I won't get sidetracked trying to arrange myself in seductive poses on the sofa. I won't risk being sprung as I sneak into Oliver's bedroom for a rummage. Why would he want me there without Niamh as a buffer? I'll have no control over Operation Allure then, and a premature launch could be disastrous.

'Helena? Did you hear me?'

'Yes.'

'Yes? You'll come to dinner?'

'Um . . . yes.' *Good work, brain.*

'Great. I'll be done here in fifteen minutes so just come round whenever.'

'Right. Bye,' I say, hanging up and praying fifteen minutes is long enough to recover the power of normal speech.

'Who was that?'

I turn to find Edme (thankfully clothed) filling the doorway, her hands planted on her hips. She's fresh in from school; her man's shirt is smudged with charcoal and there are paint spatters in her haphazard bun. She doesn't smell like a distillery, but then it is only four o'clock.

'Um . . . it was Oliver.'

Edme rolls her eyes. 'I gathered that from the gormless way you were speaking to him. Before that – who was it?'

How long has she been standing there? 'It was Anna,' I answer uncertainly. I grip the hallstand. I don't know what I'm bracing for, but I'm sure there's something unpleasant coming.

'I see. This is the girl who has your baby?'

She spits the word 'girl' as though Anna's little more than an infant herself. I can handle the barbs Edme seems to find such pleasure in flinging at me but if she's about to have a go at Anna I may just have to kick her arse.

'That's right.' I lift my chin in defiance and meet her beady eyes. *Bring it on, lady.*

'And how is she?'

'Well, she seems to be okay. Her boyfriend —'

'Not Anna, the *baby*! How is your child?' Exasperated, she raises her arms to the ceiling as though showing God where to aim the thunderbolts that are surely reserved for morons like me.

'Oh! She, um . . . I think she's fine.'

Edme regards me with suspicion. 'You didn't ask about her, did you?'

My gaze drops to the floor. I contemplate making up some excuse – for about a nanosecond. Edme has an unnerving talent for seeing straight through my bullshit. If she's going to vent her spleen, there's nothing I can do to stop her at this point.

'I couldn't.' There's no point trying to explain why.

When Edme doesn't respond, I look up in anticipation of the inevitable tongue-walloping. But she doesn't look angry. She doesn't even have that resigned 'I'd expect nothing else from you' look on her face.

She looks concerned. Maybe even a little sad. And then she steps forward and puts one hand gently to my cheek.

'Don't worry,' she says softly. 'You're getting there.'

My eyes widen; I'm as shocked as if she'd slapped me. But before I can reply, Edme snatches her hand away and sweeps into the kitchen. Moments later, I hear the clink of glass as she retrieves the sherry bottle from where I've hidden it in the pantry.

Am I high on the fumes from the oil heater or did Edme just show a glimmer of compassion? I'm so stunned that I forget all about the major beautification required for my Niamh-free evening with Oli; I pick up my bag and drift out the door.

Oliver's cottage in the centre of Gairloch is filled with rich, heady aromas when I wander in nearly an hour later. I've dawdled the two miles from Edme's place, trying to get my head around what just happened. Did I dream it? Did she really treat me like a fellow human being?

'I hope you like curry,' Oliver says as he opens the door.

'I do as long as there's no dead flesh in it.'

'Nope, it's paneer,' he says proudly.

'Paneer? I don't mean to impugn Gairloch's proud multicultural heritage, Oli, but the most exotic thing I've seen in this village in the last two weeks is the newsagent's chihuahua, and even it's called Lachlan. Where on earth did you find paneer?'

Oliver shrugs nonchalantly. 'Niamh was in Inverness yesterday for a conference so I asked her to get some because I know you like it.'

He knows I like it. And he's looking particularly like Ewan McGregor this evening in skinny jeans, battered motorcycle boots and a long-sleeved T-shirt that says 'Jesus is my homeboy'. There's no way I can dump my latest woes on him now.

'Well, thank you,' I say tightly.

'You're welcome.' He gestures for me to follow him through to the kitchen, where he pours me a glass of white wine and busies himself stirring and chopping.

'So where is Niamh tonight?' I lean against the kitchen counter next to him.

'Actually,' Oliver says conspiratorially, 'she met a bloke. They're on a date.'

'Really?' I'm surprised at how elated this information makes me feel. I guess, despite Oliver's repeated assurances that he and Niamh are nothing more than friends, I have a hard time believing a good-looking guy and a sweet, pretty girl could live under the same roof and not be sleeping together. Or at least want to be. 'I can't believe there was an eligible man in Gairloch and I didn't know about him!'

'He's from Ullapool, about thirty miles from here,' Oliver says. Then, casually, 'Are you looking to meet a bloke then?' He doesn't look up from his stirring, but his question hangs teasingly in the air.

'Why, are you offering?' I titter nervously.

Oliver laughs too, and looks at me at last. I want him to say something glib and funny and burst this bubble of tension between us. Instead, he says, 'You look great, Hels.'

It's such a left-field thing to say that I look down at my clothes to check I'm wearing what I think I am. Sure enough, it's just black jeans tucked into flat brown boots, several vests, T-shirts and long-sleeved tops designed to keep out the insidious Gairloch cold, and a woolly green scarf. All of which are creased and marked and probably a bit smelly, having not seen the inside of a washing machine for two weeks.

'Are you mad? I look like I've been stacking shelves at Safeway.'

Oliver shakes his head and puts down his spatula. Then he leans over and kisses me. Just like that.

It's a soft, tentative kiss. It feels like his lips are asking mine for permission. And mine give it. I press my body to Oliver's and his kiss deepens.

Eventually, he pulls away. 'I've wanted to do that for two weeks,' he says huskily.

'I should go,' I reply.

Anna

The thing about babies is they really don't do very much. Apart from sleep, eat, scream and poo, that is. I might get an hour or two of Ivy being hilarious, pulling faces and blowing bubbles and burbling away to herself as though she's solving the world's problems in a language only she can understand, before she's back to sleeping, eating, screaming or filling her nappy. And now that I've got a basic understanding of how often and for how long each of these things occurs, my life is a lot easier.

'In fact, I'm almost a bit bored,' I say to Jen as we lace up our running shoes outside her house. It's a classic London spring morning: bright and clear, with a bracing sharpness to the air. It's the first sunny morning in days, but there's not yet any real sense that summer is on its way, even though the calendar claims it's just a few weeks away. If there's one thing I've learned about English weather, it's that seasons are a decision rather than genuine weather phenomena: 'I'm going to wear shorts and flip-flops, even though it's twelve degrees and drizzling, because it's August, damnit!'

Jen's husband, Andrew, watches us through their sitting room window. He has Ivy in one arm, Elodie in the other, Milo zooming trucks around his feet and a look of mild panic on his face.

'I know exactly what you mean,' Jen says, giving Andrew a jaunty wave as we begin a slow jog down the street. 'When I first had Milo, I thought every second of my day would be chock-full of mum stuff. But once he got into a routine and I wasn't so knackered all the bloody time, the days felt endless.'

'I love Ivy to bits but she's just sort of a lump, you know? I've been watching an awful lot of daytime TV.'

'I hear you.' Jen's breathing quickens as we step up our pace. It's amazing how much conversational ground we cover on our runs, considering much of the time we're panting too hard to speak at all.

'So what did you do?'

'Sprint!' Jen streaks ahead, aiming for the stately white mansion that sits smack-bang in the middle of our local park. I dig in my heels and race after her but she's much better at sprints than me and reaches the front door of the house a full ten seconds before I do.

'Apart from sprinting, what did you do?' I ask, resting my hands on my knees and sucking in lungfuls of air.

'Well, it was a little different for me, An. By the time Milo was Ivy's age I was already pregnant with Elodie, so I had scans and pre-natal stuff and getting her nursery organised to keep me busy.'

Jen doesn't sound nearly as wheezy as I feel. This is my first run since Ivy arrived three weeks ago, and it shows. I can't quite believe how fast the weeks have flown by, especially given I haven't really *done* anything with my time off work. That's the weird paradox with babies: each day feels about ten years long, but the weeks whiz by in nanoseconds. 'Um, I'm not about to get knocked up just so I'll have something to do with my time.'

'Really?' Jen looks at me knowingly.

'What do you mean "really?" Of course not!'

She shrugs and steps into a deep lunge. 'Why not? You said

yourself you've fallen head over heels for Ivy. You've loved having her.'

'I've loved having her because I know I can give her back in a week!'

'Okay, but you've done such a brilliant job with her. Are you seriously telling me it hasn't made you wonder even a little bit what it would be like to have one of your own?'

I feel a bit glowy that Jen thinks my stab at pseudo-motherhood has been in any way successful. Sure, there haven't been any real disasters, except possibly that chicken tikka masala thing, but I've definitely been flying by the seat of my pants. Ivy's still in one piece but most of the time it feels like that's an accident rather than the result of any genuine maternal instinct. If I have wondered during the past three weeks what it might be like to have my own kid, it's purely out of some perverse curiosity: could I possibly be as clueless with my own flesh and blood? But that's not what I tell Jen. 'I'm too young.'

'You're twenty-six.'

'Exactly.'

'I was twenty-six when I had Milo.' She stops stretching and gives me an 'I dare you' glare.

'Yes, but you had an adoring husband to help you.' Phew.

'And you've got Finn!'

Now it's my turn to glare.

'What? You've been together five years. Andrew and I had been together less than a year when we had Milo.'

I can feel myself getting cranky. Why is Jen pushing this? Surely she can see comparing her lovely, devoted Andrew to my . . . Finn is like comparing Prada with Primark.

'You might have got hitched and popped out a baby in five minutes flat, Jen, but remember Andrew changed his whole life for you. You and the kids have always been his top priority. I don't think I'm even close to the top of Finn's list any more.'

I jog away, blinking back tears and hoping Jen will drop the subject. But she catches up to me in seconds and the lump in my throat makes my chest tighten, so I have to slow to a walk. Trapped.

'I'm sorry, hon,' Jen says, squeezing my arm. 'I didn't mean to make you all sad again. You haven't said much about Finn in the last week or so – I thought you were getting used to him being away.'

'I'm not,' I admit, sniffling. 'I thought I'd be fine, especially with Ivy to distract me, but I've had more time to think about him than I expected.'

Jen nods sympathetically. 'And what have you been thinking?'

Now there's a question. 'I've been swinging between missing him madly and feeling totally abandoned. Then I'll feel horribly selfish for not supporting his career, and then completely angry that he picked a stupid job over us.' In truth, I've never felt so unhinged in all my life.

'That's totally normal,' Jen says soothingly. 'It's a hell of a lot to deal with and that's without the added complication of a baby.'

'This from the woman who, two minutes ago, was advising me to get up the duff!'

'That's different,' she says. 'I really think a child of your own would bring you closer together. Just look at that mate of Finn's – Jim?'

'Jez.'

'Right. You said yourself he and his girlfriend have been getting along much better since their little boy was born.'

'But that's them. What if a baby didn't change anything for Finn and me? That's a pretty big risk to take.'

But Jen has her baby goggles on. Because her kids are adorable and her husband worships the ground she walks on, she's always flying the flag for procreation. There's no reasoning with her.

'Have you told Finn how you're feeling?' she asks.

'Sort of. I mean, I've tried, but . . .' But what? How can I explain that I've clocked up a grand total of about fifteen minutes of actual conversation with Finn since he left ten days ago? That when I actually do get hold of him he's invariably too busy or too tired to discuss our relationship? That he cancelled his planned trip back to London last weekend to go to some team-building weekend with his fancy TV mates in the Irish countryside?

'He's doing so well over there. I don't want to take the shine off by constantly dragging him into deep and meaningfuls about the state of our relationship.' I start jogging again. Jen matches my stride but I can still feel her looking at me dubiously.

'Anna,' she says at last. 'If you're not telling Finn how you feel and you haven't been talking to me about it, who *have* you been telling? You can't just bottle all this stuff up. I know Ivy's advanced for her age, but I don't think she's going to be able to shed much light on this one.'

I giggle. I have had several 'conversations' with Ivy actually . . . and Nui . . . and my own reflection in the bathroom mirror. Jen's right; none of my confidants has been particularly useful.

'Oh, have you been chatting with Helena?' Jen asks. 'She must be on the phone constantly, checking up on Ivy?'

'Actually, I haven't spoken to her that much. She's dealing with a lot at the moment so I'm kind of just trying to let her get on with it,' I say in what I hope is a sympathetic tone. I'm not about to reveal to Jen that the bizarre phone call a few days ago was the sole contact I've had from Helena since her midnight flight. And I'm certainly not going to tell my kid-obsessed neighbour that Hel didn't even ask about Ivy. Of course I thought it was unutterably selfish, but I also kind of know where she's coming from. I've known Helena more than ten years and this is how she's always dealt with painful things: swept them under the carpet until she's ready to face them. But Jen already has a lower-than-low opinion of Helena; if I tell her that Hel seems totally uninterested in her daughter's wellbeing, Jen will inevitably take it upon herself to give Helena a tongue-lashing when she returns to collect Ivy.

'Fair enough,' says Jen, though the look on her face makes it clear she doesn't think it's fair at all. 'So you've just been keeping it all to yourself then?'

I clear my throat, suddenly nervous. 'Actually, I've run a few things past Luke.' I cast a sidelong glance at Jen, whose mouth, predictably, is agape. 'Just, you know, to get a male perspective,' I add quickly.

I'm trying to discourage Jen from launching a full-blown inquisition into precisely what Luke and I have discussed, but in all honesty my previously irritating neighbour has proved to be a real surprise packet. Since we finally buried the hatchet and took that walk, I've seen him most days. He's become my go-to guy on everything from how often I should be bathing Ivy (apparently three times a day is too much, no matter how hectic her pooing schedule) to whether Finn understands why I'm so hurt by his defection to Ireland. Our friendship might have had a decidedly rocky beginning, but it turns out Luke is actually pretty fantastic.

'Luke? Luke Parker? From next door?'

'Yes.'

'The same Luke you once wished would succumb to a medieval testicle-withering curse?'

'That's him.'

'This guy is now your sounding board?'

'Uh-huh.' My desire to be evasive is greatly assisted by the fact that our running pace has now rendered polysyllabic speech almost impossible. For me, at least.

'I see. And what does Luke make of the Finn situation?'

'Well, he thinks Finn is definitely still invested in our relationship or he would have just called it off before he went to Belfast.'

'Did he actually use that phrase, "invested in the relationship"?'
Jen's voice is scornful.

'Er . . . I think so. Why?'

She rolls her eyes. 'Tool.'

'Jen!'

'What? Why are you even listening to this guy, Anna?'

I steal another glance; Jen looks genuinely miffed. I stop dead.
'Jen, are you jealous?'

'Get over yourself!' she calls over her shoulder as she strides
ahead.

I summon the last of my stamina and dash after her. She gathers speed until I'm practically hyperventilating just to keep up with
her. When she sees that I'm turning a fetching shade of crimson, she
finally stops.

'Okay, you're right,' I wheeze. 'Luke was a complete tool for a
very long time. And I appreciate you looking out for me.' I draw
in raspy breaths; it feels like a billion angry fire ants are staging a
demonstration in my lungs. 'But we're good now. You don't have to
hate him on my behalf any more.'

Jen still looks incredulous. 'I don't buy it,' she says flatly.

'What's to buy?' Now I'm confused. 'We're friends. Really.'

'That's what bothers me.'

I shake my head. I'm sweaty, I can barely breathe and my legs
apparently have anvils strapped to them. I'm seriously not in the
mood for cryptic conversations with Jen.

'What's going on, Jen? Spit it out.'

She sighs irritably. 'Call me a conspiracy theorist, but I find it a
little convenient that a bloke you'd have crossed the road to avoid
a few weeks ago is now your NBF.'

'NBF?'

'New best friend.'

'He's not my new best friend! What are we, twelve? Though I

guess I'm in the market for a best friend since mine's vanished into
thin air and saddled me with her kid.'

'And what am I, chopped liver?'

Evidently we *are* twelve.

'No, Jen, you're brilliant. You've been unbelievably supportive
and are without a doubt my oracle on all things baby,' I say firmly,
gripping Jen's biceps to punctuate my point. 'Luke is a friend too,
but he's not a patch on you.'

Jen smiles at last and the tension leaves her face. 'I'm sorry, hon,'
she says. 'I just worry about you. You've had to take on an awful
lot in the past few weeks and you're vulnerable. I'd hate to see you
taken advantage of.'

'Who's going to take advantage of me?' I ask, frowning. Maybe
it's the rush of exercise-induced endorphins to her brain, but Jen is
making precious little sense today.

She looks at me like she can't fathom how someone so naïve
manages to put one foot in front of the other. 'Luke.'

'Luke! What are you on about?'

'Oh come on, Anna.' She rolls her eyes. 'You're a gorgeous girl
on her own with a baby. You've hit a rocky patch in your relationship. It's the perfect opportunity for a dashing bloke like him to
swoop in and play your knight in shining armour.'

I suppress a smile at Jen's description of Luke. Dashing? Useful,
definitely. Not entirely hideous-looking, maybe. But dashing? I've
certainly never thought of him that way. I blink in shock. 'Have you
gone mental? I only have Ivy for another week or so, which Luke
knows. He's not preying on single mums, or sort-of mums, because
he thinks they're easy targets.'

'How do you know?' Jen says pointedly. 'You've really only
known him for three weeks.'

I don't answer but turn around and start jogging towards home.
It's not Jen's low opinion of Luke and his motives that bothers

me – it's her lack of faith in me. Does she really think I'm going to swoon at the feet of the first man I see just because my life is a little challenging at the moment? Sure, it's nice to spend time with a man who seems to appreciate rather than tolerate my company. A man who's interested in what I have to say. A man who goes out of his way to help me, unlike my boyfriend, who went out of his way to *get* out of my way.

'My relationship with Luke is purely platonic, Jen,' I call over my shoulder. 'He's a friend. *Just* a friend.'

But even as the words leave my lips, there's a tiny voice in the back of my mind whispering, 'Who are you trying to convince?' Jen's arched eyebrow and dubious smirk tell me she's wondering the same thing.

It's just this mess with Finn that's got me second-guessing myself. Jen is right that Finn and I have hit a rocky patch. I've been trying not to think about it but that rock feels roughly the size of Gibraltar. Maybe I've been too cavalier, expecting Finn to make all the effort to get us back on track just because he's the one who left. He's told me a thousand times he's still one hundred per cent committed to us; maybe it's time I took him at his word.

And if there's even a skerrick of truth to what Jen says about Luke, maybe it's time to make the point to him that, while I may temporarily be a mum, I'm hopefully still a long way from being single.

'Okay,' I say when Jen catches up. 'Say I want to get things sorted out with Finn. What should I do?'

'When's he back next?' she asks.

'Tomorrow afternoon.'

'Why is he waiting til Saturday? I thought he worked Monday to Friday. Why isn't he coming back straight after work tonight?'

I shrug. 'Some team dinner he couldn't get out of.' The truth is, Finn's been vague about why he changed his flight from Friday night to Saturday morning.

'Never mind. That could actually work in your favour. More shopping time,' Jen says conspiratorially.

'Oh yeah? And what am I shopping for?' I hope she's not about to suggest chocolate body paint or a French maid's outfit.

She smiles mischievously. 'Lingerie. And the racier the better.'

Jen's shopping brief may have specified the, er, briefest of briefs, but I'm not about to shop for crotchless knickers with my infant god-daughter looking on. What would Helena think?

I wheel Ivy's pram down Richmond high street, crowded even for mid-afternoon on a Friday, past the saucy smalls in the window of Ann Summers and into the classier La Senza. I'm relieved to see there's no PVC or edible undergarments in sight.

This is not me. Lingerie girl, that is. I still wear the trusty Bonds briefs I brought with me from Australia five years ago. They're grey from overwashing and the elastic is going in most of them, but they're comfy and familiar and I won't bin them until I absolutely have to. Which, says Jen, is entirely my problem. My knickers drawer is a metaphor for my relationship with Finn: safe, familiar and thoroughly devoid of sex appeal of any sort. She stopped short of saying Finn might not have been so eager to get to Belfast if things were more exciting in the bedroom department, but I could tell she was thinking it.

Jen and Andrew are one of those infuriating couples that are forever making googly eyes at each other at dinner parties; you just know they'll be tearing each other's clothes off the second you're out the door. She never talks about their sex life, which is how I know it's amazing. The people who talk about it are never actually doing it.

But if Jen and Andrew are red-hot between the sheets, Finn and I are more like the cup of tea you make and then forget to drink: luke-warm and kind of congealed. The night before he left for Belfast we made love for the first time in weeks, but I was so filled with fear and resentment, I imagine it must have been like shagging an ironing board.

'Can I help you?' says the stunning salesgirl, who undoubtedly has an entire chest of drawers full of lacy G-strings and balconette bras. And a steady stream of stallion-esque suitors to admire her in them.

'I'm looking for something for, um, a special occasion,' I mumble. I feel about sixty; if she directed me to the support stocking section I wouldn't be at all surprised.

She looks at Ivy in her pram, then looks me up and down. 'I think I've got just the thing,' she says. 'Thirty-two D?'

'Uh, thirty-four C actually.'

She actually winks at me. 'Trust me, darling, you're a thirty-two D.' She gestures for me to follow her to the fitting rooms at the back of the store, plucking tiny scraps of fabric from racks as she goes.

She ushers me into a curtained cubicle and hands over an armful of lingerie. 'I'll keep an eye on bubs,' she says, drawing the curtain across.

I open it a crack so I can see Ivy's pram reflected in the mirror and strip down to my smalls. Any passing perverts are likely to cop a view of my backside but I know better than to leave Ivy out of my sight. At least some of the more basic tenets of parenting have penetrated my brain.

I'm dubious about this whole size thing but I slip the first bra on anyway. It's a coffee-coloured microfibre number with a satin trim, and it hoists my boobs somewhere up near my chin.

'Let's have a look,' says Miss Perky, thrusting her head inside the curtain without warning. 'Ooh, stunning. I wish my bust looked as good as yours after my kids,' she says wistfully.

Kids? She looks about fifteen. Which, this being England, she might well be.

'Oh, she's not mine,' I admit. 'I'm her godmother.'

'Oh, right. I don't have to be completely jealous of your great figure then,' she says good-naturedly, and I instantly blush. 'Why don't you pop the boylegs on with that bra?'

She hands the matching knickers through the curtain and I slide them on over my own shabby pair. The effect is appealing, though somehow more sporty than sexy. And I really need to bring sexy back.

'What do you think?' Perky calls from outside the cubicle.

'It's really pretty, but I'm looking for something a little . . .'

'Hotter?' she replies, quick as a flash.

Fifteen or not, this girl is damn good at her job. 'Exactly.'

'One sec.' I hear her bustle out of the fitting rooms.

Ivy is singing cheerfully to herself in her pram and I pop my head out of the cubicle to watch. She really is such an angelic child. Sometimes I struggle to understand how Helena found it so difficult to cope with her. Maybe I could be a good mother to a child of my own after all.

I turn back to the mirror and cast a critical eye over my body. Years of running have honed my figure, though I'm neither naturally athletic or thin; given the choice I'll always gravitate to prolonged periods of sloth and excessive Tim Tam consumption. I run a hand over my flat stomach, trying to picture myself with a big pregnant belly. The thought makes me feel faintly nauseated. And my boobs, which look quite impressive thanks to this bra – could I willingly condemn them to a life of sagginess and stretch marks? I don't know that I could, and surely rampant vanity is reason enough not to have a child.

My mobile phone trills from the depths of Ivy's nappy bag. Wrapping myself in the curtain, I lean out of the cubicle and grab the bag from underneath the pram. The noise and commotion star- tles Ivy and she immediately bursts into tears.

'Oh no, no, no, Ivy. It's okay, my love,' I coo as I fumble for my phone. I retrieve it at last and squint at the tiny screen. The call is coming from my office number.

'Hello?' I answer uncertainly.

'Anna,' Nicki Ford-Smith's clipped voice responds. She would know to call while I'm half-naked and trying to calm a squawking baby. It's like she has ESP: Evil Skank Perception.

'Oh, hi. You're sitting at my desk now?'

'Um, I'm acting showbiz *editor*, Anna. I need to be able to access your computer and answer your phone,' she says primly.

It's the first time I've spoken to Nicki since I banned her from the Benedict Cumberbatch premiere. Judging by the tone of her voice, I'm not even close to being forgiven.

'Having fun babysitting?'

'I'm not babysitting, Nicki. I'm —'

'Whatever. Girish said I had to call you because you got an invite.'

Miss Perky returns, brandishing a leopard-print bra and suspender-belt combo. I shake my head sharply and signal her to turn around immediately and find me something a little less 'Amsterdam shop window'. She looks crestfallen but dutifully spins on her heel.

'I get a lot of invites, Nicki,' I say with a sigh. I've barely thought about my job in the past few weeks. Whatever C-list event I've been invited to suddenly seems laughably trivial.

'I know that, and I told Girish you wouldn't be interested, but he said I had to tell you because it was addressed to you personally and it's on the day you're due back.'

'For God's sake, Nicki, just spit it out, will you? What's the event?' I'm trying to keep my voice level because Ivy's still whimpering and I don't want to alarm her even more, but really I'd like to hop in the next taxi to Canary Wharf and inflict a zillion paper cuts on Nicki with this mystery invitation.

'It's Cat Hubbard's album release party,' she grudgingly reveals, then adds hastily, 'I told Girish I'm more than happy to cover it.'

'I bet,' I say wryly. 'But it's fine. Tell Girish I'll be there and please send the invitation on to me.'

Though Cat's PR agency probably would have put me on the guest list anyway, I'm touched to think that perhaps Cat remembered her casual invite at the movie premiere. I don't trust Nicki to RSVP on my behalf so I give her my home address and hang up just as Perky reappears. She looks hopeful and presents with a flourish a black silk camisole edged with cream lace, and matching French knickers.

'It's perfect,' I breathe. I peel off the coffee-coloured set and slip on the buttery-soft silk. The ensemble is undeniably sexy but in a 'saucy secretary' rather than 'Soho streetwalker' way. I'd definitely do me in this. Feeling bold, I fling back the curtain and strut into the main changing area, where there's an enormous mirror covering an entire wall.

'Special occasion, you say?' Perky asks, subtly averting her eyes.

'Mmm-hmm,' I reply distractedly, admiring the way the silk clings to my curves.

'Your boyfriend's a lucky man,' she says pleasantly. 'What's his name?'

'Luke.'

'Well, Luke will —'

'Finn! My boyfriend's name is Finn.'

Oh. My. God. Miss Perky looks perturbed. She clearly suspects I'm not the full enchilada. I can see how taking someone else's child lingerie shopping, strutting around like a peacock in my underwear and forgetting my boyfriend's name could create that impression.

Finn

Mate. In LDN 2mrw. Beers?
Sorry mate. E away 4 w/end so Iv got the lad.
Bring him 2!
Nah. Ur Mrs wont let u out anyway!

I frown and delete Jez's last message. I'm really not sure I like this new version of my best mate. Not so long ago he'd have been the first one to tell me to ditch my 'bird' and head to the pub with him, even if I have been away for two weeks. Now he's trying to force me to spend quality time with Anna. Except that it won't be quality, because Ivy will be causing a ruckus and there'll still be a simmering anger in Anna's eyes.

That's why I didn't bother flying back to London after my first week in Belfast. I could have skipped the team-building weekend, but I sensed Anna needed more time to cool off. I've been trying to give her space so she can get used to our new arrangement, but judging by the few frosty phone calls we've had in the past fortnight, somehow I just seem to be making her angrier.

I guess I've not really done myself any favours. Anna says I'm not very communicative on the phone at the best of times, and it hasn't helped that I've been absolutely shattered since I started the new job. The adrenalin-fuelled morning person died a horrible death halfway through the first week, replaced by Mr Look-at-me-before-I've-had-caffeine-and-I'll-rip-your-freaking-head-off. I know I need to lift my game where Anna is concerned, but I also know I'm too tired for a fresh dose of drama. So when Fiona announced tonight's strategy planning session ('attendance compulsory') I was secretly overjoyed.

The leafy cul-de-sac where Fiona lives in a posh suburb of Belfast is lined with cars when I arrive, late. In a vain effort to claw my way out of sleep debt, I've taken to having little granddad naps in the afternoon. By Friday it's near impossible to get out of bed after-wards, and this evening was no exception.

I recognise Mary's black Audi and Roland's old banger parked outside Fiona's smart terrace. I really need to get myself some wheels. The chauffeur service was just a first-week perk and I've been taxiing to the studio ever since. Anna would be horrified; I could easily walk to work in under twenty minutes.

'Awright,' Roland says gruffly as he opens the door.

A sharp jerk of his head tells me I should follow him into the house. As I'd suspected, the cheerful Roland I'd seen on my first day didn't last long. By day three, he'd been replaced by a surly git who is virtually monosyllabic unless he's kicking your arse over some minor transgression. And that happens a lot. Not often to me, miraculously. But the floor team get a tongue-lashing at least once a day and even Mary's been on the receiving end of some of his pricklier barbs. The only person who never seems to cop it is Fiona, probably because she's his boss.

I trail behind Roland into the living room and I'm surprised to see only Mary and a couple of the more senior members of the production team, Gary and Patrick.

'Evening, all. Where's the rest of us then?'

'We're it,' Mary says, and the look in her eyes tells me she expected a bigger turnout, too.

'We don't need the *little people*, Finn,' Fiona says, laughing, as she sweeps into the room carrying a platter of dips and cut-up vegetables. 'I wanted the key team members to have the chance to blue-sky the direction of the show going forward.'

Fiona always looks pretty nicely put together, but tonight she looks hot. She's wearing a black wrap dress that plunges suggestively over her cleavage, and shiny black knee-high boots. I can hardly take my eyes off her, and I gather from the hush that descends that the other blokes in the room feel the same way.

Nevertheless, I have to hide a major eye roll at Fiona's use of godawful management speak. Who actually says 'blue-sky' when they mean brainstorm? (Come to think of it, who even says brainstorm when 'think of ideas' are perfectly good words?) I mean, come on. And when did 'going forward' become the new thing? What's wrong with 'in the future' or even just plain old 'next'? Jez and I have a pact that if either of us ever starts speaking like a wanker, the other is well within his rights to administer a punch to the face.

'Drink?' Fiona takes an open bottle of Carlsberg from a tray on the coffee table and, leaning forward, hands it to me. I cop a proper eyeful down the front of her dress and, I admit, my gaze lingers a fraction too long.

'Thanks.' I take a long swig, then another. I've got a feeling this could be a long night.

'Okay, you all know we've been rating through the roof for the last fortnight,' Fiona says, crossing her legs as she sits and exposing a sliver of smooth, tanned thigh. 'Our challenge now is to weather the inevitable plateau and keep growing.'

She looks at Mary, then at me. 'You guys are doing a great job, but I want to get you out there more. Mary, we'd like to get you involved in some high-profile charity stuff. Establish you as *Belfast*

Breakfast's "TV angel".'

Mary nods thoughtfully. 'I'd definitely be open to that,' she says. 'I already work with a couple of children's charities and there's certainly potential there for some *BB*-backed campaigns. Real heart-strings stuff.' The others murmur appreciatively.

'Great. Can you come back to me with a proposal? Talk to your charities and see what they've got,' Fiona says.

'No problem.' Mary pulls a notebook from her handbag and begins scribbling.

'Now Finn,' Fiona continues, turning to face me. 'I've something a little different in mind for you.'

I drain the last of my beer and reach for another. 'Uh-huh. And what's that?'

'Our research shows our female viewers are responding really well to you. They like this "cheeky chappy" thing you've got happening.'

She makes me sound like a Dickensian street urchin. It's probably the pastel shirts. 'I thought you said they didn't like me because they couldn't understand my accent?'

Fiona waves her hand, dismissing my question. 'That's just the old biddies. The urban twenty-somethings think you're quite the heartthrob, and they're the ones our advertisers are selling to.'

'Okaaay . . . so what's the plan?' I'm suddenly afraid my professional future is going to be filled with nothing but lame stories about those fat women who lose hundreds of kilos by eating African gnats or whatever.

'You're going to become a sort of male Carrie Bradshaw,' Fiona says with a smile.

'Kerry who?'

'Carrie Bradshaw!' Mary pipes up. 'Oh come on, kangaroo boy. I know you're a true-blue Aussie bloke but I refuse to believe you've not heard of *Sex and the City*.'

I groan inwardly. They've got to be kidding me. Anna owns all four million episodes of that show on DVD and, from what I can tell, they're all identical – just a bunch of spoilt women moaning that they can't find a man. Then, when they do get one, moaning about why he's no good. And the Kerry one has her head even further up her bum than the others, forever droning on about shoes and handbags and how her rich boyfriend isn't nice to her. Fiona wants me to be like *that*?

'I'm not quite sure I follow,' I say, trying to mask the sneer in my voice. I neck most of my beer; maybe being half cut will make me more receptive to whatever's coming next.

'You're going to navigate the Belfast singles scene for us. I see you speed dating, internet dating – however the cool kids are meeting each other, that's what we want to see on *Belfast Breakfast*. There's so much scope for you here, Finn.'

'But the thing is, I have —'

'Great! Okay, Roly, I know you've got a couple of issues you'd like to discuss.' Fiona angles her body away from mine, letting me know our conversation is over.

I swallow what's left of my second beer and look around for another but the tray on the table is bare. Perfect.

'More drinks, guys?' I ask.

Everyone but Mary raises their hands. 'Driving,' she whispers.

I escape into the kitchen and open Fiona's fridge. It contains nothing but beer, champagne (Moët, of course; even Anna would approve) and cottage cheese. Either Fiona has an eating disorder or she doesn't spend a lot of time at home. Somehow I suspect it's the latter. She strikes me as a woman with a healthy appetite.

I retrieve four bottles of Carlsberg and twist off their tops. Though we've all been drinking straight from the bottle, I search Fiona's cupboards for glasses. I need to buy some time to figure out how to tell Fiona I can't be her Breakfast Cupid, or whatever inane name she'll undoubtedly give me.

I can read between the lines. I know what Fiona really means when she uses phrases like 'heartthrob' and 'navigate the singles scene'. She wants to paint me as some sort of serial shagger, so I'll get column inches in the local tabloids. I've seen it done with other commercial TV presenters, though usually only when their shows are on the skids and they're desperate for new viewers. It's not a tactic I'd have thought palatable for a breakfast TV audience, but then Fiona seems hell-bent on breaking the mould with our show.

But it's not just the fact that becoming 'dating guy' totally undermines everything I've ever tried to do with my career. It's Anna.

As if I haven't disappointed her enough in the last few weeks; how can I now turn around and tell her I've got to pretend to be single just to pull in the ratings? 'How was my day? Great! I spent it trawling Belfast's seediest meat markets trying to pick up chicks!' Not bloody likely.

The kitchen door swings open and Fiona strides in. 'Finn, we thought you'd got lost!' she says in a singsong voice. She takes the replenished beer tray from the counter and moves to return to the sitting room.

'Ah, Fiona?'

I'd have liked at least one more alcoholic beverage under my belt before I tell my boss to get stuffed, but there's no time like the present.

She pauses and looks over her shoulder at me. 'What's up?'

'It's about your plans for me. I'm not really, you know, very, um . . . comfortable with them. Sort of.'

Eloquent as always.

Fiona frowns, setting the tray down. 'And why's that?' she says a touch defensively.

'Well . . .' How can I say it without sounding like a fifteen-year-old who's been offered an illicit snog behind the bike sheds? 'I've got a girlfriend. I can't.'

'Oh Finn.' Fiona sighs and offers a patronising smile. 'Tell you what. Hang about after this lot leaves and we'll talk about it, okay? We'll work something out.'

I nod mutely as Fiona collects the drinks and pushes through the door. My stomach starts churning, whether from nerves or the effects of guzzling two beers in about two minutes, I can't be sure. Fiona is a formidable woman; the thought of a showdown with her – on her turf no less – is not one I relish.

Four beers later, my guts are still bubbling away – I think it's safe to assume it's definitely the alcohol now – and my head's spinning. Probably I should stop drinking but more beer currently feels like my only option if I'm going to make it through this interminable discussion about the show's running order without banging my head on the coffee table out of sheer boredom.

Close to midnight, Mary yawns theatrically and picks up her handbag. 'I hate to love you and leave you, gang,' she says, the fatigue evident in her voice, 'but I've been awake for, ooh, going on twenty hours now. If I don't leave this second I'm going to fall asleep and start drooling on myself. Nobody needs to see that.'

Sensing their escape route, Gary and Patrick spring to their feet, bid hasty goodbyes and scuttle out the front door behind Mary. Which just leaves me, Fiona and Roland. Even in my drunken state I detect a sudden weird vibe in the air.

'Do you want me to call you a cab, Finn?' Roland asks pointedly. 'Ahh . . .'

I look to Fiona for assistance. I'm not sure if she wants Roland knowing about our scheduled follow-up meeting. He'll probably want to stick around and offer his two cents' worth, and I get the feeling Fiona wants to keep our chat private. At least, I hope she does. The last thing I want is Roland telling the rest of the crew how the pretty-boy Aussie refused an assignment because he feared the wrath of his missus.

'Finn and I have more to discuss,' Fiona says smoothly. 'You go home and get some sleep, Roly. I'll see you tomorrow.'

Roland frowns at Fiona and shoots me a look that would be best described as loathing. 'Fine,' he says eventually. He pecks Fiona on the cheek and she walks him to the front door.

When she returns, instead of settling into the leather armchair she's been sitting in all night, Fiona sits close to me on the couch. Really close. She presses her thigh to mine and rests her hand on my knee.

'Now Finn, what are these concerns of yours?'

'Tomorrow's Sat'day.'

'Er . . . yes.' Fiona regards me with that long-suffering expression commonly employed by sober people trapped in conversation with drunks.

'Why would you see Roland on a Sat'day? S'no show on Sat'day,' I slur.

'Roland and I occasionally see each other socially,' she says casually.

'Whassat mean?'

'Don't worry about that, Finn. Tell me what's bothering you.'

This is where I'm supposed to deliver the little speech I've been practising in my head for the past two hours: 'Fiona, the fact that you seem to want to position me as some sort of Lothario is insulting in itself, but even more so is the fact you would ask me to do that when you know I'm in a committed long-term relationship.'

That's what I want to say. That would really tell her. But I don't say that, because my boozy brain haze won't let me construct proper sentences.

Instead, I say: 'My girlfriend.' And I know I deserve the flicker of condescension I see in Fiona's eyes.

'Your girlfriend?' she repeats.

I nod. 'I can't do it to her. She's mad enough as it is.'

Fiona removes her hand from my knee and drapes it across

my shoulders. 'That's a very telling statement, Finn. Your girl-friend – Annie, is it?'

'Anna.'

'Right. So Anna is angry because you accepted this job in Belfast and moved away from London, correct?'

'Yesssh.' And because I didn't tell her about it, then did tell her but promised not to take the job. And also left her on her own with a baby. Let's not forget that.

Fiona pauses a moment, like she's not sure how to say what she wants to say. 'But doesn't that make *you* angry? That this person who supposedly loves you won't support your decision and be proud of your achievements?'

I think about this. It's true I was pissed off when I first told Anna about the job and she flew off the handle, because I knew she would. But since then the sheer scale of Anna's fury has been so overwhelming I've kind of forgotten about my own. These days I mostly just feel guilty.

Maybe Fiona has a point. Maybe I'm entitled to throw a little ire in Anna's direction. But Fiona's wrong about one thing.

'Anna doesn't "supposedly" love me; she definitely loves me. That's why this whole thing became such a disaster in the first place,' I tell her.

I feel Fiona's fingers creep from my shoulder into my hair. She nuzzles in closer and looks at me gravely.

'Well then, I guess there's only one question left to ask yourself,' she says.

I can smell her perfume; it's even more intoxicating than the beer and I feel myself responding to her in a place that has no business responding to anyone but Anna.

'What's that?'

'Do you love her?'

'What? Of course!'

'Oh come on, Finn!' Fiona shouts, leaping up from the couch.

She stalks across the sitting room to the fireplace. Resting her hands on the mantel for a moment, she turns to face me.

'If you really loved this girl, you'd be cuddled up next to her on your sofa in London, instead of with me on mine. Why don't you just admit it and cut the poor girl loose?'

I stare at her, slack-jawed. Her words take a moment to sink in and, when they do, I'm not sure what's more shocking: what she's said or the impassioned way she's said it.

'What are you talking about?' I shout back when my brain and my mouth finally reconnect. 'I'm not "cuddling up" with you. I'm not doing anything with you!'

'Stop kidding yourself!' Fiona says. 'I can't imagine what your relationship is based on, Finn, but anyone who's met you here can see it's not love or even respect. The day I offered you this job, Anna could not have been further from your mind. You couldn't sign the contract fast enough. And you *never* talk about her.'

'That's called being a professional, Fiona,' I fire back. 'Mary barely mentions her husband or their kids. And I don't see you giving us all the details of your "social excursions" with Roly.'

Fiona holds my gaze a beat longer, her eyes flashing. Then she smiles sweetly. 'Finn, you've misunderstood me,' she says. She returns to sit beside me once more. 'I'm not criticising you. I've told you before I admire your ambition.'

She runs the tips of two fingers down one side of my face. My head is throbbing trying to keep up with her. Something else is throbbing, too. She's obviously a complete bitch – and a mad one at that. So why do I want to tear her clothes off?

'I'm saying it's okay, I get it,' she goes on.

'Get what?'

'That your relationship isn't as important to you as your career. You don't have to pretend with me.'

'Fiona, this is a pretty extreme reaction to my saying I don't want to do a stupid speed-dating story.' I really want her to stop touching me. I think.

She throws back her head and laughs. 'We're so alike,' she says huskily.

'How's that?'

'We both want to do the right thing. We want to be all things to all people.'

She may be on to something there. Trying to keep everyone in my life happy lately has felt about as easy as juggling machetes. With a similar success rate.

'But the thing is, Finn, sometimes you just have to put yourself first.'

She's so close now I can see the light smattering of freckles across her nose. I know in that instant what's going to happen next. I know it's beyond wrong. But I also know I won't stop it.

I turn to face Fiona and she kisses me hungrily. I kiss her back; it's almost a reflex action. It doesn't feel like my brain has any part of this. Another part of my body is doing all the thinking for me. Fiona presses her body to mine and I feel the familiar stirring below decks. Her fingers deftly unfasten my shirt buttons – salmon-pink today – and she yanks the shirt roughly from my shoulders.

I let my hands roam over Fiona's toned body. She feels so different to Anna. While Anna's body is lean, she still has some feminine softness – Fiona is all sculpted muscles and hard edges. I slip my hand inside Fiona's dress and feel the rough lace of her bra. Her breasts are small, the nipples hard. She groans softly in my ear as she kisses my neck. I run my other hand up the inside of her thigh. It feels like an experiment now, like I'm testing Fiona to see how far she'll let me push this.

She wriggles out of her dress, then her underwear. That far then. Fiona reaches for my belt buckle, smiling wickedly when she feels how hard I am.

'This has been a long time coming,' she says, unzipping me and sliding off the sofa onto her knees at my feet.

I don't reply. Have I wanted this, too? Fiona is gorgeous and sexy and powerful, all of which make her a pretty attractive package. But Anna is beautiful too. And she can be sexy, when she makes the effort. And Anna has loved me for the past five years. I don't think Fiona's interested in loving me for even five minutes. I get the feeling this is all a game to her: she's the haughty cat and I'm just the piece of string. Am I really going to throw away everything I've got with Anna for a bit of a roll-around with a woman I know has no real interest in me except as a pawn in her own weird power games?

Fiona takes me into her mouth and for a split second I think that, yes, I will throw away my relationship and anything else Fiona cares to nominate as long as she doesn't ever stop what she's doing right now.

But then she pauses, looks up at me and says, 'See? Isn't it great to think only about yourself for a change?'

And the wind dies. The little puddle of guilt in my gut suddenly rears up into a great wave. Fiona has reminded me of what I've been trying my hardest to forget: I've been putting myself first for weeks.

She looks at my limp excuse for an erection, then looks up at me, puzzled. 'I thought you wanted this?' she says.

'I've got to go,' I say, pulling up my trousers and throwing on the hideous pink shirt.

'Excuse me?' she snaps, getting to her feet. She makes no attempt to cover herself; her body really is spectacular.

'I'm sorry, Fiona. You're gorgeous and amazing and so, so sexy . . .'

'Forgive me, but I thought those were good things.' She crosses her arms, which thrusts her breasts forward.

'They are. But I have a girlfriend,' I say. 'You know that. It's not fair of you to do this.'

She scoffs and reaches for her dress at last. 'Oh right, I'm being unfair. And getting a blow job from your *boss*' – she emphasises the word – 'that's okay, is it?'

I shake my head, which makes the throbbing worse. A wave of nausea rolls through me. I'm going to feel like death tomorrow, even though I now feel alarmingly sober.

'No, it's not okay. None of this is okay. But us sleeping together is *definitely* not okay.'

'I know you're attracted to me, Finn,' Fiona says, straightening her dress and smoothing her hair. 'I think you know it would be more than just sleeping together. But I haven't got time for your schoolboy guilt. When you decide you're ready to be a grown-up, let me know.'

I open my mouth to try to explain myself, but she looks unsubtly at the front door. Out in the street, I draw in a deep breath of frigid night air. I pull out my phone to call a cab, then decide to walk. Maybe the exercise will send some blood to my brain; right now it all seems to have been appropriated by another part of my body.

If Fiona hadn't reminded me *in flagrante* that I'm possibly the most selfish collection of cells ever to crawl the earth, there's no way I'd have stopped her. She's hot and it felt amazing but, more than that, it just felt good to be wanted, to feel like I'm vaguely desirable rather than an endless source of frustration. I need to talk to someone about this, but it's nearly one in the morning. I decide to take a punt on Jez being up on 'Daddy duty'.

'You are so fucking lucky I'm already awake,' Jez says by way of greeting. 'Do you even realise how highly prized my sleep is these days?'

'My boss just gave me a blow job.'

Silence.

'Jez?'

'Holy balls. Hang on, let me put the lad down.' There are muffled sounds. 'Am I going to need a beer for this?'

'Better make it a vodka.'

'Right. Call you back in thirteen seconds.'

While I wait for Jez to call me back, I huddle against the cold in the nearest bus shelter. My phone buzzes.

'What the fuck are you doing?' is Jez's opening gambit.

I sigh and outline the evening's catalogue of disasters. When I finish, Jez gives a low whistle.

'This Fiona sounds like a piece of work. It's a bit eighties, isn't it? Throwing herself at you like that?'

I laugh hollowly. There is something a bit *Wall Street* about Fiona. But her take-no-prisoners approach is part of what makes her so bloody enticing.

'I'm just glad I stopped it.'

'Why did you?' Jez asks.

'What do you mean?'

'What do you mean what do I mean? I mean why did you stop when this bird was all set to give you a no-strings blow job?'

No strings. That seems a hilarious concept where Fiona's concerned.

'Because I don't want to cheat on my girlfriend!'

'Yeah, but why?'

For crying out loud. I'm beginning to regret this phone call. 'I don't know, Dr Phil, you tell me.'

'I'm not trying to mess with you, mate. It's a serious question. Did you stop because you genuinely don't want to risk your relationship with Anna? Or was it only because you want to be able to look at yourself in the mirror tomorrow morning without feeling like a royal shit?'

'Does it make a difference?'

'It makes a hell of a difference. If you stopped it because of Anna, you need to pack in this job, come back to London and give your relationship a proper go.'

'And if it was the other one?'

Jez pauses. 'If it was the other one, you're a selfish twat and you might as well go back and let her finish you off.'

'Thanks, Jez. Insightful as always.'

He sighs. 'Look Finn, I know you want me to do the best-mate thing and tell you to do whatever the hell you want. But I can't do that any more. Anna's a lovely girl, and one way or another she deserves better from you.'

I hear Jez's little boy, Danny, start wailing in the background.

'What do you mean "one way or another"?'

'Shh, you're all right, lad,' Jez soothes his son. 'I mean, either treat her right or let her go. I mean grow a pair and make a fucking decision.'

My stomach twists angrily. I've had a gutful of Jez's holier-than-thou attitude. Not so long ago, he was no stranger to receiving the occasional, er, favour from women other than Ellie.

'You're hardly one to lecture,' I say through gritted teeth. 'As long as I've known you, you've been umm-ing and aah-ing about dumping Ellie. I didn't see you being Mr Decisive.'

Jez chuckles. 'Aye, that's fair. But I made my decision when Danny came along, mate.'

It's as if his words flick a switch in my head. Of course. Anna's found a whole new purpose since she's had Ivy. I'm looking for a new purpose in our relationship. Like Jez, I need a reason to stop looking elsewhere.

I need to be a dad.

Anna and I need to have a baby.

Helena

What usually happens when people get something they really, really want is that they're really, really happy. I know there are all those old clichés: 'Be careful what you wish for, you might get it' and 'Money can't buy you happiness', but really — that's crap. Most people who get what they wish for are overjoyed. People who have loads of money can buy ponies and helicopters and gold-plated toilets, and at least one of those things must make them a tiny bit cheerful. Normal people are happy when they get what they want.

Which is why I'm about as far from happy – and, it's becoming abundantly obvious, as far from normal – as a person can get.

Oliver kissing me is definitely what I wanted. I've wanted it since the moment I clapped eyes on him, to be honest. But then he went and did it. And now I'm in a shame spiral.

He's phoned me approximately fifty-seven times since I bolted from his house two nights ago. He even came to Edme's cottage yesterday and, when I didn't answer the door (and he thankfully couldn't raise Edme from her drunken stupor), he slipped a note underneath.

I tore it up without reading it. I know what Oli wants to tell me and I can't bear to listen to it. At best, he'll tell me it was a mistake and it can never work between us and we're better off as friends. And he'll be right.

At worst, he'll tell it like it really is. That a basket case like me has no business throwing herself at a beautiful, properly functioning member of society like him. That he has no interest in raising another man's child. That I should pull myself together, collect said child from her long-suffering godmother and stop wasting his time. And he'll be right about that, too.

The phone rings in the hall. I've switched my mobile off so Oliver is now risking catching Edme with her booze hat on, such is his desire to tell me to get stuffed. But if there's one thing I'm good at, it's avoiding confrontation. I'm due back in London in three days, and I'm pretty confident I can keep Oli at arm's length until then. From my foetal position on my bed, I hear Edme muttering as she huffs into the hall. That's the one advantage of sharing living quarters with a woman who bellows when she's had a few: it makes eavesdropping so much easier.

'Oliver,' Edme answers gruffly. 'Lucky guess . . . No, she's still not surfaced . . . no, I haven't . . . How the blazes should I know . . . I'll tell her . . . All right . . . all *right*.'

She slams the handset back into the receiver but instead of padding back into the sitting room I hear her footsteps creaking up the stairs. A moment later, there's a soft knock at my bedroom door.

'Helena?' Edme's voice is uncharacteristically gentle. 'May I come in?'

'Okay,' I agree, more out of curiosity than any real desire to speak to my great-aunt. I'm not used to hearing Edme speak to me in anything other than her usual flinty tone.

The door clicks open a crack and she peeps in. Apparently satisfied that I haven't swallowed the entire contents of the medicine cabinet, she enters the room. 'Tell me,' she says simply, perching on the edge of my bed.

I sit up. My instinct is to tell her nothing's wrong and send her on her way. But when I open my mouth to do just that, the words just tumble out. 'I'm in love with Oliver.'

'I know.'

I reel back in surprise. It's terrifying enough that I've realised I'm truly, madly, properly in love with Oliver, without realising Edme evidently spotted it well before I did.

'You know?'

'Of course. I'm not blind, Helena.'

No, just drunk.

'But . . . but how?'

Edme looks mildly affronted, as though I've been wearing an 'I love Oliver' T-shirt for the last month and didn't think she'd notice. 'Helena, you arrived on my doorstep nearly four weeks ago barely able to string a sentence together,' she says.

Leave it to Edme to call a spade a shovel.

'You were so pale and drawn, and there was all that crying.'

I duck my head, embarrassed.

'You thought I didn't see it?' she says.

I shrug. The crying was pretty constant. I guess I knew she couldn't have missed it. 'You never said anything.'

'I know.' She offers me a sad little smile. 'I've not been of great use to you, have I?'

It's delivered as a statement rather than a question; she doesn't need me to agree with her. As if I'd disagree. The woman has been no use to me whatsoever.

'I have problems of my own,' she goes on, mercifully sparing me from having to respond.

'I gathered.' I wait for Edme to continue but she falls silent, like she's deep in thought.

'As I was saying,' she says eventually, 'I've seen you change since you befriended Oliver. You've more colour in your cheeks now. You seem almost happy, even with me to put up with.'

So at least she knows she's a nightmare. I never would have pegged my great-aunt as being so self-aware.

'So if you've noticed the way I feel about Oliver . . . do you think he has?' I brace myself for Edme's answer.

'Oh yes. Certainly.'

I groan and throw myself face-down on to the bed. 'That's what I was afraid of,' I wail into my pillow.

Edme lays her hand on my back. 'What happened?'

I sit up again, sniffling. 'He kissed me. The other night when I went round for dinner. And I did a runner. And now he's calling and calling so he can tell me it was all a mistake and he never wants to see me again.'

Edme purses her lips and I'm sure I see a hint of a smile.

'Helena,' she says gravely. 'I would imagine Oliver wants to speak with you for a very different reason.'

'What?'

'Silly girl.' She takes my chin in her hand and tilts my head so I'm looking her square in the face. 'Oliver is quite smitten with you. Do you honestly not see it?'

God, the woman really has lost her marbles. The last few minutes of conversation must have been a fluke. 'He feels sorry for me, that's all. How could he possibly be, you know, romantically interested in someone like me?'

'Someone like you?'

'Yes! Look at me. I'm fat – well, usually – and unemployed and an emotional wreck. Oh, and there's my daughter, who was the product of a fling with an idiot. Yes, it's a wonder Oliver didn't sweep me off my feet the moment he laid eyes on me.'

Edme presses her hand to her mouth and I'm sure I see tears

welling in her eyes. 'My dear girl,' she says softly. 'It's a terrible thing if you truly believe all of that.'

I pick at the embroidery on the bedspread. 'I don't know what else I'm supposed to believe. The evidence is pretty compelling.'

'For a start, you are not fat. I think scrawny would be a more appropriate description. You need a few hearty Scottish meals, my dear. And secondly, why would Oliver kiss you if he wasn't interested?'

'I don't know,' I say with a shrug. 'Maybe he just thought I'd be an easy conquest.'

Edme shakes her head firmly. 'No,' she says. 'I know Oliver well. He's not that sort.'

'You're giving him too much credit, Edme. In my experience, they're *all* that sort. And as you said to me when I arrived, I'm not likely to be picky, am I?'

A shadow crosses Edme's face; she looks almost anguished for a moment. Neither of us has ever mentioned the day she called me a slut, but I know neither of us has forgotten it either.

There's a long silence. Finally, Edme says, 'I had a daughter.'

Well, tie me up and slap me with a haggis. That is *not* what I was expecting. As far as I know, my dad's only cousins are the children of his uncle Robert – the brother of Edme and my grandmother, Maggie. Edme has never married and I assumed she'd never had kids. Talk about skeletons in the cupboard.

'I didn't know that,' I say.

'Nobody does. Not your father, not Bob or Maggie. No one.' Edme's voice is strained, like she's trying hard not to cry. 'I gave her up.'

As she says it, it's like my vision zooms out. Edme suddenly seems tiny and far, far away. 'But . . . why? What happened?'

The tears spill over and Edme shakes her head sadly. 'It was 1960. I was twenty and living in Paris, playing at being an artist,' she says.

'I suppose I was quite good. I had an exhibition and I attracted the attention of a wealthy businessman. He was older, much older than me, and married. He promised me the world but failed to deliver it.'

'Oh, Edme.' I'm filled with a wrenching sadness for my great-aunt, for her lost daughter, for Ivy. And for myself.

'I was penniless, of course. It all seemed wonderfully bohemian and fun until I realised I'd have another mouth to feed. So when she was born, I gave her up.'

'To who?'

'To him.'

My breath catches in my throat. '*Him?* Why?'

Edme grows very still. 'He had so much money. He could feed and clothe her, send her to the best schools. Give her opportunities I never could.'

Her voice is flat, her words sound rehearsed. It's like she's speaking about someone else. I know this tactic well. I've used it when talking or thinking about Ivy lately. It's easier somehow.

I reach out to Edme and clasp her hand in mine. 'Did he keep in touch?'

'No. He told his wife the baby had been abandoned by one of the maids. I'm sure she suspected there was more to it, but she agreed to the adoption. They couldn't have children of their own.'

'Do you know what happened to your daughter?'

'I believe she became a lawyer and then a judge. But it's been difficult to keep track of her over the years,' Edme says.

'Why?'

'He changed her name. I called her Alice, after my mother, but he changed it to Antoinette. I didn't find that out until many years later.'

'But . . .' I shake my head, trying to take in everything Edme has told me. So many things suddenly make so much sense. The party girl I remember from my dad's photos, the drinking, the stalled career as an artist, the obscure teaching job, this hermit's existence in the middle of freaking nowhere. If I'd lost my daughter for good, I'd want to shut the world out, too.

'But you could contact her now! She'd be in her fifties. She's probably been desperate to find you all these years.' I'm growing excited at the prospect. I want desperately to make it all okay for Edme. If I could do that, maybe it would mean there's hope for me.

'Oh no!' She laughs dryly. 'He never would have told Alice that his wife was not her real mother. And she would have her own children now, maybe even grandchildren.' Edme shakes her head resolutely. 'I think about it often, but I don't feel it would be right.'

'So you're just going to sit here in this cottage and drink yourself to death instead?' I clamp my hands over my mouth a second too late; my harsh words have already escaped. I expect Edme to bristle and snap back at me but instead she smiles.

'I know no words of apology can make up for the things I've said and the way I've treated you, Helena,' she says softly. 'And I'm not looking for your sympathy. I made my choices and it's too late for me. But it's not too late for you.'

'What do you mean?'

'Don't make the same mistakes I did. Be a mother to your child.' She holds my gaze steadily and the desperation in her eyes is plain. She thinks I can offer her absolution.

In one way, Edme's story has had the desired effect. She's succeeded in making me want to run from the house all the way to Inverness and leap on to the next train to London to be with my daughter. But in another sense she's failed, because all the fears that led Edme to give her daughter up, I've had for Ivy, too. There's a very real chance I'll wreck my daughter's life through my own incompetence. Edme's sad tale actually reassures me that I did the right thing by leaving Ivy with Anna while I get myself together. The difference between us is that I know I could never give Ivy up for good, so she's stuck with whatever I've got to offer her. I don't know if that makes me braver than Edme, or weaker.

I muster a smile for Edme. 'I *am* her mother, for better or worse,' I tell her. And, maybe for the first time, I mean it.

'Good.' She wipes the tears briskly from her eyes. 'Now, what of Oliver?'

The woman is truly barking. One minute she's telling me not to repeat her mistakes – which clearly include bad taste in men – and to step up and protect my child. Next thing, she wants to gossip about boys.

'It doesn't seem important,' I say with a wave of my hand.

'Oh no, it *is* important,' Edme says. 'You are in love with this man. I'd wager he's in love with you. If you have a chance of happiness with him, a chance to give Ivy a father, you must take it.'

She speaks so earnestly that I wonder whether it's me she wants to see coupled up, or whether she's talking to some younger ghost of herself. Her words make me cringe, because it's not the first time I've mentally weighed up Oliver's potential suitability as a father.

Well before we kissed, I'd pictured us walking in a park with Ivy. I'd seen him bouncing her on his knee, dropping her at the school gates, interrogating her spotty teenage suitors, walking her down the aisle at her wedding. I've imagined Ivy's entire life in my mind, with Oliver slotted in as Daddy. Which makes me mistrust my feelings for him. Have I fallen for Oliver, or for the imagined family he and I could create for Ivy? Have I ranked the fact that he's sensible and gainfully employed and has no criminal record above what I really feel for him?

Do I even have a clue what I really feel for him?

'At the very least,' Edme goes on, 'you ought to let him explain himself. He's obviously in a lather, if all those ruddy phone calls are anything to go by.'

On cue, the phone in the hall starts shrieking again. Edme looks at me with one eyebrow raised, as if to say, 'I'm not getting it.'

With a groan, I heave myself up off the bed and trudge down-stairs. 'Hello.'

There's a pause. 'Helena?' Oliver sounds genuinely astonished to hear my voice.

'Yes. Hi.'

'Hi . . . how are you?'

'I'm okay.' *I'm in love with you!*

'Look, about the other night,' he begins, at the precise moment I say, 'I'm sorry I haven't called.'

We both stop and laugh. I sense the nervousness in his voice and my heart flutters a little.

Oliver lets out a long breath. 'I'd like to see you.'

So it's to be a face-to-face 'get stuffed'.

'I'll come over,' I reply. At least if I'm on his turf I get to be the one who walks away.

'Helena!' Niamh says, swooping in to peck me on the cheek at the front door. 'Did you and Oli have a row?'

'Um . . . no.' What has he said to her?

'He's in his room.' She ushers me inside. 'He's been there for days. I'm having some friends round for dinner and invited him to join us but he said no. He *never* turns down food.' Her eyes are full of concern.

'I'll get to the bottom of it,' I say with fake jollity, scurrying upstairs to Oliver's bedroom.

I've used the walk over here to figure out what I'm going to say. Or rather, what I'm not going to say. I'm definitely going to speak first, for one thing. I need to say our kiss was a mistake before Oli does. That way, when he agrees that our snog was a catastrophic error on his part, I may be able to save the tiniest bit of face. If by some miracle it's not a 'Thanks, but no thanks', I'm going to be sensible about it. I'll think only of my feelings for Oli, and not any excellent pseudo-father qualities he may possess. And I'm definitely not going to use the 'L word'.

It's a good, rational plan. I'm proud of my resolve. Except then I push open Oliver's bedroom door and see him sitting on his bed, strumming his guitar. He's wearing slippers.

Slippers.

Game over.

'Edme seems to think you have feelings for me,' I blurt. *Way to stick to the plan, Hel.*

'Edme's right,' Oliver replies without missing a beat.

'Oh! Okay . . . Are they good feelings or not-so-good feelings?'

He considers this for a moment. 'Well, I guess that depends.'

'On what?'

'Well, I've fallen in love with you,' he says simply. 'So if you feel the same way, they're good feelings. But if you want to run scream-ing from the house, then it's not so good. For me.'

He doesn't move from the bed and the expression on his face is nonchalant. But his right hand flicks his guitar pick over and over and over. He's terrified. God bless him.

'Good feelings then.'

Oli raises his eyebrows. 'Yeah?'

I nod. 'Yeah.'

Still he doesn't move. He's waiting for me to say it; to tell him I feel the same way. But if I say it aloud, there's no going back. I'll be laying my heart at his feet for him to do with as he pleases. He could stomp it into dust for all I know, and it wouldn't take much – it's pretty battered already. I should play my cards close to my chest, kick into self-preservation mode.

Or not.

'I love you, too.' I'm surprised at the conviction in my voice.

Oliver's cool facade instantly crumbles. He crosses the room in one stride, gathers me up in his arms and kisses me so hard he almost knocks the wind out of me. The hesitancy of our first kiss has vanished. I can feel how much Oliver wants me. I don't think I've ever felt that from a man, and it feels amazing.

There's hands and lips and tongues everywhere as we paw frantically at each other's clothes. As we tumble on to Oliver's bed, I hear a burst of laughter from downstairs. Niamh's friends. I'm so glad they're here to drown us out. There's nothing worse than hearing your flatmate getting it on.

Oliver kneels above me and swoops off his jumper. My breath catches in my throat and I can't take my eyes off his lean torso and chiselled arms, not because they're fit and toned and gorgeous (which they are), but because they're literally *covered* with tattoos.

From his collarbones to his waist, and his shoulders to his wrists, there's not a bare patch of skin. There are names and symbols, Latin phrases, tribal patterns and intricate, brightly coloured scenes. He's a walking work of art, and it's unbelievably sexy.

Oliver watches me studying his ink. 'Does it freak you out?' he says at length. 'It's not exactly the norm for a rural high-school teacher.'

'Not at all,' I say, shaking my head. 'It's beautiful. Though it does answer the question of why I've never seen you in short sleeves.'

Oli laughs. 'Turns out the Scottish climate comes in handy when you need to cover up five days out of seven.'

I want to examine Oli's tattoos further, but it feels like it would take days. And right now, I just want him inside me. I pull him down on top of me and kiss him urgently, arching my back and pushing my hips into his. He gets the message.

'You sure?' he says, pulling back and looking searchingly into my eyes.

I nod.

Oli smiles and, levering himself up onto one elbow, reaches over to his bedside table. He extracts a condom from the top drawer and I silently thank the universe for giving at least one of us a couple of brain cells. Contraception was the furthest thing from my mind, which is ironic given the situation that brought me to Gairloch in the first place.

I wriggle out of my jeans but leave my T-shirt on. While the whole 'so miserable I forgot to eat' thing has rid my body of the weight I gained during pregnancy, I don't think I need to introduce Oliver to my 'mummy tummy' and stretch-marked boobs just yet.

But when he's completely naked and has put the condom on, he pushes up my T-shirt and actually kisses my saggy skin.

'No!' I say sharply.

Oli looks up at me, alarmed. I laugh nervously and cross my hands over my belly. 'Sorry. It's just . . . it's not my favourite body part.' Understatement of the evening.

'Helena, you are so beautiful,' Oliver says.

I scoff and roll my eyes. 'You've already got me half-naked, Oli. You don't need to start lying now.'

I'm joking – sort of – but he props himself up on his elbow again and looks at me. Damn me and my big mouth. If I'd known it would stop the kissing I'd have kept my trap shut.

'I mean it. You're gorgeous,' he says.

He gently lifts one hand from my belly and guides it between his legs. 'See what you do to me?'

I feel rather than see, and it's impressive. Drawing a deep breath, I sit up and peel off my T-shirt, then unclip my bra. Physically I've only taken my clothes off, but emotionally I'm now completely and utterly naked.

I watch Oli's eyes sweep over my exposed flesh – ugly purple stretch marks, saggy boobs and all. Weirdly, he doesn't seem repulsed. In fact, the look on his face is sort of reverent.

'You're incredible,' he says, and at last starts kissing me again.

I feel my body tense as Oli's lips cover my boobs and tummy with kisses, but I don't stop him. And when he enters me, I can't think about anything except how good it feels.

It's not long before a delicious tingling starts to build in my pelvis. Chalk up another first for Oli – an actual orgasm. With other guys I've had to fake it and finish myself off after they've fallen asleep. The wave breaks over me and Oli smothers my cries with deep kisses. He comes a second later with a guttural moan that sends little electric chills right to my toes. He rolls over and wraps his arms around me, fitting his body around mine.

I want to say something memorable and profound to let him know what a huge deal this is for me. But what comes out is, 'That was amazing.' I cringe at my own cliché.

'Yes, it was,' Oliver replies, kissing my neck. '*You're* amazing.'

I lie there in post-orgasmic bliss for about three minutes, aware of nothing but Oli's warm breath on my skin and how absolutely, unutterably incredible it feels to be engulfed by his tattooed arms. But then my brain whirs into life and ruins it all.

Who am I kidding? This can't work. All we've done is sleep together – we haven't actually got anywhere. Oli may think he's in love with me, but this me isn't real. I can only ever be a holiday fling for Oliver, because *I'm* not real. This is me without my daughter. It's only a tiny, tiny fraction of my story.

I know Oli must see me as fragile and in need of fixing and he wants to make it right. But will he still feel that way when he's sleep-deprived and up to his elbows in shitty nappies and we haven't had sex for weeks?

That's assuming he even plans to stick around long enough to see that stuff. In a perfect world, I-love-yous and amazing sex are generally followed by some sort of relationship. But a perfect world doesn't tend to involve illegitimate children and the small issue of living in different hemispheres. I'm going to have to ask the question no man wants to hear after sex.

'Oli?'

'Hmm?' he murmurs.

'Um, where do you see this going?'

He squeezes me tighter. 'I see us both going to sleep for a bit, then waking up and doing that again. As many times as possible.'

I don't reply.

'You're serious, aren't you?' he says after a few seconds.

'Yes,' I say apologetically. I roll over to face him. 'I'm sorry to have to get all deep and meaningful on you, but . . .'

'Time is against us.'

I nod. I've promised to collect Ivy and, beyond that, I guess I should go home to Adelaide and face my parents. I'd love to be able to be the breezy, 'Hey, let's just relax and see where it goes' girl but I've got bigger decisions to make. Like what I'm going to do with my life to avoid wrecking my daughter's.

'I could come to London with you,' Oliver says.

My heart soars briefly at the thought that Oliver wants to go somewhere, anywhere, with me – then crashes to earth with a thud.

'But what about your job? You won't be able to just leave at a moment's notice.'

'I could try to arrange cover,' he suggests but I can tell by his tone that he knows the idea isn't feasible.

And anyway, I can't just turn up on Anna's doorstep with Oliver in tow. I've got so much ground to make up after the way I ran out on her and everything she's done for me in the meantime. I can just imagine the look on her face if she opens the door and sees me standing there with what she'll assume is the latest in a long line of loser boyfriends. If she sees Oli's tattoos, her head might explode.

Plus, there's the other thing. The thing the loved-up lunatic in me doesn't want to consider but the pragmatic mum can't ignore. Oliver coming to London with me would be just a stopgap; it's what lies beyond Blighty that matters.

'I've got a baby daughter, Oli. I don't expect you to be a father to someone else's child,' I say.

'A father?' he repeats.

'I know it's a scary concept but if we're going to be together that's what you'd be. It's not like she has any other male role models in her life.' I'm sure my dad will be more involved in Ivy's life in time but as long as my mother remains the puppeteer, he's not going to be much good to her.

'I'll be honest, I hadn't really thought about that side of things,' Oli admits. I can't read his expression in the darkened room. 'Is Ivy's real father around at all?'

For all the insights into my soul he's had in the past three weeks, Oliver doesn't know much about Adam. I've told him our relationship was short-lived and that Ivy and I haven't seen much of him since. But I haven't told him the full story.

'Adam has nothing to do with Ivy and if he ever tries to come anywhere near her, I will kill him.'

'Whoa.' Oli rolls away and clicks on the bedside lamp, then returns to lie next to me. 'What's the story?' he says, leaning his head on his arm.

God. I've got to tell him now. I have to reveal the thing that not even Anna knows.

I take a deep breath. 'Adam was, uh, not happy when I fell pregnant,' I begin slowly. If Oli thought I was broken before, he's going to think I'm beyond repair after this. 'He tried to get me to have an abortion and, when I wouldn't he resorted to threats and . . . things.'

'What kind of things?' Oli sits up, his face clouding. His voice is full of fear, but I don't feel afraid when I think about it anymore. I feel numb, like it happened to someone else.

'Well, I don't have any actual proof it was him but . . .'

'Helena.' Oliver takes my hand. 'What did he do to you?'

'I came home from uni one night to find my flat ransacked. I was about four months pregnant and all the baby things I'd bought or been given were destroyed or damaged.'

Oli's grip on my hand tightens. I can feel the anger radiating from him, but he doesn't speak.

'I don't have a lot of money and I couldn't afford to replace it all, even though most of it was secondhand anyway. Ivy still doesn't have a pram or a cot. It's lucky she's little and still fits in her bassinet.'

'What happened to this guy?' There's cold fury in Oliver's voice. 'I hope you went to the police.'

'And tell them what? Like I said, I didn't have any proof it was him. And even if I did, I wouldn't have pressed charges – I didn't want to give him even more reason to want to hurt me or my daughter.'

Oliver just shakes his head. 'But Helena, he deserves to be punished.'

'I know. But by trying to punish him I could have been risking Ivy's safety. That's not something I'm even willing to consider. And anyway, his punishment is never having the chance to be a father to my amazing little girl.'

Does he think I haven't thought about this? I search Oli's face for a sign that he understands. That he knows I wanted to hunt Adam down and rip him to pieces – still do – but that Ivy's life is more precious to me than any brief feeling of satisfaction that vengeance may give me. But all I read in Oliver's expression is confusion.

'I know what you're thinking,' I tell him.

'You do? What's that?'

'You're wondering why, if I'm so gung-ho about protecting my baby, I dumped her with my best mate and pissed off to Scotland.'

He's not the only one; I ask myself the same question about a hundred thousand times a day.

'You don't give me much credit, do you?' Oli says, but there's a smile in his tone. 'Hels, I think you're incredibly brave. You asked for help. You took the steps you felt you needed to take to be a better mother. A lot of people wouldn't be prepared to be accountable like that.'

He kisses me tenderly, entwining his hands in my hair. God, he's a sexy bloke. Not just because of the tatts and the hot body and the incredible sex – though those things are definitely part of it – but because he gets me. He really sees me and he seems to like me anyway. That's an unbelievable turn-on.

Oliver's kiss deepens. He presses his body against mine and I feel him growing hard again.

'Wait!' I pull away and try to catch my breath. 'I'm sorry. I want to do that again – definitely – but I don't think we're done talking.'

I hate being Little Miss Ruin the Moment, but I have to know where I stand.

'You're right,' Oli says, trying vainly to disguise the lustful glint in his eye.

'So . . . do you want to give this a go? Us, I mean?' I try not to sound too hopeful.

'Of course,' he replies softly, brushing a wisp of hair from my face.

'Okay. So we need to think about how it's going to work.' *If* it's going to work.

'Stay,' Oli says simply.

'What?'

'Stay. Don't go back to Australia.'

'But I live in Australia.'

'You said yourself there's nothing much for you there. You don't get on with your parents, your best friend is here. Stay with me, Helena.'

It seems such a simple solution. But maybe it's too simple. Could Ivy and I really live in Scotland? What Oliver says is probably true – there's really nothing for me in Adelaide now. My mum may eventually come round to the idea of having a grandchild, but she'll never be the sort of Mary Poppins grandmother Ivy deserves because she'll never forgive me for shaming her. She'll never stop punishing me. In small, subtle ways she'll manage to remind me every day for the rest of my life that I thoroughly screwed it up.

But if I stay in Gairloch we'll have Edme. I wouldn't expect her to become a doting great-great-aunt overnight, but I know our relationship has changed for the better. I think there's potential for us both to be of some use to each other.

'But I'd have to go back to London at least to get Ivy,' I muse aloud. 'I'm supposed to leave in a couple of days.'

'Why not stay a little longer?' Oli says. 'Just another week or so. We can spend some more time together, talk it all out.'

'What, are you trying to buy some time in case you decide you can't put up with someone else's brat after all?'

'Helena, come on. How many times do I have to say it: I love you. That means all of you, whether you have one baby or six.'

He looks hurt and I silently chastise myself for being such a cynical cow.

'I'm sorry. I think it's just going to take a while to get used to hearing you say you love me. Like about a century.'

'All the more reason to stay on an extra week,' Oli says. 'There's no point rushing off to get Ivy now, only to decide in a few days that you hate Gairloch and you actually can't stand me, even though I'm spectacular in bed.' He flashes an impish grin.

It makes sense. Though part of me wants to move quickly so that Oli doesn't change his mind, a bigger part knows I need to take some time to make sure I'm not going to change mine. Courage of conviction has never been one of my strengths.

'Okay . . .' I say.

'Okay? You'll stay a little longer?'

'Um, yes.' I throw back the covers and step out of bed.

'What are you doing? I think we should celebrate this momentous decision *in* the bed.' Oli pats the mattress beside him and gives me his best 'come hither' eyes.

But this can't wait. I have to move before I lose my nerve. I've been cowardly enough already where Anna's concerned.

'I have to make a phone call.'

Anna

'Hello?'

'Anna, it's Hel.'

'Oh. Hi.' I thought it might be Finn, calling to confirm what time his flight's due in tomorrow.

'Hi. How's Ivy?'

This is a turn-up. Last time I spoke to Helena she didn't even mention her daughter's name. I glance over at Ivy. She's sleeping soundly in her pram, even though I bashed it into the door frame about six times in my rush to get into the house and answer the phone.

'She's fine,' I tell Helena. 'She . . . she misses her mum though.'

'I miss her too,' Hel says wistfully, and I can tell she means it.

'Well, you'll see her in a couple of days.'

'Uh, yeah. About that.'

I'm instantly suspicious. Something in my best friend's voice tells me I'm not going to like what I'm about to hear.

'What about it?'

'Well, it's just . . . I've met someone.'

I'm lost for words. She has *got* to be kidding me. Only Helena could go somewhere populated almost entirely by fisherman and septuagenarian sheep farmers and pick up.

'His name is Oliver. He's a teacher and he's so amazing,' she blathers on. 'He loves me, Anna. And I'm in love with him.'

'You're in *love* with him? Are you fucking serious?'

'Look, I know what you must be thinking but —'

'No, Helena. You don't know what I must be thinking. You don't have a clue what I'm thinking, because you're too busy thinking about YOURSELF!'

I'm screeching but I don't care. It feels like my blood is boiling in my veins. I know what's coming next: she's not coming back. I can't believe she's doing this to me.

'You're not coming back, are you?'

'Of course! Of course I'm coming back,' she says. 'It's been hell being away from Ivy.'

Could have fooled me. 'What then?'

'Huh?'

'Well, if you're coming back in a couple of days like you said you would, why are you ringing to tell me about the amazing Oliver?'

'Can't I just ring my best friend to tell her I'm in love?' Helena sounds pissed off.

Once upon a time she definitely would have called just to dish about her latest dubious boyfriend, to tell me breathlessly that he's definitely The One. But that was before she had Ivy and hightailed it to Scotland; before I was left alone, literally holding the baby. Call it godmother's intuition, but this whole thing stinks to high heaven.

'Helena, just tell me what's going on.'

'I need you to keep Ivy an extra week,' she blurts as though the entire sentence is a single word.

'What? No!'

'Please, Anna! I just need a few more days with Oliver. I need time to work out if we have a future together. He loves me and I love him, but it's not that simple. I don't want to rush into anything.'

'Helena, I have to go back to work! I've used up all my leave and I'm broke. I have a life, you know!'

'Well . . . could Finn help?'

'Finn is *gone*. I'm doing this by myself.'

Helena is silent a moment. 'Please, An. For Ivy's sake.'

Manipulative so-and-so. 'You did not just say that.'

'Sorry. I'm sorry,' she says quickly. 'It's just . . . I can't explain it. Everything has changed in the last month, Anna. I've got the chance to make a proper life with Oliver, to give Ivy a family. I know I'm the worst best friend ever and I shouldn't be asking you this but . . . well, I *am* asking.'

Damn her. God *damn* her. She's turned my life upside down by forcing her child into it. My career's in the toilet, my relationship is teetering on the brink of oblivion. All because of the tiny bundle dreaming away in a pram in my hallway. But how can I say no to Helena? Yes, she has a chequered history of choosing thoroughly rotten boyfriends and she's proclaimed that every last one of them is Mr Right at some point. But what if this one really is different? She went to Scotland an absolute mess. The fact that this Oliver bloke managed to get through all that to reach her is a miracle in itself. And she's never been this sensible about any of the previous losers. Two years ago she wouldn't have even bothered telling me she'd be late back; she'd have just disappeared for another week, leaving me terrified she'd been dismembered or brainwashed by a cult.

But that was before Ivy. And if Hel is asking me to look after her daughter for one more week so she can decide if this guy is fit even to breathe the same air as Ivy, I don't see how I can refuse. The alternative is demanding Hel come back in a couple of days as planned, and if that means Ivy might miss out on having a man in her life who adores her like his own child, I wouldn't be much of a godmother.

'One week,' I say through gritted teeth. 'If you are not on my

doorstep by' – I check my watch – 'nine p.m. next Friday, you and I
will be having serious words.'

'Anna?' Helena says.

'What?'

'Out of all the people on this planet, I love you second most.'

'I know. Now piss off.'

Saturday morning dawns unseasonably warm and I'm woken by
Ivy chirping away like a songbird in her cot in the corner of my
bedroom. I pray her good mood lasts until Finn arrives. I'm debut-
ing my sexy lingerie, which will hopefully be followed by hot sex.
A squawking baby would be a bit of a passion-killer.

I fling back the bed covers, disturbing the little nest Nui has fash-
ioned for himself at the foot of the bed. He glares at me, most put out.

'Oi! You're lucky you're even up here, haughty little bugger!'

Suitably chastised, Nui closes his eyes and instantly falls asleep
again. Finn never lets Nui anywhere near the bed. He'd be horrified
if he knew the dog has developed somewhat amorous feelings for his
pillow. But hey, when the cat's away, the Boston terrier and the bitter girlfriend will play.

'Good morning, missy,' I greet Ivy as I throw back the curtains.
I peer into her cot and she rewards me with a gummy grin. She still
hasn't sprouted any teeth, thank goodness. If the horror stories I've
heard about teething babies are true, I'm not sure how well I would
cope. 'How's tricks?'

'Mum,' she says, clear as day.

'Uh . . . what's that now?'

'Mumumumumumum. Mum!' She grabs her foot and tries to
jam her big toe into her mouth, clearly proud of her efforts.

Oh my God. She called me Mum. This is unbelievable. Seven
months old and she can talk. Okay, so she's got it all wrong, but you

can hardly blame the poor lass for being confused, given she hasn't seen her real mother for a month.

But does Ivy calling me Mum break some sort of friendship code? I'm no expert, but it would probably be irksome to have your kid believing some other woman is her mother. I need a second opinion.

I lift Ivy out of her cot and sniff her business end. Fresh as a daisy. (It's always grossed me out when women do that, but I quickly learned it's definitely preferable to sticking your hand into a potentially soggy nappy.) I hoist Ivy on to my hip, jam my feet into ugg boots and head downstairs.

I step out the front door and am about to cross the road to Jen's house when I remember she and Andrew have taken the kids to the New Forest for the weekend.

Damn. I whirl around. It'll have to be Luke then. But just as I'm about to hop over the wall that separates our gardens, I hesitate. After my Freudian slip in the lingerie store, I'm not sure if running to Luke is the wisest course of action. Plus, at this hour of the morning I'm not exactly dressed for calling on attractive male graphic designers.

But I swore black and blue to Jen that Luke's and my relationship is purely platonic. I need a friend's advice right now, and if Luke really is a friend I guess there's no harm in it. Right?

'Ugh, enough with the analysis, Anna,' I mutter. Ivy offers me a quizzical look. 'You're quite right, poppet,' I tell her in a much jauntier voice than the chaos in my head warrants. 'Aunty Anna's overthinking things yet again. She should just get over herself, shouldn't she? Yes, she should!'

Squaring my shoulders, I walk briskly to Luke's house and hammer on the front door. He takes an age to answer it but when he finally does it's obvious I've dragged him out of bed.

'Bugger,' I say.

'Top of the morning to you too,' Luke replies, grinning sleepily. He's wearing baggy blue PJ bottoms and a white T-shirt and he looks kind of cute. In a rumpled, morning-breath sort of way.

'Sorry. I didn't realise it was so early.'

'You breeders never do. So selfish.' He's smiling as he says it.

Ivy squeals with delight at the sight of Luke. She'll probably start calling him Dad next.

'Anyway, I need your help,' I say. 'I think I've wrecked her.'

'What's up?' Luke's expression changes from cheeky to concerned and he reaches for Ivy.

'She just called me Mum,' I wail, handing her over.

'So?' He lifts her over his head and she flaps her arms like she's trying to take off.

'So? So I'm *not* her mum! Where did she learn this? Helena will think I've brainwashed her child!'

'Chill out there, stressy,' Luke says. He turns Ivy on to her belly and supports her with his forearm so she looks like a little superhero in mid-flight. 'You talk to her about Helena – her *mum* – all the time. She's probably just put two and two together.'

'And come up with five,' I mutter.

'Kids are like sponges. They pick up on everything,' Luke says. 'So you might want to reconsider greeting your neighbours with "bugger" first thing in the morning.' He ducks his head close to Ivy's and blows gently in her face, which she loves. She flutters her little eyelashes like a movie star.

'So I haven't ruined her? Helena won't hate me?'

'Helena should be giving you a medal after everything you've done for her,' Luke says under his breath. Then, 'Sorry, it's not my place to say. But no, you haven't ruined her. If anything, you should be happy she's such a little brainiac. Seven months is really young to start talking.'

'Mumumumumumum!' Ivy says on cue.

'Now you're just showing off,' Luke says, kissing Ivy on the nose and handing her back to me.

'Okay. Thank you,' I say, embarrassed that once again I've panicked for no reason. 'You can go back to bed now. Unless you fancy popping over for a coffee? You know, as thanks for answering the door to your crazy neighbour at such an ungodly hour.'

Luke squints into the early-morning sunlight. 'Why not?' he says, stepping outside and pulling his front door closed behind him.

'Oh! Okay. You didn't want to change first?'

'Ahem.' Luke looks pointedly at my sleeping attire, which consists of my cherished Van Halen T-shirt and a pair of men's boxer shorts. I'm deeply grateful I stopped to put a bra on before racing out the door.

'Point taken.'

I walk back to my house with Luke in tow. Once inside, I hand Ivy back to him and head to the kitchen to make the coffee. Luke follows, sitting at the kitchen table with Ivy on his knee.

'So, Van Halen?'

'I love them.' I'm daring him to diss them, and he knows it.

'Hagar or Roth?'

I give him my most withering look. What a stupid question. 'Um, Roth. Duh.'

'Did you just say "duh" to me?'

'Shut up and drink your coffee.' I plonk the steaming mug in front of him and plonk myself in the chair opposite.

Ivy immediately lunges to grab the cup but Luke scoots it beyond her reach. 'Check out the reflexes on this one! I never thought I'd say this but I reckon I'm going to miss you, little madam, when your mum comes back in a few days,' he tells Ivy.

'Mumumumumum!' she hoots.

'Actually, Ivy's staying another week,' I say.

Luke looks up, his face a mixture of surprise and delight. 'Really? How come?'

I recount last night's conversation with Helena, trying to keep my scorn to a minimum as I tell Luke about Hel's latest Mr Right.

'Well, that's just luverley,' Luke says to Ivy in his best cockney-geezer accent. 'Another week of fun for us then.' He launches into an enthusiastic game of peekaboo that quickly has Ivy howling with mirth.

I don't know that 'fun' is the word. While I must admit I'm happy that Ivy's sticking around a little longer, I don't know how I'm going to finagle another week off work.

I sip my coffee and observe Luke for a moment. He looks completely natural with Ivy in his lap, one arm looped around her waist like he's not even thinking about it. I, meanwhile, still want to strap a crash helmet on her every time I pick her up in case I drop her. Much as I love having Ivy, I just can't get used to it.

I realise I really don't know much about Luke at all. Most of our conversations to date have involved my yelling at him, moaning about Finn or decrying my faux parenting skills. I guess he struggles to get a word in. He's certainly never revealed why he's so freakishly competent with my goddaughter. For all I know, he could have a football team of his own children.

'Do you have kids?' I ask.

Luke splutters into his coffee. 'Where did that come from?' he asks through a fit of coughing.

I shrug. 'Sorry, it's just you're so good with Ivy and you said once you've had experience looking after kids. I didn't mean to pry.'

'No, no – you're not prying. You just took me by surprise.' Luke bounces Ivy up and down on his knee and gazes out the window.

'So . . . do you?'

'Do I what?'

'Have kids?'

'Christ no!'

'Oh.' I'm taken aback by the vehemence of his response. You'd have thought I'd just asked him if he enjoyed wearing women's underwear or something. I wait for Luke to continue but he's absorbed in tickling Ivy's tummy, making her squeal like a stuck pig. Taking the hint, I reach down to give Nui, who's sitting patiently at my feet, a scratch behind the ears.

'The thing is,' Luke says after what feels like an hour of awkward silence, 'I was pretty involved in bringing up my sisters and brother.' He speaks quietly and doesn't meet my gaze.

'Right . . . Can I ask why?'

He picks up his coffee cup and looks at me at last. 'When I was fifteen, my —'

'What the hell is this?'

I leap at least four feet in the air. Nui scrambles to his feet and begins barking furiously. Luke sploshes coffee on to the table. Even Ivy looks alarmed.

I turn to see Finn standing in the kitchen doorway, looking homicidal, his overnight bag at his feet.

'Good lord, Finn! Don't sneak up on me like that!' He shoots me an angry glare. 'Sorry babe,' I say as my heartbeat slows to something approaching normal. I walk over and kiss him on the lips. 'You just startled me. I wasn't expecting you 'til at least lunchtime.'

'Clearly.' Finn doesn't move or return my kiss. He just stares steely-eyed over my shoulder. I follow his gaze but all I see is Luke, sitting at the kitchen table drinking coffee. In his pyjamas.

Suddenly I see what Finn sees. Me and Luke, heads together over coffee, Ivy on Luke's lap. One happy little family.

'Oh! No, babe, it's not what you think. That's just Luke. From next door?' I gesture towards Luke in a 'Look what you've won!' sort of way.

'Awright, mate,' says Luke. There's no warmth in his greeting, which, weirdly, I find kind of gratifying.

'I know who he is,' Finn spits. 'What's he doing here, half-dressed, at seven in the morning?'

I know it must look a bit dodgy, but the fire in Finn's voice still surprises me. Surely he doesn't really think I've taken up with the bloke next door the second his back's turned? It's not like Finn to jump to conclusions – especially when the conclusion he's jumped to is such a cliché.

'He just helped me out with the baby, so I invited him in for a coffee. That's all.'

Finn is still glaring at Luke so I use my index finger to swivel his head to face me. 'That's. *All*.'

'Know a lot about babies, do you?' Finn asks Luke, hardly registering that I've even spoken.

'I do, as it happens,' Luke replies coolly. His south London accent makes his polite words sound menacing.

'Yeah?'

'Yeah.'

Finn seems to be spoiling for a fight but I'm relieved to see Luke's not taking the bait. He drains the last of his coffee and sets the mug on the table.

'I should be getting on,' he says. He stands up and hands Ivy to me. She's grown sombre, clearly enthralled by the proceedings. 'Thanks for the coffee, Anna. I'll see you around.'

'You don't have to go, Luke. Finn!' I toss my boyfriend an exasperated look but he doesn't say a word, just stares back at me with a petulant look on his face. 'Oh, for goodness sake.'

Luke pushes past Finn and I follow him into the hall. 'I'm really sorry about this,' I whisper as he opens the front door. 'I don't know what's got into him.'

'Don't worry about it,' he says, but his smile is guarded. He caresses Ivy's cheek. 'See you later, bubs.' She flashes him a big grin.

Luke lingers in the doorway. He looks uncomfortable. 'If you need anything . . .' he says quietly, nodding towards the kitchen, where I can hear Finn slamming cupboard doors and rattling crockery.

'Thanks, but don't worry about him. He's just tired and cranky. We'll be fine.' I hope my flippant tone hides the dread I feel.

'Anna, I know I shouldn't say this,' he says, lowering his voice to a barely audible whisper, 'but that guy is an arse. You deserve better.'

He walks away before I can respond.

Although I feel strangely flattered that Luke seems so concerned about my welfare, I also find it kind of irritating. Who is he to tell me what's good for me? I can practically hear Jen's voice in my head: 'See? I *told* you he fancies you!' But I still can't believe it. Luke may have listened to me whinge about Finn pretty much 24/7 for the past few weeks, but he must realise I'm just venting; that my complaints reflect only a tiny part of Finn's and my relationship.

As I walk back into the house, I resolve to put my grovelling hat on for a change. Finn might have overreacted, but I can't really blame him. I'd be pretty unimpressed if I walked into his kitchen in Belfast and found him and some woman looking like they'd just rolled out of the sack.

I find him in the kitchen, picking up Ivy's toys from the floor and flinging them into the washing basket that doubles as her toy box. I'm so surprised to see him tidying up that I stop in my tracks, my planned apology abruptly forgotten.

Finn looks up and sees me in the doorway. 'I'm sorry. I didn't mean to fly off the handle like that,' he says.

Now I'm really flummoxed. Not only is he tidying and not sulking, *he's* actually apologising to *me*.

'No, gorgeous, I'm sorry. I can imagine what you must have thought.' I walk over to him and wrap my arms around him.

'I didn't think, I just reacted,' Finn says into my neck. 'If I had thought about it I'd have realised there's no way you'd ever be interested in Parcel Nazi.'

Again, I find myself feeling inexplicably peeved. I want to tell

Finn that Luke's not the guy we had him pegged as – that he's actually funny and warm and doesn't mind me asking silly questions at all hours of the day (and sometimes the night). But in the interests of relationship preservation, I manage to hold my tongue.

What is wrong with me? One minute I'm annoyed at Luke for acting all proprietary, and the next I'm annoyed with *Finn* for not appreciating how special Luke is. It's like moaning about your mum: *you* can do it 'til you're blue in the face, but no one else is allowed to even think about it.

It's exhausting, and I resolve to stop thinking about it for the time being. I just want to enjoy having Finn in my arms for a moment. The weeks he's been gone have been full of such hurt and confusion and resentment they've felt like years. Now that he's here again, I realise how much I've missed him. 'I'm so glad you're home.'

'Me too,' he replies. Then, clocking my Van Halen T-shirt, 'Didn't I chuck that out? Like about forty times?'

'Oh, you love it really.' I duck out of his embrace and settle Ivy into her bouncy chair on the kitchen table. But I am annoyed at myself that Finn's arrived home when I look such a mess. I'd planned to be fake-tanned, blow-dried and wearing my new racy smalls when he turned up. Van Halen and boxer shorts is not exactly the 'must have you now' scenario I'd played out in my mind. Not that Finn seems to have bedroom shenanigans on his mind anyway. He watches me seriously as I buckle Ivy into her chair.

'What's up, babe?' I ask when it becomes unnerving.

Finn throws the plastic frog he's holding into the washing basket and sits down at the table. 'Sit down, An,' he says. 'There's something I need to talk to you about.'

Instantly, my heart starts thumping double-time. This can't be good. 'We need to talk' is never good. I need to feed Ivy. And bathe her, change her and dress her. But I sit.

Finn takes a deep breath and takes my hand in his. 'I know

things haven't been easy lately,' he says. 'And I know that's mostly my fault. Because of the Belfast thing.'

Like I need it pointed out.

'But even before I got this job things weren't quite right between us,' he goes on. 'We've been growing apart for a while.'

Oh. My. God. He's breaking up with me. 'We've been growing apart' is right up there with 'We need to talk' on the all-time break-up cliché charts. Next thing he'll tell me 'It's not you, it's me'.

'It's not you, Anna. It's me,' he says.

A strangled little cry escapes my lips. Finn looks alarmed.

'What?' he says.

'Are you breaking up with me? You are! You're breaking up with me, aren't you?!'

Hysteria is so becoming.

'What? Anna, no! Of course I'm not breaking up with you.'

His words are a little too emphatic for my liking. 'Then what? What's with all the end-of-relationship clichés?'

Finn buries his face in his hands. 'Christ, I've really cocked this up,' he mutters to himself.

'What is going on, Finn? Just spit it out!'

The pitch of my voice is reaching glass-shattering proportions. I'm not surprised to see Nui hightail it out of the room.

'This was supposed to be a happy moment,' Finn says with a sheepish smile. He clasps my hand again. 'I have a proposal to put to you.'

My poor heart stops its panicked pounding. In fact, I think it stops altogether for a moment. He's not breaking up with me. He's going to propose to me.

The prospect of marrying him fills me with more dread than the idea of not being with him. My stomach turns over and I feel like I'm going to vomit. Which isn't exactly the fairytale response to a marriage proposal.

It's not like I haven't thought about marrying Finn. Of course I have. In the heady early days of our relationship, it was all I thought about. We went to Las Vegas on holiday about a year into it and if he'd suggested getting hitched in the Little White Wedding Chapel, I was so in love I'd have done it without a second thought. But all that seems like such a long, long time ago. In the last year or so, the thought of one day becoming Mrs Cassidy hasn't really entered my head.

'An, I think I know how we can be close again,' Finn continues. 'Get things back to the way they were. We've always been so great together, don't you think?'

I nod mutely. If I try to speak I'm likely to blurt out 'nononono-noNO!', Tourette's style.

'Okay. So, what I want to ask you is . . .'

Oh God oh God oh God oh God oh God oh God.

'Anna, will you have my baby?'

What the *what*?

'Sorry?'

'I think we should have a baby,' he repeats. He's grinning like a nutter, as though he's just suggested we make a lasagne instead of a child.

'I thought you were going to ask me to marry you,' I murmur without thinking.

'What?' Finn looks as horrified by the idea as I am. 'Oh. Um, no. But having a child together would be an even stronger commitment to each other than some pointless piece of paper,' he says.

I shake my head vigorously in the hope it will induce a stroke and I won't have to continue with this conversation. No such luck.

'Finn, why on earth would you suggest having a kid? You *hate* kids.'

'I don't hate kids,' he says, though he looks slightly embarrassed. 'I think kids are great. And, more importantly, I think you're great with them.'

'So? I'm pretty good with sushi too, but I don't hear you suggesting we open a restaurant.'

'I'm serious,' he says, ignoring my lame attempt at humour. 'I've seen you with Ivy this past month. You're a different person. It's like you're, I don't know, fulfilled.'

'But you *haven't* seen me with her, Finn. You haven't been here. Are you saying that, if we were to have a baby, you'd quit your job and come back to London to be a dad? Or that we'd go home to Adelaide?'

I'd wager the thought hasn't even crossed his mind. But if it occurs to him now he doesn't show it.

'We'll work that stuff out. None of it would be important compared to the little life we could create.' He sounds so earnest. It's like he's swallowed one of those *A Mother's Love* books.

'And what about my career? I'm not about to just become some housewife.'

'You've said yourself you're ready to take a break from the showbiz stuff,' Finn says smoothly. 'This would be the perfect opportunity.'

I can't believe it – he actually does expect me to give up my job to look after his kid. I mean *our* kid.

'Take a break to do something different! Not just hang up my notebook and express breastmilk for the rest of my life!'

Finn gives a long-suffering sigh. 'Enough with the jokes. I'm not kidding here, Anna. I want to have a child with you.'

'But why? Why now?'

He looks away. 'I can't really explain it. Maybe it's like some male biological clock. I see you with Ivy and you're so fantastic with her, and I just know I want you to be the mother of my children.'

Child*ren* now? Is he imagining a Brangelina-style brood of anklebiters? Well, I'm no Angelina and Finn is a long way from Brad

Pitt. And even they didn't get the happily ever after.

I look over at Ivy, snoring softly in her bouncy chair. She is beautiful. And smart. And hilarious. And I'm definitely a lot more confident with her now than I was a month ago. But confident enough to want to do it full-time? With my own kid? My career would be over. Even if I went back to work, I wouldn't get far up the ladder. The women who become newspaper editors, or even assistant editors, devote their lives to it. They work ridiculous hours, sometimes even longer than the men because they're so desperate to prove themselves. Gender inequality and sexism is rife in the news media. Women with kids do not become editors. Women with kids become casual sub-editors or restaurant reviewers or gardening columnists. I don't know anything about gardening.

And I guess, if I'm totally honest with myself, I don't know that I can see Finn as the father of my kids.

During the fleeting moments I've ever pictured myself with rugrats of my own, I've always imagined them having a fun, hands-on dad who'd watch SpongeBob SquarePants with them in the morning and give me a damn good seeing to after dark. I just don't think Finn is that kind of guy.

Obviously the fact that I don't want to marry Finn and am ambivalent about producing a Cassidy heir opens up a whole other can of worms. But I can't even contemplate having the 'Where is this relationship going?' analysis marathon yet.

'I don't know, Finn,' I say, shaking my head slowly. 'There's so much to think about.'

'That's all I'm asking, babe. That you think about it,' Finn says. 'Promise me you will?'

I nod. As if I'll be able to think about anything else.

Helena

Oliver throws a copy of the *Highland Express* on to Edme's coffee table. 'Found it,' he says triumphantly.

'The newspaper?'

'Yeah,' he says, rolling his eyes. 'After an exhaustive search of the *Highland Express* rack at the Gairloch newsagency, I somehow managed to locate a copy.'

'Ooh, sarcasm. Clever.'

He throws a cushion at me and sits down next to me on Edme's worn couch. 'It's what's *in* the paper,' he says, planting a kiss on my forehead. 'Our house.'

My stomach lurches. 'Our . . . our house?'

Oli flips to the back of the paper. 'Check it out.' He taps a three-line listing in the 'Property for rent' column.

Gairloch, 2br ctg. O/F. Int ldy. Mdn ktch. Gdn. 500pcm.

'Office furniture? International lady? Golden? You want me to live in a golden house?'

Oli laughs and wraps his arms around me. 'Shall I translate?' he asks. 'We're looking at a two-bedroom cottage with an open fireplace, internal laundry, modern kitchen and a garden. For five hundred quid a month.'

'That sounds reasonable.'

'It's dirt-cheap! And in Gairloch!' He shakes his head in amazement. 'This being the Highlands, we don't have an especially dynamic rental market. Houses like this don't come up very often.'

'Well, that's lucky then.' I hope my voice doesn't sound as hollow to Oliver as it does to me.

'I'm going to call them,' he says, getting up and darting into the hall. 'We should see it as quickly as possible.'

As he picks up the telephone and dials the number, I quietly exhale. The tears I've been blinking back ever since Oli walked through the door spill over. I weep quietly as I hear him telling the owner of the cottage that he's looking for a family home for his partner and baby daughter.

What the hell is wrong with me? I should be dancing with joy that this gorgeous man not only loves me but wants to make a home for me and Ivy. So what am I doing sobbing into Edme's Afghan throw? I feel lower today than I have at any point since I arrived in the UK. Why? It doesn't make any sense.

Okay, I guess things have moved a bit quickly. We decided on Friday night that I'd stay an extra week and we'd try to get our heads around it all; now it's Tuesday afternoon and we're practically picking out our wedding china. From first roll in the hay to shacking up in three and a bit days is speedy, even for me. It's movie star pace – normal people just don't cover that sort of relationship ground so quickly.

But it's not the speed of things that's sent me spiralling back down to the depths of god-knows-where. It's not like I haven't set land speed records for declaring my undying love before, after all. It's something else, something I can't quite put my finger on. But whatever it is, it's not showing any signs of going away.

'Are you up for a walk?' Oli says, bouncing back into the sitting room. 'We can check out the cottage in an hour if —'

He stops speaking abruptly as he takes in my tearstained face. Curse my hyper-sensitive complexion. One tear and I puff up like a facelift gone wrong. Anna, meanwhile, could weep for a week and you wouldn't see a trace of it on her infuriatingly flawless skin.

'Hey, hey, hey,' Oliver says. He hurries over to me and folds me into his arms. 'What is it?'

'Oh, don't worry about me!' I wipe the tears from my eyes and give an 'I'm such a drama queen' laugh. 'Just a minor relapse,' I tell him. I'll say anything to avoid revealing that this whole thing is totally freaking me out.

Oli kisses me tenderly. 'I'm going to make you so happy, Helena. You know that, don't you?'

I nod and attempt a watery smile but don't reply. I can't, because if I try to speak I might scream.

'I'll go and look at the cottage on my own then,' he says, standing up. 'If it's great, we can check it out together later on.' He kisses me again and leaves with a wave.

The thing I couldn't put my finger on? Oliver has just bashed the nail on the head with a sledgehammer.

He's decided my happiness is his responsibility. He sees it as a job he has to do. I thought he'd seen through my frailty and brokenness and fallen in love with the kernel of the real me that lurks somewhere underneath. But he just wants to fix me the way he fixed the leaky tap in Edme's kitchen last week. And what happens to us when he realises parts of me just can't be mended?

I'm going to make you so happy. That's why the idea of living with Oli makes me cry. Have I made him think that I want to be fixed? By telling him I love him, and by letting him love me back, have I accidentally given him the impression that I need him to sort my life out for me?

I flinch as the front door bangs open. Edme sweeps into the hall looking windblown and ruddy-faced. Half of her long, russet-coloured hair has escaped its bun and her vivid woollen shawl and the hem of her skirt are covered with brambles and bits of twig.

'Helena, dear, you should be outdoors. It's such a glorious day!' she proclaims, rolling her r's in that exuberant way all Scots seem to do.

I can't help but smile at the enthusiasm in my great-aunt's voice. Since Edme told me about her lost daughter, it's as if a veil has lifted. She's somehow lighter and more vibrant; at times she seems almost happy.

She joins me on the sofa and the acrid odour of stale sherry stings my nostrils. She's still drinking – there haven't been any more naked meltdowns in the past few days but I know it will take more than one heart-to-heart to exorcise all of Edme's demons. In the meantime, I just keep hiding the sherry bottles and putting her to bed when she can't stand up.

'I'm not really in an outdoorsy mood today,' I say weakly.

She regards me gravely. 'What is it?' she asks gently. 'Where's Oliver? Did you have a quarrel?'

'No, no. Nothing like that. The opposite in fact. He's out right now looking at a cottage for us to rent.'

'Then why do you look so glum? Don't you want to be with Oliver?' She frowns.

'Yes! I think so. Oh, I don't know.' I hug my knees to my chest as Edme waits patiently for me to make some sense.

'I love Oliver. I do. And I want us to be together. It's just . . . it's all gathering so much momentum and I feel out of control.'

'I see,' Edme says.

'I don't feel like I chose any of this. All my life I've just kind of drifted into things without any say in it. I want this to be different. The irony is I probably would choose this anyway – me and Ivy, living with Oliver in our own little house.'

'But you feel Oliver has made that decision for you,' Edme says.

'Yes.'

'And you feel that, after everything that has happened of late, you're under tremendous pressure to make the right decisions for you and for Ivy.'

'Exactly.'

Edme smiles sadly and I know she's thinking of her own gut-wrenching decision nearly sixty years ago.

'You must tell Oliver,' she says matter-of-factly.

'No way! Are you serious? He'll think I'm the most ungrateful cow in history.' Clearly Edme's brain is still addled by the booze.

She presses her palm to my cheek and looks intently into my eyes. 'Helena, I want you to listen to me,' she says. 'You do not need to be grateful to Oliver for loving you. You are not undeserving of his love or anyone else's.'

Her words hit me like a broadside. It's true. I have been walking around feeling like Oliver's doing me the world's biggest favour by deigning to give me the time of day.

'Oliver loves you for you,' she goes on. 'I can see it. Every woman under forty in this village has thrown herself at him at some point in the past two years and he's not looked twice at any of them. You must believe me, my dear: Oliver is grateful to *you*.'

'So . . . you think he'd understand if I told him how I've been feeling?'

'I'm sure he will,' she says. 'Oliver is not a domineering fellow. You should see him at school – the children run rings around him, which is really quite unfortunate given he's the assistant principal. He wouldn't want to railroad you into anything you're not comfortable with.'

I'm suddenly so glad Edme's there to offer me some perspective – even if she is looking at the situation from the bottom of a sherry bottle. If anyone has the right to enrol at the All Men Are Bastards school of thought, it's Edme. But she always sees the best in Oliver. I feel faintly ashamed that she's had to convince me to do the same.

'I need to go back to London,' I say, more to myself than to Edme. 'I need to be with Ivy and figure all this out.'

Edme doesn't say anything, but I know the irony of my comment isn't lost on her. I left my daughter and came to Gairloch to find answers but all I've got are more questions.

'I need to go now. Tonight.' Now that I've said it aloud, I can feel my resolve crystallising by the second.

'If you feel it's the best thing,' Edme says. 'I shall miss you though, I must say.'

I look at my great-aunt, startled by her words. A month ago I'd have been less shocked if she'd recited *Fifty Shades of Grey* backwards. In Latin. But Edme's expression is sincere. The really weird thing is, I know I'll miss her too.

'You won't have a chance to miss me – I'll probably be back in a couple of days with my screaming kid in tow. Then you'll miss the peace and quiet!'

She smiles politely at my weak joke but her expression says she knows better. She doubts I'll ever be back.

And I don't know if she's right.

Hasty departures have become my thing, and I admit I'm tempted to leave without talking to Oliver. I don't trust myself to find the right words to explain to him why, even though I love him more than I've ever loved any man, I have to leave. And why I don't know when – or if – I'm coming back. But I know I owe it to him to try. Running away without a word to Oli would be the worst bad thing I've done to anyone.

Plus, I need him to drive me to the train station at Inverness.

I set off along the windswept road into town, hoping I'll meet him before I reach the village and the little house he wants to make our home. If I see the cottage and start picturing Oli reading storybooks to Ivy in front of an open fire, I fear I'll be signing the lease faster than I can say 'domestic bliss'.

My heartbeat quickens as I spy Oliver loping towards me about half a mile down the road. His face lights up when he sees me; he waves and breaks into a jog.

'Hey, beautiful,' he says when we meet. He wraps his arms around me and lifts me off the ground, twirling me around. 'Did you decide you want to see the cottage after all? We can head back into town. The landlord lives on the same street.'

'No, I was just . . . looking for you.'

'Cool. Well, the cottage is perfect! There's a little study off the main bedroom where Ivy can sleep until she's big enough to go into the second bedroom. Oh, and there's —'

'Oliver.'

'— a great bay window in the sitting room which looks out over the loch. But the —'

'Oli.'

'— best bit is the garden. It's massive! We could get a swing set for Ivy out there and —'

'*Oliver!*'

The volume of my voice surprises even me. He falls silent and stares at me, perplexed. 'What's the matter?' he asks.

'Nothing. Well, not *nothing*. I'm just . . . I kind of feel . . .' Great start, Hel.

'Helena, I know something's up. You were crying earlier, now you're yelling at me. You need to tell me what's going on.'

'I'm sorry. I didn't mean to yell,' I say glumly.

'What is it? You're starting to worry me.' There's anxiety in Oliver's voice.

'I need to go back to London to see Ivy.' The words tumble out on a rush of breath.

'I know. On Friday, right?'

'No. Not on Friday. Now. Today.'

'Why? Has something happened to Ivy?'

I shake my head. 'No, she's fine. At least, I think she's fine. I don't really know. That's the thing, Oli. I've been away from her for a month, so really, I have no idea.'

He strokes my arm. 'Look, I know you miss Ivy but —'

'I don't just miss her, Oli. I'm absolutely lost without her. I feel like I'm missing a limb.' I search for words that will better explain how profoundly I feel my daughter's absence but come up empty-handed. 'I came up here to sort my head out and I've done that. I know what I have to do now.'

'And what's that?'

'I have to be a mother, a proper mother, to my child.'

Oliver is quiet a moment. 'So what does that mean for us?' he asks softly.

I turn away from him and look out over the loch. It's bathed in the strange half-light that's so unique to the Highlands, where either dawn or dusk could be just a breath away at any given moment. It's a stunning vista, and I know I could be happy gazing at it every day from the bay window of our little cottage. But I can't just think about myself any more. It's taken me seven months, but I finally get it: every decision I make from now on, from where I live to what I eat for lunch, has to be made with Ivy in mind.

'It means I love you,' I say, turning back to Oliver. 'It means I want to be with you. But it also means I need time to decide whether moving to Gairloch is the best thing for my child. I can't afford to let other people make decisions for me any more.'

'I didn't mean to —' Oli starts, but I hold my hand up to stop him apologising.

'I know you didn't. I love that you want us to live with you. And I hope in time that's what will happen. But I need to think it through. Properly, you know?'

He nods.

'Aside from anything else, there's the practical stuff to consider. I have no money. We'd need residency visas. And what would I do for work? I don't really have any useful skills and it's not like Gairloch has a booming job market.'

'Sounds like you've made up your mind then,' Oli says, a trace of bitterness in his voice. It's his turn to look away, his face grim.

'I have.' I can't explain myself any more; I'm exhausted.

Minutes pass without either of us saying a word. The late-afternoon breeze has picked up and my skin prickles with cold. I silently berate myself for dashing out without my coat.

At last, Oli faces me again. 'I think I understand,' he says.

I throw my arms around him and kiss him deeply. He's said the perfect thing. Knowing he gets it means more than a million I love yous.

'But you are going to come back?' His voice catches as he asks.

I bite my lip, unsure how to reply. I know I love Oliver, but is my future in Gairloch? Is Ivy's future here? Suburban Adelaide isn't exactly cosmopolitan, but compared to Gairloch it's New York City. I don't know if I want Ivy to be a country girl. I want her to have every opportunity life can offer, and as beautiful as it is, a rural Scottish hamlet may be a little short on opportunities as she grows up. Splendid isolation isn't quite so splendid when you're fifteen and bored rigid. And if I decide not to come back, what does that mean for me and Oliver?

'I don't know,' I answer honestly. 'All I know is I want to be with you and I hope we can find a way to make that happen that's right for both of us.'

What I'm really saying is *I don't want you to rescue me.*

Oliver nods again and rubs his hands wearily over his stubbly chin. 'So when will you go? Tomorrow?'

'Today. I hoped you might drive me to the train.'

I know I'm pushing my luck and Oli looks incredulous for a moment, as if he can't believe I'd have the audacity to ask. Then he sighs and says, 'You won't make the last train to London tonight. I'll take you first thing in the morning.'

I stand on my tiptoes and kiss him on the forehead, trying valiantly to swallow the lump in my throat. 'Thank you.'

I move to pull away but Oli grips my shoulders and holds me in place, my lips still grazing his skin. 'Will you stay with me tonight?' he asks quietly, not looking at me.

My throat constricts even more and I feel tears prick my eyes. Oli's sadness is palpable; he thinks tonight is the last we'll spend together.

'Of course,' I tell him, wrapping my arms around his waist.

God help me if he's right.

Anna

On closer inspection, Cat Hubbard is something of a giantess. She must be at least six foot two, and in her Blahnik stilettos she looks positively Amazonian. She's all olive skin and enormous, liquid-brown eyes. Her hair, impossibly dark and glossy, plummets to her waist in artfully dishevelled waves. I may be slightly in love with her.

But what's most mesmerising about Cat Hubbard is her hips. As in, she has them. Not starved-to-perfection jutting supermodel hips, or the vaguely rounded variety that prompt magazine hacks to proclaim some skinny starlet a 'real woman' – but honest-to-God, child-bearing hips. She's like Nigella Lawson with a guitar.

I know I'm not the only one noticing this Earth Mother quality as Cat Hubbard works the room at her album launch party. The skinny girls watch aghast, as if offended by such a public admission of carbohydrate consumption; the men sneak furtive glances and adopt beatific expressions, no doubt picturing some clinch involving Cat in a meadow on a spring afternoon.

It does appear, however, that I am the only one seeing Cat Hubbard's hips in triplicate. I have broken the cardinal showbiz journalist's rule of reporting on such events: if you're going to quaff eighty thousand flutes of champagne, don't make the mistake of thinking one salmon blini is 'dinner'.

It had started as a nerve-calming tipple. I've been out of the loop for a month, and even after two years of rubbing shoulders with London's A-list they can still scare the bejesus out of me. But then Nicki Ford-Smith had swanned in, clinging like a limpet to the lead singer of some painfully hip indie band (there was no way she was going to miss another star-studded bash), and I was suddenly, crushingly reminded that I'm dateless once again.

Finn is supposed to be here with me. Though at pains to point out – regularly – just how trivial he thinks my work is, he's not above kissing the collective arse of movers and shakers if he thinks they can help him. Finn being a breathlessly ambitious television news reporter, and this being a bash entirely populated by powerful media types, he practically fell over himself in offering to escort me when the invitation arrived. And yet Finn is not here. After a weekend involving lots of discussion about whether or not we should procreate, and zero time actually spent between the sheets, Finn is back in Belfast, probably picking out wallpaper friezes depicting frolicking jungle animals for our hypothetical child's nursery.

But our talkfest really got us nowhere. I'm still utterly bewildered about whether I want to have Finn's baby. Or any man's baby, for that matter. Ever.

Shock, confusion, sheer desperation – I've felt them all since Finn dropped his baby bombshell. Mostly I feel angry; seriously pissed off that he's sprung this on me and not even had the decency to stick around and help me make this massive decision.

Now I'm firmly in the penultimate phase of the anger-confusion cycle: getting absolutely, positively, steaming drunk. (The ultimate phase being the nauseating hangover and associated humiliation I'll undoubtedly experience in the morning.)

'Ann-aaaah!'

Oh goody, it's Nicki Ford-Smith, gliding towards me clad in what looks like lingerie. This surely is the woman for whom the term 'snake-hipped' was invented. Her whip-thin figure and ability to wear spaghetti straps without the need for masking tape to keep her bust in place makes me want to move into the nearest Krispy Kreme store.

'I was just telling Pad all about you,' she breathes. 'Pad, this is my colleague, Anna Harding.'

Strangely, there's no animosity in her voice. She's either forgiven me from banning her from the Benedict Cumberbatch premiere, or she's even better at fake friendliness than I gave her credit for. I suspect it's probably the latter.

'Passnoraname,' I slur.

'Er, what's that, Anna?' says Pad, who is really rather gorgeous.

'Pad. It's not a name. It's stationery.'

'Right. Um, well, it's short for Padraig. It's Irish.'

'Ha!' I snort. 'And are *you* Irish?'

'Pad's from Belfast, Anna. He's with that new band, The Chevrons. You wrote about them last month. Before your little . . . hiatus.'

'Belfast, is it? That's very interesting because my bast—'

'Oh look, Pad. It's Lily Allen. Let's go say hello!' Nicki shoots me a death stare and steers her conquest away.

I fumble my way through the dark bar and slump miserably on a chair in a corner. I really don't want to be here. Well, that's not entirely true. I *did* want to be here when I first got Cat's invitation. I thought then that tonight would be my glittering return to the showbiz scene. Helena would have returned for Ivy, and I'd be rested and raring to get back to work. My scandal radar would be fully recharged and I'd dig up some first-class dirt and get myself back in Girish's good books.

Except that, like everything else in my life in the past month, it hasn't worked out the way I planned it. At all.

Helena hasn't turned up to collect her child, who is currently with Luke. Though he's fast become Ivy's favourite playmate, I've never left her with him for any length of time. I wouldn't have done it tonight, but Jen's at some black tie work function with Andrew and Luke was my only option. At least forty thousand of the flutes of champers were downed in an attempt to assuage my guilt at having abandoned Ivy with yet another random.

I even tried to get out of coming tonight, but when I pleaded with Girish for a few more days off, he would only agree if I'd cover the party. Apparently Nicki still hasn't redeemed herself in the wake of the Benedict Cumberbatch disaster, and a personal invite from pop music's current 'It Girl' is too valuable to entrust to a grown woman who admits she's a One Direction fan.

But as I watch Nicki now, seamlessly working the room with Mr Stationery on her arm, chatting away with celebrities it would take Showbiz Anna all night to muster the courage to even look at, I wonder if perhaps she *is* better at this than I am.

Obviously she's dumber than mud and couldn't write her way out of a Chanel clutch bag, but she sure seems to have the passion for schmoozing. I don't have that – I don't know if I *ever* had it. Most famous folk will wave you away when they find out you're a tabloid hack, but this lot are chatting with Nicki like she's their next-door neighbour. You can't put a price on that sort of access.

'Ohhh God. My feet!'

Cat Hubbard flops into the chair next to mine and kicks off her Blahniks. 'Oh sorry! Hope you don't mind me crashing your corner,' she says, mistaking my confused and inebriated expression for annoyance.

'No worries, Cat!' I say too enthusiastically.

Cat frowns slightly. 'We've met before, haven't we?'

I try nodding but it makes the room spin. 'At the *Sherlock* thing.'

I'm not surprised she doesn't remember me. Celebrities never do, even the ones I've met several times. I have a forgettable face. Which is probably handy, given how many of them I've written truly salacious things about.

'Of course! You're Anna. The writer, right?'

'Ahh . . . right.' Another lie comes back to haunt me.

'I'm glad you could make it,' Cat says warmly. 'It's nice to have another normal person here. I can't bear these fucking sycophants. "Ooh Cat, your album's so brilliant! Ooh Cat, let's do lunch! Ooh Cat, who are you wearing?" *Who* am I wearing? I'm just wearing a fucking dress, you know?'

'Totally,' I say, even though I have no idea what it's like to be swathed in designer couture. *Free* designer couture.

'I mean, I'm not complaining, because hopefully all these ridiculous PR exercises will translate into album sales. It would just be nice if even one of these arseholes gave a toss about the actual music.'

Cat's obviously had a few beverages too because her usual plummy north London accent is melting into an almost cockney drawl that's not unlike Luke's. I make a mental note: has our golden girl not been entirely honest about her geographical origins?

'Well, I *have* heard the album and I *do* think it's brilliant,' I say in what I hope is a heartfelt, non-sycophantic arsehole way.

'Thanks, babe,' Cat says. 'I appreciate it coming from you because you know what it's like, don't you?'

'Um . . . do I?' Oh yeah, I'm *totally* familiar with the life of a rock princess.

'Yeah, man! We're both writers, innit? I write songs and you write . . . things and we're both just artists with mouths to feed.' She punctuates every other word with stabbing hand gestures and even in my tipsy state I sense I should move my champagne flute out of harm's way.

'Oh, right. Absolutely. We're artists trying to put food on the table.' I gulp my drink so she won't see my shame. Artist indeed.

'How is your little girl, by the way? Decided not to bring her this time?'

The woman has a memory like a steel trap when it comes to the fibs I've told her.

'She's great. She's at home tonight.'

'With Daddy?'

'Ah, with a friend actually.'

'Oh.' Cat gives a knowing smile and taps her index finger against the side of her nose. 'Say no more. My kid's dad's not in the picture either.' She rolls her eyes in an 'all men are bastards' fashion.

'You have a kid? I didn't know that.' I try to sound casual but my heart starts to pound the way it always does when I'm poised to make a fresh celebrity kill.

'No one does. I'm not supposed to talk about him,' she says.

'Why not?'

'Oh, you know, he doesn't fit in with the sexy rock-star vibe or some bollocks. And also because I haven't always been Mother of the Year material.'

Oh God. I feel like a tiger circling a wounded gazelle. Cat's either about to flee or expose her jugular and let me tear her throat out.

'Ha! Tell me about it.' I'm trying desperately to keep her talking. 'I tried to feed my – Ivy a curry once.'

'Well, there were times when I didn't try to feed Riley at all.'

I stare at her in a most unladylike fashion. 'What do you mean?'

'I used to be into the drugs,' she says and there's not a trace of reticence in her face or voice as she prepares to confide in me. The booze has clearly numbed all her inhibitions. 'My loser ex-husband had disappeared into thin air. We were living in a shitty council flat in Lewisham and I was spending most of my money on crack. Riley was about three, way underweight, sick all the time. Eventually the council took him into care.'

'Oh my God,' I say, but it's not Cat's awful story that astonishes me. I knew about her past drug problems. Everybody does – the 'bad girl made good' story is a key element of Cat's carefully choreographed public persona. And it works. The fact that she kicked drugs and now calls some of London's brightest young things her friends makes her a source of endless fascination – and tabloid fodder. I even knew about her ill-fated marriage, thanks to Nicki.

What blows me away is that I had no clue about her child. I'm grudgingly impressed that her 'people' have managed to keep his existence under wraps. I'm also disgusted. I can't believe her publicity machine would be so cynical as to play up her drug addiction like it's a badge of honour but force her to hide her son like some dirty little secret. That's low, even for this business.

I'm suddenly consumed with a renewed loathing of celebrity culture and all the bastards that propagate it. Myself included. But I'm also astounded no tabloid has found out about Riley. Cat's people must have him locked up tight.

'Does Riley live with you now?' I ask.

'Oh yeah. He was only in care a few weeks, but they were the longest weeks of my life. It was one hell of a wake-up call for me. I got clean quick-smart after that and haven't touched an illegal substance since,' she says. 'Riley's nine now and an absolute little champion.'

I do the maths and realise Cat must have had her son at seventeen. Teenage pregnancy! Drugs! Kid taken away! A million-selling album! It's just too juicy for words. It's the story that will save my career. I can see the headline now: *Bad Mother Hubbard*.

'I'm just going to nip to the loo,' I tell Cat. 'Want me to bring you back a drink?' The least I can do is 'buy' her a free cocktail.

'Thanks, babe, but I don't touch the hard stuff.' She raises her champagne flute. 'This is just fizzy water. Anyway, I've gotta go mingle. I can see my publicist giving me the evil eye from the other end of the bar,' she says. 'Good talking to you, though.'

'You too.' She doesn't know just *how* great.

Cat stands and smooths her designer dress, then squares her shoulders and swaggers back into the crowd. She's immediately enveloped by a swarm of buzzing hangers-on. I grab my mobile phone and dart to the back of the venue, frantically punching in Girish's number as I step out into the back alley. It's late but I know Girish will still be in the office; the man has no life outside *The Mirror*.

'Hello, this is Girish Thakkar, news editor at *The Mirror*. Please leave me a message.'

I wait impatiently for the beep. 'Girish! Call me back immediately. Massive scoop! Immediately, do you understand? *Immediately* . . . oh, um, it's Anna.'

I snap my phone shut and ponder what to do next. Though it seems unlikely, I suppose there's a slim chance Girish might have actually left the office and won't get my message.

Should I just go to the office myself? Or go home and file the story from my laptop? It simply has to go in tomorrow's paper; it definitely can't wait until Thursday's edition. This is proper 'stop the presses' stuff. And if Cat's feeling as loose-lipped with any of the other reporters here as she was with me, it might not be our exclusive for much longer.

'Has anyone ever told you that you shout when you're drunk, Anna?'

I pivot on my heel to see Nicki leaning casually against the club's back door, baring her teeth in her inimitable style (and blocking my escape route).

'Where's Post-It?'

She narrows her eyes. 'If you mean Pad, he's inside talking to Rita Ora.'

'Shouldn't you be draped over him?' I flash my most condescending smile.

'It's not like we need to spend every second together, Anna,' she says, rolling her eyes. 'Unlike some people, I know that when my man leaves he's actually going to come back.' She plants her hands on her skinny hips and tilts her chin defiantly.

'What's that supposed to mean?'

'Anyway,' she says, ignoring my question. 'If I were you, I'd be less concerned about Pad's whereabouts and more worried about why Girish isn't answering his phone.'

I look at the phone in my hand, then back at Nicki. Something stinks in Soho and this smug little wannabe is obviously behind it.

'Why don't you enlighten me?' I say coldly. I'll be damned if I'm going to let her see me sweat.

Nicki walks around me in a slow circle, clearly relishing every moment she has me at her mercy. Eventually she stops dead in front of me, her nose just a polyester-hair extension-width from mine.

'I would imagine,' she purrs, 'that Girish is not at his desk because he's in Nigel's office, asking him to hold the front page.'

'And why would he be doing that?' I'm close enough to knock out her perfect white front teeth with one punch.

'Because Girish has a hell of a story on his hands.' Her smile vanishes, replaced by a look of sheer, unadulterated hatred.

'For Christ's sake, stop acting like some bad Bond villain and just tell me what you've done.'

Her steely expression falters for a second as she realises I'm not about to just lie down and beg for her mercy. I don't know what it is about Nicki that allows me to override my usual fear of confrontation and just tell her exactly what I'm thinking. My total lack of respect for her, probably. Whatever it is, I like it.

'It's the showbiz exclusive of the year, Anna,' she says, recovering quickly. 'Cat Hubbard has a kid who was taken into care because she was a crackhead.'

I think Nicki keeps talking, keeps relaying my story back to me, but I can't hear her. It feels like the street beneath my feet drops away and I'm falling, tumbling and twisting through the air with no idea where or when I'm going to hit the ground – but knowing with absolute certainty that I will. And that it's going to hurt.

'But . . . how? How did you know?' My question seems to come from somewhere far behind me.

'Like I said, you shout when you're drunk,' Nicki says gleefully. 'About half the bar could hear the pair of you. But most of them are Cat's mates and already know all the nasty details of her murky past. Not one of them realised she was baring her soul to the lowest sort of trash hack. Which is lucky for me.'

'You've told Girish then?'

'Of course. Tomorrow's splash: *Bad Mother Hubbard*.'

She looks so thoroughly satisfied with herself it's disturbing. There's not the faintest glimmer of regret that she's stolen my story and most probably sunk my career. Which is probably to be expected. But, even worse, Nicki's gormless face displays not even a trace of recognition that with one phone call to Girish she may have put a mother's relationship with her son in real danger. She just does not give a shit. Is that what *I'm* like? Would I really have thrown Cat under the metaphorical bus if Girish had picked up the phone?

At once, the feeling of freefalling gives way to an agonising, technicolour clarity.

No.

That's not what I'm like. It's what I *was* like, without question. I've screwed over more celebrities than I've had pedicures, for the most part without a second (or first) thought about the damage I might cause. And yes, I was all set to do the same thing to Cat. But not anymore. I can't be Showbiz Anna anymore.

I don't know whether it's having Ivy or not having had a job for the last month. Maybe it's Finn or Helena or even Luke. But I do know that Showbiz Anna isn't who I am.

Everyday Anna is all I've really got – all I've ever had, I realise – and from now on that will have to be enough.

'Congratulations, Nicki,' I tell her. 'Great scoop. Definitely worthy of promotion to showbiz editor.'

Her face is a mask of confusion. 'What are you talking about?' she spits.

'I'm saying the job's yours. You've wanted it for a year and you're welcome to it. You are now officially the lowest sort of trash hack. Well done you.'

I push past her and dive back into the mass of bodies in the bar. Scanning the darkened room frantically, I spot Cat standing to the side of the makeshift stage, waiting for her cue to perform her latest single.

'Cat!' I shout but my voice is swallowed by the white noise of two hundred voices. I shove my way through the crowd, elbowing Premiership footballers and stomping on the polished toes of Page Three girls. Eventually I reach her. 'Cat!'

I grab her arm and she spins to face me, startled. When she sees it's me and not some crazed fan (though the crazed part definitely applies), she visibly relaxes.

'Hey, Anna,' she says. 'You made me jump. I'm just about to play a song but I'll catch you after?' She holds up her guitar as if to prove she is indeed about to perform.

I shake my head. 'This can't wait,' I say.

Cat frowns, whether from confusion or annoyance I can't tell. Probably both. 'What is it?'

'I've been lying to you, Cat. I'm not a writer. I mean, I am but not of anything important or even useful,' I blather.

Now her expression definitely says 'confused'.

'I work for *The Mirror*.'

'And?'

And? Can't she see what I'm getting at? I'm starting to question whether it really was just fizzy water in her glass. 'And you just told me all that stuff about your son, stuff no one's supposed to know.'

Cat bristles. 'You didn't tell anyone, did you?'

'No, but I was about to. I called my editor but he wasn't there, and then I realised that I didn't want to tell him anyway. I didn't want to . . . to do that to you.'

Cat considers this for a moment. 'So there's no problem then,' she says slowly.

God, she's actually considering letting me off the hook after I've been such a two-faced bitch. I want to fling my arms around her and thank her for letting me believe I still have an ounce of humanity in my twisted soul. But, of course, I haven't told her the worst bit.

'Well, there *is* a problem. My . . . *colleague*' – I still can't believe I have to refer to Nicki as my professional equal – 'overheard our conversation. She told my editor.'

Cat sighs impatiently. 'What exactly are you telling me here, Anna?' she shouts above the bar's monotonous R&B soundtrack.

'It's tomorrow's front page. *Bad Mother Hubbard*.'

Cat smiles at this. She actually smiles. I was expecting a slap across the face. Or some hair-pulling.

'I am so, so sorry, Cat.'

A leggy publicist suddenly appears by her side. 'Ready, Cat?' she trills. 'Leon's all set to introduce you.'

'Give me thirty seconds, Holly,' Cat replies.

'It's Molly.' The girl pouts as she sashays back into the crowd.

Cat turns back to me. 'Thank you,' she says.

'Huh?'

'Thank you,' Cat repeats. 'I know who you are. You're Anna Harding, *The Mirror*'s showbiz editor. I've known all along – ever since we met at the premiere. I sent the invitation to this little shindig to your *work* address, remember?'

And I'm in freefall once again. The background hubbub seems

to recede so that everything Cat says is crystal-clear.

'But then . . . why tell me all that?'

Cat shrugs. 'I'm sick of lying about my son. I can't even take him to the park any more in case a pap snaps us together. It's not fair to Riley and I've had enough of it,' she says.

'So why not tell the press yourself? Or let one of the paps get that shot?'

'It's a condition of my contract with this lot' – she jerks her head towards the gaggle of record-company suits lounging by the bar – 'that, whenever speaking publicly, I maintain that I am single and childless. They think I'll lose my cred if people find out I spend my Friday nights watching *Dr Who* DVDs with my kid. Or that the public won't be of a mind to forgive me and will stop buying my records if the story I told you gets out.'

'That's crazy.' I just can't get my head around any of this.

'Is it? Would you be as interested in Brand Kanye West if you knew he was reading bedtime stories to his kids every night instead of whatever insane thing he's done this week? People like their rock stars to come with a side order of nuts. But *women* rock stars have to be selfless, devoted mothers above all else. That's why they made such a big thing out of my drug use and buried the rest.'

'But everyone will find out about Riley now. And not just that he exists, but that there was a time you couldn't look after him. Even if you didn't breach your contract, you know people will judge you.'

'Well, my plan didn't unfold entirely as I'd hoped,' she admits. 'When I saw you at the premiere with your little one, I thought perhaps if I told you about Riley you might handle it a bit more sensitively than any of these other hacks.'

God, if sensitivity is what she's after, she's definitely not going to like whatever drivel Nicki Ford-Smith churns out.

'I've got to tell you, Cat, the girl who's writing the story has all the sensitivity of a serial killer.'

'You know what, Anna? That's cool. I don't care what happens now. Riley is the most important thing to me. If all this' – she gestures to the fancy venue and the sycophants and arseholes – 'disappears tomorrow, I'll just get a day job. I'll start again. I've done it plenty of times already.'

Hips *and* principles. I am definitely a little in love with Cat Hubbard.

The leggy publicist reappears by Cat's elbow. 'Um, Cat?' she says. 'Leon's getting impatient.'

'Well, we wouldn't want that, would we?' Cat replies with a wink. She slings her guitar strap over one shoulder.

'Cat, wait.' I grab her wrist. 'So are we okay? Do you forgive me?'

I don't know why it matters; I've never apologised to a celebrity before, no matter how severely I've screwed them over. And besides, I was just a pawn in Cat's grand scheme. But somehow, knowing she doesn't hate me suddenly matters a hell of a lot.

'Well, no. We're not *okay*, Anna,' she says, wresting her arm free of my grip. 'You lied to me and, whether you meant to or not, you've probably done my career some serious damage.'

I hang my head in shame. I'm a cockroach. No, worse than a cockroach. I'm a dung beetle trailing behind a cockroach hoping to pick up its droppings.

'But,' Cat goes on, 'I know why you did it. You did it because you've got a job to do and a mouth to feed, just like me. So in that sense, yes – I forgive you.'

And just like that, she sweeps on to the stage to rapturous applause, leaving me slack-jawed in the wings. Even though her for-giveness is based on yet another of my lies – that Ivy is my biological child, or at least my permanent responsibility – I can't believe she would be so magnanimous. I know with certainty there's no way I could turn the other cheek if someone betrayed me so spectacularly.

As Cat tears into her latest single, I leg it. On the street, it's started raining but I don't hail a cab. Instead, I walk to Waterloo station, which takes a good forty minutes. When I arrive, I'm sodden and cold but mercifully sober. And I've made up my mind.

I step onto the next fast train to Richmond and pull out my mobile phone. Again, Girish's number diverts to voicemail.

'Girish, it's Anna. I know Nicki has thrilled you all beyond words with the story about Cat Hubbard's son – which, by the way, she stole from me. I also know there's no chance you won't run it, so I won't bother asking. But I am asking you not to completely crucify Cat. You're a parent, Girish. Just go a tiny bit easy. Also, I quit. You were probably going to sack me anyway but I quit nevertheless. Effective immediately. I can't do it any more. Well, I can – I just don't want to. I don't want to be this person. Anyway, I'm rambling. The point is, I'm done. You can call me back if you want but I probably won't answer. Goodbye.'

He does call me back, within about fifteen seconds in fact. And he keeps calling all the way to Richmond, though I switch my phone to silent after the third call. He leaves messages too, but I don't listen to them.

I'm sure I'm breaching the terms of my contract and that by law I'm probably required to serve a 999-year notice period and give up a kidney or something, but right now I don't care. That's Tomorrow Anna's problem.

The train pulls in and I jump in a black cab at the front of the station. As the cabbie drives towards my house, blatantly sneaking glances down my top in the rear-view mirror, I try to formulate some sort of plan.

I would say I've roundly dashed my chances of ever working for a national newspaper again, not that I particularly want to. Which leaves the suburban rags, magazines and online publications or PR. And I would rather pull out my own fingernails than work in PR. At least I've got options. There are always options. Whatever happens, I'm feeling surprisingly good about my decision.

Until I walk in my front door and see Luke sprawled out on the couch, fast asleep, with Ivy snoozing on his broad chest. Damn it all to hell.

What was I thinking? I can't leave my job! I have a baby to look after, at least for a few more days. And maybe after that, I'll have a child of my own to prepare for. I have rent and bills to pay, plus a garbage disposal of a dog to feed.

Perhaps I emit some sort of desperate little squeak, because Luke wakes with a start. I think he'd have leapt off the couch as well, but fortunately he remembers Ivy at the last minute.

'Anna,' he says sleepily, looking suddenly awkward in his prostrate position, like a turtle flipped onto its back. His black hair is sticking up in all directions. 'What time is it? How was the thing?'

I can't answer. It feels as if I'm rooted to the spot, sheer panic threatening to engulf me.

Seeing the look on my face, Luke sits up slowly, cradling Ivy and gently placing her on the seat next to him. She stirs momentarily but doesn't wake.

'What happened? Are you okay?'

I shake my head as fat tears roll down my cheeks. Lordy, I am pathetic. Why, why, *why* is Luke always around to see me freak out?

'Come and sit down.' He raises himself half up and reaches out for my hand, guiding me to the sofa. I sit gingerly, Ivy between us.

'I just quit my job,' I tell him. It's the first time I've said it aloud and it comes out more like a question than a statement.

'Whoa. That's great,' Luke says.

Not quite the reaction I was expecting.

'I'm sorry?'

He shrugs. 'You're better than that job, Anna,' he says simply.

I can't bring myself to argue; I know he's right. It's just weird to hear him say it – Finn never would. To him, any occupation that puts someone in the public eye is something to be hung onto at all costs. But knowing that I'm capable of more than ranking boy band members on a Shagability Meter isn't going to put dog biscuits in Nui's bowl.

'I'm a fraud. I told a terrible lie that could cause real problems for someone who doesn't deserve it. My editor would've sacked me if I hadn't quit.' I hide my mascara-streaked face behind my hands as the tears flow harder.

'But on the bright side, now you can spend all your time with Ivy and not have to worry you're missing some earth-shattering celebrity scandal,' Luke says cheerily.

I know he's trying to cheer me up, but it just makes me feel worse.

'What good am I to her?' I spit. 'This entire month has been a nightmare. The sooner she's rid of me, the better off she'll be.'

Luke looks taken aback. 'Are you for real? Name one thing about this month that's been nightmarish.'

I catalogue the disasters on my fingers. 'Um, best friend's done a runner. Career's officially over. Boyfriend's pissed off to Ireland.'

'I mean in terms of Ivy,' he says, exasperated.

'Ha! How long have you got? Let's start with the infamous chicken tikka incident, shall we? Then there's the fact that she hasn't slept through the night since she's been here. And, of course, the small matter of my dumping her with a total stranger so I could go to a party.'

Luke looks a little crestfallen.

'I'm sorry,' I say wearily. 'You're not a stranger. You're . . . a friend. A good friend.' Even as I say it, I feel like I'm treading on dangerous ground. 'Though I don't know why you put up with me when I've been badgering you with constant, stupid baby questions for weeks.'

'I don't mind that,' Luke says softly.

'She's probably better off with you than she is with me anyhow.'

'Stop selling yourself short,' he says, rubbing my back. 'You're amazing. With Ivy.' He clears his throat. 'You're amazing with Ivy.'

'Oh, what would you know!' I start sobbing again; it's his being so nice to me that's done it.

'I do know,' he says. 'I raised my brother and sisters after our parents died in a car crash.'

His words hang between us. It feels as if all the air has suddenly been sucked out of the room.

'Oh my God. Luke . . .' But there are no words.

'It's okay. It was fifteen years ago,' he says lightly, but there's a lingering sadness there.

'How did you manage?' Without thinking, I reach out and clasp his hand.

'We just did. The alternative was being split up. I was old enough to live alone, but the little ones would have gone into foster care,' he says. 'I couldn't let that happen.'

'But what about university and girls and . . . your life?'

'There wasn't much of that for a few years,' he admits with a wry smile. 'Maybe that's why, as you so astutely pointed out once, I'm a little bit lacking in the social skills department.'

I'm filled with renewed shame about how badly I've misjudged Luke since I've known him. He's been so kind and endlessly patient with my trivial baby/boyfriend/job dilemmas, when all the time he's been lugging this anvil of heartbreak around with him.

'Didn't you resent it? Having to put your life on hold like that?'

He shakes his head. 'I was happy to do it. But that's not to say it was easy. I know now that I'll never have my own kids,' he says.

I stare at him, stunned. 'Why not?'

'Well, part of me feels like I've done enough child rearing for one lifetime,' he says with a smile. 'But also because I saw how hard it was for my siblings, how much they missed Mum and Dad. I couldn't bring a child into the world knowing there's a chance I might not be there when they need me.'

I can't help thinking of Helena; she should definitely talk to Luke. 'Are you still close to your siblings now?'

'Oh yeah. Matt and Vanessa are only a couple of years younger than me, so they're off doing their own thing,' he says. 'But Belinda was just a toddler when Mum and Dad died, so I guess I was sort of like a dad to her.'

'Where's Belinda now?'

'She's just started university in Birmingham,' he says, smiling proudly. 'You'd like her. You're very similar.'

'How's that?'

'She's stubborn and bloody-minded and insists on doing everything herself.'

'Excuse me?' I shriek. Ivy's eyelids flutter and she expels a deep sigh.

'Hey, it's a compliment!'

I laugh through my tears and wipe at my panda-ringed eyes. When I look up again, Luke isn't smiling any more. He's looking at me oddly, as if he wants to say something but can't quite find the words. He reaches up and tucks a stray lock of hair behind my ear, his fingertips brushing softly against my cheek.

'What?'

'Um . . .' he says. Then he leans forward and kisses me. I'm so shocked that for a second I don't react. A second after that, I'm aware of his hands in my hair and my lips kissing him hungrily back. One second more and I realise what the hell I'm doing.

'What do you think you're playing at?' I shout, pushing him back with such force he slams into the wooden arm of the sofa.

He blinks, dazed. 'I'm sorry. I thought —'

'What? You thought you'd tell me your sob story and I'd leap into bed with you?'

The second the words leave my mouth, I wish an A380 would crash into the house and pulverise me. I've never said a crueller thing in all my life.

Luke obviously thinks so too. Without a word, he stands up from the sofa and walks out the front door.

Finn

What is it with babies and planes? How come, no matter how happy they've been in the airport lounge, the second they get into an aircraft cabin they become screaming little demons from hell? Why do their parents just sit there like vegetables and watch them do it? And why are they always, *always* seated next to me? It's as if the check-in staff size me up as someone who's likely to be short-tempered and sleep-deprived, and figure the best place for me is smack-bang in the middle of an airborne crèche.

When I'm a father, I won't allow it. I grew up knowing it was my job to be polite and immaculately behaved in public, and not to speak until spoken to. My kid will be the same.

I really should be keeping a list of all these paternal pearls of wisdom; they've been coming to me thick and fast the past few days. I could compile them into a book: *How Not to Raise a Total Brat*. It'd be a bestseller for sure.

HOW NOT TO RAISE A TOTAL BRAT

1. Don't be one of those prats – sorry, parents – who thinks every burp or fart his kid does is sheer genius. It's not.

2. Never take said kid to a cinema/wedding/restaurant unless a) its jaw is wired shut or b) it fully understands the meaning of the phrase, 'One more peep out of you and you're sleeping in the shed.'
3. Lock kid in bedroom until at least eight a.m. on weekends.

Oh yeah, Anna's and my baby will be positively angelic.

'Sir, you need to turn off your laptop now. We're preparing for landing,' the blonde stewardess says, leaning over the seat in front of mine and treating me to an extended glimpse of her ample cleavage. At least I have the sense to avert my eyes this time. Maybe if I'd kept my eyes out of Fiona's frock when I had the chance I wouldn't be in my current predicament. As the hostie moves on, I subtly rearrange the contents of my boxer shorts, which have, er, pricked up their collective ears at the sound of a silky female voice.

I can't wait to get home and get started on baby-making practice with Anna. This last week in Belfast has been pure agony. In other words, I'm gagging for it.

I thought my rejection of Fiona a week ago might encourage her to back off. I half feared she might even go to the other extreme and avenge herself by picking on me in front of the rest of the team. A woman scorned and all that. But she appears to have interpreted my affirmation of my commitment to Anna as some sort of challenge and has been coming on stronger than ever.

She's been sending me racy texts at all hours. Actually, racy isn't even the word – some of them have been downright pornographic. On my way to the studio the Monday after our encounter, my phone beeped to announce the arrival of this little missive: *Barely had my fingers out of my knickers all weekend. U don't know what ur missing.*

Meanwhile, poor old Roland's been following her around like a puppy at work, aware something's up and trying desperately not to end up in the pound.

At team drinks last night, Fiona followed me into the gents and just grabbed me. *All* of me. Knocked the breath right out of my body.

'Going back to London for the weekend?' she'd breathed, pressing her tits into my chest.

'Uh, yeah.'

'Well, just remember this is waiting for you when you get back.'

Like I'm going to forget.

Which is why I've called in sick today and hopped on the first flight to Heathrow. It's thoroughly unprofessional, especially given I've only been in the job a month, but I don't care. I have to see Anna. The likelihood of my having sex with Fiona seems to be increasing by the day and I need to know if Anna intends to give me a reason not to. More than ever, I need a distraction from Fiona, from the job and the whole weird little bubble that my life in Belfast has rapidly become.

Anna hasn't said much about 'Operation Baby' when we've talked on the phone this week. In fact, I'm starting to think she's avoiding my calls. She's probably just been distracted by having Ivy for an extra week. I can't imagine how she's persuaded the paper to give her another five days off. Hopefully the extra time with the baby has sealed the deal, convinced her she wants one of her own.

She doesn't know I'm coming home today. I'm due back tomorrow and Anna knows I want an answer then; I just hope she's prepared to give it a few hours ahead of schedule. If she hasn't decided, or her answer is no, who knows what will become of us.

The house is a pigsty when I arrive, brandishing a bunch of lilies hastily bought from the petrol station around the corner. But at least it's quiet; Ivy must be asleep upstairs. Unless she's with Luke the Baby Whisperer from next door. Anna looks a bit of a mess too. Her frumpy tracksuit bottoms and hoodie are covered in chalky dried baby spew, her hair is unwashed and it looks as if she hasn't slept in a week. But at least she's not wearing the Van Halen T-shirt.

'Surprise, babe!' I greet her with a peck on the cheek as I survey the bombsite I've walked into. 'How's things?'

'Fine,' Anna mumbles. 'It's been a pretty full-on week.'

'Looks like it.'

I drop my bag and start straightening the piles of newspapers strewn across the floor. Some of them are open to the employment sections and I notice several job ads have thick red rings around them.

'Anna?' I call. 'What's this?'

'What's what?' she replies from the kitchen.

'These job ads. Are you looking for a new job?' And hasn't she heard of the internet?

She appears in the kitchen doorway, grinning broadly. There's a wild look in her eyes. 'I quit!' she announces.

I drop the newspaper I'm holding. 'You quit? When? Why?'

'On Tuesday. It's a long story, but basically I was just over it,' she says, as though throwing in your job is as normal as nipping to the pub for a pint.

'You were *over* it? What does that mean? Don't you think this is something we maybe need to talk about? We might have a baby soon, Anna. You've just done yourself out of paid maternity leave.'

Anna's face clouds. 'If you can accept a job in another city without telling me, I think I'm entitled to leave one without telling you,' she says stiffly.

Ouch. I guess I deserved that.

'So what do you propose to do now? How are you going to pay the rent? I can't cover both of us forever,' I say.

'Well, that's the thing,' she says, the crazed grin returning. 'I was thinking I'd move. To Belfast.'

A cold wave of fear washes over me. The thought of Anna and Fiona living in the same city doesn't bear thinking about. 'To

Belfast?'

'Why not? I've been in London too long,' she says. 'And I miss you, Finn. I want us to be together. Especially if we're going to have a baby.'

She almost whispers the last sentence, but she might as well have shouted it through a loudspeaker.

'You want to have a baby? You mean it?' My heart's thumping; she's offering me the Get Out of Jail Free card I need.

Anna hesitates a moment, then says, 'I do.'

I grab her in a bear hug and lift her off the ground. Thank God. I'm all for getting started straight away, but as I kiss her neck, Anna wriggles out of my embrace.

'What's that?' she says, looking pointedly at my crotch.

'Uh . . . do you really need me to explain it to you?'

'Not that,' she exclaims, swatting me playfully. 'Something's buzzing in your trousers.'

'It sure is, baby,' I say in my best Barry White voice.

'Seriously, Finn,' she says, laughing. It seems like months since I've heard Anna laugh.

I put my hand in my pocket and, sure enough, my phone is vibrating. I pull it out and glance at the screen: FIONA MOBILE. I hit the reject button and 8 MISSED CALLS appears on the screen.

Jesus, I only switched the phone back on half an hour ago. I shove it back into my pocket. Thank goodness it's set to vibrate and not ring.

'Who's after you?' Anna says.

Ha. If only she knew.

'Oh, it's just work. I chucked a sickie to come here – they probably want to know if I'm going to be okay for Monday,' I lie.

Thankfully, Anna buys it. 'And are you?' she asks, one eyebrow raised seductively.

'Well, now, that all depends.' I slide my arms around her waist again. 'I respond very well to incentives.'

She laughs again. 'I just need to jump in the shower,' she says. Seeing my deflated expression, she quickly adds, 'Come on, babe, I'm not exactly a glamour puss this morning. Give a girl a chance to put on her glad rags!'

'Why? I'm only going to take them off again.'

'Finn!'

'Okay, but be quick,' I say, pouting.

'I will. And when I come back, I'll incentivise all day if you like.'

She bounds up the stairs, giggling as she goes. I carry the flowers into the kitchen, shove them inelegantly into a vase and take the arrangement back into the sitting room. I'm killing time. As soon as I hear the shower running, I retrieve my phone and dial Fiona's number.

'Well, hello there, sickly child,' she answers.

I pinch the bridge of my nose. 'Hi, Fiona,' I say, trying to sound sinusy and miserable.

'Oh, poor boy,' she coos. 'How are you?'

'I've felt less like death in my time.' I figure a little embellishment can't hurt.

'I was calling to see if you'll be back on deck for Monday, but by the sounds of you, I imagine you'll need a few days off.'

'You're probably right,' I say, with a heavy sigh and a cough thrown in for good measure. Give the man an Oscar.

'Mary can hold the fort. Get yourself back to bed and rest.'

'I will.' She's being far less predatory than usual. Maybe even femmes fatale respect illness.

'Oh, and Finn?'

'Yes?'

'Dream of me, won't you? Naked.' She hangs up.

For God's sake. I fled back to London to escape Fiona and now she's got me thinking about her sponging my fevered brow with a cold compress. And I'm not even sick.

I toss my phone on to the sofa in disgust and walk through the kitchen to the back door. Nui, having heard voices inside, is scratching furiously at it, but when he sees it's me he turns on his paws and huffs off to the other end of the garden.

'Bugger you then,' I mutter, following him onto the back patio. I plop into one of the awful wrought-iron garden chairs we inherited with the house and wish I still smoked. A cigarette always helps at times like these.

Five minutes later, Anna's voice jolts me from my reverie.

'Finn, your phone's buzzing again,' she calls from the sitting room. 'Want me to answer it and pretend to be your doctor or something? I do a great Oirish accent, to be sure!'

No. I leap up from my chair.

'Oh, hang on, it's not a call,' she goes on. 'It's a text. It's from . . . Fiona?'

No, no, no! I race into the house but it's like the world is suddenly spinning in slow motion. My legs feel like they're made of lead.

By the time I reach Anna, only seconds have passed – but it might as well have been years. She looks at me like I'm a stranger, a horrified expression on her face. My mobile phone lies in her open palm.

'I can explain,' I say.

'Can you?' she asks flatly. 'Can you explain' – she squints at the screen – '"Just wrapped. Perhaps Nurse Fi should come over and administer a medicinal blow job"?'

'It's . . . it's not what you think.'

'Really? That's good. Because what I think is that you're SCREWING YOUR BOSS!' She throws the phone at me as hard as she can and it glances off my collarbone.

'Ow! Anna, for God's sake, let me explain,' I shout.

Her confused expression has given way to a look of cold fury. She crosses her arms and waits.

'Nothing has happened between me and Fiona. *Nothing!* I swear to you.'

'Then why is she offering to suck your dick?' she spits.

'I don't know, she's deranged or something. She's decided she fancies me and she's been hassling me for weeks.'

'Weeks! Why didn't you tell me? Or, more importantly, tell *her* you're in a relationship and to leave you the hell alone?'

Anna's voice, though still at a startling pitch, is starting to wobble. I fear tears aren't far away.

'I *have* told her that. It makes no difference. If anything, she seems to see it as a challenge.'

She clenches her jaw and looks away. I can tell she's weighing up whether or not to believe me.

'The second you get back to Belfast,' she says through gritted teeth, 'you need to go to her superior and file a sexual harassment complaint. She can't be allowed to get away with this.'

I feel my throat constrict. 'I can't do that, Anna,' I say.

'Of course you can! If this has been going on for weeks and you've given this crazy bitch no indication that her attention is wanted or reciprocated then she's . . .'

She trails off. I've always worn my guilt on my face and Anna knows it. She can see it now.

'Oh my God,' she whispers and the tears flow. 'What have you done?'

'Nothing! Just some stupid fooling around. I was smashed, An, and I stopped it before it could get out of hand. I swear. *I did not sleep with her.*'

A sob escapes Anna's lips and she squeezes her eyes shut tight. 'How could you do this?' she says.

'I didn't do anything! I've just told you. It was —'

'I mean THIS!' she roars, waving her hand wildly between the two of us. 'How could you surprise me in the middle of the week and bring me flowers' – she extracts the lilies from their vase on the coffee table and flings them at my feet – 'and ask me to have your *baby* when the whole time you've been shagging another woman!'

'I'm not shagging her! I asked you to have my baby so I WON'T shag her!'

A strange stillness descends on Anna. She stands in front of me, utterly motionless, a glint of total, agonising comprehension in her eyes.

'I . . . I didn't mean that. I meant that I wanted to get our relationship back on track and I thought —'

'Get out,' she says quietly.

'I knew we just needed some way to be close again. The way we used to be, you know?'

'Get out.'

'No, Anna. Please. Listen to me. Let me explain.'

'GET OUT!' The stillness shatters and Anna launches herself at me, scratching at my cheeks, pummelling my chest with her fists. Then she's picking up whatever she can lay her hands on and pitching it at me. I raise my hands in front of my face to shield myself from baby toys, shoes, the TV remote.

'You bastard, you bastard, you bastard!' she screeches.

'Anna, please don't do this! I love you, An. I love you!'

'Are you going to leave or not?'

'No! We need to talk about this!'

'Fine then. I will.' She turns around and bolts.

As she wrenches open the front door, Luke from next-door looms into view and she smacks straight into him. Why is that guy always skulking around the place?

'Anna, what —' he says.

'Oh, just piss off, the pair of you,' she sobs, shoving past him.

He watches her dart down the street, then turns to me, looking simultaneously astonished and suspicious.

I expect him to give me a serve. He seems to have appointed himself Anna's protector and I'm clearly the bad guy, standing here surrounded by debris with a smashed bouquet at my feet.

But Luke doesn't play the heavy. Instead he says, 'Where's Ivy?'

'Ivy?'

'Yes, Ivy. Anna's goddaughter? The baby who's been living here for the past month?'

'Uh . . . I don't know,' I admit. 'I guess she's upstairs.' If she is, I can't believe she's slept through this.

Luke doesn't respond but walks purposefully upstairs. He returns a minute later with a groggy Ivy swaddled in a fluffy pink blanket. 'I'm taking her next door,' he says. 'I look after her a bit. It'll be cool with Anna.'

'Hang on a minute —' I step forward to argue but Luke holds up his hand.

'Look, I don't know what's been going on here,' he begins. I know what he really means is *I don't know what you've done but I'm sure it's bad.* 'But assuming Anna comes back at some point, I imagine the blazing row I've just had the pleasure of listening to is likely to continue. I don't think Ivy needs to be here for that, do you?'

I don't know what I think at this point. About anything.

'Whatever,' I tell him. 'Take her if you want.' At least if the baby's gone, I can leave too. I don't want to be here for round two.

Luke heads for the door, then turns back. 'I don't know how anyone could be stupid enough to do the dirty on her,' he says, as if to himself. 'What a prat.'

Anna

Of course I fled the house in the most unsuitable house-fleeing clothes I own. I was going for an 'effortless sex kitten' look, so after my shower I put on mushroom-coloured fitted yoga pants and a baby-pink fine cashmere wrap top. I'd be toasty warm if I was in my house, especially as I'd expected to be getting hot and heavy with Finn at this moment.

Instead, I'm outside and absolutely freezing, huddled against the sharp wind as I run, blindly, as fast and as far as I can. I'm not remotely hot, but I definitely feel heavy. At least my feet are warm – I jammed them into my trainers as I bolted out the door.

I'm supposed to be making babies right now – or at least practising. Instead I'm roaming the streets dressed like some yoga-school drop-out, while the baby actually in my care is probably frightened and bewildered at having found herself in the company of yet another complete stranger. What kind of mother would I make?

Luke must have come over because he heard Finn and me fighting. Maybe he's taken pity on Ivy and rescued her from Finn – possibly the one person on the planet even more clueless about kids than

I am – even though I'm a horrendous person who doesn't deserve another iota of help from him.

How did it come to this? Unemployed, unloved, boyfriend shagging his boss, accidentally snogging the next-door neighbour. When did my life become such a soap opera?

I spot a park bench and realise I've run all the way to the river at Twickenham, a good two or three miles from home. I plop down on the seat, suddenly exhausted. I feel as if I've been running an emotional marathon for the last month and it's only just dawned on me there's no medal at the finish line. There's just sweat, tears, confusion and yet more hard work.

I watch the murky-brown water of the Thames swirl past, carrying bits of flotsam and rubbish in its current. The occasional duck bobs by looking confused, as though it just dipped a toe in to check the temperature and got swept downstream. I know the feeling.

Now I'm seeing parallels between my own life and a duck's. That's encouraging.

I jump as my phone buzzes in my pocket. I retrieve it, expecting to see Finn's number pop up on the screen but it's a number I don't recognise. Against my better judgement, I hit answer. 'Hello?'

'Anna? Where are you? Are you okay?'

'Who is this?'

'What do you mean "Who is this"? It's Hel! What's wrong?'

The voice on the phone sounds vaguely like Helena's, but at a volume and pitch I'm certain only dogs should be able to hear. She sounds hysterical.

'Nothing's wrong. I mean, everything's wrong but . . . oh, I'll tell you later.'

'Is Ivy with you?'

'No. She's at home. Why?'

'She's not at home, Anna. I'm at your place, there's no one

here and I can see through your front window that the place is all smashed up,' Helena says.

'You're at my place? Why? I thought you weren't coming back until tomorrow night.'

'Forget that!' she howls. 'Where is my daughter?'

Without registering, I've risen from the park bench and turned for home. Now I break into a run once more; the panic in Hel's voice chills me.

'I . . . I don't know,' I admit.

And I really don't. I never figured Finn would actually leave the house – so much for wanting to explain himself. And I can't imagine he'd have taken Ivy with him. He wouldn't even know how to unfold her pram.

'You don't *know*? Jesus Christ, Anna! You're supposed to be looking after her!'

The words 'pot' and 'kettle' are on the tip of my tongue, but I manage to hold them in. 'Finn must have come looking for me. She must be with him.'

'Why is he looking for you? *What is going on?*'

I sigh. Where do I even begin? Before I can attempt an explanation, I hear a muffled deep voice at Helena's end of the line.

'What?' Helena snaps at the interloper. Then, '*Who* are you?'

'I'm Luke,' my neighbour replies, evidently now standing next to Hel. 'We've met. Ivy's asleep next door. At my house.'

Bless you, Luke, I want to shout. But there's stony silence from Helena. When she finally speaks again it's to me, not Luke.

'Who is Luke and why is my child asleep in his house?' she asks frostily.

'He's my neighbour, Helena. You met him the night you arrived?'

'Met' is hardly the right word, considering Luke was still in his Parcel Nazi guise back then and Hel's mental state was teetering somewhere between 'rock bottom' and 'caverns of hell'.

'He looks after Ivy sometimes,' I say, as if that explains everything.

'He looks . . .!' She's breathless with incredulity. 'You've been letting Parcel Nazi look after my daughter?'

I cringe. Thanks, Hel.

'Can I speak to Anna, please?' Luke asks brusquely in the background.

'No! Hel, don't give him the phone! Don't —'

'Anna?' Luke's voice comes on the line.

On the list of people I really don't want to speak to right now, Luke is second only to Finn. We haven't spoken since he kissed me last night and I said that terrible, terrible thing to him. I couldn't bear to have him yell at me right now on top of everything else.

'Hi,' I say feebly.

'Are you all right?'

'No.'

'Do you want me to come and get you?'

'Huh?'

'Do you want me to come and pick you up?'

'What, like, in your car?'

'No, Anna. On my BMX.'

I can't believe it. Even though I was nastier to Luke than I've ever been to anyone, even though he's once again been lumbered with my goddaughter and even though he now has her irate mother to contend with, he's still being nice to me. Which makes me feel even worse, obviously. I can't bring myself to accept any more of his charity.

'No, thank you,' I say, trying to maintain my composure. 'It won't take me long to jog back.'

'Okay. See you in a bit.' He sounds glad that I've refused his offer.

'Well, maybe —' But Luke hangs up.

I'm knackered but I dig in and find a burst of speed, practically sprinting the last of the way home. It's not going to be fun explaining to Helena what's happened, and reliving the humiliation of Finn's anti-cheat baby scam, but the thought that maybe Luke doesn't despise me after all somehow makes me believe I'll get through it.

But Luke's not there when I reach home a few minutes later. The street is oddly quiet and there's no sign of life at his house. My place, however, is a different story. I must have been out longer than I realised; it was broad daylight when I left and now it's the edge of twilight and every light in my house is blazing. The front door is wide open and Nui is darting fitfully between the hall and the front garden, clearly perturbed by whatever's going on inside.

'Come on, mate,' I call to him. He skitters out to me, whimpering, as if he's trying to tell me not to go inside.

I scoop Nui up in one hand and close the front gate with the other, noting with irritation that Hel has left it open as well. It's lucky nothing interesting is going on in the street or Nui would have been straight out and potentially under the wheels of one of the huge SUVs so popular with the bored housewives in this area.

I step gingerly into the hall, expecting to see the detritus of my earlier meltdown. But the hall and the sitting room beyond it are pristine. Like, cleaner and tidier than they've been in weeks. Or ever.

In the middle of this sparkling scene, sitting primly on the sofa, is Helena. Looking like she wants to beat me to death with a scatter cushion.

'Start talking,' she says grimly before I've even had a chance to say hello.

Instantly, my stomach twists into an angry knot. What's with the attitude? I've been thinking about it all the way home, and if Helena thinks she's going to be all high and mighty after the way she's behaved – and especially after the twenty-four hours I've had – she is mightily mistaken.

'Hey, Hel, it's great to have you back! I wasn't expecting you for another couple of days.'

'That's pretty obvious,' she replies crossly.

I'm giving her one last chance to redeem herself. Then it's gloves off. 'Is Ivy upstairs?' I ask brightly.

'She is. No thanks to you. She could have been anywhere.'

'Well, that didn't seem to bother you a month ago when you skulked off in the middle of the night!'

Gloves *well and truly* off.

Helena leaps to her feet. 'Are you for real?' she hisses, her eyes blazing. 'What choice did I have, Anna? I'd practically had to beg you to look after Ivy in the first place. I had to leave before you woke up and realised, "Oh, a baby doesn't actually go with what I'm wearing today!"'

'What do you mean by that?'

'I mean I was a mess when I turned up here, Anna. A proper raving loony. I'd come halfway round the world to see you, for God's sake. But you've still not let me forget what a huge favour you're doing me. You can't just be my friend and help me out. It's always about how it affects you!'

Her gall takes my breath away. I actually feel winded. 'That's not true! I've been there for you all the way, Helena. Ever since you got pregnant in the first place. And yes, a little thought for me wouldn't have gone astray, since I've turned my life upside down for you.' I'm genuinely stunned by how unreasonable she's being. Can she really be this deluded?

Helena scoffs and rolls her eyes. 'You mean ever since it took me three weeks to even tell you I was pregnant, since you never return my calls or answer my emails? Ever since I had to "sell" the idea of being Ivy's godmother to you by telling you what was in it for YOU!'

'Oh, spare me your tale of woe, Helena. I've heard it a million times,' I spit.

Now Hel's looking at me as if I'm the unbalanced one. 'What are you talking about?' she says, her eyes narrowing to flinty little slits.

'I'm talking about the train wreck you call your life! It's been one disaster after another for as long as I've known you. Don't like your uni course? Just quit! Don't like your boyfriend? Ditch him! Can't look after your own kid? Leave her with Anna! Met some bloke and can't be arsed coming back for your daughter? No worries. Anna will sort it out! Anna always DOES!'

Helena gives me a look of abject fury. I'm sure if I was standing closer to her she'd physically lash out at me. I'm being totally unfair; I'm well aware of that. I know leaving Ivy with me was undoubtedly the hardest thing Helena has ever done. But right now I don't care. I'm sick of her sanctimonious attitude – I've been sick of it for ten years, come to think of it. Hel's put most of her life in the too-hard basket and now it's overflowing all over my sitting room floor.

'When are you going to take some responsibility for yourself?' I rail as she stares at me, dumbfounded. 'You're twenty-six years old, for Christ's sake. The people in your life don't exist purely to bail you out of trouble. I've got problems too, you know!'

'Problems!' Helena shouts. 'You have got to be kidding me. Posh house in London, fancy job, TV star boyfriend. Oh, my heart just *bleeds* for you.'

'I've worked for those things, Helena. Unlike you, I don't expect to just drift through life and miraculously have a roof over my head and money in my pocket.'

Her eyes widen in indignation. 'I do not —'

'Anyway,' I yell, cutting her off. 'If you'd bothered to keep in touch in the last month and ask me even once how I've been doing, you'd know the job's gone, Finn's gone and, as I now have no source of income, it probably won't be long before the house is gone too.'

She falters mid-retort and regards me suspiciously. 'Gone? What are you talking about, *gone?*'

'I quit my job. I used up all my leave looking after your kid, then I made an enormous balls-up and walked before they could sack me.'

'And Finn?'

'Sleeping with his boss.'

Helena takes a step back, as though the barrage of information has knocked her off balance.

'Yeah,' I say bitterly. 'And you don't hear me whining about my lot in life, do you? I just get on —'

But Helena holds her hand up to silence me and cocks her head towards the hall. 'Did you hear that?' she says.

'Hear what?' I snap. This is a classic Helena avoidance tactic.

She shakes her head. 'I thought I heard a —'

Then I hear it too. A tiny whimper, almost inaudible. And there's something not right about it.

Helena's gaze meets mine and in an instant we're both sprinting up the stairs. The door to the spare room is ajar; I fling it open.

Ivy's whimpering is louder now. In the dim, dusky gloom I can't see her, but I can hear that something is terribly wrong.

'Where is she?' Helena cries, flipping on the light and pawing frantically through the piles of clean washing I've dumped on the bed.

A flicker of movement at floor level catches my eye. I drop to my knees and peer under the futon.

There's Ivy, lying face down. She's tangled up in a towel, her tiny right arm twisted at an unearthly angle behind her.

'Oh my God,' I breathe. I feel paralysed for a moment.

A split second later, Helena is on the floor beside me. 'Ivy!' she cries. 'Oh, no. No, no, no, no.'

She gingerly disentangles her daughter from the towel and gathers her up in her arms. Ivy is floppy and still, her injured arm now hanging limply by her side. She whimpers occasionally but doesn't open her eyes; she's drifting in and out of consciousness.

As if I'm on autopilot, I stand up and run back down the stairs. I grab the phone from the hall table and punch in 999.

'Ambulance!' I scream when the operator picks up. 'My god-daughter, she's seven months old, she's hurt. Send someone! Please send an ambulance!'

'Madam, can you tell me what happened?' the operator says curtly.

'I don't know. I think she rolled off the bed. I . . . I wasn't with her.' No, I was too busy screaming at her mother.

The operator asks some more questions and I must reply, because what seems like years later she tells me to remain calm, that an ambulance is on its way.

I hang up and race back up the stairs. I can only have been out of the room for a minute or so, but Helena has sprung into action. She's wrapped Ivy snugly in a blanket, her poor mangled arm tucked securely by her side.

Ivy's eyelids are flickering and her little face is screwed up in pain. Her soft mewling is growing louder; it's like music to my ears.

'The ambulance is on its way,' I tell Helena. Even as I say it, I can hear the siren wailing in the distance.

Wordlessly, Hel stands up and, clutching Ivy tightly to her breast, walks downstairs. I trail behind her, feeling impotent and unnecessary.

Only a few hours ago, Ivy felt like mine. I'm a little embarrassed to realise how infrequently Helena has entered my thoughts in the past few days. I'd almost forgotten she'd ever be coming back for her daughter. Now, watching her with Ivy, it's as if they've never been apart.

Helena strides purposefully out of the house and perches on the low brick wall at the front. She rocks Ivy gently and whispers in her ear. She doesn't say a word to me.

The whining siren grows steadily louder until, just a few minutes later, the street is bathed in the eerie red and blue light of the approaching ambulance. When it screeches to a stop in front of the house and the siren stops, the silence feels abrupt and oppressive.

Two paramedics jump out and approach Helena. 'Miss Harding?' says one. 'You're the mother?'

Oh God, did I really tell them that? I step forward. 'I'm Anna Harding, Ivy's godmother. This is Helena Stanley, her mother,' I say quickly, gesturing towards Hel. She flicks me a thankful glance; I don't think she's got it in her to talk details at the moment.

'Okay, Miss Stanley. I'm Paul,' the paramedic says, reaching for Ivy. 'Let's have a look at the little one.'

Helena reluctantly hands her daughter over. 'She rolled off the bed,' she says dispassionately.

Paul carefully peels back Ivy's swaddling and glances at her arm. 'Oh yes, that's a break,' he says in a weirdly jovial tone. He's probably trying to keep Hel calm, though it doesn't look like she needs much help in that respect. She's standing there like a sack of potatoes, looking at Ivy the dispassionate way she might regard a bundle of clothes she's just handed to the dry cleaner.

I want to slap her face to snap her out of it – until I really look at my best friend and realise she's scared out of her mind.

'Okay, Miss Stanley. Ivy will need hospital treatment. Would you like to come with us?'

Helena nods and starts walking robotically towards the ambulance. I follow without thinking but the second paramedic, a woman, clutches my arm.

'I'm really sorry, but only immediate family can accompany a patient,' she says. 'We're going to West Middlesex Hospital if you'd like to meet us there?'

I nod. Of course I can't go with them. There's no place for me in any of this.

'I'll see you there, Hel,' I call as Paul swings the big van doors shut. But Hel is bent over Ivy's tiny body and doesn't hear me.

The ambulance pulls away and I'm left standing there on the kerb. I might have lost my job and my boyfriend in the last few days, but I've never felt a more crushing sense of loss than I do at this moment. Dazed, I watch the flashing lights of the ambulance retreat. I barely notice Jen bounding from her house across the road.

'Anna!' she screeches. 'Are you all right? What's happened?' She reaches me and, without waiting for my response, envelops me in a fierce hug. 'I didn't want to stick my beak in while the ambulance was here,' she tells my shoulder.

'It's Ivy,' I say when she finally releases her grip. 'She fell or . . . rolled off the bed or something. Her arm . . . it's . . . she wouldn't wake up . . . I don't know if . . .' Despite my best efforts, my composure crumbles and I dissolve into sobs.

'What was she doing on the bed? I gave you Milo's old travel cot,' Jen exclaims. As if this is the time to point that out.

'I don't know . . . I–I–I wasn't heeeere!' I wail. 'Finn's cheating and – *hic* – I left and – *sniff* – Hel came back while I was gone.'

Jen makes a good point, though – what *was* Ivy doing on the futon in the spare room instead of the nice, secure cot in my bedroom across the landing? I know the spare room was where Helena left Ivy when she did her midnight flit, but that was a month ago. Ivy's so much more mobile now – she can roll over and sit up and I can tell any minute now she'll start to crawl. Surely Hel must appreciate that?

'It's all right, hon,' Jen says, one arm still firmly around my shoulders. 'Let's just get to the hospital and you can tell me the rest of it then.'

By 'the rest of it' I know she means the Finn saga; what a joy it will be to rehash that particular nightmare again.

'Okay,' I snuffle, charmingly wiping my runny nose with my

sleeve. One glance down the street tells me Andrew must be out in his and Jen's four-wheel drive, and I've never bothered to get a car. You don't need one in London. Except, of course, at crucial moments like this. 'I'll have to call a cab.'

'Why don't you just ask Luke to drive us?' Jen suggests. 'He won't mind. He's been peeking out of his sitting room window every ten seconds for the last five minutes. As have I.'

I shake my head sadly. 'I can't ask him. He hates me.'

Jen stares at me, incredulous. 'He hates you? Why on earth would you think that?'

'Because he kissed me and I kissed him back and then I said the most hateful thing to him,' I say, hanging my head in shame.

'Okay, the fact that you snogged him is a conversation we will definitely be having over a bottle of wine some other time. But Anna, seriously,' Jen says firmly. She grips both my shoulders and shakes me. Hard.

'Oi! What?'

'Luke is mad about you. Any idiot can see that.'

'Huh?'

'The bloke is, like, ridiculously in love with you!' she hoots. 'Why else has he been hanging around like a bad smell for the last month?'

I think I detect a note of jealousy in her voice. Which is stupid because she's blatantly wrong.

'He's not in love with me, you nutter. He's got a lot of experience with kids, that's all. He's just being helpful.'

'Anna, I don't care if he's Supernanny. No 33-year-old single guy willingly spends that much time with a baby unless he's either really weird or someone else has captured his attention. And Luke's not *that* weird, though the hair leaves a lot to be desired.'

I shake my head. Jen can't be right. Before Ivy arrived, and for a while after, Luke and I clashed every time our paths crossed. He was just Parcel Nazi – why would he suddenly decide he fancies me? I open my mouth to tell Jen this, but she cuts in before I can speak.

'Look, just go and ask him to give us a lift,' she says knowingly. 'If he agrees – which he *will* – you'll know he doesn't hate you, at the very least.'

'Okay,' I say reluctantly. 'I'll do it, but only because a taxi will take too long to get here. And to prove that you're mental.'

I square my shoulders, spin on my heel and stride briskly to Luke's front door. Before I can knock, it swings open and there's Luke, car keys in hand.

'I was just coming to get you,' he says. 'Let's go.'

Helena

'Mrs Stanley? Helena Stanley?'

The harsh voice stuns me from my catatonic stupor in the fluorescent-lit hospital waiting room. I leap up from the exquisitely uncomfortable plastic chair to face a diminutive Indian woman wearing green scrubs and a pristine white coat.

'Yes! I'm Helena, uh, *Miss* Stanley.'

'I'm Doctor Basih,' she says, eyeing me critically. 'You're Ivy's mother?'

'Yes. Is she all right? Will . . . will she be okay?' I can barely squeeze the words out. Now that I've asked the question, she'll have to answer it – and if the answer isn't good, I don't know what I'll do.

Dr Basih frowns. 'Can you tell me how this happened?' she asks.

I don't know where to begin explaining what brought us here. Did this happen because I stupidly left an inquisitive seven-month-old baby alone on a bed? Or do I have to go back even further than that – to my fight with Anna, my arrival in London a month ago? Hell, why not go right back to the night I got knocked up? It suddenly strikes me that my life has an air of Shakespearean tragedy about it – as though a truly catastrophic event like this has been inevitable from the very start.

'She rolled off a bed,' I tell Dr Basih. Something tells me she's not the sort who'd appreciate my maudlin musing. 'It was a futon,' I continue. 'Only about ten centimetres off the floor. She's slept on it before and I thought she'd be okay. Is she okay?'

'I see,' she says gravely, scribbling notes on her clipboard. 'And why was Ivy not properly secured in a cot or bassinette?'

Because I'm a bad mother, I want to scream. She's obviously already drawn that conclusion anyway. Uppity cow.

'I – I don't think there was one. We've been staying with a friend who doesn't have children.'

Why won't she tell me how Ivy is? I'm trying to be polite, but I don't know how much longer I can pretend to be calm.

'And you left Ivy unattended?' Dr Basih murmurs, still scribbling.

'Yes. Yes, I left her unattended. All by herself. While I was living it up downstairs in front of *Antiques Roadshow*. Okay?'

'Miss Stanley, I appreciate that you are anxious, but this is a very serious injury for such a small child. I am required to investigate,' she says crisply.

I cover my face with my hands and draw a deep breath. This is not a woman I want to piss off, that much I know at least. It's obvious she thinks I did this to Ivy. And I guess, in a way, I did. Being scared and confused and mad at the world is no excuse for failing – again – to be there for my child.

'I'm sorry,' I tell her. 'I'll answer all your questions, tell you anything you want to know. But please, I'm begging you, just tell me if Ivy's okay.'

A flicker of sympathy crosses Dr Basih's face and instantly I know that she has children too.

'Ivy has fractured her arm. We have sedated her for pain relief and to keep her still while we set it,' she says. 'Fortunately it's what we call an incomplete fracture, which means it's relatively small and should heal well.'

'Oh, thank God,' I whisper. A wave of relief washes over me.

Dr Basih hesitates a moment. 'I need to tell you, Miss Stanley, that the police will be notified about this. It's standard procedure when a young child presents with a serious injury.' She sounds vaguely apologetic.

'It's okay,' I assure her. 'I have nothing to hide. My best friend – Ivy's godmother – was there too. She can confirm what happened.' If she's still talking to me. 'When can I take her home?'

'Unfortunately I can't permit you to see Ivy until the police have attended,' Dr Basih says.

My stomach flip-flops. 'But she's all by herself.'

'She is sedated, so she's not aware of her surroundings. There are nurses with her,' the doctor says patiently. 'It won't be long. The police should be here soon.' She gives me a 'there, there' smile and squeaks away down the vinyl-floored corridor.

I slump back down in the chair. I feel completely numb; I can't even cry. My baby, my beautiful little girl, is lying broken and bruised in a hospital ward in a strange country and I can't even be there to comfort her. And what if the police decide this was somehow my fault? What if they think I hurt Ivy? I don't think I could survive if they took my daughter away. And the irony of that – feeling I'd die without her when I've just spent a month voluntarily away from her – is not lost on me. The universe is reminding me what I stand to lose.

There's a sudden ruckus at the far end of the corridor and I look up to see Anna, flanked by Parcel Nazi and a tall red-haired woman, thumping her fist on the reception desk. 'Ivy Stanley!' she's saying hotly. Then, 'Yes, I'm family. I'm her godmother!'

'Anna,' I call weakly, standing up and waving to her. She turns, sees me and sprints down the hall towards me. She has such a thunderous look on her face, I'm sure she's going to tear into me for being so irresponsible and generally shit at mothering. Instead, she flings her arms around me with such force she nearly knocks me off my feet.

'Where is she? Is she okay? What have they told you?' she cries.

'Whoa, Anna, you're cutting off my air supply!'

'Sorry,' she says, pulling back from her bear hug and holding me at arm's length. 'What did they say?' Her face is a mask of fear and anxiety.

'She's going to be fine,' I say, and relay Dr Basih's diagnosis.

Anna lets out a whoosh of breath and presses her hands to her heart. 'Thank you,' she whispers, and I don't think she's talking to me.

Parcel Nazi and the red-haired woman hover behind Anna.

'Hi, Helena, I'm Jen,' Red says, stepping forward and extending her hand. 'I'm Anna's neighbour. How are you doing?'

'I'm okay,' I lie. 'The thing is, they have to get the police involved.'

'*What?* Why?' Anna exclaims. 'Do they think you had something to do with this?'

'Didn't I?'

Anna looks thoroughly outraged. 'What are you on about, Helena? I was with you the whole time. It was an accident.'

'Yeah, but all of this . . .' I gesture around me to indicate the hospital, this city, this country. 'It's all because of my stupid, selfish decisions.'

'Jen, shall we grab a coffee?' Parcel Nazi pipes up. He might be speaking to Jen, but he's looking straight at Anna.

'Good idea,' Jen replies. 'Anna? Helena? Coffee?'

We both nod, and the pair of them retreat.

'This is my doing, Anna,' I say when they're out of earshot. 'Of course I'd never hurt Ivy on purpose, but I've done a pretty good job of it anyway, haven't I?'

Anna sits and pulls me down next to her. 'Listen to me, Hel,' she says. 'All those things I said to you before? I was wrong. You're not weak or flaky or irresponsible. And you're not a bad mother. You're the bravest person I know.'

I look sharply at Anna, half expecting to see her smirking or giggling. I mean, come on. Me, brave? That's about as sensible as calling Donald Trump humble. But Anna's face is earnest. 'You're kidding, right? How is dumping my daughter with someone who knows absolutely bugger-all about kids – sorry, but it's true – how is that brave?'

Now Anna does smile, but it's a sheepish grin. 'It's taken me a while to see it – and you're right about me and kids, by the way – but I mean it, Hel. You were struggling back in Adelaide, you knew you needed help and you went out and got it,' she says. 'That took some serious balls. Especially given there were, ahem, certain people who would have been first in line to say, "I told you so".'

I grimace involuntarily at Anna's euphemistic mention of my mother. God knows how I'll even begin to explain myself to her.

'I guess so,' I venture. I'm still not convinced that 'brave' is the best way to describe my actions over the last month. To me, bravery implies some sort of conscious decision-making process – like knowing the house is on fire but deciding to risk rescuing the family dog anyway. Everything I've done has been the opposite of decisive. It's been all about flying by the seat of my pants and just getting as far away from my demons as possible. Except, of course, the little buggers followed me. And they'll keep following me until I stop trying to outrun them and start trying to banish them for good. I know that now.

So while I'm pretty sure I'm not the fearless warrior princess Anna's trying to make me out to be, maybe I'm not the weakling I thought I was either. Ivy has definitely been better off with Anna these past few weeks than she would have been with me, I'm certain of that much. That, at least, was a good decision.

'Helena,' Anna goes on, 'I'm really sorry I said those terrible things to you tonight. I've been such a head case about Finn and work and everything, and then when you rang and said you were in London I think I just lost the plot. I – I thought you'd take Ivy back and I'd be all by myself.'

'No, *I'm* sorry,' I say, clutching her hands in mine. 'I've been selfish and ungrateful. I'll never forgive myself for not being here for you while you've been going through all this. Especially since it's probably all my fault you *have* been going through this.'

'It's not,' Anna says firmly, shaking her head. 'I've been over the job for ages. I was secretly really glad of the break.'

'And Finn?'

'Ahh . . .' Anna groans and rakes her hands through her hair. 'That's a whole other nightmare. I'll tell you about it later. Wine will be required.'

'So you forgive me then?'

'Of course! Do you forgive me?'

'Definitely. I honestly could not cope without you, An.'

Anna wraps me up in a tight hug and I squeeze back just as fiercely.

'Is it just me or do you feel like we're in a John Hughes movie circa 1983?' Anna says after a few moments.

Laughing, I let her go and wipe away the tears that have sprung from nowhere. 'You mean the bit at the end where everyone learns the big lesson and vows to be best friends forever? Totally.'

'So,' Anna goes on when we've composed ourselves, 'why *are* you in London, Hel? I wasn't expecting you til tomorrow. Or, you know, three months from now.'

I make a face. I guess I deserved that; I don't have great form when it comes to sticking to a schedule. And if I'm honest, I still haven't quite made sense of why I left Gairloch in such a hurry. It's not an easy one to explain. But if anyone will get it, it's Anna. 'I met the love of my life in Scotland, so I left him there to make sure it's real,' I say.

Anna nods sagely. 'Ivy?'

'Uh-huh.'

'You want to make sure he's the right man to bring into her life?'

'Yes,' I say with a sigh. 'You said it yourself, An. I don't have a great track record where guys are concerned. I just don't know if I can trust myself on this.'

'And this guy – sorry, I've forgotten his name . . .'

'Oliver.'

'Right, Oliver. Have you told him all this?' Anna asks.

I shrug. 'I tried. He says he understands, but I don't know if he really does. I don't know if it's even something you can understand if you're not a parent.'

Anna is quiet for a moment. 'But you *are* a parent. You're Ivy's mother and you know you have to do what's right for her,' she says slowly. 'Don't get me wrong, I want you to find Mr Right, but both you and Ivy have been through so much . . . maybe it needs to be just the two of you for a while?'

She flinches as she says it, like she's expecting me to go off at her again. But I just smile because Anna has managed to put into words exactly what I've been thinking about ever since I kissed Oli goodbye at the train station in Inverness.

Half of my heart shattered as the train doors slid closed and I watched Oliver waving miserably as the carriage pulled away from the platform. But the other half was soaring because I was on my way back to my girl. I couldn't wait to see how much she'd grown and the new things she'd learned. However bereft I felt without Oliver next to me, it was almost cancelled out by my excitement at being reunited with Ivy.

'What are you smiling at?' Anna asks, grinning herself.

'I want to go home,' I reply.

'I don't think we can, Hel. We've got to wait for the police,' she says, scanning the corridor for any sign of uniformed officers.

'I don't mean now. I'm not leaving this hospital without Ivy in my arms,' I say. 'But after all this is sorted out I want to go home to Australia, to Adelaide.'

'Wow,' Anna says, her eyes wide. 'Really? But . . . but your mother lives there.'

'I know. And obviously there's a world of issues there. But that doesn't mean I should deny Ivy the chance to know her grandparents.'

Anna has her supportive face on but I can tell that, personally, the idea of living in Adelaide again horrifies her.

'I'm not like you, Anna. Travelling isn't my thing. For you, home is wherever you make it. But for me it's where I feel safe and have familiar faces around me. Ivy needs a support network and so do I. I can't keep pretending I can do this all by myself.'

'Hey, I'm not arguing,' Anna says. 'I completely agree with you. Why would you raise Ivy in the wilds of Scotland when she could grow up by the sea, running around barefoot and playing outside 'til it gets dark?' She sighs wistfully. 'I miss that.'

'Me too.'

'But what about Oliver?'

My heart doesn't give its usual little lurch at the sound of his name. For once, I feel one hundred per cent confident about something. 'Oliver loves me,' I tell Anna with certainty. 'We'll figure it out somehow.'

'Um, Anna?' says a deep voice. We both look up to see Parcel Nazi looming over us, bearing two cardboard cups of steaming coffee. 'Sorry to interrupt,' he says. 'But the police are here.'

Behind him, I see two officers chatting amiably with the desk nurse.

Anna squeezes my hand. 'Let's get this over with,' she says. 'You'll be fine.'

'I know,' I reply. 'I'm not worried.'

And, for once, I really mean it.

Anna

'So,' Jen says primly. 'What have we learned from all this?'

'You know, for a cocktail waitress-turned-Richmond housewife, you sound remarkably like a schoolteacher,' I say wryly.

'I know, I think I missed my calling. Now answer the question.'

'I . . .' I search for the right words but turn up nothing. 'I don't know, Jen. I'm sure there's some great philosophical lesson to be gleaned from it all, but right now I'm still too close to it. My head's still spinning a bit, you know?'

Jen smiles sympathetically at me across her kitchen table. 'I do,' she says. 'Maybe when it all dies down a bit, you'll see what I see.'

'And what's that?'

'An awesomely strong – some would say bloody-minded – chick who was handed a shitload of lemons and somehow managed to make lemonade. Or maybe vodka with a twist.'

'Thanks . . . I think!' I say, laughing.

'You're welcome.' Jen looks at her watch. 'What time is Helena's flight?'

I glance at the clock on Jen's kitchen wall. 'It's at three. The taxi will be here soon,' I say.

'Are you sure you don't want me to drive you?'

'Thanks, mate, but I've, um, actually got to go somewhere straight from the airport.'

Jen narrows her eyes. 'Do not tell me,' she says in a low voice.

I shrug. 'I have to see him, Jen, even if it is just to tell him it's over. I need to finish it properly.'

She sighs. 'That arsehole doesn't deserve anything from you,' she says vehemently.

'I'm not doing it for Finn, I'm doing it for me,' I tell her. 'Five years is a long time. Too long to just never speak to him again and pretend like we never happened.'

'Fair enough,' she replies. 'Where are you meeting him?'

'He's staying with his mate Jez in Chiswick this weekend. I'm going there.'

'Write down the address,' Jen says, sliding a bit of paper and a pencil across the table to me. 'If you're not back by five o'clock I'm coming to find you.'

'Jen! What do you think is going to happen? Finn's not going to do me in!'

'It's not you I'm worried about,' she says darkly. 'It's him. I've seen you angry, Anna.'

I roll my eyes and sincerely hope she's joking. I'm not that scary. 'Look, I'll text you on my way home. How's that?' I drain the dregs of my tea.

'Done,' Jen says, standing up and clearing the mugs away. 'Say goodbye to Helena for me, won't you? And try not to sob all over your goddaughter.'

'I can't make any promises,' I reply. I say it with a smile but my heart is heavy. Watching Hel and Ivy board that plane is going to be gut-wrenchingly hard.

I give Jen a wave and jog back across the road to my own house.

In my sitting room, Ivy is on a rug on the floor, shrieking with wild giggles as Helena blows raspberries on her bare belly. Hel laughs too as Ivy claps her hands together, the resulting sound a dull thud as her free hand meets her tiny plaster cast.

'I can't believe it's only been a week since her accident,' I say. 'It obviously hasn't affected her sense of humour.'

'She's definitely a happy little camper today,' Hel says, squirting baby powder on to Ivy's peachy behind. 'I think she knows we're leaving. We're heading home at last, aren't we, Ivy? Yes we are!'

'Oi! What are the rules?' I cry.

'Ooh, sorry,' Hel says, cringing. 'No mention of the L word in the house.'

'That's right.'

The L word: leaving. It's too hard to hear it.

The week since Ivy's accident has been both amazing and heartbreaking. The amazing bit has been watching Hel reconnect with her daughter. As I suspected the day she came back from Scotland, it's as if Hel has never been away. As soon as Ivy regained consciousness in the hospital and saw Helena leaning over her crib, she flashed her impish little grin and said, 'Mumumumumum.' I've never seen Helena look happier. I don't think I've ever seen *anyone* look happier.

The police were easily satisfied that Ivy's broken arm was an accident. I didn't let on to Hel, but I'd been secretly terrified they'd think she'd done it. The injury itself is easily explained, especially as I saw the whole thing, but in the context of the preceding month . . .

But maybe the officers who came to the hospital that day saw what I've seen every day since: a woman utterly besotted with her child. Or maybe, after Hel told them she was going home to Australia, they just decided it was easier to let her go than drown themselves in paperwork. Call me cynical, but I know which scenario my money's on.

'Right then, possum,' Hel says to Ivy as she finishes wrangling her into a fuzzy green bodysuit. 'You are all set and ready to, uh . . .' She looks at me guiltily.

'Leave,' I supply.

'Yeah. Sorry.'

'It's okay,' I say resignedly. 'I've got to get used to it eventually. Although' – I scoop Ivy up from her blanket – 'I can't promise I won't try to hide you in my handbag.'

'You could fit her in there without much trouble,' Hel says, cocking her head towards the enormous Miu Miu tote bag on the hall table.

If there's a positive side to Hel and Ivy leaving, that's it: I've been able to bring out all the fabulous accessories I had to temporarily retire to save them from gooey fingers and milky spew. I've worn vertiginous heels every day since Helena came back and it feels *good*. But being able to reacquaint myself with Jimmy Choo doesn't ameliorate the heartbreaking bit. Ivy and Helena will soon be on the other side of the planet. And I'll be . . . where?

'Oh, I almost forgot to tell you,' Hel says. 'Guess who called while you were over the road?'

'Who?'

'You're not going to guess? You never guess.'

'You've got a plane to catch,' I remind her with a smile.

'Fair enough. Well, it was Edme. And you'll never guess what's happened!'

I raise my eyebrows.

'Oh, right. She's decided she's going to try to find her daughter after all. Can you believe it?' Hel is positively beaming. 'She said my commitment to taking responsibility for the mistakes I've made in my life had inspired her to do the same. She actually called me inspiring!'

'That's brilliant, Hel. And Edme's right. You *are* inspiring.'

Helena ducks her head, but I can see her proud grin. We smile goofily at each other until a single, firm knock at the door ends the moment.

With Ivy still in my arms, I walk into the hall and open the door to see a taxi driver walking back towards the van idling at the kerb. Instantly, my chest tightens. This is it then.

'Cab?' Helena calls from the lounge.

'Yep!' I say with false brightness. 'Time to hit the road!'

'Anna,' Hel says sternly. I turn to see her loaded down with bags. 'You don't have to pretend to be cool about this, you know. I'm gutted, too.'

I smile gratefully at her; I don't trust my wobbly voice to manage actual words.

'Can you bring Ivy? I've kind of got my hands full here,' she asks.

'Sure. I'll just put Nui out.'

'Oh, don't worry. He's already out,' Helena says quickly.

'Oh cool, thanks, hon. Okay, missy,' I say to Ivy. 'Are you ready to fly?'

She screws up her face and blows a raspberry. It's a charming trick I suspect came from Luke. I'd hoped it was a passing phase, but it appears to be here to stay.

'Oh, did you want to nip next door and see Luke?' I ask Hel. 'I'm sure he'd love to say goodbye to Ivy.'

'We popped over while you were at Jen's,' Hel says, teetering towards the front door with her baggage. I follow her with Ivy on my hip and pull the door closed behind us.

'You know, Anna, you should really talk to Luke,' Helena says. 'It's been over a week now.'

She doesn't look at me as she says it, busily loading her bags into the back of the taxi, but I can tell by her careful tone that she wants me to pay attention.

'I know, I know. And I will. I just . . . there's so much going on, you know? I'll talk to him when I've got everything else sorted out.

I couldn't cope with him telling me what a despicable person I am on top of everything else.'

'He's not going to —' Helena begins sharply, but stops herself. She smiles. 'I'm sure you'll work things out,' she says.

We ride to Heathrow in virtual silence, both pretending to be engrossed in entertaining Ivy. Anything but acknowledge the thickening atmosphere of sadness in the van.

At the airport, Helena queues to check herself and Ivy in, while I take the opportunity for one last cuddle with my goddaughter. 'Now madam, you have to be on your best behaviour on the plane. Nobody wants to be friends with a screaming baby,' I tell her.

Ivy regards me solemnly, as if she can feel my sorrow. Then she grins and says, 'Anna!'

Okay, what she actually says is, 'Fnnnaaar!' But I know what she means. Clever little thing.

'I'm going to miss you so much,' I tell her, burying my nose in her downy hair and breathing in her violet-sweet scent. 'But guess what? I'll see you again in a month or so.'

'WHAT?'

I turn – as do several dozen other travellers within earshot – to see Helena standing behind me, a look of rapturous excitement on her face.

'You'll what?' she repeats at a volume less likely to shatter the airport terminal's plate-glass windows. 'Are you coming home?'

'Uh, yeah,' I mutter. 'I was going to tell you when we got to the gate.'

'Oh my Goooood!' Hel shrieks, waving her and Ivy's boarding passes as if they're winning lottery tickets. 'When did you decide?'

I shrug. 'I don't know. There was no big eureka moment. I guess I've been thinking about it for the last couple of weeks. I think I've worn out my welcome in London. I want sunshine and warmth and properly refrigerated beer.'

'Yay!' says Helena, still beaming. 'When will you come?'

'I'm not quite sure. Once I've got everything organised, I guess. Three or four weeks maybe?'

'So you'll arrive home around the same time as Oliver!'

I can see she thinks all her Christmases have come at once. Oliver decided he can't live without Hel and is making the move to Adelaide as soon as he's finished the school term. And now she'll have me on the same continent as well. She looks as if she may literally burst with joy.

But then her expression turns sombre. 'What about Luke?' she asks.

'You mean Finn.'

'No, I mean Luke.'

'Er, what about Luke? I'm sure I'll find another next-door neighbour, Hel. In fact, I'd say it's guaranteed.'

Helena stares at me for a long time, one eyebrow cocked. When I don't say anything she simply says, 'Okay.'

She reaches for Ivy. 'Won't it be exciting to have Aunty Anna back?' she trills. Then, to me, 'Ooh, you can babysit!'

'Steady on there, Miss Hastypants! You've only just got your kid back – don't you think I deserve a break? And anyway, I'm not coming back to Adelaide. I thought I'd give Melbourne a go.'

'Awesome shopping,' Hel says knowingly.

'Precisely.'

She turns around to peer at the departures board. 'We're boarding in thirty minutes. We'd better go through,' she says.

The now painfully familiar lump instantly returns to my throat. 'Okay,' I say tightly. 'I – I might just leave you here then. You know . . .'

'I know,' Hel says, her eyes shiny with tears.

We look at each other for a moment, neither willing to be the first to say goodbye. The announcement for Helena's flight comes over the tinny PA and curtails our standoff. Laughing, we wrap each other in a final hug.

'Thank you,' Hel whispers in my ear.

'Thank *you*,' I reply.

I kiss her cheek and the crown of Ivy's head, hand Helena her carry-on bag and walk away with a smile and a wave. I don't look back.

But I do cry. A lot. Loudly and snottily, all the way to the Tube station and then halfway to Chiswick. I finally stop weeping at South Ealing and frantically reapply my mascara. If Finn can tell I've been crying, I definitely don't want him to think it's over him.

I'm not angry with Finn any more; I'm just sad. Sad that five years of being together has ended like this. Sad that we've done this to each other. Sad because I'm just as much to blame as he is.

Okay, so I didn't almost sleep with someone else and hatch a hare-brained baby plot to try to cover my tracks. But I did hide behind the safety net of 'having someone', instead of admitting our relationship was over long ago, and being brave enough to go it alone before it all got so awful. Maybe that's just as bad.

The small front yard of Jez's terrace house is littered with neon-bright child's toys and an enormous pram parked next to the front door. My knock is answered by Jez's girlfriend, Ellie, looking tired and harassed.

Instantly, I realise who inspired Finn's ridiculous plan. Ellie and Jez have been on the rocks as long as I've known them. At least, they were until Ellie had Danny. Now Jez has allegedly turned over a new leaf. I say 'allegedly' because I'm not convinced. What's that they say about leopards and spots?

'Hi Anna,' Ellie says wearily. 'Finn's upstairs in the spare bed-room. Sorry, I've got to . . .' She holds up her hands, which are covered with what I sincerely hope is chocolate, and hurries back into the house.

I climb the stairs to the second floor, thanking my lucky stars as I go. If I hadn't found out about Fiona, this could have been me – knackered, housebound and forever wondering how long the baby Band-Aid would hold my broken relationship together. Maybe it works for Ellie and Jez but it's more obvious than ever that it never could have worked for me.

Though I can happily admit I fell for Ivy hook, line and sinker, I was also happy to hand her back to Helena. Being permanently responsible for a child is *exhausting*. I feel as if I need to sleep for a year. And watching Hel with her daughter, I saw something in her that I know I lack. It's that all-consuming desire to exist solely for the good of another human being. Once I spotted it in Hel I started recognising it in women everywhere – Jen, women pushing prams in the street, even (beneath her harried exterior) Ellie.

I don't have that and I don't know if I'll ever have it. Maybe it's terribly selfish, but I think I've got my hands full for the time being just trying to work out how to make myself happy. I'm a work in progress, and if my time with Ivy has taught me anything it's that I can't rush that process. It takes a long time to grow into the people we're meant to be. If children aren't in my future, I'm okay with that. Not every woman is destined to be a mother. Some of us choose parenthood; some of us have parenthood unceremoniously thrust upon us. And some of us are just meant to be really, *really* awesome godmothers.

Maybe that's the lesson Jen was so keen for me to put my finger on: I'm not the maternal type. I'm not cut out for it. I might be great with other people's kids but I don't know if I'll ever have my own.

I rap lightly on the closed door of the guest bedroom.

'Come in.'

I step inside and see Finn tapping intently away at his laptop keyboard. He doesn't look up.

'Uh . . . hi?'

'Hey Anna,' Finn replies. 'Sorry – one sec. I just have to save this.'

I grit my teeth and fight the urge to slam the laptop shut on his bony little fingers. I'm right on time and Finn knew I was coming; he couldn't have saved his work five minutes ago?

I perch on his unmade bed and wait for him to finish. At last he hits enter and turns to face me.

'So . . .' he ventures, wearing a look that says 'What a silly old mess we've got ourselves into.' Like it's all some hilarious misunderstanding.

'So?' I'm not giving him an inch. Not this time. I guess I am still angry after all.

'I'm so sorry, Anna,' he says, redeeming himself slightly. 'I'm sorry for all of it. For the Fiona thing, obviously. For the baby idea. For taking the bloody job in the first place.'

'Okay . . .'

'I love you. I want us to be together. Come to Belfast with me.'

'And you think that would fix things, do you? Me in Belfast?'

Finn shifts uncomfortably in his seat. 'Well, maybe not immediately. But it's a start. We're never going to work things out if we're in different cities,' he says.

'So why don't you move back to London then?' I say hotly. 'All my being in Belfast would achieve is, well, me being in Belfast, while you carry on exactly as before.'

'But you're not working and my job's going really well and . . .' he trails off, looking helpless.

I sigh. Even as he's pleading with me to stay with him, it's clear he has no idea why he wants us to be together. He's just saying what he thinks I want to hear.

'This isn't why I came here today, Finn,' I tell him honestly. 'I don't want you to make all sorts of declarations and promises you can't keep. That you don't *want* to keep.'

'But I do —'

'Finn.' I hold up my hand to silence him. 'I came to tell you it's okay. Our relationship is over – you can admit it.'

He shakes his head. 'No. It doesn't have to be. I'll change,' he says.

I swallow the laugh that bubbles up from my stomach. 'I don't think you can,' I manage to say with a straight face. 'And anyway, I don't want you to. Yes, your taking the job and all the rest of it was hurtful, but we should have called it quits long before that happened. Before any of this happened.'

Finn blinks, surprised – though I suspect he's less surprised by what I've said than the fact I've actually said it aloud.

'We've been growing apart for a really long time, Finn,' I continue. 'Be honest – would you have even considered taking a job in another city five years ago when we first fell in love?'

Finn stares at the floor. 'No,' he admits. 'I wouldn't have wanted to be away from you.'

'Exactly.'

'But that doesn't mean I want to be away from you now!' he protests.

'Maybe not. But taking this job didn't exactly scream that you want to be *with* me, did it?'

He sits in guilty silence.

'It's okay. That's what I'm saying. We're different people now. We should have figured that out before it got this far,' I say gently.

I know Finn agrees with me; he's just so bloody stubborn. He'd give up his hair gel before he admitted he'd failed at something. And he *loves* his hair gel.

'We want different things, Finn. You want a glittering career and you should have it.'

'And what do you want?'

'There's the million-dollar question,' I say with a rueful smile.

'I'm not entirely sure yet. But I do know that I want to go home.'

'Home? To Australia?'

'Yeah. Helena and Ivy have just left and I plan to be hot on their heels.'

'Wow . . . uh, I don't know what to say to that,' Finn mutters.

It takes me a moment to decipher his odd response. Then it hits me – he thinks I'm scurrying home to lick my wounds.

'I'm not leaving because of you, you arrogant git!' I snarl, my benevolent mood instantly dissipating. 'Don't credit yourself with driving me out of the country! This is *my* decision.'

Finn looks relieved, if not entirely convinced. 'Okay. Well, give me a call if you want a hand sorting out the furniture and stuff,' he says.

I groan inwardly. In my excitement about returning to my home turf, I'd forgotten I have to pack up an entire house. I loathe moving.

Finn stands awkwardly, handing me my cue to leave. But there's one question I have to ask before I go.

'So . . . this Fiona. Are you going to be with her now?'

I don't know why I care. I don't love Finn anymore, I know that. But some morbid curiosity compels me to find out whether he loves somebody else.

'I don't know,' he says, not meeting my gaze. 'Maybe.'

In Finn-speak, that's a yes. I'd expected Finn's affirmation of his feelings for Fiona to feel like a punch to the stomach, but weirdly, I don't feel anything at all. Not hatred, not anger, not even jealousy. Standing there in Jez's tiny spare bedroom, looking at the man I loved for five years, I feel a strange sort of pity. I feel sorry that Finn was so readily tempted away from real love by a fresh pair of legs and a different set of boobs.

'Well, good luck with that,' I say, standing up. 'I've got to go.'

'Can we still be friends?' he blurts, because he has a cliché for every occasion.

I can't believe he would even ask. Sure, I've let him off the hook, but he's still behaved like a total cad. Then again, I'll be on the other side of the planet soon. It's not like I'm going to have to talk football over a beer with him, or go for dinner parties at his and Fiona's place.

'Sure,' I say. 'If you like.'

I let him peck me on the cheek and then I leave. I walk back to the Tube station without crying. I still feel a bit sad, but that has more to do with Helena and Ivy leaving than with Finn. Where he's concerned, I just feel an overwhelming sense of relief.

When the train stops in Richmond, I dawdle the long way home along the Thames. Summer has finally decided to make its presence felt. It's a warm day and the riverside pubs are alive with chatter and laughter and the clink of glasses. I'm almost tempted to step into one and order myself a pint. I feel like I should be celebrating. It's a historic moment: the first time in my life I have no ties and no plans. I'm liberated.

My whole life, I've always known what I'm supposed to do next. Finish school, get a cadetship to avoid having to go to university, qualify as a journalist, spend four years being the office dogsbody, go to London, earn more, do more, *be more*.

And I've had a boyfriend pretty much constantly since I was seventeen. First came the typical parade of short-lived high school romances, where the fact that we patently had nothing in common didn't matter as long as we each had someone to grope on a Saturday night.

For the first year or so of my cadetship, there was Pete. He was sweet, eager and really, really dull. I stuck with him because he was a journalist too, and back then anyone who was already doing what I so desperately wanted to do was fascinating to me. Unfortunately for Pete, I think he was rather smitten. He apparently had no problem with the fact that we had precisely nothing in common. By the end, our relationship had become a kind of warped experiment on my part to see how mean I could be before he'd finally stand up to me. He never did and I got bored and pulled the plug.

And then there was Finn. I was only twenty-one when I fell head over heels for him. When I look back now, at the ripe old age of twenty-six, that girl seems like a totally different person.

So now I'm free of all that. Free to go wherever, do whatever and be whoever I want. I thought I'd feel terrified, but I feel oddly serene.

Maybe that's because now I can be *with* who I want, too. Maybe it's because, probably for the first time, I know who that person is. And maybe, even though I've been so utterly foul to him, he might not be averse to that idea.

Anna

My theory that I might be forgiven for my bad behaviour is scotched when I reach my house and see a crudely scrawled note taped to the front door.

We have your dog, it says. A panic-fuelled surge of adrenalin rushes through me.

If you want to see him again, proceed immediately to number 26.

Number 26. Luke's house. I should have known.

I stomp next door and hammer on Luke's door with a closed fist. If he hates me, I guess I can deal with it. But you don't mess with man's – or girl's – best friend.

After what feels like an age, Luke's front door swings open. 'Anna,' he says nonchalantly, leaning against the doorframe with his arms crossed. He's looking particularly delicious today, in jeans and a cowboy-style checked shirt. And – am I imagining it? – it even looks like he's had his unruly hair trimmed.

'Don't you think dognapping Nui is a bit juvenile?' I snap.

'This from the woman who says "duh".'

'I'm serious. It's something a twelve-year-old would do.'

'Whereas kissing someone and then refusing to talk to him for a week is the height of maturity.'

'You kissed *me*!'

'You kissed me back,' he says smoothly.

'I was drunk.'

'No, you weren't.'

I sigh, exasperated. 'Just give me my dog back.'

'No.'

'Luke!'

'Not until you talk to me,' he says. 'You can't just ignore me forever, Anna. We're neighbours.'

'Not for much longer,' I mutter.

'What do you mean by that?'

'I mean I'm moving back to Australia.'

A strange expression clouds Luke's face, just for a moment. From where I'm standing, it kind of looks like panic.

'When?' he asks in a weird voice.

'As soon as I can get everything sorted.'

He steps aside and holds the front door open. 'Come in,' he says. 'Please, Anna.'

He obviously hasn't forgiven me for what I said. He wants to tell me exactly what he thinks of me while he still has the chance. I don't think I can bear it, and it's not just because the way I feel about Luke is the polar opposite of how he surely must feel about me. I also feel a sudden sense of urgency to get on with the plans for my move. Now that I've decided I'm going home, I need to ring airlines and find out what shots Nui will need and whatnot. And my mum. I should probably let my family know I'm returning at some point.

But Luke looks so, I don't know, *desperate* that I find myself following him into his house. I do need my dog back, after all. And I'm secretly grateful that, if he's going to give me a serve, he's at least going to do it away from the eyes and ears of prying neighbours.

Luke's house isn't at all what I expected. I can't believe I've never been inside before. For all the time we've spent together in the last few weeks, our friendship has mostly been conducted on his front step or in my kitchen.

'Please sit,' he says, gesturing to a very cool retro armchair. The entire sitting room is furnished with quirky mismatched furniture and funky artwork. It should look like a dog's breakfast but somehow it works. The man's got style.

I perch in the chair, expecting Luke to sit down opposite me, but he paces the floor agitatedly.

'Is your bloke going back too?' he asks eventually.

'My . . . Oh. No. He's not my bloke anymore, actually.'

Luke stops pacing. 'Really? Since when?'

I laugh despite the weird, tense atmosphere, because putting my finger on exactly when Finn stopped being 'mine' is about as easy as defining precisely when Tom Cruise went from being 'shaggable' to being 'creepy Scientology guy'.

I settle for the black and white response. 'Officially, since about an hour ago.'

'And unofficially?'

I give him a level look. 'Much longer, but I've only realised it in the past few weeks.'

'And how do you feel about that?'

'Who are you, Dr Freud?'

Luke ducks his head. 'Sorry.'

I wait for him to continue but he just stands there, staring at the carpet.

'Luke, what's going on?'

Still he gazes at the floor.

'The other night,' he says at last, and I know immediately which night he's referring to. 'You *did* kiss me back.'

Oh, Lordy. Cards-on-the-table time.

'Um, yes.'

He's looking directly at me now, his gaze boring deep into mine. 'So, what then? Why have you been avoiding me ever since?'

I squeeze my eyes shut, hoping to find an easy answer to Luke's question stamped on the back of my eyelids. 'Because I said that terrible thing to you about your family and you walked out. I was too ashamed of myself to talk to you, even to apologise,' I say miserably. 'I thought you'd hate me.'

'I think it's pretty obvious I don't hate you,' he says softly.

'But what I said – it was totally cruel.'

'I know you didn't mean it.'

I shake my head. 'Luke,' I say. 'Why do you put up with me? I've pretty much been either a bitch on wheels or a whiny moron from the moment we met.'

'Those are the qualities I look for in a woman,' he replies, grinning.

'I'm serious!'

'So am I,' he says. 'Anna, it's never been a matter of "putting up" with you. I fancy the arse off you. You must know that.'

I laugh nervously, but Luke looks completely calm. I get the sense he's been waiting a while to say this.

'Sorry, I don't speak cockney. Is fancying the arse off someone a good thing? Is that your eloquent way of saying you like me?'

'I more than like you, you cheeky minx,' he says in his best Dick Van Dyke circa *Mary Poppins* accent.

He sits down at last, on the arm of my chair. 'If I kiss you now, are you going to insult me and then not speak to me for a week?' he asks gravely.

'Hmm . . .' I pretend to consider this. 'Try it. See what happens.'

So he does. He tilts my chin up gently with his thumb, leans down and kisses me softly. Just like our last kiss, Luke's lips are tentative at first, but almost without thinking, I melt into his embrace.

I feel like I could literally spend a good three to five years in this exact position, just kissing this divine man.

But soon I'm on the move. I stand and pull Luke up with me, not breaking lip contact for a moment. My hands take on a life of their own, fumbling for his belt buckle and freely roaming the flat plane of his stomach.

'Wait, wait,' Luke says, pulling away.

'Wait? Are you kidding me?'

'Sorry, it's just . . . I have to ask you something,' he says, breathing hard.

'Okay . . .' This sounds ominous.

'Australia.'

'What about it?'

'Are you still going to go back? Does this – do we – change anything?'

The thought hadn't even entered my head. I was too busy enjoying the kissing.

Will I still go home? I want to feel the touch of Luke's hands on my body right now more than I've ever wanted anything, but I know that our connection is more than just physical. This won't be just a fling. This could be forever. But am I prepared to put my plans on hold to find out for sure?

I don't think I am. I've spent too long allowing my life to be governed by other people's decisions and whims. Not any more.

'I am still going to go home,' I tell him. I try to read his expression, but whatever thoughts are racing through Luke's mind, he's keeping them to himself.

'Fair enough,' he says at last. 'Can I come?'

My jaw drops. 'Come to Australia? With me?'

Luke shrugs. 'If that's all right,' he says.

'Shouldn't we maybe go on a date or something first?'

'Well, I heard Van Halen are touring. Why don't I get us a couple of tickets? You could wear that T-shirt you love so much.'

'Hagar or Roth?'

'Roth. Duh,' he says, drawing me into his arms again. 'And after we've been on our date, can I come to Australia?'

'But what about your job?'

He rolls his eyes. 'I think we established during the "Parcel Nazi" period of our relationship that I work for myself,' he says, grinning. 'I'm a graphic designer, Anna. I can do that anywhere.'

'But your siblings – could you handle being so far away from them?'

'They're all grown up and doing their own thing. They don't need me to hold their hands. And anyway, Australia's only a day away.'

I shake my head, still not quite believing it. Luke wants to move to the other side of the world. For me! I feel a lunatic grin spread across my face.

'So . . . you really want to do this?' I ask.

'Too right, mate!' he crows, apparently channelling Alf Stewart.

'Don't do that.'

'Sorry.' He kisses me softly on the lips. 'I want to be wherever you are,' he murmurs, and I swear my heart actually stops for a split second.

'Well then,' I take a deep breath, 'you'd better get your suitcase, Parcel Nazi.'

'We're going to Australia?'

'We're going to Australia.'